DUNGEON DESOLATION

Book Four of

THE DIVINE DUNGEON Series

Written by DAKOTA KROUT

MOUNTAINDALE
PRESS

TABLE OF CONTENTS

ACKNOWLEDGMENTS

There are many people who have given a huge amount of encouragement to me. An extra special thank you to Steven Willden, Nicholas Schmidt, Samuel Landrie, Justin Williams, Blas Agosto, Andrew Long, Dennis Vanderkerken, Andrew Reagan, Fred Lloyd, William Merrick, Mikeal Moffatt and all other Patreons for your support! You not only help me make better stories, but you are a great group of people that have become my friends.

To the amazing individuals who have given their all to help me get where I am – beta readers, street team members, and regulars on my social media – thank you for your support and promotion of my work. You make my life fun!

Thank you to my wonderful wife, who not only encouraged me to write but joined me in the terrifying leap of self-employment. Now we work harder than we ever have, but I'm so blessed because I get to spend every single day with you and our beautiful daughter.

Lastly, a heartfelt thanks to you my reader. I could not have done it without you and I hope to keep you entertained for years to come!

Prologue

"I'm *not* happy, Dale." Princess Brianna of the Dark Elven nation barged into the meeting room, the anger in her voice causing all other noise to cease. "Do you know *why* I am unhappy?"

Dale was sitting at the head of a long table that had been expressly designed for the council. The sharp words being directed at him - singling *him* out though the room was full - grated against his overstressed mind. It showed in his snappish response. "Please, *allow* me to *guess.* Nothing would make me happier than playing *games* right now. Could it be you are unhappy because nearly *every* human government has been toppled at the same time? Would it be the fact that the necromantic army now controls almost all of the surviving humans and we don't know what is going to happen to them? *Perhaps* your unhappiness is because the High Elves were able to push our foes back and we were not?"

"You can't believe that the general population would hold that against *us.*" Tyler - the only non-cultivator on the council - looked around nervously at the important people filling the space. "We aren't even a full fighting force! This was a dungeon for beginners... what? Only a few months ago?"

"*I'm* still in shock that we lost *Frank.*" High Mageous Amber sighed and leaned back into her chair, though it was impossible for her to get sore from remaining seated too long. "He was the only reason we didn't have high-ranked Guild leaders sniffing around looking for scraps."

Dale nodded at that. "I am already having trouble dealing with the Guild. The main branch is trying to send a replacement and is demanding to have a vote on *my* council. I gave Frank that position because he *earned* it, not because of his Guild membership. Now, I saw Frank's final moments and am still surprised that a single, chantless invocation was enough to kill him. I had it on good authority that he was in the A-ranks, but now I am hearing conflicting reports."

Putting his face into his hands, Dale continued speaking, "Apparently, it was 'well-known' that he was in the B-ranks? I even knew that at one point, but I remember being told very specifically that he was in the A-ranks nearly the first time I met him. Does anyone know what his actual cultivation was? If he *was* A-ranked, are the individual steps in each rank *that* much more potent? If not, I thought that their equal power levels would make it much harder for one of them to gain the upper hand. Can anyone explain what happened?"

"I'm sorry, did you say *equal* power levels? In the A-ranks, that is not a 'thing'. Even at the same rank, the power levels vary wildly." Madame Chandra, the A-ranked cultivator who owned the *Pleasure House* restaurant in town was frowning at him and had a slight tinge of pity bleeding through her tone. "Dale, do you remember when I told you that I trained Frank for almost a decade?"

Chandra leaned forward, making sure he was focused on her. Dale nodded sharply, and she continued, "Frank *was* a B-rank Mage. He was not a High Mageous, or he would have held a much more important position in the Guild, a position far too high for what was a backwater dungeon like this. Who told you that he was A-ranked?"

Dale thought back, his eyes narrowing when he finally remembered. "... Hans. Of course it was Hans. I'm going to kick his-"

"It's likely that he was trying to 'wow' you, Dale. What would the difference between A and B rank be for you if you were in the F-ranks? Don't be too hard on him, just understand where your confusion comes from and rectify the issue." Chandra sighed and pulled another report toward herself. "Also, I'd still like to learn how you got back into town. I know that portal collapsed, and by all accounts... you died. Are you finally willing to explain yourself?"

"I'm not," Dale firmly announced his decision. The other people in the room, including scribes, couriers, and even the servers who had brought lunch, all slunk back into their normal positions or started walking again. This was a rumor that all of them had heard, and each had heard gossip wilder than anything they could imagine to be true. To be fair, only one of them was overly imaginative, and he was pretty close to guessing correctly. "How are we progressing on talks between the various races? Do we have any information on how to arrange a counterattack against the necromancers?"

"*Excuse* me!" Brianna lightly rapped her knuckles on the table, leaving a small dent. In reinforced marble. Dale rolled his eyes; that was the fifth time that had happened. He'd need to get an Earth Mage to come over and fix it yet again. "Did we forget the *reason* this conversation is happening?"

"Please, Brianna. Tell us why you aren't happy." Dale tried to placate the B-ranked Assassin Princess.

Speaking in a loud voice, she took a moment and tried to lock eyes with all the members at the table, "It's been three weeks since the battle. Not only have we not made *any* progress in finding a base of operations or launching a counter-initiative, do you know what I saw when I looked off of this floating island? Ocean. *Ocean*! We are no longer over the continent, Dale. The dungeon is *running away*."

Chapter One

I felt the need to fix a problem, but none of the beings around me could provide ideas or results fast or varied enough to help me. They still needed to sleep, *for celestial sake! Since my mana concept is an amalgamation of all other principles of mana, I decided to try my figurative hand at using a bit of 'creativity' mana. If I hadn't found out that there was a higher tier at the last second, it would have been my top pick. So why not explore it? My thoughts were along this line: why should* I *be the only one who comes up with the ideas all the time? I could just be the one who* creates *the being that comes up with a solution for a change!*

I first tried making the screaming rocks a bit more imaginative, but that just made their screams more varied and expletive with mixed reactions that were hard to replicate. From there, I found that the Bashers did not take well to creation mana altering their structure since they had no intelligence in the first place. On an unrelated note, they did start growing mohawks, braids, and other colored patterns in their fur. After that, I tried on a willing Bob. Sadly, after a hefty dose of creativity, Bob just wanted to paint the dungeon walls, and then he cut off his own ear... who knew creativity could be so hard to manage?

Since the main issue was that I didn't want to have to actively devote attention to listening to speeches made by all of the various sources of bad ideas, I created a quill which could write by itself! After a few failed attempts where it would just endlessly draw a picture of itself drawing itself - it seemed to enjoy recursion - I finally got it to start writing words instead. Nothing on its own, but it would write out anything spoken in the area around it. Progress.

"Cal? *Cal*! Pay attention to what I am saying!" Dani was shouting at me. I 'blinked' and looked around. Had I just been... dreaming? Or was that a vision of some sort? I don't dream; I don't lose focus like that. Something was going on. "It is *time* for an *intervention*!"

<Oh, come on. You *want* me to intervene? It's so *cute,* though!> I knew exactly what she was talking about, but I thought it was harmless fun. Our newest addition, a tiny Wisp named Grace, was zipping around the dungeon driving the Cats wild. Take the susceptibility of normal cats to moving lights, add on the alluring power of Wisps, and you might have an idea of what we were dealing with. Combine *that* with a limited ability to *order* the Mobs to play with her... <Oh, just let her play. She isn't hurting anyone!>

"She just led over a dozen Cats into two different adventuring parties! They were *slaughtered*! She shouldn't see that sort of thing at her age!" Dani was turning from purple-pink to purple-red, showing me that she was becoming *actually* angry instead of playfully angry. "Are you ignoring me in there?"

<I meant that she wasn't hurting anyone that *mattered*,> I clarified for my lovely bonded Wisp. She was so *funny* sometimes! Sure, she was more empathetic now, especially since each day wasn't a struggle to gain enough Essence to survive on, and she was a parent now...

"*Cal*." Uh-oh, she was now e-nun-ci-a-ting, and I knew for sure that she was serious. Time to get to work.

<I'm on it.> I ordered the Cats back to their rooms, then pouted a bit when Grace looked around and saw all of her friends wandering off without her. Her light dimmed, making me feel like a lousy Core. She couldn't speak yet, but her emotions were easy to understand just by looking at her. Since I knew that Dani wasn't looking, I generated some air-aligned Essence and

sent it into the tiny ball of light, knowing that it would tickle her. I couldn't do this very often because it had a similar effect on her that candy did on human children. Sure enough, soon the Wisp was zipping around the lower level at high speeds. Leaving her to play, I turned my attention to Bob. My Goblin Shaman was busy working on a multitude of projects for me, and it was time to see what was working.

"Great Spirit?" Bob was now sensitive enough to the fluctuations of Mana around himself to be able to detect when my full attention was resting on him.

<Hi there, Bob. How are we doing?> I looked at what he was working on, a map, and was impressed by the level of detail shown on the vellum rendering.

"Decent, and by that, I mean that we are getting *close.*" Bob pointed at the map, where tiny golden lines were traced out. "There is a spot here where we *should* be getting a large amount of Essence due to ley lines converging and expanding, but instead, we are only getting a trickle of power. As you know, I am not *entirely* certain what is there, but I *do* know that this is an issue that needs to be fixed. We need to find a way to scout ahead; we could be moving toward something that could swat us out of the air like a fly."

<Agreed. We'll be extra careful as we get closer, but this needs to happen. This was supposed to be a new Node for the increased expansion of the ley lines. I can only think of one or two things that could be taking all of that Essence, but my bet is that it is a dungeon of some sort. If there is a single entity there, a monster or some such that can absorb all that power, we will have a much harder time taking control of the area.> I looked over the map a bit longer, doing a double take when I saw that the golden lines had expanded a tiny bit.

"Ah, yes, this is actually enchanted to update as your 'ley lines' expand. Thank you again for access to that book of Runes; all the Bobs have been able to make excellent progress on various utility and war Inscriptions." Bob gestured at the map. "For instance, this map is not hand-drawn. We are taking an image through a Core and having the map update based on what we know and can see. The less well-detailed areas are what we have taken from various standard maps, and those areas change as we go along and gather data."

<*Very* impressive, Bob.> I tried to think about any other use for this map but decided to leave it to him and went to work on other projects. I had been tinkering with and altering a few of the floors as we flew, and what were currently the bottom two levels were coming along nicely. They were platforms connected by various paths, and each platform had a guardian based on the concept of Mana represented by the connections that led to each platform.

There were multiple ways to arrive at each guardian, denoting the myriad ways to attain each combination of Essence, the knowledge of which would allow for more natural ascension. Whew. That was a mouthful. Simple terms: follow and measure a path, try to have that ratio of Essence in your system when ascending to the Mage ranks. Simple to say but not really easy in practice. I hadn't expected that there would be such a strong reaction to such a simple setup, but people had been *stampeding* to the lower levels for a chance to document my structure each day.

The amount of people *not* attempting to descend to the lower levels had increased to the point that I made Inscriptions that blurred the space between the paths and platforms. If they wanted to learn the secrets, they would need to *work* for it! More specifically, they would need to *fight* for it! People had been sitting on the sidelines and *drawing* out of the reach of the monsters! Drawing! I was still grumbling about that.

Changes to the levels were twofold. First of all, I had been working to upgrade my golems with the new materials that Bob had nearly died researching. These components allowed for more Mana and corruption to be imparted to the golems, making them stronger, faster, and overall deadlier. Lots of '-ers'. I needed to incorporate multiple types of minerals and alloys into their creation; otherwise, they became fragile and brittle. I was trying to shore up their weaknesses but needed more time to experiment so that the changes were Mana-cost effective. The second significant change on the bottom floors was traps and wandering monsters that were placed merely to keep non-combatants away or punish them for coming in the first place.

The people I was specifically referencing were those who stayed on the outskirts and hung around the reward kiosks especially thickly. When I had first made these floors, higher ranked cultivators were getting rich by charging a fee to lower rankers for taking their tokens to lower levels to redeem them for higher quality and more expensive gear. So many of the weak people were slain that the few adventurers that *were* strong enough were able to charge a premium. This system worked well... except abyssal *Hans* kept showing up at the kiosks - having completely avoided the Mobs - and used a bunch of tokens whenever he was sure that Dale had gone to sleep and wouldn't yell at him for risking himself. He threw off all of my *calc*ulations and tended to frustrate me to no end.

I was startled to hear a chiming tone, and, speak of the little...! There he was, throwing a handful of gold coins into the air and letting them shower down on him as he closed his eyes and danced! I yelled at him, knowing he couldn't hear me.

<Hey! Get off this floor, *C-ranker*! You don't belong here! Cats! Where are the Cats? Go get that Assassin!>

Looking around for the Cats that were *supposed* to be guarding against this *specific* annoyance, I found that they were distracted by playing with a small bag stuffed full of... mint? No! *Catnip*! I absorbed the bag and its contents with a *pop* which caused the Cats to become confused... then angry. They looked around for Hans, as did I so I could send them after him, but all I saw was the shimmer of a closing portal.

<...I'll get him next time.> I promised myself silently, knowing that it was likely a promise I couldn't keep.

Chapter Two

Dale was sitting in the ground, yes, *in* the ground, coated in rock up to his neck. Right now, he was *supposed* to be working on his control of an earth technique but was finding it hard to concentrate with his grumpy old Moon Elf instructor slapping him every few seconds. Blood leaked from Dale's broken nose, and he was pretty sure a few teeth were getting loose.

"You'd better get yourself out of there soon, *Human*," his teacher punctuated the last word with a particularly vicious slap that left Dale seeing stars, "or I am going to start using something that will *really* hurt."

Dale's eye flicked to the bucket of *something* bubbling over a fire behind the Elf. He was pretty sure that there was some form of tar in there. He redoubled his efforts, managing to form his most well-practiced technique. As he began to send the shaped Essence into the stone around him, a particularly vicious smack and a harsh tone stopped him. "Fool! You are trying to *shatter* the stone that you are coated in? Are you trying to kill yourself? Thousands of stone shards shooting into you *will* accomplish that nicely. You probably think you're a wit, but you're only half right! Stop trying to cut corners, and do this properly."

The verbal abuse kept mounting, and the slaps began increasing in severity to the point Dale was actually worried that he would be killed from one of the blows if they continued. With a burst of inspiration and power, Dale *shoved* the stone away from him. Unlike the barely-controlled explosion of energy leaving his body, the stone sank away smoothly. The slaps and acidic voice stopped, and Dale was allowed to clamber out of the hole he had been in.

"Finally." The Elf seemed to be more exhausted than Dale was, but Dale knew the Elf was at *least* a Mage and so must have been acting. "You have *finally* taken your first step upon non-somatic casting. *Now,* do you understand that all of your enormous motions and gestures for using your techniques are merely a crutch that you should not rely on?"

"I understand that I apparently don't need to make the motions, but... I'm not sure how to replicate what I just did." Dale winced as he spoke, knowing that it was likely that the pain would soon begin again.

The Elf glared at him, only relaxing after Dale was fully panic-sweating. "Good. After all, that is what this training is *for.* Now that you have had a taste of the *proper* way to use your Essence, it will be easier for you to accept the teachings we will impart to you. Once something is shown to be possible, the body and mind will accept it much more easily. Let's continue with the next exercise, but you may need some pain reduction if we are to continue. Stefan! Get over here and administer a swelling reduction potion; he needs to be able to see for this next part."

A man Dale had never met before came walking over at what seemed to be a laborious pace for him. Dale had never seen someone who embodied absolute exhaustion like this 'Stefan' did. "Did I hear pain relief?"

"Don't worry about that; I changed my mind. Swelling reduction only."

"Yes, dark lord." Stefan groaned as he reached into a bag at his side. Dale honestly thought the man might be a zombie. "I have been making up more potions, but-"

"We are busy, *Stefan.* When you graduate from Pharmacist to Alchemist, we will speak again. Until then, you are just an assistant and will be regarded as such." The Moon Elf's tone was bland, but his words were so sharp Dale was surprised the man didn't start bleeding. "Dale, drink that and get ready to dodge."

The sun was coming up by the time Dale wobbled on unsteady legs away from his brutal instructor. He felt entirely drained of Essence, and his meridians felt abused. Then again, he had functioning meridians, so he really shouldn't be complaining too much. Overusing the ability to crush and absorb the power in Cores had caused him to burn out his meridians, which had led to his recent death. Also, the loss of all of his weapons and armor, which was *almost* as horrifying. Dale stumbled into his bedroom, dropped onto the bed, and cursed the fact that stairs existed. Everything should be on the same level so that when he was exhausted, he didn't need to bother with such inconvenience. He looked out of his window and saw only an expanse of blue, reminding him of his next unpleasant task.

"Cal," Dale groaned into the air, hoping that the dungeon would respond before he passed out. They had recently discovered that they were originally the same person and had been trying to get on better terms. It had been a very confusing time and involved a portal through time and space generated via chaos. Something they literally could not *intend* to happen... had happened. On the plus side, Dale no longer had an irrational fear of the dungeon. "Cal, buddy, my other half, we need to talk."

<Hello there, Dale.> The voice resounded in Dale's head. <By the way, I wouldn't call you 'half'. Maybe... I don't know, my other tenth? One-eighteenth?>

"You always say the nicest things." Dale closed his eyes, the stone ceiling above him not interesting enough to continue keeping his eyes open to stare at. "Question for you: why are we out over the ocean instead of hunting the undead and their masters?"

<About that... look, as much as I'm mentally ready to go seeking revenge, the only success we had was against the reserve units that were holding a decimated city. This 'Master' guy is the strongest necromancer in the world - most likely - and has a bunch of other people that aren't *that* far off from his own strength. I'm circling the issue here, but the fact of the matter is that we aren't actually strong enough to fight him, even indirectly. We don't have a single S-rank individual on the entire... island? Should we call this flying mountain an island? We do have a lake...> the voice trailed off, so Dale hurried to keep the dungeons attention.

"Cal, hey! Don't go running off. This is Mountaindale." Dale waited a moment, but there was no instant response, so he decided to play along. "How about a 'skyland'? Combine 'sky' and 'island', and I think you are the only one."

<Ooh, I like that. What about a 'Neverland'? Because I'm never going to land.> The voice was back, so Dale quickly jumped into conversation.

"I don't think people would call us a 'Neverland'; they don't have any context for understanding the name. Plus, what happens if someday you have to touch down? Listen, Cal. I need a few more details from you about why we are out over the ocean." Dale paused and stopped speaking entirely, something that he knew bothered the dungeon. It did *not* like to waste time.

<Ugh, fine. When our souls rejoined, I got all of your memories, and I feel like you got at least a *portion* of mine, right?> Dale nodded in confirmation. <Alright. Listen, the ley lines that I have been creating to regulate the world's Essence and Mana should eventually cover the surface of the entire

planet. Then it will dig, getting to the center of the planet eventually. That part will take a long time, *decades* at least, but the surface should be covered in mere weeks. Something is blocking the advancement of the lines, and we are on our way to destroy it. I say 'something', but this is happening in multiple locations. So. Some*things*?>

"I see. So this will benefit you and, indirectly, *us*, correct?" Dale spoke thoughtfully. "Also, even the memories I did get from you are… vanishing."

<Fleshy memory devices. Terrible design. As for the blockage, this *particular* annoyance is sitting at the crossroads of a half-dozen lines. When it is removed, I estimate that the surface Essence on '*Mountaindale*' will increase in density by thirty percent. It'll go even higher in the deep layers of myself, so less 'indirectly' beneficial and more 'instant gratification'. Speaking of, real nice pick for naming the mountain, you narcissist. Why not 'Mountaincal'?>

"Pretty sure I get that arrogant tendency from *you*," Dale muttered while tapping at his mattress. "That's a pretty large benefit; I should be able to get the others to calm down with that information. I have a small issue, though. If there is something we need to fight at this location, I have nothing to fight with or defend myself with."

<You want me to fix every little issue you have? You have money, go *buy* some gear.> Dale rolled his eyes at this statement.

"We both know that there isn't anyone that can match the quality of the gear you are able to provide. If I leave here and die outside of your influence, you lose a chunk of your soul, and I am gone forever." Dale knew this argument was guaranteed to produce results. The dungeon was nothing if not concerned about self-preservation, and adding on flattery didn't hurt.

<You do have a tendency to die for just... *no* reason. Yeah... fine, you have a good point. Take a nap; I'll think of something. You'd better help me out on the issue I'm having, or I'll make sure that you have *no* clothes. Ever.> Dale nodded and closed his eyes, his exhaustive training assuring that he was asleep in moments.

Chapter Three

Screams resounded through a small town as orderly ranks of the undead closed in on them. The gates were barred, and any cultivators in the area moved to a defensive position. Protecting the people was their duty, their calling. Heavy feet pounding, exposed bone scraping over stone, and moaning zombies all ensured that a cacophony of sound nearly drowned out the cries of fear.

All at once, the undead stopped. The echoes of their movement reverberated for a long moment, but total silence fell within seconds. A few of the undead shuffled out of the way, allowing a festering demon to stalk toward the town. As soon as it was seen, the people behind the walls understood that they were dead. There was no one around this small population center that could fight on equal terms with something like *that.*

"Human filth." The demon called lazily. "I am here as an ambassador of The Master. I have been *instructed* to give you all a choice. You are to join us, or you will die. These are your only options, and not choosing or delaying will ensure your demise. You have one minute to answer."

Frantic shouting came from the town, and as the seconds ticked away, they became more furious and louder. The Demon decided that enough time had passed, and spoke once more. "Your *choice*?"

There was a pause, but then one of the people on the wall shouted, "We'll never join you!"

"Incorrect, but I am *so* glad that was your choice." The Demon took a step forward, and the ranks of the dead did the same. The wooden walls surrounding the town were demolished in seconds. The highest ranking cultivator in the town was a C-ranker, everyone else being a D-rank, F-rank, or just a normal person. All of them joined the ranks of the dead that day.

The Demon, coated in rapidly drying blood and viscera, gave a happy sigh as he bit into a femur and crunched on a chunk of bone. "I *love* it when they struggle like that. It makes everything so much more... satisfying."

CAL

I snorted a soft chuckle as Dale passed out. I suppose his previous career of counting sheep made it really easy for him to fall asleep whenever and wherever he was.

<Let's see... he fights with his fists and relies on high mobility to survive. Can't really say that has worked out for him, though. Well, he's totally out, so I can at least fit him for gear. Alright... hmm... chainmail? Too noisy and noticeable. How thin can I make this stuff... oh, wow, pretty thin. Okay then, let's pretend to be a tailor. I can't believe I am going to spend all this time making him armor. So boring. Could be building a new floor right now.> I continued to grumble as I spun aluminum thread into a set of silvery clothes. I used his nearby uniform as a model and even went so far as to put his crest in the proper place, seeing as he couldn't exactly pin it onto this outfit.

<There! Shirt complete. More like tunic, really, since it was modeled... pants, right! On to pants. He better not overeat; these can't be altered after I make them. Not that he could gain much weight, thanks to his constant need for nutrients right now. No, better to make both of these a bit looser. He could potentially put on muscle. Now he would need a belt, though...>

I made shoes next, then a balaclava. I was pretty proud of this piece. It looked similar to what the Moon Elves wore to hide their features, and since the material was so thin, Dale could wear it around his neck and still have it hidden beneath his collar when it wasn't in use. When he needed to protect his head, he could just pull it up and have it cover his entire head. There was a layered portion so he could leave his eyes uncovered if he wanted to, but given the fact that eyes were such a weak point... I wanted to give him the option to protect them.

Gloves came next, but I made the material much more sturdy and rigid, turning them into battle gauntlets. He would need to take them off when he didn't want to be in combat, so I added a hook for them to hang on his belt in the same place a weapon such as a sword or mace would typically go. That covered the puny human's needs pretty well, so it was time to wake him up and explain the gear to him.

<Dale! *Look out!*> I screamed into his mind. For some reason, he woke up *violently*, a wave of earth Essence rippling out from him and shattering the walls, floor, and ceiling around his bed. I was actually impressed; that would have caused serious harm to anyone that was actually trying to get the jump on him. Of course, he was showered with rubble but was still mostly unharmed since I had created the armor around his sleeping form.

"Ow!" he coughed wetly as a large chunk of stone landed on him. Oh right, this gear mainly protected against piercing and slashing effects. Sadly, it wouldn't do too well against kinetic impact. You really needed something sturdier for that. He should go get armor that would fit over this, though his mobility *was* his strength...

<Hey there! I'd like you to tell me what you think about your brand new armor!> I called happily into his mind.

"Ow," Dale repeated obnoxiously. Seriously, he did it to himself. "Just... where is it?"

<You are already wearing it! Can you really not see your armor?> Exactly as I had hoped for. No one should suspect that he was covered in a continents' ransom of Mithril.

"I see that I am wearing an odd head wrap and gloves. Did you make my armor invisible?" Dale voiced quizzically.

<I understand you are just waking up, but please regain your standard level of intellect. Your 'clothes, Dale. They look totally normal to you?>

"...Yes?"

<Well, they are made of Mithril. That 'head wrap' rolls down to be a thin cloth around your neck, and the gauntlets have a chunk of unbelievably Essence-conductive minerals wrapped in Mithril to create three wedges on each glove. In order: earth, fire, infernal on the left glove; wind, water, celestial on the right. To help *you* out, they are color coded. Direct your techniques through those, and they should amplify the damage to levels you can't manage otherwise.> I paused a moment to let him admire his new weapons, then continued to praise myself.

<The entirety of your armor has two layers; the top layer should funnel any affinity-typed attack into the second layer, which should absorb the Essence out of the blow. You could stand in a gout of pure fire for ten minutes without getting *warm*. At least until the Cores collecting the Essence are full. Then you burn. So. Oh! Side note: basically, you can't be stabbed while wearing this clothing. No, wait, correction. Though nothing is going to *cut* you, people can still *stab* you.>

< Let's see... blunt force trauma is going to be your biggest weakness since this has no real sturdiness. So... you might want to get a helmet or something. Also, try not to get crushed. This would protect you enough to keep you from becoming a pancake but not enough for you to survive the experience. As for the armor itself, the weave of the cloth is so tight that you

could drink water out of a sewer and the liquid should be filtered well enough to leave behind only pure water. Actually, you should test that; I'd like to be sure.>

"Hard pass."

<Ingrate! I do all of this work for you, and you can't do a simple thing for me? Tsk, tsk.>

"Why can't you make me some armor to go over this that will help if something hits me?" Dale kept the whine from his voice, but I still detected it.

I decided to show my ire with words. <Just so you know, you ungrateful aspect of me, it took the Essence equivalent of fourteen C-ranked people dying in the dungeon to create *this* armor for you. Mithril is not cheap to charge with power, even though you seem to think I should be tossing it to anyone who wants it. You can thank the newest Wisp down here for the contribution. Also, there were two groups that just got wiped out on the third floor just so that you could be a bit more protected.>

"You killed two *parties* of *people* to make this?" Dale looked down at his clothing with disgust.

<Make me armor! Do it with your personal energy supply! Don't hurt anyone else! Make up your mind, Dale. *Nothing* is free. How about you just try not to lose this armor and actually make sure to wear it instead of just complaining. It's already made, after all. Good luck.> I really had to go; there were lots of things to get done, and Dale talked *really* slowly.

Perhaps it wasn't that he spoke slowly; it could be that the enhanced cognition and processing speed associated with not only being a Mage but also being a Dungeon Core caused everyone to *seem* so slow. Well, not my fault they couldn't keep up. I had golems to design! Well, that wasn't strictly accurate. The golems were designed, but I was continuing to fail at creating a more potent version of them. I had some greater success with the golem controlled by the mind of a bunny-loving Elf that had died here, but while she was an impressive fighter, there were just too many flaws in her body.

Mainly, she was fragile. Not... well, certainly not to an average person but to a Mage that was able to make the trek to her? My Boss was a challenge to them, sure, but not a *serious* one. The issue was: I hadn't been lying when I said that Mithril was expensive to make, and that was the only thing I could think of right now that would increase her durability. That created a problem for me because if she was defeated and taken as treasure while coated in Mithril... someone would be walking away with a vast power investment. She just wasn't deadly enough to justify the potential loss. To fix my issues, I was trying to boost the density of Mana packed into golems by using our newly discovered materials, but at a certain point, they would just explode.

Perhaps all I should do was cover her in Inscriptions and give her armor and maybe a few weapons? She knew how to fight, and her body never tired. I sighed gently; it was becoming harder to create creatures uniquely suited to destroying my enemies. Perhaps... perhaps I should be focusing on empowering *myself* instead of my creatures? Should I meditate on my **law**, **Acme**, the concept of *perfection itself* for a few decades?

Nah. I decided to go make my traps more deadly instead.

CHAPTER FOUR

"Well, I now know why we are going the wrong way," Dale mentioned to the councilors at the morning's pre-conference meeting. Hopefully this information would be beneficial for the morning's post-conference meeting and perhaps even inspire people to be polite at the luncheon for the afternoon's pre-afternoon forum. Dale was sick to his stomach as he realized how many meetings he was forced to attend on a daily basis. "As I understand it, there is a dungeon that we are moving toward. If we take the Core from this dungeon and feed it to ours, we can expect a thirty percent increase in unaligned Essence on the surface of Mountaindale."

Madame Chandra rolled her eyes and spoke in an uncharacteristically sharp tone, "Now we are going to be doing the dungeon's dirty work? How will this help our goals? Were you able to get the dungeon to make any concessions for our assistance in this matter?"

Dale thought about the incredible armor that he had gained for himself and felt a bit guilty that he had something that he wouldn't be sharing with the people that were relying on him. "I felt that having an understanding of what was happening coupled with the benefit that we will see from increased Essence would be enough. Realistically, what can we do right now? Can we fight this 'Master' directly? Can we fight any portion of his forces on equal footing? The answer to all of these questions is 'no'. Why not focus on something that we *can* do? Why not grow stronger and prepare for the day when we *can* fight back?"

"Well said, Dale, but there are facts you are not considering." Father Richard ambled toward his chair. He had been wounded multiple times in the last few months, and though he recovered quickly... it still took time and energy. "One of the most important being that The Master did *not* kill the people of the cities. In fact, from all reports, it appears that they are being treated well. This is concerning for many reasons but especially because we do not know what he intends to do with them. We know that human sacrifice is not off the table. If that is the case, we need to save the tens of thousands of lives that might be sacrificed for power due to our inaction."

"So you are saying human sacrifice is *on* the table? Or on the *altar*?" Dale looked around the solemn faces, his coy smile slipping. "I'm very tired."

Madame Chandra glanced around the room with bloodshot eyes. "Or it could be that The Master does not *intend* to hurt them in any way. For goodness sake, in his own mind he could be trying to *help* those people!"

"By murdering our families and destroying the armies?" Prince... no, *King* Henry stalked into the room, his footsteps clinking against the ground with each step. "I refuse to make concessions to this monster. We *will* be fighting a war against him, and he *will* pay for his crimes. Even if I need to spend eternity hunting him and empowering myself, I will eventually bring him down like the beast he is."

Madame Chandra could find no argument to refute him and just shook her head sadly. "I know that your loss was shocking, but at this point, there is nothing we can do against them. Pursuing peace may truly be our only option."

"*I will have war!*" Henry bellowed into the now-silent room, crashing his metal-clad fist against the table. Thanks to its recent enhancement, the table weathered the blow admirably, not even chipping.

"Your *Majesty*!" Dale loudly disrupted the shouting. "With *all* due respect, we will be doing whatever we can to *save lives.* If that means that we find a peaceful option, we *need* to consider it. Otherwise, it is the people that *you* were sworn to protect that will suffer. *Your. People.* The ones counting on *you* to rescue them from the predation of the infernal. Please, think on that... Your Majesty."

"You... you people *don't...*" Fuming and trying to surreptitiously wipe his eyes, Henry turned on his heel and marched out of the room, exuding a bloodlust that caused the ordinary people in his path to freeze in place.

"War isn't off the table, and neither is a peaceful option," Princess Brianna bit into an apple with a wet crunch, swallowing before finishing her sentence, "but have you thought of a *third* option? The one where you ask the Elvish Assassins you live with to intercede?"

There were many glances thrown around the table, and it was surprisingly the merchant Tyler who spoke, "Are... are you offering? Do you even have anyone who could take out an above S-ranked necromancer?"

"He *isn't* a necromancer." Madame Chandra rubbed at her eyes once again. "At least... he never *was* one. The **law** he is bound to is far too strange for it to be so simple."

"Then what is he, Madame? Where does his specialty lie?" Father Richard seemed excited to finally have a starting point; surely they could find a counterpoint to his **law** and use it to weaken the S-ranked 'Master'.

Chandra shook her head hard, "I don't know. He has always just been good at... *knowing* things. I do know that he has access to the void, but I am uncertain how or what that means for him... or for us."

"Sorry to say, but assassinating The Master is off the table. Simply put, none of you could afford the cost, as it would involve sending my *mother* after him. No, what I am thinking is more to the effect of a war of attrition. We can go after his generals, his leaders, and strike them down. Without competent leadership, his plans may fail." Princess Brianna only started to get serious near the end, her flippancy giving way to strategy.

"*Assassins*? I cannot condone..." Father Richard looked around at all the faces that were turned toward Brianna. "Surely this cannot actually be up for debate!"

Tyler turned his intense stare upon the priest. "Father Richard, I know that this issue is serious for you, but I don't think you understand quite where some of us are standing on this issue. The necromancers had my neighbors and myself trapped in a basement as the building above us crumbled. We did everything we could to keep ourselves alive, not only because we wanted to stay living but because of what happened to our dead."

Heaving a few deep breaths to calm down, Tyler continued speaking, "Two of my new employees were struck by falling rubble and were slain. They turned into *jelly* and oozed out of my building to join into an *abomination*. We were afraid of dying for more than the normal reasons at that point. We were afraid that our *souls* would be used as ammunition against our people. *That* is the reason I am here right now, and I will push for anything that allows me to sleep without waking up in terror. If that means a distant necromancer dies without getting anywhere near me, then I say *so be it*; send in the Assassins. I believe I can and do speak the will of the people."

The room was quiet again, so after a few tense moments Dale cleared his throat and moved the conversation along. "We will discuss this later, in a closed session. For now, we have another issue to think on. The academy is full, but the classes are becoming a bit sporadic. We need a Headmaster to run things there and rein in the instructors. We have had dozens of applicants, but after background checks, knowledge tests, and determining general amiability, we have narrowed it down to these three." Dale handed out a packet of information to each person, who scanned through each and determined who they wanted to offer the position to.

"We can rule out the High Elf off the bat, can't we?" Brianna tossed a small booklet of information into the fire. Dale watched it burn with resignation; that had cost quite a bit of money in terms of paper and research.

"*Please* don't burn things that I give you. It's... rude." He stopped himself from shrieking but only just barely. It wouldn't be a good idea to yell; Brianna had guards in the room that might react poorly. Dale had gained a few benefits from the dungeon that he didn't think even Cal knew about. One of those was the ability to connect to the dungeon's senses and use them as his own. It had a *very* limited range, but he could sense the disturbances in the areas' Essence as the invisible folk continually scanned the room for threats.

"This one is promising. Emilia Nerys... A-ranked blood cultivator." Tyler shook his head in wonder. "She is far and away more than qualified. A healer, a background in taking on F-rankers to mentor..."

"There are complications, unfortunately," Father Richard spoke up as Tyler trailed off. "My order has been working to recruit her, as she specializes not in healing, but in hunting necromancers. She holds a deep grudge against them, and I feel that if you are serious about opening an infernal wing, she would slay any applicant. Either way, I cannot say she is suited to the position."

"She applied for a professor position, as an instructor of water and healing," Tyler pressed onward. "Can we consider her for the dean of one of those wings?"

The others agreed to his proposition and decided to offer her a pick of the two availabilities.

"That leaves this man... Artorian?" Amber flicked the paper, and it lifted into the air and hung there with a picture of a man on it. "Why is he even being considered? He is in the C-ranks."

"These people aren't necessarily being considered for their cultivation bases; they are being considered for their ability to run an academy." Dale knew it would come to an argument; typically, cultivators didn't respect others that were at lower ranks.

Amber's eyelids fluttered as she thought. "How is he supposed to keep the students in line? Let the *other* teachers do it? Who would keep *them* under control?"

Dale slapped the table, much less impressively than the others had been able to do. "By being an *administrator*. I don't want a school to be run only by those that can use *force* on others; that will lead to a corrupt faculty nigh instantly! Look at the treatise by the Scholar D. Coda; his study done on the Amazonian Queendom clearly lays this out. If they hadn't only given authority to people with the physical power to back it up, their capital would not have fallen, and they wouldn't have lost half their population in a cataclysmic uprising. Let's learn from the past, not dive into their mistakes in the present."

"A *scholar*! That's a good one! You are citing history that I was *there* for, Dale. It is the history of The Master as well. In any case, I think you have used enough memory stones if you are able to learn about esoteric case studies and find a way to use them in general conversation." Madame Chandra chortled, then read some more of the information from the document. "It says here that Artorian developed his own cultivation technique when he was in his *fifties*. Goodness. I can't even imagine how corrupt his center was at that point. He was a philosopher and bedridden for three years until he suddenly decided to become a cultivator…"

"I like him," Tyler stated as the others silently read.

Brianna shrugged, "At least he isn't the High Elf. I say go for it."

"We'll give him a three month probationary period then," Dale stated with relief. "We're finally done. Thank goodness. I'm going to go do other things, no more full meetings for at least a week." He left the room, searching for his team to prepare them for the upcoming raid on a new dungeon.

CHAPTER FIVE

"Where are we? The dungeon has stopped moving forward and is sinking toward the waves. Is it going to drown us?" Hans was lying flat on the ground, looking over the edge of Mountaindale's cliff at the ocean below and speaking in a conversational tone. "At least that would be a novel experience. It's been nothing but blue for *days*. Blue sky, blue water, blue feelings..."

Rose was oiling her beast-sinew bowstring but glanced up when Hans spoke. "We must be above the dungeon that Dale wants us to fight in. Is it so surprising to you that a dungeon in the ocean is surrounded by water, Hans?"

"No, I'm more worried that this place doesn't exist, and Dale is having a strange fantasy... oh, hey, look! There is a teeny-tiny island down there. Must be the entrance. Neat." Hans smiled up at the party, trying to dazzle them with a brilliant smile.

"The 'Dale is crazy' routine is getting really old." Dale had his arms crossed and was staring the Assassin down. "We have seen definitive proof that I am not making this stuff up."

Hans ignored him and looked over the edge once more. "I'd say that we have about ten minutes before we get close enough to survive the fall. Not sure why we are going to jump off the cliff instead of going down the path to the flat area. Sure, we save time, but is it really time that we would rather use this way?"

Dale shrugged and gestured at a raft they were going to be sitting on. "I have a plan; I've done something similar to this before."

"That's *wonderful*, but I think I'll just go ahead and drop under my own power. You know, since I can just float down on the wind. Your suicide raft over there would sure be *fun* to get on..." Hans started making motions like he was getting to his feet, but extra slowly.

"Dale, what are you *doing*?" Rose lunged at Dale as she saw him begin to equip a familiar item. "Why in the world would you put on those cursed gauntlets again?"

"No, these are different." Dale attempted to soothe her. "New and improved version."

"Not cursed gear? You sure? Those symbols look... pretty similar." Adam leaned in for a closer inspection, squinting at the intricate runes.

"I see lots of corruption in the Cores, but nothing in the gloves themselves. Might be fine, might be cursed. You should get them looked at," Hans nonchalantly added, flopping back down to the ground instead of standing as he had planned.

Dale looked at the gauntlets that he was just about to empower. "They better *not* be cursed." Sending Essence through the Inscriptions, his heart fell as the gauntlets tightened and latched onto his wrists. "Oh, *come* on!"

"Really, Dale? *Really*?" Hans slipped to his feet in a whirl of flesh and loose clothes. "What did I *just* say?"

<Sorry, Dale, but you have a track record of failure, to the point where if I ever die, I want you to be the one to lower my body into the ground, just so that you can let me down one last time.> Dale's face went red as he listened to the dungeon. <On the plus side, I built these so that they will slide up under your sleeves when you aren't in combat. Yes, the hook on your armor designed to hold them was a distraction. It comes right off. Oh, also, try channeling each type of Essence through the gems in the gauntlet. All at the same time, if you don't mind.>

Fuming, Dale did as instructed. His knuckles lit up in various colors, and he was hit by a wave of fatigue as a large amount of Essence was drained through him and into his armor. The gauntlets wove themselves into his 'shirt', and his shirt wove into his pants, shoes, and balaclava. The previously dull colors of his outfit changed, becoming vibrant and showing various Inscriptions placed throughout the entire material. After a moment, the color in the Runes faded, but the hue of the outfit remained. Dale punched the ground and shouted, "Seriously! This entire *set* is cursed gear?"

<Punching my mountain doesn't hurt me. Also, to answer your question: yes it is, but now it cleans both itself and your body. You never *need* to take it off now! You're welcome. It also helps to regulate heat. Not in, you know, lava or a blizzard, but in normal situations.> In Dale's opinion, his origin was *entirely* too cheerful about this.

"*Cal.* What if I need to use the latrine?" Dale growled softly, already getting shifty looks from his team. He didn't need to be shouting into the air for the dungeon to hear him.

<I *did* say they were self-cleaning, didn't I?>

"*No.*"

<Fine. Just tell them 'toilet mode', and the necessary areas will become exposed. Also, that only works if *you* tell it; some random person can't do it to you.>

"What about if *you* instruct it?" Dale's eyes were narrowed so tightly that he may as well have his eyes closed.

<Well... oh look, time for you all to go after the dungeon down there!>

"Dale, stop being strange and let's get going. Nice outfit by the way; bright reds and purples are *great* for maintaining stealth." Hans' eyes were rolling hard. When Dale didn't budge, just continuing to stand in the same spot mumbling, Hans grabbed him and put him on the raft with the others. "Hope you're ready!"

Hans shoved the raft off the edge, jumping after them only a moment later. As the wind rushed past him, he chuckled at the screams coming from the lower ranked cultivators. "I'm sure they'll be fine."

Dale was forced to snap out of his funk, and he reached into his bag and pulled out a Core. Focusing on sending out tendrils of Essence with air corruption in them, Dale waited for the right moment and shattered the Core in his fist. *Bamph.* He directed the explosive influx of Essence into the tendrils he had created, thickening them and doubling their length in an instant. The invisible tendrils caught at the air around them, slowing their fall from 'deadly' all the way to 'uncomfortable' just before the raft slapped into the water.

The group was drenched as the raft sank a few feet into the water before springing back upward. As the water ran off the now-damaged craft, Hans landed lightly and looked around at the sputtering group. "That looked fun!"

Rose formed her hand into a scoop and splashed water all over the Assassin. Hans looked shocked as she burst into laughter. "It actually *was* fun, and you deserve to be dunked for not joining us."

Adam, meanwhile, was looking at Dale and making sure that he didn't have any severe injuries or issues from using his new trick. "That was beyond foolish. You, more than anyone living, should understand that using Cores like that is wasteful and dangerous."

"I know that, but I only had an issue when I used a Core filled with Mana. I can handle this," Dale brushed off Adam's concerns.

"Spoken like a true power addict," Adam replied softly. "Let me guess, 'you can stop whenever you want'. You don't *need* the Cores."

"Well, *obviously*." Dale looked over at the small island, instantly seeing a path to get underground. "There's our target, everyone. Let's get in there and finish this place off quickly."

After paddling through the waves, they arrived on an island that appeared to be perfectly circular. Only sand and two palm trees were present, and the trees were on either side of what seemed to be a ramp sloping down into the unknown. The Northern Barbarian, Tom, stared at the perfectly smooth ramp and spat to the side. "Hey. You think a human has ever gone in there before? I think this could be difficult for all sorts of reasons we aren't considering. Perhaps we should allow another team, trained professionals, to scout the dungeon below?"

"Unfortunately... we don't have that kind of time." Dale adjusted his gauntlets and strode into the ground. "If there is something we can't handle, we will just have to deal with turning around."

They walked on the downward slope, interested to see that there was decent lighting in the area. It was shimmering and reflecting off the water, but they could see where they were walking. As they entered the first floor, it was clear that the walkways were mainly natural formations from the tide moving through the area. Tide pools filled a vast cavern, various life forms in the shallows.

"See any traps?" Rose nudged Hans, who was looking around with a smile on his face.

"None! This is the only dungeon I've ever seen that has traps and creatures only designed to prey on the *environment*. Look at this!" Hans pointed at a pool where a huge moray eel was zipping around. "If we fall in the water, we might be in trouble, but we are apparently totally safe on the sandbar!"

With this being said, they moved through the cavern and avoided fighting in all but one instance. They had to ford a small stream to get to the next downward sloping ramp, and an oversized piranha tried to go for their legs. Dale punched it several times, each strike breaking through scales and allowing him to tear Essence away from it and into himself. When the fish died, a small item drop appeared seven feet away. Hans rushed over and looked at it, rolling his eyes before tossing the item into the water behind them.

"Fish food." Hans sighed and trudged toward the ramp. "Unsurprisingly, the rewards are things that are useless to us. Most attackers here are *fish*. So the rewards are tasty fish food. I hate it here already."

Down the ramp they went, and after a few turns, the air began to get moist and musty. Walking onto the next floor, the walls opened up to reveal an expansive space filled with water. There was a path around the room that sloped slightly toward the water, apparently designed to direct any liquid to flow down into the pool. For them, it was a convenient path to avoid the vast shapes moving under the surface below them.

"This entire place is *stuffed* with water Essence," Rose commented carelessly. "Dale, seriously, even though we are on a mission, you might as well take in some of this. It's obvious that no one has ever cultivated here."

"I will at the exit of this floor. Let's make sure not to get caught off guard because we haven't really needed to fight yet." Dale was uneasy. "This is a dungeon, and it should *certainly* have something to defend itself with soon, something that could fight us on at least equal terms. The Essence in here is just too *dense* not to have some powerfully evolved creatures, so we can't forget to stay vigilant."

"True, very true." Hans looked around the cavern, yawning and fiddling with his daggers. "How's your aura going, by the way?"

"Ugh, it's a gigantic frustration." Dale pulled a face and continued walking. "I know to break into the C-ranks we need to force the excess Essence we collect into our bodies and aura, but for some reason, mine is expanding *so* slowly compared to anyone else I've ever heard of. It's actually hard to maintain expanding it when I see such poor results."

"Hmm." Hans tapped the tip of his dagger against his teeth, producing a sound that made Rose wince. "Well... I'm no Craig, but I am in the C-ranks. Hey, Dale, you know what makes your aura expand really fast? Impure Essence. Yup. Instead of weaving a tapestry inside your body, you just add corruption and slap stones together to make a wall."

There was confused silence for a moment, and right as Dale was about to ask what Hans meant, the man continued, "Guess what makes people bad at cultivation and actually attaining higher ranks? You may have guessed it: corruption. You see, your Essence is so pure that there is no wasted space, no 'extra' that *isn't* being filled with Essence. That's likely why it is going so slowly. On the positive side, when you *do* increase in rank, you can expect to be more powerful than others at that same level. Again, you should really talk to Craig about this. He's the expert. I just... dabble."

Dale contemplated this advice. "Thanks, Hans. Motivation is exactly what I needed. I think."

"That's nice, but you should really look out for that tentacle." Hans stated this in such a bland tone that Dale didn't register the threat right away. He was whipped across the back and tossed into the wall, needing to work hard not to slip off the slope and into the pool below.

"What was *that*?" Dale roared as he got to his feet, spinning around to see tentacles lifting out of the water.

"Some kind of octopus. I've got it." Rose drew an arrow, collected a ball of chaotic Essence on the tip, and smoothly fired it into the cephalopod's head as it breached the water. The tentacles spasmed and the water blackened from ink, but it then toppled over and began floating listlessly in the muddied pool. "Shall we?"

Chapter Six

The group reached the lowest level of the dungeon without much incident. This place, while likely an amazing predator in the ocean, was simply not built to defend against intelligent fighters. There was *one* last challenge ahead of them, and it was a doozy. A massive king crab was waiting for them, snapping its pincers in their general direction. Beyond having eight legs, it was mutated to have four pincers and have a glistening, diamond-hard shell.

"Would anyone be opposed to me attempting to handle this challenge on my own?" Tom loudly drawled to the others. He didn't wait for an answer, and instead, pulled his oversized warhammer out of a bag that was far too small to contain it. The Barbarian started jogging toward the crustacean, picking up speed as he moved. Just as he got in range of the pincers, Essence that he had been gathering at his feet exploded into flames and sent him soaring at the monster with a speed he couldn't naturally attain. The pincers missed closing around him, clacking together hard enough to create small shockwaves.

Tom spun and used his momentum to swing his hammer. Like the moons circling the earth, the warhammer turned with utter inevitability, landing against the shell with enough kinetic force to cause a localized earthquake. Unbelievably, the shell held firm. No cracks could be seen, and no blood came pouring out. The crab had stopped moving though and, after a few moments, toppled over as the others watched in awe.

"Good, you remembered my lessons." Hans stepped forward and clapped Tom on the back. "If the exterior is overly armored, it is likely that they are compensating with weak internal defenses. You landed that blow right over its eyes, so you rattled its brain hard enough to kill it. Now, where did you go wrong?"

"Using that ability while surrounded by water and water Essence reduced the effectiveness by a great amount." Tom furrowed his brow and thought harder. "Beyond that, I... did I do anything wrong?"

"You didn't make sure it was dead." Hans moved slightly, and a massive pincer was suddenly bearing down on Tom.

"Ahh!" Tom yelped, falling backward into a puddle in surprise.

"Ha! Gotcha!" Hans was holding the pincer in front of Tom, wiggling it around and pretending to clamp the Northman. "*Rawr*! I'm just joking. Really though, a lot of beasts like to play dead to lure in prey, so use caution. Gimme one second; I'm gonna see if this thing has a Core."

"I think I've found the dungeon Core!" Adam called from behind the crab as Rose and Tom both fumed over Hans' antics.

"Grab it and let's get out of here," Dale called over. Adam nodded and created a ring of glowing celestial Essence on the end of his staff. Poking the wood underwater, he fished around for a few moments and pulled up a brightly shining blue Core. After handing the large Core to Dale, Adam turned and led the way back up to the surface.

"What's that sound?" Rose's slightly pointed ears were twitching, and her warning was taken to heart instantly.

"I think the tide is coming in," Hans calmly explained, continuing forward. A moment later, his steps faltered, and he looked back. "Oh. We are pretty far below sea level, and there is now a hostile dungeon Core in your pocket. Let's run."

"The Core shouldn't be able to influence anything in the dungeon right now. My aura should prevent it from interacting with anything!" Dale bitterly complained as they ran up the ramp. Water was trickling down it, the speed and volume increasing by the second.

"It doesn't need to! The tide coming in probably fills the entire dungeon twice a day!" Hans shouted over the sounds of rushing water. "It probably absorbs all of it and converts it to Essence! With nothing absorbing the liquid, this place will fill up and *stay* full."

They re-entered the floor that held a miniature ocean, noting that water was pouring in from all sides. The walkways were waterfalls now, and the water was rising rapidly. Huge shapes were in the water, and the octopus they had slain earlier was bobbing up and down as huge chunks were torn off it to be eaten by the other monsters.

Hans saw what was eating their kill, and his eyebrows rose in surprise. "Whale, whale, whale, what do we have here?"

Gigantic fish that Dale had never heard of were breaching the water, blowing geysers from holes on their heads. Their walkway was cut off, but Dale had another, possibly foolish, idea. "Follow me!" He jumped off the ledge, landing lightly on the huge fish and running across it like a bridge.

"Dale, you are an *abyssal* crazy person!" Tom roared with laughter as he followed his leader in a headfirst dive off the ledge. "I love it! I get to use a fish as a bridge!!"

The fish didn't even seem to realize that there were creatures walking on them, causing Dale to shiver. The sheer scale of these things was terrifying; their size on par with the largest Abominations he had ever seen. The thought of necromancers getting ahold of these and using their flesh and bones in an amalgamation was horrifying. Hopefully their foes remained on land.

"This is surprisingly e-*fish*-ent!" Hans called as they raced against time. If they didn't get up the next ramp soon, either the water would rise too high or the whales would submerge themselves. In both cases, drowning would soon follow. Hans looked at the creatures they were on with a glint in his eyes, then pulled out his daggers and murmured, "You think these things have Cores?"

"Hans, now may not be the time to satisfy your curiosity," Adam stated as they jumped to a new whale. This one reacted to their presence, almost immediately beginning to thrash around. It seemed to realize that it could just go underwater, and as it nose-dived the people ran up its tail and *jumped...* landing on the ledge next to the ramp. Water was pouring down from the upper level, but they were able to power through the current with their enhanced bodies.

As they returned to the first floor, Tom stopped them from moving forward and plunging into the waist-high water. "This level may not be as simple this time."

There were no more walkways. The water had also reached a point where all the creatures were able to move about freely, and dangerous creatures were already striking out toward them to rescue the dungeon Core. Gigantic eels were the fastest, flashing toward them with needle-sharp teeth leading the way. Hans moved forward, his speed so high that he skipped across the water. His daggers plunged downward into the water, opening gaping wounds in their bodies.

Hans was singing as he slew the dungeon monsters. "When a big slimy eel a-bites you on the heel, that's *a moray*!"

"Don't bastardize *love songs*!" Rose shouted at him in the cavern, the word 'songs' reverberating and echoing a few times.

"We need to move faster, everyone." Adam pointed at a wall that was beginning to spray water. "I think that the walls are mainly held in place by the dungeon's will, so right now, they are in serious danger of failing."

"This entire place is an *abyssal* deathtrap." Dale glared at the Core in his satchel before quickly pulling the drawstring tight and diving into the now-chest-high water. He wasn't a particularly good swimmer, having lived on the slopes of various mountains his entire life, but the threat of drowning turned his doggie-paddle into a breaststroke. Luckily, his clothes didn't seem to hold water; therefore, he wasn't dragged down very much. Adam was having significantly more trouble, his large robe soaking up water and dragging him toward the bottom. He had recently broken through to D-rank six, so luckily, his strength was more than enough to allow him to power through the rising water.

While Adam and Rose focused on moving through the currents, Dale and Tom needed to work to defend them from sharp teeth and various poisonous creatures like jellyfish. After a few instances of vicious bites only being stopped by the armor concealed in his clothing, Dale tried to move the water around him in a manner similar to the stone that he had been encased in during his last training session. As he had hoped, the water around him reacted similarly by creating a current that moved away from him. This made the creatures coming at him move much slower while also removing the strain of going against the flowing water. It did *not* help his team, though, so he tried to restructure the water into flowing in a single direction.

It worked to a small degree, but creating functions that work exactly as you want them to was an exhaustingly tricky, time-consuming, and potentially dangerous process. By the time the team worked their way to the ramp, the water level was only a few feet from the roof of the cavern. A wall had given out, creating a cross current that was draining their stamina quickly. If they weren't able to escape as intended, there was the possibility of using the new breech to swim upward if they could avoid the pull of the ocean. They had to dive down to get into the tunnel and then swim upward while enduring constant assaults from normal-sized piranha with oversized fins. These variant fish moved faster through the water than a projectile from a harpoon launcher and were able to shrug off water-slowed punches from Dale.

Rose had a dagger out and was killing off fish every few seconds, but her speed through the water had significantly slowed. Adam was thrashing upward, evidently near the limit of holding his breath. Dale pushed them forward and upward, following the others after attracting the attention of most of the predatory fish. Their bites couldn't get through his armor, but he was confident their mutated jaws were enough to leave behind severe bruises and blood blisters. After a few more strokes, Dale burst through a curtain of water, gasping for air even as he fought to stay above the water line.

A steady hand grabbed Dale and pulled him upward onto the raft. Hans slapped his back hard. "Breathe, breathe. You doing alright? Swallow any water?"

"I'm fine." Dale coughed hard into his arm. "Is everyone out?"

"We're all here," Rose confirmed for him. "We're caught in a whirlpool right now, so I'm uncertain how long we will *be* alright, but..."

Hans waved off her concerns. "We won't be stuck for much longer. The last room was almost full as is. *My* concern is: how the heck are we getting back up there?" He gestured at the island that was floating a few hundred feet above them. Mountaindale and the surrounding land it had taken was hovering in the sky, blotting out the sun and giving off a truly dangerous feeling. Dale supposed that anyone would be nervous when a gigantic chunk of rock could fall out of the sky and crush them at any moment.

Dale simply shrugged. "Cal said he'd take care of it."

"I think I know. I see our ride." Tom pointed at something falling toward them. "Vines? Someone must have told Madame Chandra that we needed a lift."

CHAPTER SEVEN

<Are you in there?> I prodded the captured dungeon Core with a tendril of Essence. It attacked the Essence savagely, doing all it could do to absorb the pure power. This wasn't unusual, I had been given several Dungeon Cores as gifts from Minya. Apparently they were a hot item on the black market. <Hello? I'd hate to destroy you if you can think. No? Do you have a Wisp? Alright... let's see. If you want to survive, if you can hear me or understand the impressions I'm sending you, *don't* try to eat this.>

I extended a small thread of **Acme** mana, which the Core instantly tried to absorb. Instead, it cracked in half and exploded into a massive storm of Essence. I sighed sadly; so far, nothing I did had reached these Cores. At least I had learned to contain the blast of power after I had lost a dozen Goblins by trying to be nice out in the open. Now Essence only raged through a room designed to contain it, and the power was swiftly pulled through the dungeon, purified, and used to empower the various mechanisms of my traps and spawners. Any remainder came to me as a tasty treat, not even enough to be called a snack.

This Core had been C-ranked, but the mind had been from something like a shark. If it had ever had a Wisp, it had eaten it long ago. This Core had been decades away from achieving capabilities needed to actually think and would have required nurturing that no one - especially me - was willing to commit to. Ah well. I was glad that Dale had handed the Core over to me right away; I had been seriously concerned that he would do something foolish like attempt to absorb it himself. Maybe coming back and forming a complete soul had imparted some wisdom or extra intelligence to him? I didn't know for sure, but I was interested in what was going to happen next.

According to all available texts and rumors, when a Core was torn out of a dungeon, one of three things would happen. The first option was *usually* the most likely, where the backlash of losing the controlling Core would kill all of the Mobs, turning the creature with the highest ranked Core into the new dungeon Core. This made the dungeon into a new, weaker version. This wouldn't happen here, as far as I could tell from Dale's story, there should only be one creature in there with a Core, and Hans had taken it.

The second option was that the accumulated Essence would be released into the environment slowly, mutating and empowering the nearby... everything. Even the water could gain some mystical properties. That was the least likely option normally because option number three was the apparent go-to.

In this scenario, the accumulated power was released all at once. *Boom.* Cataclysm. Mana storms, cats and dogs living together peacefully, rain turning into diamonds. Also, fire. Lots of fire, and in almost every circumstance. I was trying to avoid this because I was attempting to create a fourth option.

In what I was unbiasedly calling the best case 'Cal option', my ley lines would insert themselves and regulate the various Essences in the area. There was already a framework all around the dungeon's location, and now that there wasn't an active influence eating away at my Inscriptions, they should be working to connect and drain the excess Essence into *my* dungeon. Even though I was directly above the dead dungeon, the power wouldn't reach me for several days. It would follow the ley lines back to my mountain's original location, then the condensed Essence would pour through a small portal that connected me to my growing reservoir of Essence.

I say reservoir, but it was currently more like a funnel. There was hardly any Essence in there, as I was able to absorb it as fast as it appeared. Perhaps it would accumulate over time as my network of lines connected fully, but for now... well, for now it just waited. The skyland was starting to move again, but as always, it gained speed just as quickly as it slowed down. Eventually, I would be able to make the entire thing a part of my dungeon, but that was going more slowly than I liked. At least I had boundaries and a goal for myself. Eat. Entire. Mountain. Tearing it out of the earth and making it fly was one thing, but most of the Essence I would need to use to expand my influence went instead to keeping the place afloat.

I looked at the shattered remnants of the dead dungeon Core one last time before absorbing them. Now that this task was out of the way and Navigation Bob had charted a course to our next destination, it was time to try out some of my new... features. That sounded better than 'killer golems and deadly traps', right? Oh, and before that, there was another group going to challenge Manny the man-eating Manticore! This should be fun. The five Mages looked fresh, determined, and excited for the battle that they would be fighting. They must have come to this floor via a keygem and portal and seemed to think that they were going to get a sneak attack off on the floor Boss. This made me chuckle darkly. Manny knew they were coming. Manny was waiting. Manny... was *hungry*.

"This thing is in the B-ranks, right?" One of the men was polishing a weapon that gleamed in the sparse light of the room. I had no idea why he was doing so; even *I* couldn't see any imperfections on the surface of the blade. Although the edge could have used a bit of sharpening.

"Yeah. B-one, if the new info is correct." These people must be in the B-ranks at least, but I was thoroughly uncertain how they got the keygem. Either they bought it or stole it, and since I had never seen them before, I had no idea what form their mana would take. On the plus side, they were seemingly unaware that most of my creatures were far stronger than others of their same ranking. Any of my Mobs in the B-ranks had at least rudimentary intelligence, which translated into adaptive fighting styles. Cats could pounce, and Manny could skewer you by sliding his tail through a hole in the wall or floor and ambushing you. He had also learned a new trick where he waited on the mirrored ceiling and dropped rocks on people.

"Shouldn't be an issue. Let's get the bounty and check out the next floor. Not too many people have the Manticore keygem, so getting down to the next floor is costing an arm and a leg." This came from a man who was the apparent leader of the group, although it seemed that there was some contention, as another spoke nearly instantly.

"Better than paying with an *actual* arm or leg." This man sneered at the leader, making me happier with every passing second. Contention in the group! That should make this easier.

The leader rolled his eyes and jumped back as a projection of light appeared in the air before them. It wasn't anything malicious - mainly because I couldn't seem to weaponize the illusion - but it held some information that Manager Bob collected for me. "This Boss has a forty percent pass rate? What does that even... oh, the words changed. For every ten prepared parties that enter, only four groups survive. Then... what's this, 'challenge rating'?"

I growled to myself at that. I had made Bob update the list after Chandra came down here and killed Manny all by herself to gather 'exotic meats'. The challenge rating meant that people who fought and won a hard-fought battle earned more and had a higher spot on the leaderboard than people who might come down with a group of A-ranked people and blow my Manticore to smithereens.

"Who cares? Let's do this and get moving." They pushed open the massive door and stepped through into the Boss battle arena. Manny was waiting for them patiently, sitting on the floor and staring at the approaching Mages. "Pff. It is so scared that it's just waiting to die! Let's oblige him, boys!" The sneering man ran forward, plainly attempting to steal command out from under his current leader. Two of the other men cursed and darted forward to join Mr. Speedy Man, but the leader and what must be their group's healer didn't move.

"Something's wrong." The healer was trembling as he stared at the Manticore. "I can sense no Mana from that beast. Boss, you need to call them back. ...Boss?" The healer looked over, just as the man he was talking to slipped to the ground. Before the healer could shout a warning, a potently poisoned spike tore into his back. He slumped to the floor, joining his leader on the ground.

The charging men got in range of the Manticore, who seemed to be almost *smirking* at them. It didn't even bother to move as a Mana-infused sword sliced through the air and stabbed into... a mirror. The reflection shattered, and to their credit, the men whirled around nearly instantly. They saw that two of their number were already dead, then their eyes traveled up a bit. The Manticore was sitting on a ledge that was placed above the doorway, mimicking the pose it had been using in the angled mirror. A deep chuckle resounded through the room, and the men began to sweat. "Get it!"

Manny crouched and sprang forward at them like a tiger, opening his wings with a snap and *zipping* toward the Mages. There were abrupt curses, and the men scattered out of the way before launching their own assault. Oh, now this was interesting! I was starting to classify Mages by the tier their **law** was residing on, which I had learned was a common practice. Now, I didn't get a chance to interact with *every* node in the Tower of Ascension, but I had a pretty good feel for their general location. The more I interacted with various forms of Mana, and the more I grew to know my own, the better I could gauge Mages.

Two of them were 'tier one' Mages, basic Mages that had accepted a **law** from the first level. One was a fire Mage, the other a wind Mage. The final man was a tier three, and his abilities were more abstract and powerful. He was a 'force' Mage, someone who could transfer force from one position to another. After the first two sent a blast of elemental destruction toward Manny as a distraction, they all wound back and punched into the air with as much power as they possibly could. This force was redirected across the distance, and Manny took the entire synchronized kinetic load of three B-ranked Mages on his chest. The area it hit was the size of a pinhead, so it blew through his armor and splattered his innards against the back wall without hardly moving his body at large.

Manny collapsed with a shudder, coughing wetly and weakly. In a few moments, he stilled. I was stunned at the outcome of the battle. I would have *never* expected a couple of sneering jerks to survive against Manny. For some reason, I was *certain* that he would rally at the last minute and have a fantastic comeback. I guess the only comeback he'd get was when I *brought* him back. Wow. Oh, right, they won. I formed a keygem and let it clatter to the ground at the top of the stairs leading downward. Put in the work, get the reward... even if you *are* a sucky person.

Chapter Eight

The Mages walked down to the next level and halted. They stood there for a few moments, gawking at the various paths they could take. Obviously, they were frustrated by the concealment Runes I had made, but even the simple paths that *were* visible seemed to entice them *almost* to the point of self-destruction. Not being able to see the way clearly was surely frustrating, and in fact, they nearly stepped on the trail and started walking in order to see and understand more of them. That would have undeniably spelled doom for them, but sadly, they realized their current weakness in time to make an inglorious escape.

Too bad. The portal closed behind them with a *fizzle*, and my lowest levels were once again mercifully empty. Mostly empty. I still pretended not to see the Dark Elf guards that 'protected' the Silverwood tree that grew over my position. They tried so hard to be stealthy; I just couldn't bear to break their hearts. Heh, that made me think of bears and bear jokes. Maybe someday I would make an entire area devoted to that. Then if they did something wrong I could make a *pun*ishment! It might be funny. No, it *would* be funny! I just couldn't let Dani know about it 'til it was too late, or she would try to stop me.

I briefly glanced upward, looking over the first few levels and smiling at the massive amount of fighters that were moving around the area. I usually left those floors to be managed by the Bobs, but it was fun to see all these students struggling against Bashers. Seriously, how do you have a hard time fighting rabbits when they didn't come in overwhelming numbers? Just then I saw a Hopsecutioner decapitate an instructor with a sneak attack.

I winced; Dale was going to be sad that they needed to find *another* instructor for... lutes?

What in the world was *her* class doing here? You know, besides getting beat into the ground? The students lasted longer than the teacher, but not by much. There was only one survivor, a Dwarven earth cultivator. He coated himself in stone and was ignored by the Mobs. He escaped after they left the area, I tracked his progress directly to the tavern. Now, a serious question, why were the Hopsecutioners this far up in the dungeon? Hadn't I assigned them to hang out with Raile or something? ...Yes. I had, but... they were rank C-zero mobs and only came out when they were bored, or a too-powerful group attacked Raile. Technically, these things were stronger than Snowball, at least in cultivation, but... they were rabbits. If they were this bored, I thought it would be fine leaving them as wandering monsters... so I looked for something else to work on.

At that point, I was waiting on the results of the self-writing quills I had designed based off my vision. It had been fun to access creativity mana because I was suddenly able to envision Runes that I had never seen nor heard of. Not to brag but I had a copy of *every* Rune known by the Spotters, and their lists were extensive. So suddenly being able to take an idea and write out an unknown Rune... pretty amazing. The combinations I had made had produced these new quills after only a few failures, and I didn't even accidentally summon a creature when I powered the new Runes! Sure, I had blasted a hole out of the mountain, but that just made it easier to fill that space with my influence. Sure, I had been testing in a reinforced experimentation room, but this was Mana so powerful that it was located at the highest, well, *second* highest tier in the Tower of Ascension. Even a *drop* of it was more potent than a river of tier one mana.

To be fair, I shouldn't have powered the Inscription with that type of Mana, but I was *so* excited! I probably should have used Essence and did on the next trial, but still! Now I had a self-writing quill in each of the workrooms that I had set up for non-Mages. They recorded everything anyone in the area said or did, and it was kind of funny to see the annotation 'Spotter attempted to grab quill and screamed in frustration when defensive Runes took hold'. That was all *over* the place on the papers. The Spotters that could see the pens moving were salivating over the thought of new Runes. Heh. I'd make sure to give these out as a reward on the lowest levels, but I would put the Inscriptions on the interior of the quill and make it from some kind of material that would take weeks to peel away. That should keep 'em busy for a while.

"What are you doing, Cal?" Dani interrupted my chuckling and diabolical plans, and I went silent instantly.

<Just, uh, going over the results of the Runes and such that I've been working on!> I must have sounded a little too innocent because she didn't seem to believe me.

"Is that what you *should* be doing? Or should you be working on what *we* decided you should be doing?" Her voice had a dangerous inflection, and I sighed at the reminder.

<Dani, you see, sometimes, I just need a break. Expanding influence is so slow and boring and time-consuming! I just-> I was cut off quickly; she knew that I could find any number of things to say about this.

"It isn't a *break* when you are doing it all the time. Take a break from your 'break' every once in a while and do actual work. There's an idea! You doing work is actually a break from what you *normally* do." Dani's voice was a whiplash.

<Demanding little thing, aren't you?> I muttered quietly. Not quietly enough. Apparently.

Dani flashed red. "Excuse *me*? You are the one that asked me to keep you on task for the deadline *you* set! I-"

<You are excused, thanks for the apology! Listen, I have a lot of work to do, so I'm going to grab all this Essence and sink down into the stone, 'kay? Love, love! Bye!> A hurricane of Essence followed my mind as I dove into the ground beneath my Core and began converting Essence into influence. I heard a growl from above, and the floor vibrated. Dani was in the Mage ranks with the same access to **Acme** that I had. Scary. To work and quickly!

I had *almost* enough space converted to make a new floor, but I was holding off until I could think of a good theme for it. I could continue with the Tower of Ascension theme, but what I had between the sixth and seventh floor currently listed out options all the way to the ninth tier. I initially had all of them on one, but that had been too crowded for me to really *enjoy* watching the battles. Now, the platforms were more extensive, and I was able to fit a changing roster of options onto each floor.

I had only seen two beings besides myself that were in the upper tiers, hinting at the fact that most people *couldn't* get to that point. It made a certain kind of sense. As I had climbed the tower, the concepts became more abstract and powerful. At a certain point, a fleshy brain wouldn't be able to turn away from the deepest desires of their mind and would suddenly wake up bound to a **law**.

I would bet money - if it had any value to me - that most people who got to those tiers blocked out the memories of the other things they had seen. Heck, *I* wanted to block out a few of them. Madness had been so... *alluring*. It had an innocence, a compelling sweet sound... but it had been full of rot and corruption. The dichotomy threatened to damage my mind if I thought on it too hard. No wonder the Madness cultivator,

Xenocide, had been so strange. If he hadn't started that way, going to places overflowing with madness just to study it and draw it into himself would undoubtedly do it.

Maybe I would make this into a rest room. Not a toilet area, but a pleasant and comfortable space. That sounded kind of ideal, and since I hadn't made any areas for Mages, maybe I would do something like that here. Blocking the Mages from the workshops and training areas still made sense, but perhaps I could create some extravagant manors, giant personal workshops, and a pool! That would be nice, a small communal area so the Mages didn't get all cagey and introverted. I snorted at that. Like *I* had room to think about others being introverted.

Also... I think that the keygems I make for this floor will be tied to the people that use them the first time. I want this to be the Mage's Refuge from other people, especially the students at the academy. Oh, this will be fun. If I had hands, I would be rubbing them together in delight. There was going to be an undeniable surge of Mages trying to get to this floor as soon as it was found. With all the people that had been running here from the necromancers, all of the uppity Nobles and all the students... space on the surface was being rented at a premium. Manors deep in the dungeon? I can't even imagine how they would react.

After dutifully expanding my influence over the course of six hours, I turned to my new project with gusto. With a thought, I made a precise cut in the stone by absorbing the minerals. Taking away was much easier than creating, so the structures I was picturing began to form quickly. It looked like giant slabs of rock were falling and vanishing, revealing stone frameworks for buildings that had been there all along. Oh, this was going to be fun!

Chapter Nine

Dale was back to training, which is all he seemed to do these days. Practice, meetings, and just a *hint* of harrowing danger from charging into an unknown dungeon with the intent to kill it. His Moon Elf instructor had nearly killed him outright when he learned that Dale had gone into the oceanic dungeon, and after doling out a severe beating, he had been forcing Dale to fight against monsters constantly.

This was monster number fifteen, and Dale was already coughing blood from the repeated body blows he had taken during earlier fights. The beast charged him, and thanks to having two swollen eyelids, Dale didn't see this fast enough to dodge. He wasn't sure what this creature was, but it had reasonably simple characteristics. It was all teeth and claws, had six legs, and was surprisingly light. The being hopped on his chest and started tearing into him, or at least, it was trying to.

Dale's clothes had no tears, abrasions, or even loose threads. He could feel nasty bruises forming under the paths of the claws and teeth but was able to grab the thing and *squeeze.* Crying in a cross between piteous and furious, the animal struggled even harder for a long moment before a *snap* resounded through the area. The creature fell limp, and Dale slid to the ground as well, completely exhausted.

"Let's see here... 'the dungeon wanted me to do it'. 'I needed to get the dungeon Core and give it to the dungeon'. 'It was something I was supposed to do myself'." The Moon Elf was ticking things off on his fingers as he recited parts of earlier conversations. "We are going to try again, and if the answer doesn't satisfy me, I am going to let something nastier in. Now, tell me again why you went into an unknown dungeon, with a team in the C or D ranks, with *no* backup, and *without* explaining it to the people relying on you."

"I just..." Dale sighed and dragged himself to his feet, "I have no excuse. It was a bad idea, and it won't happen again."

The Moon Elf stared at him, nodding after a few long seconds. "That was the correct answer, finally! I thought we were going to be here all night." He pulled a lever, and a small gate opened. Out of the gate came a yowling Flesh Cat from the lower levels of the dungeon. It pounced at Dale, its Essence ability tearing open his skin and ignoring his armor entirely as it slashed hooked claws at him.

"*Ow!*" Dale twisted away from the Cat, returning the assault with one of his own. His fist hit the Cat, and the studded knuckles broke its skin. The Cat had a strange expression on its face as the blood in its body lurched and churned away from the normal paths it would be taking. A huge bruise formed on the hairless Beast before it collapsed, but when it did, Dale angrily tore it open and pulled out a Core. Glaring up at the Elf, he asked a simple question, "Why?"

"I told you that if your answer didn't satisfy me, I would let a monster in. Just because your answer was *correct...*" he trailed off, pulling another lever and making Dale blanch. Thank goodness, this time it revealed an exit from the training arena the academy had built. "This is a handy invention. Great for letting people test their limits. How do you feel, Dale? Do you feel that your limits have been... tested?"

Dale frowned, feeling at his Core. It was almost completely drained, leaving only a depressingly small trickle of Essence running through his body. "I certainly feel like I am completely exhausted if that's what you are getting at. I have almost no Essence remaining, and I haven't slept in thirty-nine hours. My limits feel tested, yes."

The Moon Elf sneered at him. “Good. Dale, if you are so weak currently, how did you not only break the Scrivener’s spine but also beat a Flesh Cat to death with repeated blows? Before you try some half-baked answer, I’ll just tell you. Your *aura.* It’s weak as of yet, but your body is becoming more directly powerful. All of this was without using Essence directly, which means you are becoming formidable. Not to mention the hand-to-hand combat style you have been learning is the most effective style for killing without a weapon that currently exists. Now, there is another aspect to the aura that you have been building throughout your body and in your immediate surroundings.”

He paused a moment, considering his next words. “Two aspects, actually. First, the Essence that you are inserting into your body is the path that your Mana will take once you actually gain access to it. This has a different meaning to many people, but the gist of it is that Mana will only empower the areas where you have stored Essence. I've seen people do a poor job of maintaining their aura, and they are torn apart when they try to move into the Mage ranks. I heard that you needed motivation; I hope that covers it. Consider yourself motivated."

"I'm feeling it." Dale's face was green, extra queasy at the thought that he had been ignoring his Essence collection recently.

“Good.” The Elf looked away, gathering his thoughts. "Second, there is a reason it is called 'aura' and not 'body preparation'. You've already been using what I am talking about, or your body would be significantly more *singed* than it currently is. By holding your Essence in multiple patterns around you and infusing them with various corruption, you are able to generate elemental ‘shielding’. This is more useful than you seem to think if your lax attitude in practicing your shields is any indication. What I want you to do is prepare the shield you've been using to block my fire traps."

Dale was relatively confident that this was another lesson that he wasn't going to like. "One small issue, teacher. I am almost fully out of Essence right now."

The Elf waved at him and growled. "Then sit down and cultivate, you infernally frustrating man-child! Not that it will matter much. Until you have a full aura and step into the C-ranks, whatever you manage to create will be a wispy shadow of what it will become."

Glad for the respite, Dale sat and began greedily sucking in all of the Essence around him, heedless of its natural affinity. The strange energies swirled around him, getting pulled to his body and covering him with colored lights if you could see them. Typically, this would make for a corrupted Center and would hamper the future growth of anyone foolish enough to cultivate in such a manner. There were a few exceptions. In the dungeon below them, the Essence was cleaned and had little to no corruption in it. Dale could take it a step further, as the tiny corruption Cores that surrounded his central Core would funnel all of the corruption away and use it to power the various cursed equipment that Dale was using.

Within five minutes, Dale was moderately sure that he could hold his shielding in place for a handful of minutes, so he stood, got into position, created the shield, and nodded at the Elf. His instructor hadn't bothered to wait for the nod of confirmation, throwing a massive fireball at the now-nervous Dale. The fire washed over him, splitting around and rebounding off of his shielding.

"I have three important lessons to teach you right now. Lesson one: like *reflects* like." The Elf held a fireball in each hand and bounced them off each other. Creating a strange watery spike, he tossed it at Dale. "Lesson two: opposites *cancel.*"

Indeed, as the water hit Dale's shield, there was a small gout of steam that rose away from the impact site, and Dale felt a bit weaker. The Elf continued to speak the entire time Dale was pondering. "It is easier and less Essence intensive to reflect than to cancel. When canceling out another affinity, you are betting that you have put at least as much Essence into your shield as your opponent is throwing at you. Lesson three."

His instructor now had a whirling tornado in his palm. He threw it at Dale, and as the wind Essence brushed against the fire Essence, a roaring flame scorched Dale's exposed hands. As Dale cursed and shook his hand, the Moon Elf snickered. "Hee... I love this lesson. Adjacents *interact.* When in combat, knowing the protections that a person has in place is the key to not only winning, but surviving. Since I knew that you had only placed fire in your defense, it was easy for me to know what would happen."

"There are only so many things that I can make!" Dale had waited until it appeared that the Moon Elf was finished speaking. He had learned long ago that interrupting the Elf was a recipe for a tooth-loosening slap. "I have access to each of the elements, but how can I possibly know what is about to assault me?"

"Two things." Luckily his instructor seemed to be in a talking mood instead of a 'beat Dale ‘til he gets it' mood. "Practice. You know how to look at a person and see what Essence is swirling around them. You simply need to get better at interacting and understanding what that means. Now, some people will intentionally misdirect you, using an element in their shields that they don't plan to use for attacking. Be wary, for all combat is a life-or-death situation. Honor is a joke in battle, and if I have taught you anything, I hope it is that you must do anything, *anything*, to survive. Winning is secondary in all cases. Next, think for a moment; if you have access to all forms of Essence, what do you need to do to protect against a larger portion of them?"

Dale didn't respond right away, instead cursing himself for not seeing the obvious answer right away. "I would guess that I need to combine them?"

"Correct. You have an advantage that others can't get without reaching the B-ranks at a minimum." The Elf lifted his hands and twined together fire and wind Essence over his hands. "Aura can be used for defense and attack. There are many, many people who focus entirely on using aura to its fullest potential. Typically, these are people without access to techniques or other forms of more efficient fighting abilities. Using aura allows you to empower your body as well as offer other simple short-to-medium range means of assault without the need for extensive training. Observe."

Dale watched as the Elf increased the swirl of wind. Pointing his hand away from himself with his palm aiming at a training dummy, the Assassin forcibly ejected a river of fire that acted like a twister, creating a blazing cone that engulfed the mannequin and quickly burned away all the flammable portions. Liquid metal began to drip, and the fire suddenly stopped sprouting from the delicate-seeming hand. "Now, the trick is to learn how to combine elements in your shield without doing *that* to your body. I'm sure you understand the inherent risk involved here, so please practice near a healer or at least away from highly-populated areas if you plan to do something *extra* foolish."

Staring at the ruined dummy, the thought that he could have easily started a conflagration on his skin of the same intensity caused Dale's eye to twitch nervously. This had been an excellent lesson: no practicing until he was well-rested and thinking clearly.

CHAPTER TEN

After getting a very rejuvenating three hours of sleep, Dale decided to find one of the few people he knew of that could help him with exact requirements for his shielding. "Good morning, Craig. Do you mind if I take a few minutes of your time?"

The Monk looked up from his breakfast of tea and broccoli, seeming a bit surprised by Dale's words. "Oh? I believe that our next session was supposed to be tomorrow, but if there is something I can help with, I am always glad to do so."

"Thank you. I am attempting to create aura shielding, but I am concerned that I may damage myself. I was hoping that you could give me some information to make this a bit easier." Dale was trying to keep his voice down; several people were already looking over at them, exchanging coins, and chuckling. There was a simple explanation for this. Dale no longer ate in this area but he still *technically* had a standing order from the cook to bring him herbs, meats, and rare ingredients that may be found in the dungeon. Dale was attempting to keep a low profile because the man would always charge at him and demand service if he knew that Dale was here. It had become something of a game for the cook, but the threats he made were genuine.

"Oh, we were going to start going over that tomorrow night anyway. I suppose you were given a more... practical lesson from your... combat instructor?" Craig had initially been excited for Dale, as the Moon Elf hand-to-hand combat forms were considered to be the most thorough and deadly martial arts in the world. After seeing Dale's patchwork of new scars and the constant damage he sustained, Craig had grown more concerned. Not to mention he was starting to dislike the Moon

Elf that would inflict such punishment on his former team member and current student.

"I did, and I am very excited not to turn myself into a wreck of a person. I've died too many... I mean, I've come close to dying too many times to want to put myself into that sort of situation again. I'm also fairly certain that he is standing over in that corner watching me, and if I were to try it alone he may very well cut off an arm or something as punishment." Dale had gestured at a corner of the large tent they were eating in, and moments after he did so, the tent flap opened and closed 'by itself'. Sure. Invisible freaks.

"I think that we can do some work on that this morning." Craig swallowed his tea, standing and walking outside with Dale by his side. He had Dale explain what he knew about shielding, nodding begrudgingly at the straightforward explanation that Dale had been given. They walked to the academy and took an entire stone room for themselves. Craig explained that learning aura control was the purpose of this room, and so it had been specially reinforced. Dale winced. As helpful as this shielding sounded... no turning back now, though; he was committed to improving himself every day.

"Let's begin." Craig had Dale sit down in the lotus position, then place his hands out in front of him with his palms facing upward. "The most common mistake when learning to combine elements is to use your entire body to practice. In a safe location like this, it is fine to retract your aura or focus it into your palms. Do so now."

It took a few minutes because Dale had never needed to control the aura around him in this manner. Typically, it was a consistent coating of energy that was the same thickness throughout. Once he got the hang of it, it was simple to retract the aura, though it made him feel vulnerable in a way that he hadn't been expecting. He had been building his aura for weeks at this point, and it had grown to be a familiar friend that protected him from dangerous things. Craig was watching closely and nodded when he saw that there was no aura leaking from Dale's body. "Very good. I am surprised at your instinctive level of control; many people have a much harder time learning to do even this much."

"I do have to say that the daily life-or-death training has helped me to know myself better." Dale had a rough time most days, but it was all in an effort to become stronger and protect himself, the people around him, his land, and the dungeon. Which was also kind of like defending himself, but unfortunately, the memories that he had initially gained from combining with Cal had been fading day by day. He had written down a small portion of information that he had deemed essential to remembering, but in general, he was back to being just Dale. He hadn't told anyone about the memories he had gained at the time and was now glad that he hadn't done so. If they wanted information, secrets, leverage... he had lost all of that by this point and would have been seen as a disreputable source.

Knowing himself as only himself wasn't terrible, and what little he did remember about Cal's ability to use Essence with a master's ability compelled him forward and heightened his own understanding of his skills. In everything he did, it was just a *little* easier to get better. Craig was now speaking, so Dale returned his attention to where it belonged. "Exact proportions are needed, every time, in order to create a powerful shield that does not damage your body either through its own creation or during another's assault. Also, not every combination is useful as protection."

"What do you mean by that?" If he got a combination wrong, he could be leaving himself entirely vulnerable?

"It's very simple, and I can give you an example right now." Craig smiled, waved, and vanished entirely. Dale looked around uncomprehendingly when suddenly, Craig's face was floating in the air in front of him. "Boo!"

Dale flinched backward with a stifled yelp as Craig became fully visible again. Craig smiled at him. "I've been wanting to try that ever since Hans told me how much fun it was. Allow me to explain. That type of shielding is a simple interaction of fire, celestial, and water Essence. The fire and water interact to make a film of steam around the body, and the celestial works to enhance this while bending light. This type of auric invisibility is fairly weak in terms of actually *hiding*, as it creates a 'shimmer' in the air whenever the person using it moves. And guess what? Breathing counts as moving. The Moon elves have a different 'recipe' that they use for their invisibility, and it is - as you have learned - far more difficult to see through. I was actually quite impressed when you were able to point one out earlier. So, as you can see, though it offers little defense you gain excellent utility."

"That's... that's amazing!" A whole new world of possibilities was opening up for Dale, and he was excited to see where this would take him. "How do I know which combinations are going to be useful for helping to survive battles?"

Craig tapped his chin, then steepled his fingers. "It is possible that I was not being as clear as I should have been. Even the invisibility that I was just using is beneficial in some combat but realistically only against those who need to see you to attack or those that weaponize light in one way or another. As this particular technique bends light around you, so long as you are able to output enough power, you would be able to survive a lance of light that can melt a hole in a mountain."

"Each situation calls for a different type of shielding, but the fact is that most people are unable to generate shields with such a plethora of affinities. You may have access to *all* of them, and learning to use as many as possible will make you more versatile but will also weaken your ability to practice them to perfection. What you should do for now is practice the most common types of shielding you will need. Utility and specialized shields will simply have to come later."

"I see. Thank you for this. Can we work on a few of those shields?" Dale needed to get started; he had other responsibilities creeping up on him, and while theory was important, practicality needed to come first.

"Yes. Let's work on bio, magma, ice, mud, and regenerative shielding. Normally, I would exclude that last one for a long time, but... looking at you makes me think that you will be needing it." Craig ignored Dale's wry look, explaining what was needed from the young Noble. "Bio shielding is similar to plant shielding but is more difficult to hold correctly. When you make this aura type correctly, you will be able to grasp the others much more easily. This requires earth, water, celestial, and wind corruption to be added in a ratio of three, four, half, and two."

"I would suggest that once you get a good feeling for the power you expend, you decide upon a metric for determining what a 'single unit' of Essence is. This is different for each person, but the ratios remain the same. Some people simply create stronger shields when they add 'one unit', but I would suggest making a single unit into a tiny portion of your Essence. You can always increase the units that you add, but that is harder to do when just one takes a full third of your Essence. Please try it now."

Dale began sending Essence to his hands and noticed the color of the energy changing swiftly. It had started as green but then transformed into brown... then grey. As soon as it began turning grey, Craig sliced his hand forward, somehow *removing* the Essence and throwing it against the far wall. A thick bramble bush was suddenly sprouting from the point of impact, and the wall cracked as roots dug into it. The bramble vanished after a moment, but the damage remained. Dale looked at the wall in horror. "What was that?"

"That, Dale, was an Essence construct. It is a representation of the Essence that created it and has no real substance. As you can see, as soon as the Essence sustaining it runs out, the construct fades." Craig sighed and looked back at the wall. "At least that wasn't your hands. Looks like you are going to have to work just as hard as anyone else at this. Let's get started. Try again."

"I have some other meetings that I-"

Craig cut him off with a slicing motion of his hands. "Reschedule. You have work to do *here*."

Chapter Eleven

It was hours before Dale was allowed to leave the training room. When he did, he seemed revitalized, calm, and focused. He was actually mightily struggling to maintain the regenerative aura that he was projecting, but it was very beneficial to him to continue using it. Not only did it *very* slowly and passively heal his body, but it also did the same for anyone that came near him. This was felt by the receiving person as a soothing presence and tended to help reduce stress and fatigue in them. This type of aura was almost exclusively able to be used by clerics, as it required significant control over celestial Essence. Even then, it was a rarity because of the requirement of being able to generate 'blood' Essence.

The ratio needed in this particular recipe was six parts celestial, three parts water and earth, and one part fire. Maintaining the balance of Essences was mentally taxing, but after it was in place, the aura would help to relieve that burden. It was a positive feedback loop that would lead to swift mastery of this type of aura, and Craig had thought he needed a rapid win to avoid depression - which in fact this aura also helped fight against. Once it was mastered, Craig asked if he would be so kind as to sit in the academy where students congregated during finals. The boost to their bodies and mental states might be precisely what they needed to survive in the high-pressure environment. For now, Dale was going to use this in any meetings, gatherings, or interpersonal event of any kind. War looming on the horizon was a significant stressor, and recently people had been snapping at each other more than usual.

"Excuse me, young man. I was hoping that you would be so kind as to help me find my way around the academy?"

Dale looked over to see an older man with a massive series of bags on his back. Dale was so shocked by the size and amount that he was speechless. Why in the world didn't he just use a spatial bag? "Young man? This burden is not getting any lighter, and I would like to be set up for classes by morning if at all possible. Oh, a regenerative aura? It's rather weak, but... a young cleric, perhaps? Or have you found a more interesting path to take? Yes... I think it is the second option." A small smile appeared on the old man's face coupled with just a hint of impatience.

"I'd be happy to assist you, elder." Dale grinned softly as the man rolled his eyes and muttered something too softly to be heard.

"Yes, well, perhaps we go with 'Headmaster' for now. Elder seems very... almost *condescending* with the number of Mages in the area. I'm only in my eighties after all! I'm a spry young bird compared to those old fogies!" He hopped in place, coming down and landing with almost no noise, though the bags on his back shook and rattled.

"Ah, you must be Headmaster Artorian!" Dale smiled as the other man looked at him quizzically, as if his mind had just snapped back to reality after being absorbed in thought. "I am actually the Baron of Mountaindale, owner of this mountain and the dungeon that it contains. I was the one who hired you, and it is a pleasure to be one of the first to be able to greet you."

The man's wizened gaze sharpened as understanding appeared on his expression. His hand rose to shake Dale's as warmth and good cheer slowly filled Artorian's face. "How fortuitous! As they say, it is better to be lucky than to be good! Personally, I find that being good *and* lucky is my preference. Would you happen to know where my personal quarters are located? I brought everything I owned with me and would like to set it down." A cursory glance was taken of his surroundings filled with the scrutiny of someone that had suddenly realized they were lost.

Artorian didn't seem to be having any issues holding his gear, but Dale understood what he was getting at. They walked through the gates of the academy, hearing chuckles every once in a while by students who didn't have as much intelligence as they should. When the Baron of the mountain and the Headmaster of the academy were walking together, respect should have been a given. Luckily, the two were deep in conversation and didn't particularly care about the derision of students.

"It simply doesn't explain the hostility and overall tendencies of these necromancers! Even if they were downtrodden, why would they not take the opportunity they had to sue for peace and perhaps start their own civilization? Is it so *unlikely* that they would have been left alone if they didn't initiate an assault?" Dale's voice was frustrated, and his aura wavered for a moment before he caught himself and devoted himself to holding the flowing Essence correctly.

"Young man, that is a rigid perspective. They did not *want* peace, and I will tell you why. It is generally believed that there are three potential goals in the philosophy of war: the cataclysmic, the eschatological, and the political goals. Now, that is not to say that there cannot be another, only that they are only three of the most common. Allow me to make this into a metaphor for you. In political philosophy, war is compared to... let's call it a game of strategy." Artorian's hands were flying about as he attempted to explain with his hands as much as his words.

"Political players look at war, and all they see are numbers. Numbers of troops, numbers of possible resources that they will be able to take upon winning the game. This... I think this is not what our foes are after, or their actions would have followed a different path."

"In terms of the eschatological, war is used as a means to an end. This could mean a war for freedom, for recognition, for *rights*. In other words, there is a *clearly stated* goal. If I understand you correctly, this is what you are thinking the necromancers would be pushing for. You are saying that they should take the rights and freedoms that they have now won, that they should now band together and raise themselves out of the positions that they had been in for so long. If they had only done this, the war would be over, and uneasy trade may have even started. Unfortunately, they seem to be after the third option."

Artorian took a moment to gather his thoughts, and even though they had stopped in front of the headmaster's new house, they didn't want to end their conversation. "Now, the cataclysmic theory of war tells us that war serves little purpose. That is, outside of causing destruction and suffering. The main outcome of this type of war is drastic change to society at large. This mentality arises from the idea that 'there is no other option', that the only thing that can possibly be beneficial is killing and destroying the previous order. From the ashes rises a new, 'better' society."

Dale shook his head. "It is impossible. Any society is going to have the same issues that plagued its precursor. Why... why wouldn't they try to affect change from within? Why not try to change society slowly instead of going back to square one and dealing with *every other* issue that society had already eradicated? King Henry, Queen Marie, they had plans for change that would have bettered the lives of hundreds of *thousands* over the years. Why not try?"

Artorian gesticulated as if he were about to fall into a long dissertation, and his entire pack moved, clanking and clattering. The Headmaster caught himself, remembering the time and seeing the exhaustion on Dale's face, and decided to shorten his answer. "Sometimes the hardest thing to cultivate is not Essence but *patience*. Perhaps even harder than bringing yourself to the Mage ranks! In all my years, patience is either the saving grace or the folly that leads to downfall."

"In short, change from *within* society also requires that they have a *place* within society. Most infernal Essence cultivators lack this, due to how they are viewed socially. I believe your settlement is the only one in the current age where their acceptance is something that has been planned for."

The old-looking man's face seemed to darken. "Even then, I did notice where their particular building is positioned. Rogue comments of the clergy have also not escaped my notice as I passed earlier. I hear there's a Father present with a keen interest in keeping an eye on them. This merely adds to what I mean about how closed off they must feel. Even here, no infernal student will be without scrutiny, and I expect strong words with at least a few of the professors to keep their biases in check. Now, Dale, this has been a pleasure, but I really need to go. I have a meeting to get to with the instructors. I'd love to do this again sometime."

"You can count on it. I am fairly certain that this is the most in-depth conversation I have ever had. I've been studying texts and reliving memories of others with no one around to help me understand them." Dale shook hands with the headmaster and turned away to head off, feeling much happier about the hard decisions he had needed to make recently.

He looked back to see Artorian undo a latch on his bag, releasing what appeared to be hundreds of pillows. They flowed from the bag like a river, somehow all making it through the doorway. Artorian looked over his shoulder, seeing that Dale was once again giving him an odd look. The older man shrugged. "I like pillows. I like them everywhere. All I have left to unpack now is a few dishes and clothes, so I'm going to get to it. Have a good day!"

CHAPTER TWELVE

<And... done!> I shouted triumphantly as the last droplet of salt water splashed into the body-temperature pool. Fifty manors cut as pagodas, similar to a city I had seen a while back when fixing a ley line issue. I had thought the city was beautiful, and so I tried to replicate the grandest elements of it into my current design. Each building had a built-in bathroom, several spacious bedrooms, and a large common area for hosting parties. There were also workrooms and comparatively small training rooms attached, but the devices in them would be enough to make most early B-rank Mages drool with greed. There were even small exchange areas set up that would allow the Mages who entered here to give up a certain amount of tokens for *specific* rewards instead of random ones. A booklet attached to the kiosk detailed all the options available, and they were not cheap. Powerful, rare, but *not* cheap.

I felt good about my actions over the last... oops, three days? I hope Dani had been managing to run everything smoothly in my absence. I felt good as I lifted myself back to my Core. I felt strong, clear-headed, and... oddly powerful. What the... I ranked up! I was rank B-three now! When did that happen? How? What did I do to become more powerful? All I had been doing was creating a new level... and making it as close to perfect for my specific goal as possible. That... alright, would that work again? I almost dove right back down, but Dani somehow knew I was poking my mind up here; she jumped on the opportunity.

"Hey! You! Cal, you... you can't just run off for days at a time! I thought we were past this!" Dani was whizzing around frantically, and I knew right away that something else was bothering her.

<What's going on, Dani?> She was doing strange things, zipping back and forth to various monsters and grumbling.

"It's Grace! She's playing hide and seek, even though I *told* her that it was time for lessons on dungeon management!" Dani flew over to a Cat and stared at it, but it merely stared back unblinkingly. I figured that Dani didn't know how much Cats liked staring contests.

A quick scan of myself revealed the location of the tiny Wisp, and I almost laughed out loud. <She's in the door over there, Dani.>

"She is? Grace, get out from behind that door this *instant!*" Dani flew over, but the door slammed shut with a tremendous *bang*. The thing weighed over five tons, so the sound was quite impressive. Dani flew backward with a startled squeak, and I laughed out loud.

<I did say she was *in* the door, didn't I?> I laughed at the uncomprehending look I got. I pulled with a thin strand of Essence, and Grace popped out of the stone. <Here you go, delivery of one baby Wisp!>

Grace had turned a light yellow, which I took to be her sulking. <Hey now! You know I hate ruining games, but I'm more afraid of her than you, so...>

"As well you should be." Dani collected Grace and went flying off. "Minya is looking for you!"

<Thanks!> It didn't take long to find Minya; she was sitting on Manny and petting him at the base of his wings. That was pretty impressive, but... I wasn't entirely sure why she wasn't under attack right now. <Minya? Can I do anything for you? What's going on?>

She glanced up with glazed eyes and a vapid smile. "Oh, he is so *cute*! Why is it that I never get to see them get made?"

<Because, from your perspective, all you would be able to see is a full-grown creature popping into existence. It looks like someone who was invisible coming out of hiding. Why are you hypnotizing Manny?> I was really concerned. I hadn't thought the Manticore could be enthralled like this.

"I'm not doing anything to him. He's just such a *good* boy!" She pet the scales under her hand hard as she said this, causing Manny to purr loudly. Maybe I had left too much feline in him. Minya looked up again, her eyes sharpening. "I'm here for my reward. I did a lot of work for you, and I think it's time that I get something more out of it."

<Oh *really*? What is it that you are after?> What was it with my dungeon born getting full of themselves? They didn't get it from me, did they?

"I started a... following. People that want to work for you, for the dungeon, in return for becoming powerful servants." Minya was beating around the bush too much for my liking. "Unfortunately, there are people on the surface that are seeing us as heretics, betrayers, and the like. They don't seem to think that the leaders working with you is as bad as working as a *part* of you. Basically, they need somewhere safe to live and work."

<You started a cult and now need a safe haven?> I cut through the fluff and watched her reaction. She didn't *quite* nod, but I got the idea. <That's fine. Really, I'm flattered. They will need to make binding oaths, of course. If that will be an issue, let them know not to come, or I'll feed them to the Cats.>

Minya smiled and thanked me, unhooking a keygem from Manny's claws before exiting the room. The Manticore jolted and hopped to his feet, looking around and growling menacingly. <Oh, so big and scary now, huh? I'm pretty sure that I heard you purring not two minutes ago you big faker.>

A raspy, growling voice came from the massive Beast, "Petting. Tricked out of treasure by *petting*."

<Eh. I've seen worse. Bye!> I had a... I don't know, a temple to make? Where do cultists sleep? Some kind of barracks? Hold on... oh, this would be funny. I went back down to the new level, the Mage's Recluse, and made comfortable apartments along one entire wall. They were beautiful homes, designed for small families, and they overlooked the beautiful tiny town I had made. They were far more straightforward than the other buildings I had constructed, and so the fifty apartments only took me around ten hours to design. Minya had decent timing; Mages were used to a certain level of... *service* when they lived somewhere. Mwa-ha-ha. The cultists probably thought they were going to become monsters or something. Maybe when they had proven their work ethic, but it would be fun to see their faces when they were assigned as servants to other humans for a good long time.

Although, until Mages started arriving, there would be nothing for them to do except for getting settled in and learn their new jobs. I worked on moving my Core and the Silverwood tree next, but I decided to have some fun with the Elves that were assigned guard duty. First, I had an Essence-rich steam pour out of the ground around my Core, obfuscating what I was doing. Then I quickly dropped the entire section and replaced it with a duplicate so that the Runescript around the room would remain fully active. As I sensed the Elves trying to get closer through the fog, I ignited the gas that had laced the mist. There was a blast and billowing flame for a few long moments, and when the smoke cleared, there was only a small mound and ashes remaining where my Core and the Silverwood tree had been.

They *lost* it. The Elves began freaking out, shouting at each other in their language and dropping their invisibility. One was crying, and I started to feel a little bad about my joke. Hmm... oh. Right. Without the tree, their race was going to become extinct. So... this joke made them think that they were all dead. Lovely. Well, to be fair, they shouldn't have burned all their bridges. Really, this tree wasn't even mature yet. Wasn't there a saying about eggs in a basket? I did hate to see grown Elves crying like this, though. It... was getting uncomfortable. Elves were not pretty criers. We're talking big sobs, blotchy faces, and bags under their eyes. That was just the males! Woof.

Before they went and told on me, I let the door I had created slowly and loudly grind open. The Elves looked at the new opening, tears drying quickly and facial expressions shifting to total embarrassment. I knew that if anyone saw how they had been acting, they would be mortified... I think I had some new statues to make and display. They walked down the stairs, apparently hopeful that they would find a new level with the Silverwood tree intact. Well... that was what they were going to get. Unfortunately for them, the new floor wasn't open for business right now. They walked along the houses, carefully searching for the threats of this level. Finding none, they eventually gathered around the tree, talked to each other a short while, shrugged, and returned to 'invisibility'. Too easy.

Chapter Thirteen

I was on my way to chat with Navigation Bob when I felt something tingle. Glancing around with a hint of confusion, I felt an expanding field of Essence pour over my newest floor. Oh! Oh, yeah! The convergence of ley lines over what had been the ocean dungeon was finally giving me Essence! It was enough that I couldn't use it all at once, and the corruption Cores that I used as filters were working overtime to clean the enormous amount of water taint that was coming through. I was worried I might need to offload some corruption collectors into the reservoir. Frankly, I was surprised that I hadn't been required to do so until now since the net of ley lines was continually expanding and growing. I had needed to fly for *days* to reach this disturbance in my network.

I'd get one of the Bobs to figure out their placement. No, actually... the amount of tainted liquid Essence flowing through the reservoir would likely pop someone who tried that with a fleshy body. I'd have to take care of it myself. I really needed to find a way to delegate this stuff. Maybe I could make a few golems that could handle the situation? That would work... if they were able to draw out the necessary Runescript. That was unlikely. I needed to talk to Bob first.

<Hey there, Navigation Bob! I was wondering where we're off to next?> I smiled to myself as Bob glanced around the room looking a bit put out.

"Pardon me, Great Spirit, but... are you giving me a name based off the work I do here?" Uh-oh. Right, I hadn't shared with them how I was remembering their individual functions.

Deciding it was better to be honest, I took a deep 'breath' and spoke, <Yes, I did. You do all of the plotting of our courses, so it just kind of stuck with me. If it is an issue, I'll come up with something else.>

Bob had tilted his head to the side. "No, no. I wasn't upset. Actually there are so many of me right now that we are having a difficult time speaking to the Goblin who is doing the work we need. We've been wearing numbers, but that has been feeling a bit degrading. Perhaps titles are what we need in order to function. Someone had suggested that we take different names, but who wants to be the one to give up a name given to them by the Great Spirit?"

<Titles, huh? I can see how those could be beneficial. I'm glad I was able to sort that out for you. Now about our destination...> I trailed off leadingly.

"Ah. Right. This one is going to be a bit harder of a sell. There is a known dungeon in this area, and there was a town in this location because of it. It isn't a Mage rank dungeon just yet, but from what I understand and from the rumors of power fluctuations coming off of it... the dungeon is not far from attaining the Mage ranks. I think that we have a couple of options. We could take the Core as it begins to ascend or nab it before it can. Grabbing a Mage-ranked Core would be much harder than taking a C-ranked one." Navigation Bob pointed at the map as he explained, and I agreed with his assessment.

<Great work, Navigation Bob,> I teased playfully. <It looks like we are a few days away, so I am going to go make preparations and get Dale to put together a team. If his beating went as his master wanted, Dale isn't going to go himself, so I need another option. Oh, maybe I can get Minya to go?>

"I'm... I'm not sure what's happening here, Great Spirit." Navigation Bob hadn't had me bouncing ideas off of him like this before. Oops. I tried to keep my manic side to those that were already 'in the know'.

<Don't worry about it! I'm off.> I probably should have just been quiet and vanished, but I was a tad embarrassed and flustered because of it. It's hard living up to the expectations of the ones relying on you and even harder to have fun with them when they are expecting that you either can't or won't.

Before I forgot to do it, I connected to the portal leading to my reservoir. Working through portals was tricky for me, but this place was *technically* still part of my dungeon. That made it manageable, even though I needed to expend a slightly higher degree of Essence and attention in order to make things happen on the other side. I needed to carve Runes along nearly the entire thing, from top to bottom, so it was a pretty draining experience. Luckily, the whole thing was mostly empty because the liquid Essence could have otherwise easily activated the Runes before they were ready. Being extra cautious, I even waited to add the activation sequences until after everything else was completed. I had to say, this place was pretty... freaky. It was neat, don't get me wrong, but someone who didn't know what it did could easily mistake it for something sinister.

The container was four hundred feet below where the base of my mountain had initially stood, and the interior was a sphere with a twenty yard diameter. This thing could contain over four *million* liters of liquid Essence at max capacity. This sucker was *huge*. The exterior was corruption-enhanced granite, followed by a layer of tungsten, lead, a *very* thin layer of Mithril, and then ceramic on the interior. To anyone scanning it with Mana or Essence, this should look like a giant ball of fecal matter. If that doesn't convince them to leave it alone, perhaps the actual night soil that I deposit around it would be enough if they started to dig. An entire city above me dumping their... stuff leaves a lot of cleanup. I could just absorb it for the Essence, but I like to think that this was more fun. I had even added some Runes to the area that would keep it 'fresh' for a few decades.

I inserted the corruption Cores throughout the ceramic layer and watched for a few minutes to make sure that everything was working correctly. The corruption in the air and liquid began rapidly decreasing, and I felt the strain of it around my own Core lessen significantly. Perfect. I was worried that there would be a buildup of corruption on my lower floors that would get out of hand and drive away my new potential tenants, not that there were many Mages strong enough to get to the lowest level. The Moon Elves were the elite of the Dark Elf race, and even they only had four guards that could take up position on this floor.

Well, I suppose that wasn't *strictly* accurate. Mainly, the difference was that other Mages were taking their time mapping out floors six and seven so they could be aided in cultivation or so their protégés could. I was also learning something interesting from the A-ranked High Mageous 'Madame Chandra'. She had come down here and begun mapping the floor all by herself. Back and forth she went, gathering all the possible ways I had learned to make plant Essence. She even seemed surprised by a few of them. Who would have guessed that earth, air, water, and fire were a way to make plant Essence? All four basic elements to form a single second tier type of power? It was because plants made breathable air by taking carbon from the air and ground. They did this from some interaction with light and water, and fire was a lower fragment of light. Fascinating stuff.

Well, after finding that out, she had gotten pretty excited and a *teeny* bit mad. From there, she had mapped all of the possible ways to achieve nature Essence, and after exhausting all possible avenues, she plopped down right there and began to cultivate. That hurt a bit because she drew in Essence like a whirlpool pulls in ships. Then... the most bizarre thing happened. She got... weaker? No... her *cultivation rank* dropped. She was pale and shaking, but when her eyes opened again and she smiled, I was in awe of her. She... she had *upgraded* her **law**! I hadn't even known that was possible! Was it because plant was a subset of nature? Could anyone enhance their powers with the knowledge I was offering? I needed to make the traps here deadlier. This... now it made sense why people kept freaking out about the paths I had made. I was going to need to put some kind of Boss monster between the tiers, or this place would be flooded with extra powerful Mages in no time flat.

Madame Chandra went from rank A-nine down to A-three, but as her power began to ripple out from her, it struck me as more condensed, more dangerous, more *whole*. She was now a tier-three *nature* High Mageous instead of a plant High Mageous. As she sat there, she seemed to be concentrating. She...! She just went up a rank! Two! She jumped to rank A-five over the course of a few hours! How? Her knowledge *of* and affinity *for* nature must be incredible!

She seemed to have progressed enough and got to her feet wearily. I could hear her speaking to herself, and I listened in closely. "All those years... and that was the key. *Fire*! I still can't believe it, but now it makes perfect sense! *He* even told me that fire had a place in the forest, and I *laughed* at him! I could have been here for a hundred years! I'm a stubborn old fool, needing to see it drawn out for me like a child. So many things that eluded me are clicking into place! My goodness, I bet fire could even be used in the growth cycle of- *oof*. Goodness me, that confirms it."

I created and dropped a jawbone on the ground just so I could visually represent the astonishment I was feeling at this moment. She had just increased in rank *again*! How deep was her understanding of the natural world, and how many revelations must she have had to reach rank A-six? I was figuratively drooling at the thought of gaining access to the memories, ideas, and concepts that must be floating around her brain. She took stock of her surroundings one more time, then began making her way into the next tier, this time frowning as she traced out the possibilities for upgrading into a higher **law**. I breathed a sigh of relief when I saw that the patterns became confusing for her. At the very least, she wasn't going to be moving to a higher understanding right now.

Still, her progress and increase in power was *sickening*. Where before she had been powerful, now she didn't even need to call upon her Mana to dominate my golems. She would walk up to them and give them a friendly pat on the chest, and they would crumble into dust. By attacking in this manner, she even shattered their Cores. The resulting blasts of Mana seemed to thrill her, and she stood in the reverberating power like someone enjoying the wind from a thunderstorm. Then she vanished.

<What in the...?> My various golems in the paths leading to the stairs exploded at that moment, the barrage of explosions shaking the entire floor and setting me back six hours. I would need to recreate every one of them individually. Let me guess: she was testing her speed. At least she was heading toward the newest floor. Maybe I would have some new residents that I could study closely. Perhaps a few memory Cores would be gently pressed against their heads as they slept... it was time to train my new servants.

Chapter Fourteen

"Hold, good folk of Basketville! Trust in your training, prepare the war hounds, and stand ready to *fight*!" The Mayor of Basketville stood on the ramparts of his town, doing all he could to bolster the spirits of his people. He knew, he *knew*, that this would be a battle they couldn't win. But he had to try; he had to inspire and give hope to the people counting on him. The Mayor looked behind him, gulping and trying to hold back the tears threatening to pour down his cheeks.

The undead were here. There were ranks and formations of skeletons and zombies, but from his vantage, he could see that there were Abominations coming up from the rear. They were marching, getting closer and closer... then all at once, the undead stopped and a Demon, an abyss-blasted *Demon* stepped out of the mass of bodies and waved at them.

"Human filth." The demon called lazily, obviously having used this same speech multiple times. "I am here as an ambassador of The Master. I have been *instructed* to give you all a choice. You are to join us, or you will die. These are your only options, and not choosing or delaying will ensure your demise. You have one minute to answer."

The Mayor listened to his people shouting, and noted the silence of his town's defenders. They were prepared to die, as long as they died fighting. No one had expected an option where they would survive the day, and this offer was breaking the resolve of more than one person. The Mayor needed to take matters into his own hands. "How do we know that we can trust this offer?"

"The Master demanded that I give this choice to all before we fought with them, and to accept whatever answer they gave us. I am bound to follow his laws." The Demon shrugged, then decided that enough time had passed. "Your *choice*?"

The Mayor looked at his people, who had just gotten a spark of hope for the first time in weeks. "We... we surrender. We will join you."

"Excellent. Open the gates so that we don't need to smash them. I am *so* glad you made the right choice." The Demon took a step forward, and the ranks of the dead moved as he did. The stone walls surrounding the town were ignored as the gate opened and the dead poured inside. When everyone was under control and accounted for, there was a slaughter that lasted mere seconds.

The Demon, coated in rapidly drying blood and viscera, gave a happy sigh as he cracked open a rib bone and sucked out the marrow. He looked around at all the slain townsfolk that were being reanimated and laughed. "I *love* it when they don't see it coming. Thank the abyss that the order from The Master was so vaguely worded. After all, they did *choose* to join us..."

CAL

Two dozen of Minya's cultists were approaching, and I was having fun watching the people move past gigantic Cats that had been ordered not to hurt them. The Cats seemed to be enjoying themselves as well, flexing their claws and releasing deep rumbling growls. Every single time they did so, all of the humans would flinch. They were *all* only humans, as it turned out. I listened in on them, laughing at what they were speaking about.

"You think that she's just bringing us here as a sacrifice to the dungeon?"

"Does it matter? If that is how I can serve the dungeon best, then so be it!" This lady had some serious advancement opportunities coming her way.

"*Finally* free from all that menial labor! Ugh, those guild members are *insufferable*! I only hope that I get the chance to ram an enchanted weapon into their guts someday when they trespass!" Taking note of *that* guy for sure; he may not like what his job was going to be down here if he couldn't stand adventurers. "If I ever had to bring them their dainty meals or tea again, I would have added as much poison as possible and made a run for it!"

Yeah, I didn't think he would last long in his new position. Maybe I should let them see their new quarters before asking them to make the oath to my service. In fact, I would give them a day in the hot spring pool that I had created, plenty of tasty food, and let them sleep in their new beds. If that didn't make them ready to say yes to anything, I didn't know what would. ...Then again, they knew what they would be getting into. In terms of the oath, that is. Minya was leading the group down the service tunnels, which were usually reserved for Goblins or relaxation areas for my Mobs. Before they could enter the eighth level, I figured it was time to get this show on the road.

<Stop them here, Minya.> She held up her hand, and the others stopped next to her. <It's time for them to swear the oath. Otherwise, they will be too excited to say anything.> The humans with her were standing in a deep gloom, their weak eyesight failing to penetrate the darkness that surrounded them on all sides. Actually, it wasn't just darkness that was all around them, this was also the recreation room for all varieties of Cats in my dungeon. Even Snowball was in the room right now, being cuddled up to by three or four lesser Cats. He shouldered them aside as he got closer to the group, wanting to be the one to get

the first kill if someone refused to swear the oath. If they had come this far, at this point, I would need to consider them traitors or spies.

One by one, Minya had them swear their oaths. I felt a connection spring up on each of them and smiled as I scanned them. Standard humans. Mostly non-cultivators looking for a cheat, a way around *working* for power. One or two of them, the real fanatics, actually had some serious health issues. One had all of his affinity channels blocked, and the other seemed to be on the verge of organ failure.

Ah. Opening a meridian would have killed her, so there was no way to cultivate past the lower levels without expensive and extensive healing. Most groups wouldn't want to devote those kinds of resources to someone who may not be able to repay them. I marked these two as leaders and looked at the last human without an oath... and grinned. Thank goodness, I had thought that my Cats would be going hungry!

The man in question was one of the worst complainers. He was fiddling with something and seemed to be getting frustrated that it wasn't working. It was either a beacon of some kind or an object that would facilitate his escape in most other situations. In this scenario, he was surrounded on all sides by corrupted stone, and I was in total control of all Essence in the area. This far down in my depths, my Mana was coating everything, and his low-ranked Essence couldn't break through even with the help of the Inscribed item he was carrying. Now he was beginning to panic. Interesting, it must have been some sort of escape device in that case. I was appreciative of the gift, but it was really too bad that- oh, there goes Snowball.

The other humans began to panic when one of their own was snatched away with a startled shriek. A snack for me *and* my Cats! <Sorry, Minya. Traitor. He had an interesting item

on him, though. Any idea what this is?> I showed her an image of the object, and she swore loudly. Whoa. She hadn't even needed to look at the Runes or anything! That didn't bode well.

"I'll tell you in a minute. We need to get these people somewhere safe *first*." Minya looked around with some expression on her face that I hadn't seen before. I'm guessing it was something like 'not in front of the new people'. That was fine. I opened the doors slowly, adding an air of majesty and wonder. The first set of doors opened by splitting in half, one part going upward, one down. The next doors opened by going to the left and right, and the final set split diagonally.

All of these were now my people and so could hear me when I spoke to them. For the very first time, they listened to the voice of the dungeon! <Welcome, my new minions. Welcome... to the Mage's Recluse! If you will follow Minya, we will get you all to your new homes.> Soft silver light from the Silverwood tree was the first thing they were able to see, followed shortly by the glowing lights along the walkways and in the beautiful manors. They stepped onto the floor, jaws dropping and eyes widening at the splendor. Small birds flew around, chirping happily although the floor was locked in what appeared to be a perpetual twilight. The cultists walked as though they were in a dream, watching everything around them in awe.

Their first step was getting close to their homes, but before they went inside, I had Minya bring them to a small hot spring that was reminiscent of - if much more modest than - the one on the Goblin's floor. They were all instructed to bathe and get into their new uniforms. All of them had matching robes that shimmered with iridescent silver. This would identify my employees, and any Mage who harmed them would quickly find themselves locked out of this floor and having a tough time in the dungeon. The next step was feeding them, and it was amusing to see them almost fight over a practically endless resource.

It wasn't overly surprising to me. After all, there were only three types of people who would make a deal with something generally considered to be a ruthless, mindless, soulless killer of people. There were your desperate people, like King Henry, who had need of great power to help others. Fanatics, who really thought that I was a higher power of some kind. Wrong, but cute in its own way. Then there were the selfish people, the people who wanted to be powerful without the hard work, without putting in the time.

While this group had a few fantastic fanatics, it was *stuffed* with the supremely selfish. If these people thought there was a way to get a benefit, they would happily kill each other for it. As they finished eating, I decided that it was time to set the rules. <Welcome, my new residents. You have now taken my hospitality, eaten my food, and pledged yourselves to me in a very binding manner. It is now time for you to learn what you are going to be doing for... well, not forever, but a good long time.>

At my words, the majority of people seemed to become wary. I guess they didn't really understand what it meant to come in here and swear oaths to me. Well, they were about to find out. I laid out their duties and roles, putting the fanatics in positions of power over the others. There was deep complaining, but when the first one to loudly shout 'I refuse to work as a servant' simply fell over, the others got *real* quiet. He was checked by one of the others, and when the fallen man was pronounced dead, the others looked around in abject fear. <Hey, I didn't force you all to swear binding oaths that would kill you if you broke them. You came down here *after* being told that was the case, correct, Minya?>

"That's correct." She seemed disgusted by their behavior, shocked that they had been acting like spoiled children. "Though I would have never guessed that they didn't understand that. Next time, I will ensure that my fellow parishioners truly *believe*!"

<I'm still *not* a deity, Minya. I have no need for that, and hubris is something I'd rather avoid.> She rolled her eyes and ignored me. I sent the cultists off to bed, letting them know that a Bob would be here in the morning to teach them their jobs. Etiquette Bob had been given memory stones from the human courts, so it was going to be his job to command and train all of these whiners. Mage's Recluse was going to be a success, or I would let the Cats in here and try again with a fresh set of... *employees.*

Looking around the area, I noticed that Madame Chandra had already set up shop in the manor closest to the Silverwood tree and furthest from the others. She was taking a nap, which, at her rank, was entirely optional. I was amazed once more by her massive increase in power and decided right then that I needed to make her a true ally. It was time to start doing things the human way. It was time to begin sending bribes.

Wait! I had nearly forgotten to learn what Minya knew about the item I had taken off the traitor! I turned my attention to her, and she grinned at nothing as she walked. "Hello there, Cal. I'm so sorry about that whole situation. If I had known they would be like that... I really thought that they were like me, wanting to see you succeed for no other reason than to have you become powerful."

<It's fine, Minya. If they shape up, they are going to live very happy lives and become more powerful than they ever could have elsewhere. I really want to know more about this... is it a bell?>

Minya stopped walking and grimaced. "It's called a 'return bell'. It is one part of a two-part item. By infusing Essence or Mana into the Runes, the activator can ring the bell and will be 'returned' to the other part of the item. It doesn't have that great of a range, though, and it has... other issues."

<Such as?>

"Well, the first thing that comes to mind is that there are no teleport protections in place for it. If you ring that and something had been placed over the return pad, you get torn into pieces and will probably fall to chunks. Also, infusing it with Essence is slow, and the further you are from the return pad the more power you need to add to it. Oh, and you leave behind an explosion of the Essence or Mana used to power it. That guy was trying to escape and kill all the humans he was around." Minya waved that information off, taking a deep breath before continuing.

"The most important point: that particular item is exclusive to the Adventurers' Guild. Only high-ranked people can get access to it, and even then, it is almost only used by guild spies or informants. If the Guild is acting like this... we are going to start having serious issues with them soon, at a time where we cannot afford to do so."

<So you are saying that the *Guild* is trying to spy on us? Literally the most powerful organization on the planet, the group that has members from all races, that has its hands in every political venture... is spying on *me*?> My voice was incredulous, and for good reason. The Guild had members that could tear this place apart, so having them *spying* on me was something I had never bothered to consider.

"Well... they are at least *trying* to."

<But... why?>

CHAPTER FIFTEEN

"I don't understand what I'm doing wrong here." Dale's entire body language screamed frustration. "This is a simple application of aura, isn't it?"

"Is anything *really* so simple, Dale? Has there been a time when you have made real progress without also suffering setbacks and consequences?" Craig was trying to help him through learning various aura signatures, but Dale kept meeting with frustration. "Aura is very difficult to master at the beginning, though progress increases rapidly as you use it properly."

"I just don't understand why such a minor difference should make such a drastic change in the outcome." Dale's voice was full of defeat, making Craig want to roll his eyes in annoyance. He held himself back thanks to his long years of training as a Monk, but it was a close call.

"Dale. The difference between blood and water is a few extra minerals and tiny meaty chunks, yes?" Craig paused only a moment before launching back into speech, "Do you think that replacing your blood with water would let you be as comfortable as you are currently?"

"Oh, come on, that's-"

"Different?" Craig reached forward and poked Dale in the head. "Of course it is! That's what I'm trying to say! Now, I understand that this is a rare application, but it will give you versatility in the lower levels of aura that are hard to match. It would be an amazing defense against nearly all forms of attack that are not purely physical. Also, you can thank your friend the dungeon that we have this information in the first place."

"Oh, what a generous donation," Dale deadpanned. "The dungeon is *amazing*, after all. Is there any more information or help you can offer?"

"Hmm. Well, I'm sorry to say that this is simply one of those auras that I am unable to create or control. Luckily, you show *extraordinary* control for your rank, so the real issue for you is maintaining and empowering your aura. I'd say you have a leg up on a few C-ranked folks." Craig patted Dale on his back and smiled kindly. "Try again."

"I'm still trying to figure out why I am trying to learn to create a disenchanting water aura," Dale grumbled as he deftly began to move strands of his aura around. He needed to ensure that he got everything correct, but he also couldn't let the water touch him. Craig had him practicing over a small chunk of cursed earth that they had excavated from the dungeon. Dale's attention had slipped during his reverie, and he was jolted back to reality as Craig tore a chunk of his Essence out of his hands once again.

"That was a nasty contact poison you just created, Dale. Perhaps my comment about your control was preemptive?" Craig was shaking his head at his student. "Are my lessons so boring that you would rather have your arms cut off than keep learning?"

"No, it's just that-" Dale was cut off as a door slammed open and a guild representative rushed in.

"Baron Dale!" The man was gasping, an impressive feat for a cultivator that had done something as simple as running. "There is a man here from Guild headquarters... he is demanding to see you and all of your councilors."

"Um. Thank you, but why is this so urgent?" Dale walked over to a nearby table to get a glass of water for the distraught man.

"He... he said that if you are not meeting with him in thirty minutes, he would tear this mountain out of the sky and drop it in the ocean." The man shuddered. "M'lord, that was *twenty minutes* ago. We couldn't find you!"

<I'm sorry, *what* now?>

Dale ignored the voice in his head and left the room at a sprint, the already exhausted Guild member running alongside him to bring him as close as possible to his destination. One final door barred the way, so Dale threw it open, smashing the wood to splinters as it impacted the wall.

A thick man in armor with deep Runescripting turned and glared at the new arrival. "*Baron* Dale?"

"Yes, I'm here." Dale shook himself out of his panic, clearing his throat and trying to appear presentable. There was a suffocating feeling given off by the man, just by him existing and being in the same area.

"Good, we are *finally* all here. Dale, by the authority vested in me as liaison to the guild, I hereby order you to stand aside in matters pertaining to the dungeon. You are also to hand over control of the city of 'Mountaindale'," the large man sneered at this obviously narcissistic naming scheme, "to someone more *qualified* to lead it. The Guild will also be assuming control of this academy and taking a direct hand in the running and maintaining of the building and curriculum. All students will be given higher quality resources as well as entry to the Guild upon completion of their academic studies and be excused from service until they reach at least the C-ranks. Until we go to the war or the war comes to us, that is. Then *everyone* will need to fight if they want to survive."

"*What?*" Dale retorted with a combination of rage and confusion lacing his voice. "You can't just-"

"I *can* and already *did*. These orders are already in place. Also, welcome to the war." The unknown man had a smirk appear on his face at that comment. "All Guild members are ordered to submit themselves to the war effort. We had *politely* asked for reinforcements against the necromantic horde, but we are past that now."

The other members of the council had also gathered in the room, and High Mageous Amber stepped forward and glared at the man. "Even so, you cannot remove him from his position. Baron Dale was confirmed in his position by two separate Kingdoms, and you-"

"*Silence*," the man cut her off with a single whiplash word. "I know exactly how he got this position, and I also know most of what has been going on here. Unfortunately, both of those Kingdoms have fallen already. I understand that surviving members of the Royal families are living here, but they have no *power*. As it stands, they could not order a single person to respect their authority. They have none. They are currently *fairly* strong civilians. That. Is. All."

The man waited a few moments so that his words would sink in. "You *will* comply with my orders, or you will be tried for dereliction of duty. By me. The penalty during a wartime situation is death. Oh, also, all titles of Nobility given to the members of fallen Kingdoms, Queendoms, fiefdoms, or political groups are now null and void. There is no more 'Baron Dale'. There is only Dale, a man who earns a five percent stipend based off of the export or sale of goods from this dungeon. You no longer are the ruler, leader, or owner of this land. It belongs to the Guild. Also, the lavish suite you were granted has been repurposed. We will hold your items for one day to give you time to find a new place to live, and your goods will be delivered if you do so."

“What?” Dale couldn’t believe what was happening. “What about my projects, the commitments the city made? The alliances we have secured?”

“All deals that have been made will be honored by the Guild. Heck, we’ll even give bonuses to the people who set them all up.” The man seemed to be getting upset by having all these low-powered fools staring at him. “In fact, the Dark Elves are going to be getting *special* deals and requests from us. It’s already been discussed, agreed upon, and sealed with their leadership.”

“I did *nothing* of the sort.” Brianna stepped forward threateningly. “Do not overstep your bounds-” She was cut off as the man unfurled a document that had the stamp of the Dark Elf Queen embossed on it. No one would be foolish enough to falsify that seal, as it would mean their death, the death of their families, and possibly being raised by a necromancer just so you could be killed again.

“I’m done now. Get out of my sight, all of you." As the others slowly started moving away, shocked by the brutal change, the man softly growled a few more lines that were almost hard to hear. "Been here living it up, relaxing, and playing with the dungeon... the rest of us have been working to save the world. Things are going to change around here. Things are going to *change*."

Brianna appeared next to Dale for an instant and murmured into his ear, “He can’t take away your *Elven* authority. Remember that, *Duke* Dale. Only my mother could, and that was not included on that document.” Then she was gone like smoke in the wind, leaving Dale to wonder how this information would help him.

A state of shock had set in as what had previously been the council walked away from the meeting room. Tyler reached out and gripped Dale's wrist. "Dale, are... are you okay?"

"You know what, I just don't know. Maybe this *is* for the best. I don't think that I have what it takes to be a Noble anyway. Take a look at my city: I either care too much about issues, or I don't seem to care at all. I could never seem to find a nice *middle* ground for moderate care distribution. Beyond that, when was the last time I went dungeon diving in *this* dungeon? I've been in meetings and training, but I haven't progressed much further because I am not actively cultivating." Dale chuckled darkly, and all the others could do to help was pat him on the back and disperse.

After all, without land, a title in the human areas, protections from multiple Kingdoms, or enormous piles of money... Dale was just a D-rank four cultivator. Everyone else was someone with *actual* power or at least responsibilities. In moments, Dale stood alone in the hallway.

CHAPTER SIXTEEN

<Well, hey there, Dale. At least you've always got me. As in, feel free to come on down and visit. Snowball, in particular, is eager to see you.> My voice seemed to startle the man out of his stupor, and he walked off with an angry spring in his step. <What's the rush, Dale? Got a hot date?>

"Nope. I just lost almost everything, and my only hope now is to become powerful enough that people can't take away the rest of it. I've pissed off a bunch of Nobles that no longer need to worry about retribution from the crown or governments." Dale started walking faster, his inherent paranoia ratcheting up another notch. "I'm already in the Guild, so my only hope *is* the Guild, even though they just screwed me over. It is highly unlikely that such a large organization holds personal animosity toward me, but I need to take precautions."

<I mean, the Dark Elves have a deal with you directly, don't they?> These guys were pretty powerful, and it was unlikely others would pick on Dale.

"I can't rely on them. As I have no political clout anymore, someone killing me off gets them out of any obligations they have to me. No, I need to do something outrageous." Dale was jogging now, which to mere non-cultivators would be an unattainable sprint. He ran into a building, right to someone sitting at a desk. Dale's abrupt appearance seemed to freak out the bureaucrat, and his next demand even more so. "Enroll me at the academy as a direct disciple to Headmaster Artorian."

"B-baron Dale?" The man sank back into his role as soon as he realized that this was a work-related visit. "Ah... while he does get the *option* to have a direct disciple, the Headmaster has indicated that he doesn't want one."

"This is an order. Register me as a student right now, and put me directly in the care of Artorian. I do *own* the academy." Dale stared the man down, but even though he started shivering, the man shook his head.

"I can make you a student right now, but this needs to be approved by the Headmaster. He has a level of autonomy that I, as a simple administrator, *can't* touch. They wouldn't want me making decisions for the high and mighty, right?" Handing over a form, the man continued, "You need to have him sign this, and your new position will take effect right away. Welcome to the Academy, cadet. Er... Baron."

"Thank you. He just needs to sign this?" Dale grabbed the paper, and when the man nodded, Dale ran out of the room. He charged over to the Headmaster's residence, pounding on the door as soon as he arrived.

"*What* is going on down there?" Artorian's head peeked over the edge of his roof, his expression clearing up as he saw Dale at the door. "Oh, if it isn't the young Noble who started the academy. Please, come on up."

Dale had no idea how he was supposed to do that when the door was locked, but he decided that he didn't care much about property damage right now. He turned away, coming back with a running start. His momentum let him get a few feet up the wall before slamming his Mithril-clad boots into the wall creating footholds. Pushing off, Dale only needed to jump twice more before he was standing in front of the Headmaster.

"Didn't you build this place? There is a stairwell in the back." Artorian was fully surrounded by pillows; in fact, the entire rooftop could be called a hedonistic hotspot. Exotic foods and drink were on display, a hookah was releasing a small amount of smoke, and not a single inch of the rooftop was visible. Pillows of various thickness and color covered it entirely. "Oh, um. Shoes off, please, if you are going to be staying."

"What are you *doing* up here?" Dale was shocked at the tendencies of the Headmaster, and this was his first day on the job!

"Cultivating and preparing for my meetings with the other faculty." Artorian took in Dale's disheveled appearance, noting the paper in his hand. "What are *you* doing here?"

"Oh. Right, I need you to sign this." Dale handed over the form, but after reading it, Artorian recoiled as if he had been handed a snake.

"Are you *out* of your *mind*? I can't devote the required time a direct disciple would need from me. No, thank you for the offer, but I am not interested." He tried to hand the paper back to Dale, but the young man shook his head.

"I don't need your tutelage; I need the protection and resources that would come with being your disciple. You don't even need to provide them, the academy will do that." Dale looked the Headmaster in the eye. "I know the *exact* requirements you need to fulfill in order to become the Headmaster permanently. I also *need* to join the Academy, and I need you to sign this right now."

"You are *bribing* me? Or is this blackmail of some kind?" Artorian shook his head... then grinned. "I like it. A cultivator needs to know when brute force will not work and when they will need to turn to other methods."

Artorian took the form and signed it with his essence signature, eschewing the standard use of a quill. After handing the document back to Dale, he seemed to come to his senses and hesitantly voiced the thoughts in his head. "Now that I think about it, *why* do you need to be a disciple? You *own* this place and all the resources..."

"Not anymore." Dale shook his head and sighed. "The Guild has removed all power from anyone from the 'Fallen Kingdoms', as they are calling them. All titles of Nobility are gone, all land ownership contracts are now voided because the Kingdoms are no longer in power. For example: Artorian, get off my mountain."

The Headmaster stared at him, remaining seated on his overstuffed pillows. He leaned over and took a long draw from the hookah before speaking again. "What was that supposed to accomplish?"

Dale let his head roll back and around to loosen his neck. "Before, you would have been forced to leave my mountain by any means possible, as fast as possible. Now, all I am is a D-rank cultivator with more gold than is typical for my status. I needed to join the academy, else I would have likely been sent to the frontlines by the Guild. I'm fairly certain they want me gone."

"Son, if the Guild wants you gone, I don't think this is going to stop them." Artorian closed his eyes and breathed in deeply. "Ah, that's the stuff."

"What are you doing?" Dale looked at the man lying on his pillows and smoking cultivator-specific tobacco.

"Cultivating."

"Like *that*?" Dale was scandalized; how was he going to achieve balance when he was draped over a space like that?

"Mmm. Should I be in a rigid lotus position, then?" Artorian blew out a ring of smoke, smiling as it made a perfect circle around the sun. "That's not my methodology. I'm a starlight cultivator; I need as much of my body open to the sun as possible."

"Are... are you naked under those pillows?" Dale felt slightly sick about that thought; wasn't he going to be meeting teachers soon? "Also, starlight? Why aren't you cultivating at night? What does the sun have to do with it?"

"Is this knowledge that you *truly* seek to learn? No, no, not *that* information, I'm clothed. This weave of tunic is loose enough that there is very little impediment to the sunlight. My cultivation is simply different than what you seem to think of as 'normal'." Artorian took a deep breath and smiled. "My method is much different than any other, as it was entirely designed and created by me. I was an old man, steeped in corruption and philosophy when I made my first breakthrough. From there, this has always been enough for me."

"Sunlight? I thought you said you were a *starlight* cultivator?" Dale was confused enough that he hadn't even run to return the form. "How is your cultivation method different?"

"A common misconception. The sun *is* a star. I can cultivate day or night, but I have much better results during the day, as the Essence is more abundant. Of course, this dungeon and my proximity to the dungeon are excellent supplements to my method. My cultivation is focused on the *outward* instead of the inward. If you look at me with Essence empowering your eyes, you should be able to see that there are no spirals in my cycle, only circles. My entire cultivation base is circling outward and blazing with starlight. I am a beacon to those looking at me, and the light purifies my Core and body daily. This leads to faster breakthroughs, weaker bottlenecks, and longevity that cannot be measured. The downside is that I need to cultivate every day without fail to replace the Essence that is being used. For this reason, I am still in the C-ranks and likely will remain here for years. At least... I would have if I were not here."

"Purifying light... I don't suppose you would be willing to share the secrets to the path of sunlight?" Dale hopefully questioned.

"I see no reason not to." Dale's eyes widened at the thought of using sunlight as an aura to begin purifying himself. "Twelve parts water, one part air, three parts fire, and eight parts celestial Essence."

"No way." Dale shook his head. "Are you telling me that you had four *naturally* occurring affinities? You would have never made it to your fifties."

"Heh. Dale, Dale. Why do you think that I am *still* using my Essence to purify myself?" Artorian made a 'go away' motion at Dale. "Thirty years is not enough time to remove fifty years of taint. Now, shoo. My instructors should be arriving anytime now."

Dale nodded and did a backflip, landing on the ground dozen feet below. Artorian's' voice floated down after him. "Showoff!"

Dale took off, returning to the administration building. He was apparently expected because the bureaucrat that had helped him previously was now glaring at him. "Ah. Hello there, *Baron* Dale. I've been informed that there have been some changes to your status recently. You should have never been admitted to the school; you have no backing, no extraordinary talent, no-"

"Indeed, there have been some changes," Dale cut the man's rant short. "I am now the direct disciple of the Headmaster. Here is the form." After handing over the paper, Dale waited until the man grudgingly gave him his room assignment and the tasks that he would need to complete in order to remain enrolled in the academy.

"As the Headmaster's *disciple*, you have extra quotas and deadlines for advancement. You can attend any classes you want, but the only tests are advancement. Miss the deadlines on what you need to give to the school, and you are *gone*." Now that Dale was no one of importance, the attitude toward him had already shifted dramatically. "*Good luck*."

Chapter Seventeen

<You think *so*, do ya?> I was gently scoffing at the man who was walking by himself in the dungeon, shouting *orders* at me.

"Dungeon, if you don't start flying toward the coordinates I've given you, I *will* knock this mountain out of the sky and *drag* it to where I want it to go." This was the third time he had shouted this order, and I was starting to think he was a bit too full of himself. Sure, he was an S-ranked individual, and I had no idea what he was *actually* capable of, but I *highly* doubted he would kill everyone here just because I was ignoring him. "I'm told that you have some slight intelligence, so I'll give you a small *demonstration*."

He was now on the floor my Goblins called home - level three - and I instantly gave the order for them to evacuate. I was too late. He *huffed* - just a light exhalation of air - and a miasma of green light appeared in front of him. He blew on it, and from there, the light expanded to cover the entire floor. His body went rigid, his eyes glassy, and his jaw slack. Odd. I watched everything that was going on, and it was easy to see that a few students saw the strange energy cover them. They looked down and around in confusion, but a sharp word issued from the S-ranker - somehow not from his body but from the miasma directly - and they no longer worried about anything.

I was confused. I had just lost all connection to everything on that level. There was an enormous hole in my influence that perfectly fit the bounds of that floor. I quickly shunted my influence through a makeshift portal between floors to recapture my control and worked to re-establish a tiny bit of connection on that floor. When I could see into the room, I still couldn't quite *understand* what I was seeing. The entire floor was empty. No fortifications, no Goblins, no people at all. The strange part was: I didn't get any Essence from the loss, which was even more confusing and disturbing.

Did he *not* kill everything? Just then, the green light finished returning to the man, condensing in front of him. When it was all there, it shrank down to a small ball of energy. He opened his mouth again, and the energy flew in, vanishing as he swallowed. Did he just *eat* my floor? He ate other humans too! Cannibal! Wait a moment... that was an illusion! Not in a good way, the eating of my floor and such, I meant his *ears*! This was a High Elf, not a human! Not a cannibal, *technically*. Still, I... I didn't know what to do. I have nothing that could even *scratch* this guy, nothing I... all I could think of was to get the word out, perhaps sully his reputation?

I concentrated on what was above me, *way* up to the surface, and created a statue in a public area. Technically, I made it underground and pushed it upward on a slab of stone, but the idea is the same. The figures were a detailed representation of what had just happened, showing the panic on the student's faces, the Goblins, the empty area around this Elf. I even placed his ears as they *really* were, showing that he was a High Elf. Then I returned my attention to his threats. He was sitting down and absorbing the energy he had just *consumed*, but after a moment, he stood and belched. Gross.

"As you should be able to tell by now, I have no qualms destroying every single person here if it means that I get access to a mobile flying fortress like this. Being able to launch our initiatives from the air would grant us battle superiority in most situations. One of the great weaknesses of the undead is that until they reach incredible heights of power, they are cursed to remain upon the ground. You *will* comply, or I will pluck your Core out of its position and seal it in a weapon. If the Guild cannot use this as a base, no one will. Ever." The dark undertone of his words was freaking me out. He whirled around and left the dungeon with a sonic boom trailing after him.

I made my decision. <Bob. What does our timetable look like for arrival at the next place blocking my ley lines?>

"We should be there tomorrow, Great Spirit," Navigation Bob confirmed for me quickly.

<This is the only one that we know of that is using Mana to block us, correct?> I looked over the map. With the additional power given to me through the ley lines, I had been able to empower their creation. It was a happy feedback loop that let me grow my network faster and faster.

"As far as we know," Bob confirmed once again.

<Good. After we get there and destroy that place, we will be following... a new course.> My words were heavy, and it was challenging to say this aloud.

"Great Spirit?"

<We will be... following the orders of the... Adventurers' Guild. They have threatened to destroy this entire place and tear out my Core if we don't comply.> I was really beating myself up about this. I should have expected something like this to happen the second I started to let others know that I had a mind. Dani had warned me, told me that other people knowing I could understand them would be dangerous. I just hadn't expected it to be like this. This was... I was being pressed into slavery, and I knew it. As soon as I had the chance, as soon as this S-ranker was gone... I was out of here. I would be eating that portal that connected me to other locations and running for it.

"...What?" Oh right, I was still next to Navigation Bob.

My resolve set, I spoke grimly, <Navigation Bob, I need you to gather the others. Bob Prime especially. We are going to be working on a new project together.>

"What should I tell the others this is about?"

<We are going to be looking for a weakness. We won't be shackled for long, Navigation Bob. We're going to be hunting an S-ranker.>

"That's... ambitious."

<It's also *necessary*. We'll be free one way or another.>

"I prefer the version of freedom where we remain alive."

<Yeah, well, we'll take what we can get.> I paused a moment and directed my thoughts at this S-ranked jerk, even though I knew he wouldn't hear me. <I hope you live each day like it's your last. You know why? Because I *am* going to kill you, but I'm also *awful* with dates and schedules.>

DALE

"Baron Dale!" A messenger was running up to the new cadet, but Dale held up a hand to forestall any information.

"I'm sorry to tell you this, but I am no longer a Baron. Is this message still applicable?" Dale questioned the heaving courier.

Hesitating, the man eventually made a 'no idea' gesture and relayed the information. "A statue came out of the ground in the main courtyard. It shows Guild Elder Sorbere... it depicts him killing a dozen students along with nearly a hundred Goblins and... and..."

"Spit it out!" Dale barked at him, already disgusted by the details. It was nice to finally learn the man's name, though.

That had been a poor choice of words, even if Dale didn't know what had happened yet. The messenger paled further and looked a bit sick. "It shows him *eating* them, sir."

"You're joking," Dale flatly responded, not quite able to comprehend the joke the man was telling him.

"I'm not."

"Alright. Um. Hmm." Dale went silent for a moment. "Please go find Hans, Tom, Adam, and Rose. Do you know who they are?"

"I do. Your party is well-renowned. That is, many people talk about you. Ah..." Now blushing after saying a little too much, the messenger almost ran off right away but was stopped once again.

"Thank you for letting me know you think of us, hopefully in a good light. Can you ask them to meet me at the entrance to the dungeon as soon as possible? After that, find one of the council members, not Tyler, and ask them to retrieve that statue. I am going to go down and take a look at what happened." Dale waited until he got a nod, then tossed the man a silver coin and went to get prepared. "Why are we fighting this guy? Why is he randomly killing people? It doesn't even make *sense* for the Guild to be acting like this."

Dale waited patiently for everyone to arrive and explained the situation to all of them. Hans, as usual, was the first to speak up. "How about we get the heck out of here before we piss him off? Do you know who he is? His name is Sorbere, but he is known as *Barry the Devourer*. He is able to infuse his entire cultivation and soul into an attack, converting everything affected into Essence or Mana. Do you know why he can just kill anyone or anything he wants? Because that was *part of his contract* to get into the Guild. He was so strong that they were forced to recruit him instead of sending an army of fellow S-rankers after him. For this guy to be here... something must have gone *really* wrong. The war must be going worse than we expected or were told."

"Are you telling me that sending proof that he killed a dozen people out of hand to the Guild will be *ignored*?" Dale froze up at Hans' nod, entirely uncertain how to deal with this situation.

"So, if we do nothing, we go to war. If we do *something*, he might *eat* us?" Rose almost gagged at the sickening thought.

"At least we know why he isn't going up against the necromancers directly." Adam shook his head, then flicked his eyes back and forth at the people giving him strange looks. "What, seriously? You just said that he invests his soul in his attacks. Don't you think a necromancer would be able to take advantage of that? Especially one as powerful as this 'Master' fellow?"

"Well... that was just a rumor. But... it does make sense." Hans rubbed at the stubble growing on his chin. "So now what?"

"I don't know about you, but I joined the Academy so that I wouldn't be sent off to war at my current ranking." Dale tossed his gauntlet-clad hands into the air in frustration. "Apparently, it's just as dangerous to stay *here,* though!"

"Dale, I hope you will not let this fear control you, even if the Guild controls us all right now." Tom stepped forward so that all eyes were looking up at him. "Listen, what have we done every single time something horrible and unexpected is happening? We persevere. When that Distortion Cat attacked us, when a horde of infected attacked the city, when you personally bet your life on rescuing a Wisp... why would we now let a single *known* threat stop us? We will get past this, through this, as a team."

Rose nodded at Tom's inspiring speech. "I agree. It is like my Grandma likes to say: everything you've ever wanted, everything that will make you happy, is on the other side of fear. If we don't take risks, if we don't power through this, we will never find what we need."

A new voice interrupted them, making the blood freeze in their bodies, "What pretty sentiments."

Barry was shaking his head at them as he strolled forward. "Do you have nothing else to do? A *war* to prepare for, perhaps? Move." He continued forward, not bothering to stop while talking to them. The party scrambled out of his way, which was for the best. If they hadn't, the S-ranked man would have walked through them. In a far more literal fashion than they would have liked.

Chapter Eighteen

"So. Now what?" Hans grinned nervously as Barry sauntered away. The others gave helpless shrugs and made as if to leave.

"Hold on." Dale had a bit of fire coming back into his voice. "The only way out of this sort of situation is to become stronger. When we finally get to a point where we can feel safe from that sort of person, *then* we can go relax in a corner or hide from the world."

"You do realize that he has likely been cultivating for several *hundred* years to get to the point he is at now?" Adam queried with resignation in his voice.

"So we do it *faster*," Dale affirmed gravely. "He never had the resources we do. A dungeon with no affinity? Seriously, why don't we stay down there for a few days or weeks at a time?"

"Some of us have a social life?" Hans chuckled when Dale rolled his eyes and head so hard that he almost fell over. "Hey, it isn't *my* fault you always ran off and had meetings to get to. Also, I haven't found a single decent ale or mead down in the dungeon."

"...You know what?" Adam tapped his stave while deeply considering the situation. "Neither have I. Because... who drinks in a dungeon, right?"

"Right?" Tom played right into Adam's trap with this single word.

"So do you think that the dungeon has recipes for alcohol down there? If not, we may be able to get a reward for items it has never taken before." Adam smiled, as did the other people around him.

"Finally! A *reason* to go to the tavern!" Hans cheered and turned to face the bar like a compass needle pointed to the north.

"You never needed one before, did you?" Rose acidly sniped at him.

Hans ignored her, a situation that was becoming more and more commonplace. They went to the tavern and - through a heroic haggling effort - managed to get a small cask of every type of booze and drink they made. If they had told the bartender the eventual destination of the drinks, he would have assuredly stopped them. So far, the dungeon hadn't been making anything like these, so it was assumed that it didn't have the recipes. The staff at the bar would certainly want to keep it that way.

As they rolled the small barrels into the dungeon proper, Dale heard a sigh in his mind as the dungeon took notice of them. The mental voice was the most lackluster Dale had ever heard. <Alright, what's this now?>

"Booze for the dungeon!" Hans called out loudly. "Come get your booze, *bo~o~oze* here!"

"What are you doing?" Adam asked the overly loud Assassin.

"Enticing the dungeon."

<No he isn't.>

"No you aren't." Dale shook his head, though he smiled while doing so. Hans had a way of breaking tension, and it was actually really nice of him to do so since they were all pretty tense currently.

<I have a totally empty floor right now, Dale.> Dale went still; he wasn't used to this kind of serious tone. <That S-ranker tore the entire level, everything, and *everyone* on it out of my depths. It was completely desolated; there wasn't even

Essence left in the area, and I'm needing to *reclaim* that space with influence! Unless I shut the dungeon down for a few days, it may be *weeks* before that level is back to its previous functionality. He also threatened to kill everyone here and knock me out of the sky if I don't meet his demands. I messed up, Dale. I messed up *bad.* Even the hot springs *bath* is gone!>

Dale was now placed in the uncomfortable position of needing to comfort a dungeon, which was also somehow *himself,* while others looked on curiously. "Um. There, there, big guy."

<Did I give you all my idiocy when I put your soul back in your body or something?> Dale flushed even further. <'There, there'? Really?>

"Soul...? *Right!*" Dale shouted as the others jumped away from the suddenly loud man. "Cal. I have information - really, it is only a rumor so don't get too excited - that Barry puts his entire *soul* into his attack when he does something like that. Does that sound realistic or at all familiar? We think that is why he isn't on the front lines fighting necromancers."

<It... yeah, it kind of does, now that I think about it.> Dale waited for a few moments, and just as he gave up and was going to do something else, the conversation continued, <Interesting. I may actually have something that I can do about it. Not for a while and not for certain, but... maybe. What do you want for this information? The booze too, I suppose.>

Dale looked around, and sure enough, the small barrels were gone. "Sneaky. We want safe areas on each level. We want to stay down here cultivating for days on end without needing to worry about being attacked all the time."

<Safe areas? That might have been a better idea than making an entire town down there...>

"I'm sorry, what?" Dale wasn't sure that he had heard Cal correctly.

"Don't worry your mutated little head about it. So you just want areas where you can cultivate. Who wants to sit in a room doing nothing but *breathing* all day? That sounds dreadfully boring.>

"If you'd rather just offer us Essence directly..." Dale trailed off, getting a more verbose response than he expected.

<Go fight a Cat. Do your own work, or fight and steal Essence like you were designed to do. Seriously! So needy. I hope you took all that personality trait with you when we split last time. Also, yes, I altered your meridians a bit, making them larger and more durable; drain Essence to your heart's content. You can get that stupid look off your face now.>

Dale tried to get his facial expressions under control, but the negative surprises of the day had made it hard for him to ignore even this small positive one. "Thanks for the information. I'll look for those safe areas." All he got in return was a disgruntled noise.

"I take it from your half of the conversation that things went well?" Rose smiled at Dale, bringing him back to the present.

"They did. We have a lot of work to do." Dale had fire in his eyes and a wide smile on his face. His regained confidence and his enthusiasm inspired the others, so they gripped their weapons and descended deep into the dungeon. "We are going to stop on each level and cultivate until we feel that we have gained all we can from that floor. We are going to hunt any creature with a Core, and eventually, we are going to become powerful."

"More than we already are!" Tom raised a fist into the air, punctuating his misplaced enthusiasm.

After roughly twenty minutes of exploring, Rose chuckled as she punched a wall and revealed a small silver chest.

"I've missed these. Do you guys remember when fighting standard Bashers was a challenging endeavor?"

"Wasn't that about two months ago for you, Rose?" Hans laughed as she flushed. "Nothing to be ashamed about, it just shows how far you've come."

"Oh." Obviously she had been prepared for an insult. "Thank you, Hans, that's true."

"No Cores or really *anything* of value for us on this floor." Adam was leaning on his staff, looking bored. Unless someone was injured or he was directly under attack, his main job was staying out of the way.

"If you all don't mind, I now have 'quotas' of materials, components, and Mob kills that I need to turn in if I want to remain at the Academy." Dale was stuffing the Bashers into his dimensional bag, but no one had said anything about that oddity yet. "If any of you want to join the Academy, I'd recommend making a stockpile as well."

"My Grandma just *had* to push for me to join the Guild," Rose grumbled softly. "Now I might need to join some two-copper school to stay out of a war."

"Hey!" Dale's eyes went wide. "I *built* that school!"

Hans shook his head. "Really, *really*, people. I know you don't see it, but the Guild is *awesome* to be in. This particular *situation* isn't super wonderful, but usually, the members start out just like us and work their way into recognition based on *good* stuff. This guy... Barry... I mentioned it before, but things must be even *worse* than we thought for him to be out and about. Knowing he is a High Elf - nice statue by the way - makes it even more concerning. They must think that the *entire world* is at serious risk if the upper echelons are starting to show up, or they just wouldn't care."

Tom considered his words. "So you are saying that we should try to work with him and just hope for the best?"

Hans shrugged and nodded. "I'm saying that there is likely a lot we aren't aware of, and we can't afford to be short-sighted or to actively work against Barry. If we do, there is a good chance that we will die. All of us. Worldwide."

CHAPTER NINETEEN

<Hey there, humans!> I cheerfully greeted my cultists-turned-servants. A few looked around with excitement, but the reactions were far more mixed than I preferred. <Tiny update: I have decided to stop calling you 'cultists' and have determined that you will be called my 'Attendants' from now on.>

Oops, I guess I had only been calling them 'cultists' in my head. There was an awkward silence as I waited for their reaction, and I sighed when only the two known fanatics reacted positively. Ah, well. If this group had been the cream of the crop, they wouldn't be here doing what they were doing. It was never the strong and confident people who gave up everything for more personal power, right? I needed to get their training started if I wanted to see any changes, and I had really wanted to leave everything to Etiquette Bob, but his creation was on hold while I slowly regrew the Goblin's floor.

It took a vast amount of Essence to bring the floor back from its current state of nothing, the kind I had been able to throw around before. Unfortunately, the ongoing maintenance of flying, ley line growth, and automated respawning on other floors was impeding my progress. <Okay, well, first off, we are going to work on fixing any issues that your bodies have. For most of you, that is going to need to wait until we get some of that corruption out of you.>

I could have made it really easy on them and directly placed Cores around their Center, but that was an exacting, time-consuming, and *expensive* way to fix something as simple as an overabundant taint. I decided to give them an option and made a pendant similar to the ones I had given Dale's group so long ago. Of course, I had never explained what the pendants did, and since I had never seen them again, they had likely sold them off as unidentified Inscribed items. <Alright, Attendants. You have two options.>

A clatter came from the stone table they were all gathered around, and all eyes were drawn to the two objects that had appeared there. <You can either wear a pendant and slowly purify your Centers - forgoing agonizing pain and a medium risk of death - or you can swallow a Core and get purified *now.*>

Several of the people reached for the pendant right away, but my resounding mental voice halted them. <There *is* a catch. At this level of the dungeon, the ambient Essence is *very* thick, as is the ambient Mana coming from my Core. Those of you who take the easy way out will be stuck on this level for a *very* long time as you are thoroughly purified over the course of... a *year* maybe? Those of you who take the risk will be able to begin cultivating right away - today even - during your free time and will likely advance *very* quickly. This will be in your favor, as influential people will have more options in my service.>

A line was drawn on the table, and I told everyone to choose a side to stand on. One half held the pendant, the other, a Core. Unsurprisingly, the fanatics went over to stand by the Core right away. The others slowly situated themselves, the vast majority waiting sheepishly by the pendant. There were only five willing to take the risk, and I silently snarled at Minya yet again. If you are going to create devoted minions, at least make sure they are *high quality* devoted minions! Each of those with weak willpower got a new necklace and were sent off to relax until I could get back to them. You would think that people that had left their lives behind them would be willing to take a few *risks*! Then I turned my attention to the people that would be the *actual* powers among my new Attendants.

<Excellent. Even by making just this step, you have raised yourselves in my estimation.> They seemed to perk up at that, and even more so at the next bit of information I fed them. <This is actually a standard recruitment task for the Adventurers' Guild. Most of their members need to go through something similar, so don't be too afraid. A couple of you are going to need to wait on this, although I'll give you all a cultivation technique right now. Don't use it until I tell you to, but study all the details. Even though it will be added directly to your mind, work at actively *understanding* it.>

I had two of the humans step into a side room, the ones with severe issues that had prevented them from advancing themselves. They laid down, and I put pressure on their minds through my Mana until they passed out. They wouldn't want to be awake for this part, and I didn't want to wait until they had taken medicine and fell asleep in a semi-natural manner. The first was easy; she merely had multi-organ failure. Hardly a problem for me to fix but likely nearly unbearable for her. Easy-peasy. Done.

The next guy was a little more interesting to work with, but my experience messing with Dale's innards had prepared me well for this moment. This man's affinity channels were stuffed with impurities and entirely blocked. I had no *idea* how he had survived this long. With no way to absorb Essence, he would be burning through his life force at an extra fast rate. At least this explained why a man who appeared to be in his early sixties was actually in his early twenties. Others might have chalked it up to a life of hard living, but his body had advanced *far* past that natural explanation. I went through the myriad channels in his body, scooping out the impurities and collecting them into a sealable jar. My Goblins really liked to use this black goo to poison weapons and such; it made for nasty wounds that disrupted Essence and became easily infected.

The rest of this man's body was in shambles due to having such a weak constitution his whole life. Fixing him up was far more intensive than, say, fixing a few failing organs; I *almost* didn't bother, but... if he was going to be wrangling the others, perhaps going from an 'old man' to a young one would create an incentive to do well in my service. I worked on him, then took all the impurities off both of their bodies, leaving them sparkling clean. That sparkling *may* be the glitter I dusted them with, but my point stands. I left clean robes next to them, and let them wake up.

They both examined their bodies with glee, feeling better than they could ever remember feeling. They stood without hunching, without pain. Then they both dropped to their knees and started singing my praises. No... they were actually praising *me* as if I were... <Enough of that, please; I'm not god. I have no wish to have actual angels dispatched against me or to have the Church attack, so stop it. Treat me like a really generous boss that is going to help you live forever.>

They both were beaming about that and seemed to get even more excited, so I decided to distract them. <Oh, look over here! A memory stone with a decent cultivation technique! Hey, you... the, um, male? What do I call you?>

"Call me Anders, Great Spirit," he responded as he pulled on the robe he had been given.

How in the...? <Oh, not you, too! Is that a side effect of fixing people?>

"Our spiritual leader, Minya, informed us that this was the preferred method of addressing you," Anders respectfully informed me.

<What a surprise. Just... fine. Listen, you have almost zero health issues right now. Your body is fixed, your meridians are clean, and your center is basically empty of Essence and corruption. Mainly because nothing could ever get *through* your clogged meridians, but that's beside the point. I want you to begin using that cultivation technique as soon as possible. Even now, your body is burning through your life force, since it isn't using Essence as a substitute. You are visibly aging. Go! Hurry up!> Anders seemed to fall into panic, because he grabbed the stone and nearly clobbered his head with it in his rush to begin. I chuckled at that and turned to the other.

<As for you, your center is *not* clear, but your body is finally at a place where it should survive the next steps. Go join the others; we are about to have a water drinking competition. Oh, wait, name please!> I caught her just as she was moving toward the exit.

She curtsied, which seemed a little out of place without a dress, but it was nice all the same. "I am known as Jules, Great Spirit."

<Lovely. Just so you are aware, you two are going to be in charge of the others. Make sure to survive!> She bobbed again, and I smiled. This might actually be fun!

I glanced around my caverns and tried to think of how to deal with the myriad issues popping up. There was already one manor occupied. Madame Chandra had found the open doorway leading downward before I had remembered to close it and was now living here without the amenities that I had planned for. She didn't seem to mind and was even unintentionally helping me out by growing plants all over the place as she tried to get a feel for her newfound prowess. This proved another point for me: Mages were *wasteful* with their Mana. I had suspected it for a while but had never found a proper way to test for long periods of time so I could know for sure. Even so, my theory had been one of the main reasons that I had made this floor.

When I say 'wasteful' I don't mean they litter all over the place, I just mean that they don't actually use their Mana efficiently. When they cast a spell or use their Mana for any reason, there is some that is just... wasted. No longer! Now, instead of floating free and eventually collecting into storms or mutating things randomly, I can gather the Mana and either use it directly or absorb it into my own power to help my reserves grow.

It's evident that Mana is more potent than Essence, but by testing it out, I was able to draw accurate conclusions about exactly how *much* more potent. The 'runoff' Mana that Madame Chandra had unknowingly leaked for me over an hour offered almost as much energy as the accumulated Essence I was able to gather on my first floor for a full *day*. There were now at least a *hundred* weak cultivators wandering my first floor at any given time, and they were no longer shy about diving in at night.

These Academy students seemed extra motivated to kill and collect my Mobs, and I had increased the amount available because of this. No longer did Bashers move alone, *ever*. The smallest group was now ten - as the humans had proven that, one-on-one, they could now defeat my Bashers every time. My first floors had gotten more dangerous as a result, but the people on them seemed pleased by this instead of upset and even *sneered* and *laughed* when they heard about people failing to survive. What a strange attitude to have! What was I talking about...? Right! Chandra!

This A-rank Mage was all the proof I needed to deem my new floor a success. From here, I would accelerate the training of my Attendants and hope that word got out to the

Mages above. They should really hurry up because the benefits of being here would be beneficial to both parties but especially to me. I needed to advance, and it was time to get serious about it.

Chapter Twenty

"Dale, I'm not sure this is the best idea," Hans spoke in a whiny tone as they settled in on the mostly empty third floor.

Dale glared over at Hans with a sour expression. This was the *third* time they had gone over this. "Hans, I'm serious about advancing my cultivation. The *only* reason I'm going to leave is to get new missions from the Academy, to drop off Mobs or requested goods, or attend my instruction with the Moon Elves. Or, you know, if we get hurt pretty bad and need help. Hurt by *Mobs*," he clarified hurriedly as a knife appeared in Hans' hand.

"How do you know that this 'safe area' will be honored by the dungeon?" Hans quietly inquired, twirling the knife over his knuckles and through his fingers in a beautiful display of dexterity.

"I don't, and that's why we are setting a rotating guard when we sleep." Dale shrugged and fluffed his small travel pillow. It wouldn't help much, but it was better than sleeping directly on the rocky ground. "But needing to defeat the Boss of the floor to get a token, *finding* the safe area kiosk, and the fact that it only lasts a few hours *maximum* all point to this being a serious effort on the dungeon's part."

"I've also noticed an interesting effect in the air after we inserted the token." Adam was watching apparently nothing with his strange golden irises. "There isn't any more Essence coming within the circle created when we put the token in. In other words, this isn't somewhere that we can sit and cultivate. If it is a 'safe area', it is *only* that; this is certainly not a valid cultivating area."

Dale seemed crestfallen, his expression exaggerated to the point that the others laughed at him. Tom lightly punched the ex-Noble, sending him staggering a few steps. The giant redhead was grinning. "Do you really *want* to cultivate in a safe area? You will end up like a greenhouse cultivator, unable to withstand the slightest breeze of adversity! No, we will grow against all odds, we will persevere where others would fail... like the weeds near the summit of Mountaindale!"

Dale burst out laughing and slapped the other man on his back. Tom gained a look of panic on his face - which twisted to one of pain - and he staggered away rubbing a hand-shaped bruise that was forming. Dale winced and sheepishly grinned. "Ah, right. Sorry about that, buddy. My strength is... I'm just not used to it yet. Great speech though!"

Tom nodded and tried to rub the spot on his back. "I understand perfectly, though I may ask Adam to look at this. Get some sleep; I'll take the first watch."

"Sorry...!" Dale called after Tom, who simply waved it off. Rose was laughing at him, as was Hans, so Dale decided to do as Tom directed and get some sleep. He lay down and drifted off, and a few hours later, he was shaken awake by Hans. "What? What's going on?"

"Just wanted to let you know that the 'safe area' is working as it is supposed to." Hans pointed at the edge of the circle that had appeared, where some frightening Bashers were staring at them menacingly. Dale hadn't seen these types before and recoiled in shock when he activated his Essence sight and was able to see that they were C-ranked.

"What *are* those things?" His voice made them shift anxiously, but the huge, blade-horned rabbits didn't come any closer.

"I'm thinking that they are the 'Hopsecutioners' that I've heard about. They supposedly give support to Raile when large parties try to work together against him. Now, I'm not sure what they are doing *here*, but if they *stay* here, they are going to be dead in half a minute." Hans stated the last part loudly, and the knives spinning in his hands took on a dull edge of heat. The Hopsecutioners' ears twitched, and after snorting softly a few times, they turned and bounced away.

"Did the dungeon give them new orders, or could they understand you?" Rose wondered aloud as the fluffy tails whisked around the corner.

"The dungeon didn't focus on this area, so I'm going to assume that they could understand, if not his words, then at least the threat that he offers." Adam had come over to stand by them and put forth his own interpretation, "I'm betting they are down here because this floor is almost empty otherwise. Even the Boss Goblin we had to fight to get this token was alone."

"Bugbears!" Tom sat upright, blinking owlishly in the light from their campfire as he looked around. "Wazzat?"

"Go back to sleep, Tom. We're all set," Dale gently ordered. Tom nodded once and laid back down. Dale looked at the others and talked a little softer, "Tomorrow, we are going into the labyrinth. Do you think everyone is ready?"

"Is there any rush?" Rose poked at him. "Let's cultivate for a few days on this floor."

Dale shook his head. "The density of Essence increases as we go further down. We can increase our cultivation in a shorter time if we dance on the edge of oblivion."

"How poetic. I assume you mean if we get especially close to that monstrosity of a Boss monster that has its own floor?" Hans shuddered in disgust. "I don't think it would be happy to have us wearing clothes made out of its skin..."

"Maybe it will think we are smaller versions and just let us pass through?" Rose countered optimistically.

"If we could survive on deeper floors, I would have just had us pop down to them through a portal. The fifth... sixth floor? The one after the Manticore... does his level count as a full floor? Anyway, they are too dangerous for us to cultivate on. We are only taking the scenic route because we need to load up on Mobs and plants. The labyrinth is going to be different; that is where we will end up staying for our extended cultivation training." Dale was confident in his plans.

"Works for me." Hans stretched and cracked his vertebrae. "Can't get ordered to do things if you can't be found, know what I mean? As for the floors, as far as I know, there are the two rabbit levels, this empty floor that used to hold the Goblins in their fortresses, the labyrinth, the Boss room, followed by two golem-filled floors of 'paths' from the Tower of Ascension."

"I thought there was only one floor of those at the end?" Adam voiced the question before Dale could.

"I hear things," Hans shrugged, feigning nonchalance, "so if you count all of those as floors, there are currently seven.

Dale was raring to go but feeling ever more powerless. "All I hear is that there are unexplored treasures under my feet that I can't access. I was taught my limits in here. A while back, I was in the room with the Manticore as a few Mages fought it, and its Mana was so overwhelming that I could not move no matter how I tried. I *hated* that feeling, and I want to be able to fight that thing on equal terms!"

"Give it a few decades, Dale." Hans smiled at the glare that was shot his direction. "You'll get there!"

"A few decades is too long." Dale's mouth set in a firm line. "That's where this training comes in. We, together, are going to become strong enough to protect ourselves, our interests, and each other."

"Ugh, so *serious* all the time." Hans pushed Dale on the chest, causing him to stumble. "You have the option for a near-unlimited lifespan; have *fun* every once in a while!"

"Where?" Dale blandly asked Hans instead of rising to his bait.

"I'll take you into the city and we can... hmm." Hans' brow furrowed, then a devious grin jumped into place. "We can go to the Golden Sands Broth... nope. Huh. To the Abyss with it! Necromancers should be renamed 'Joy Assassins'. They literally killed all the fun in the world. *Fine*, I'm in. Let's go get strong."

"They might have killed the fun, but couldn't they revive the area?" Rose tried to banter with him. "I heard that the tourist areas of the city were dying, maybe that is what got them all hot and bothered?"

"Dale already proved his point, Rose! Why must you taunt me with your beauty and honeyed words? Are you just trying to get close to me?" Hans fluttered his lashes at her.

"With our history, you are *still* trying that?" Rose's hands inched toward her bow.

Hans stepped toward her, shaking his head. "Rose, feel my arm. Just do it."

"Why?"

"It's part of me, so it is obviously made out of boyfriend material." Hans dodged gracefully, catching two arrows in his hands before the anger left her face. "Careful with that! You might actually hurt me someday!"

"Oh, I *will*. Dale, I'm fully on board with this *training*." The last sentence was said in an almost sickly-sweet tone.

"Well, let's not waste time." Dale woke the others, and they walked to the entrance of the labyrinth. They headed down the winding stairs, entering into the welcome room of the enormous maze. Dale felt a sudden pain and flipped backward as a Flesh Cat missed a swipe at him. He was bleeding, so perhaps 'missed' was the wrong word. Failing in its attack, the Cat ran off before a retaliatory strike could be made.

"A few weeks of this, and we will be sufficiently battle-hardened!" Tom was entirely too cheerful in Dale's opinion. After a bandage was pressed to his fresh wound, they moved deeper into the maze.

Chapter Twenty-one

I was hovering over the location of the almost-Mana-using dungeon that was on our map. Everything was ready for this dungeon to be destroyed; I just needed to make it happen. <Dale, come on. Just go convince some people to hop down there and grab the Core. You've been a constant annoyance, just help me out a *little*.>

Dale was fighting Snowball right now and wasn't taking my interruptions very well. "Quiet, you over-talkative rock!"

An arrow whistled through the air, and I nudged Snowball's mind to have him duck. Dale got slapped by a dinner-plate sized paw and tumbled away as Tom stepped in to block the Cat from pressing his advantage. <Why won't you just->

"Cal, I have no political power!" Dale wheezed, blood trickling from his lips. Snowball hit with the force of a high C-ranker. "All I am now is a low-ranked fighter."

<Well that's just *perfect* timing, isn't it?> I growled as Tom kicked Snowball in the ribs. That was uncalled for. Snowball hissed a gout of steam at the Barbarian, who had to dive out of the way to avoid being parboiled.

"Why not go bother Minya with this?" Dale bellowed as he dove back into the fight. He rolled onto Snowball's back, straddling him and punching the Cat in the head repeatedly.

<Oh, I'm sorry, I didn't realize your opinion was *in* this recipe, Dale.> I watched as Snowball tried to shake him off, failed, and then ran toward a steam vent. <You're probably gonna want to let go.>

"Not until- *Ahh*!" Dale shrieked as steam blasted onto him. His enhanced body took the heat without killing him instantly, but nasty blisters now coated his skin. Now, I know it is strange to be happy about seeing him in pain, as he is *me*, but it was oddly satisfying to watch him writhing around on the ground as Snowball turned on him. Good thing that steam was natural and not Essence-created, or Dale's armor would have just absorbed it.

A paw reared back, then dropped again as I warned Snowball about an incoming dagger. The blade stuck into the wall, and Hans laughed. "I guess it's learning our tricks!"

"That's great; *help me*!" Dale shouted in reply as he rolled to avoid a pounce. He should have gotten some rigid armor; he wouldn't have needed to prevent every little thing from striking him. Too bad *someone* doesn't listen to my advice!

Snowball tried to spring forward but yowled as he was pulled back to the ground. A golden chain - which looked too thin to hold my Cat in place - had kept Snowball connected to the ground. Adam was smiling with too-white teeth as his eyes shone bright gold. He blinked as Rose slammed the bladed end of her bow into the colossal Cat's head, killing my poor kitty. The chain vanished, and Adam's facial features returned to a fairly neutral expression.

Dale stood up, reached into the new wound, and split Snowball's skull open. He dug around for a moment before popping the Core out of the skull and into his hand. Just before he crushed it, I coughed into his mind to get his attention. "What, you annoying puddle-loving rock?"

<Wow. That was totally uncalled for, Dale. Here I am, about to offer you a better way of doing things, and you throw details you shouldn't know in my face.>

"You don't have a face."

<See, there you go, being all hurtful for no good reason. Fine, I won't tell you how to absorb that Core more efficiently.

Just go ahead and squeeze.> I'll admit, I was getting huffy, but he was being unaccountably rude. *I* didn't invite him to come here and kill all of my Mobs. That was on him. *He* was stressed? I had a soul-sucking S-ranker threatening to abyssal *eat me*. It was *my* job to eat people, not the other way around!

Dale rolled his eyes and ran a hand through his hair. He winced as he carelessly pressed against a blister. "Fine, fine. You're right, puddles are great, and bubbles are fun."

<Good choice. Just hold that Core in the Rune on your palm, then cultivate. If nothing happens, oh well, but if it works as intended, the Rune should let you pull the Essence out of the Core so long as you don't leave it alone long enough for it to gain intelligence.> I paused as he stared at the Core. <I think I actually will ask Minya for help. Thanks for the tip. I tend to forget that you are one of my weaker people, even if I have the most interaction with you.>

Dale ignored most of what I had to say, staring at the Core in his hand with trepidation. "This could become intelligent?"

I snorted at him. <*That*? Give it a couple hundred years, and sure. Just like a tree can become self-aware.> I didn't bother to stick around for what would assuredly be a *scintillating* rebuttal but, instead, went in search of Minya. It didn't take me long to find her; she was the only person that was surrounded by guards and proselytizing about the wonders of the Dungeon, or *me*. I guess I held wonders. That was nice to hear.

"Come deep into the dungeon and learn great secrets, be healed of your wounds, and have your cultivation bottlenecks shattered!" Minya was shouting above the guards' orders.

"You are under arrest for the suspected massacre of over a dozen people!" One of the men surrounding her was shouting back at her. "Be silent, *wench*!"

Minya backhanded him, snapping his jaw and sending his unconscious body to the ground. No one tried to catch the fallen human as Minya continued shouting, “The *Guild* sends a new police force, removes those in power, and sends our lives into turmoil! For stability, for honest work, and a boost in your abilities, join me in serving the dungeon!”

<You seem busy, I’ll come back later.>

I started to return my attention down below, but Minya’s eyes widened and she began yelling, “Even *now*, the dungeon speaks to me! What service is it that I can perform for the Great Spirit?”

<You’re really having too much fun with this, aren’t you? Listen, I need the dungeon Core from the dungeon we are hovering above. I’m pretty sure it's a Mage ranked dungeon, but I don’t have details. Can I get you to do this for me?> I winced as she started shrieking her answer aloud.

“The dungeon calls for a *crusade*! Who will join me in destroying the impertinent dungeon we are above? I call upon my fellow Mages!” Minya looked around, beaming at the growing crowd.

“What would we get out of it?” A B-ranked man stepped forward, greed warring with incredulity on his face.

I threw out the first thing I could think of, <Eh. I found a way that Mages can reach a higher tier of **laws**. You think they’d be interested?>

Minya’s eyes widened even further. Somehow. I was surprised they hadn’t popped out. “The dungeon offers a *path advancement* for any Mage willing to do this task!”

“You’re lying or insane.” The Mage who had stepped forward stated flatly, turning away and vanishing into the crowd.

“Mages! What risk are you taking?” Minya called over the laughter the Mage leaving had generated. “Either you do nothing and laugh at a perceived falsehood, or you are offered a path advancement! If the rewards are not as promised, it will be easy for you to tell the others that I do not speak true, will it not?"

The laughter faded to muttering, and soon enough, a few people had stepped forward. <Hey, Minya, I'm not sure that->

"Welcome friends!" she brightly greeted her temporary companions. "Shall we begin immediately, or do you need time to prepare? Can I get your names?"

"I'm Shanara. Call me Shan." A green-eyed Elf was standing next to her and staring unblinkingly at Minya. "I'd normally charge you for my services directly, and I warn you that if the dungeon does not follow through on the promise you made, I *will* charge you the normal fee plus danger pay."

"A mercenary? Ooh. A *Wild* Elf, then?" Minya grinned as other people quickly stepped away from the group with looks of fear or disgust, depending on their race. "What are you bringing to the group?"

"Poison and ice. Take it or leave it," Shan hissed with narrowing eyes. She did not particularly care to have her exile brought up in casual conversation. "I've destroyed dungeons before if that helps."

Minya's smile never wavered. "Oh, it does. I'll learn the rest of your names as we go, but let's do this!"

<I need the Core *unbroken*, Minya!> I called to her as the Mages began running toward the edge of the mountain.

"Don't worry about it, Cal." I saw the smirk on her face just as she jumped off the cliff. "I haven't failed you yet."

She and her team were outside of my perception, so I could only groan and try to avoid a headache that shouldn't exist. Since, yeah, no head. Alright. Well... if they couldn't succeed, I was going to be in real trouble. Already I could see that 'Barry' was getting impatient if his tapping foot was any indication. Each 'tap' demolished some of the ground around him, so it was an obvious threat to me. I listened in on his muttering for only a moment and shuddered.

"If we aren't there in time, I don't care *what* they told me to do. I bet the Dungeon Core in here is *delicious*. The taste of its Mana... so exquisite... so *pure*." Barry was literally drooling, likely the most disgusting thing I had ever seen. At least to me. I saw worse things practically daily, but for some reason, this hit me on a more visceral level than seeing someone get beheaded.

I had to put my faith in Minya and hope she pulled through. I couldn't wait here any longer. I had an appointment with the Guild, and it appeared that arriving fashionably late was *not* an option.

Chapter Twenty-two

Adam toppled to the floor as the room they were in *lurched*. He looked at the small Rune next to his head and winced. "That could have been bad. I found another trap here, everyone."

The others had been able to steady themselves during the sudden movement, and Tom had actually been assisted in his attack against a Cat. The Cloud Cat had been dropping at them, and the sudden shift brought it into Tom's attack range just as he swung. Gore rained down on them as the remains of the pulverized Beast succumbed to gravity.

"Thank you, Adam." Hans helped the man to his feet, then rounded on Tom. "As for *you*, how many times have I told you that using that hammer is overkill and wasteful?"

Tom hedged around the issue while storing his hammer back in his bag. "I, um. I just didn't want our team to be taken advantage of when we were off balance like that."

"Bull!" Hans was trying to be serious but failing to hide a snort. "You just like seeing your opponent *pop* like a Mage punched them at full strength."

"It... it is so *fun*," Tom admitted, looking at Hans out of the corner of his eye. "I try to use it rarely, but..."

"You're fine, but relying on that weapon will fail in an extended battle." Hans smacked Tom lightly on the bicep to get him to relax. "You'll be drained long before fighting anyone of actual strength. Wasting your ability to fight on such weak creatures... don't make it a habit."

"...they aren't weak to me." Tom's mutter went uncommented upon.

Dale had already sat down and was cultivating. Unlike when he focused on pulling in Essence from the air around him, there was currently little disturbance in the ambient power. He was staring at the Core in his hand as if it held all the secrets he had ever wanted and was doing his best to pull power directly from it. The light in the Core flickered, and Dale smiled maliciously as he 'caught' the Essence it contained and began to sap it.

"That is disturbing to watch for some reason." Rose shuddered as she sat next to him and joined him in cultivating. "It's almost as if you were eating raw meat from a creature you killed."

Dale slowly shook his head, trying not to lose focus. "There is so much more Essence in these than I had been getting! I was taking a fifth at best... now I'm *sure* I'm still losing some, but perfect conversion is probably outside my capabilities. Still... Snowball had more Essence stored in just his Core than I do in my entire body currently."

Dale focused on his cultivation technique, rotating his current overabundance of Essence through his body to grind away at the barriers to advancement. Until he was able to pour enough power into his aura to step into the C-ranks, he needed to continue weaving Essence through and around himself. It was not... *quite* as easy as it sounded. First, he needed to bring external Essence into himself and refine it in his Core. He couldn't just use ambient Essence directly, unfortunately. Then he needed to reach out and infuse his body with that power, down to the smallest particle. The only real difference in this step was the *order* you progressed.

There were three potential paths here that led to the same outcome, though each had positives and negatives. You could start the process by wrapping your externalities in Essence, which would allow you to make more powerful barriers from the outset. The downside was fairly obvious here: your body would be less well protected against injuries if your shields were breached. The second option was to start at the outermost portion of your body, the skin. This would help you gain resistance to piercing and slashing attacks but would leave you poorly defended against jarring blows or elemental assaults.

Option number three was to start on the interior of the body and work your way outward. This would help protect your inner organs and increase your recovery rate. Of course, by the time your aura was complete, all of the combined benefits would be in place. Dale had every Essence type available and so had chosen to work on his external shielding first. There was just too much benefit to be gained to ignore this path.

Since his armor protected him from most slashing attacks - intentionally ignoring the Flesh Cat - and he would eventually get the benefits of protected internals, shielding simply made sense for him. Creating the external aura was a trial in patience and eerily similar to the actions needed for crocheting, if on a much smaller scale. Weaving a tight aura was essential to creating shields that would hold up to various attacks. After each 'knot' was created and connected, Dale realized that the pattern was similar to the drawings he had seen from the memories of a flesh Mage that specialized in brain injuries. Each 'knot' was similar to what the Mage had called a 'neuron' and connected to the others similar to the 'dendrites'.

How very... odd. Did this explain why using an aura pattern was more natural as you used it more often? Were you able to get your aura to *learn* as you used it? Would it become intelligent, at least a little? Did it matter? Dale shook his head and continued to work. He would save his more esoteric questions for the next time he saw Artorian. If he wanted to discuss or ponder philosophy, he needed to do it in a safe location. Continuing to generate more 'knots', Dale soon hit a stumbling block and opened his eyes. The Core in his hand was inert, empty, useless.

He wasn't upset, just a bit tired. Dale had made a couple hundred new connections to his external aura. He needed a few *hundred thousand* before he was ready to step into the B-ranks, but he was happy to see that he had made progress. With good cheer, he informed the others. "I just made it into D-rank five!"

"That seems slow." Hans offhandedly crushed his good cheer. "I've seen the amount of Essence you are taking in; you should be at least at D-eight by now. Strange."

Dale was a little put out by this comment. "Hans, it isn't just about Essence, come on. You know I need to build my aura."

"You're *building* your *aura* in the *D-ranks*?" Hans' jaw dropped. "I thought you just had been storing power, maybe been taught a few techniques! Are you actually *infusing*? Let me look at you."

Dale was pulled close and heat blazed in Hans' eyes as he looked Dale over. "Would you look at that? You are actually building your aura! I've never seen a D-ranker with such a dense external aura before; you must be working on that, then? Interesting choice. I'm *shocked* that you have such fine Essence control."

"Hans, I was told that this was the path to getting into the C-ranks..." Dale trailed off as the Assassin had a grin play around his lips. "Are you messing with me?"

"Actually, no, I'm not." Hans gestured around the room. "Adam, Tom, how do you get into the C-ranks?"

Tom answered first, speaking as though he was reading from a textbook, "You store Essence in your body and aura.

Once you reach a critical mass of stored power, once you have expanded your aura to its maximum, you will step into the C-ranks. From there you will need further instruction."

"Any disagreements, Adam?" Hans looked at the Cleric, who shook his head. Hans turned back to Dale. "This must be the Moon Elf. Craig wouldn't have steered you wrong without reason. Well, not wrong. Steered you different. I'm sure there is a reason for the way they are making you do this, but it is not the standard way of making things happen. The D-ranks are all about the raw power necessary to achieve them."

Dale decided right there that he needed to have a *talk* with his instructors when he left this place. Until then... he barely stopped himself from doing something he would regret. *Fine.* Dale decided - extra reluctantly - that he would bear with this for now, he would trust that the people shaping him had the best results in mind for his advancement. No need to break something or come out with a substandard result because of his haste. He had an advantage currently, and even Hans had commented positively on his shielding. Time to get back to killing.

CHAPTER TWENTY-THREE

Tom looked around the corner, whipping his head back as a whirlwind of gold-tinged flame filled the hallway and melted the stone to slag. "I *truly* dislike Assimilators. They seem to be disproportionately powerful to the other creatures in here."

A detail sprang to Dale's mind from the fading memories of his time recombined with Cal. "The dungeon powers them directly with ambient Essence. They will get stronger and stronger until the Essence in the area is reduced; then they will weaken quickly. That will make it useless to cultivate in this area though, so we should kill them quickly..."

"Thanks, Dale, that's *extra* helpful." Rose stood and drew an arrow. "So your advice is to kill the thing trying to kill us? If only we had thought of that sooner!"

She leaned out into the hallway, sighting, firing, and whirling back to safety all in the span of a half second. A bolt of electricity hit the wall where she had briefly appeared, scattering sparks and discharging against the stone. Tom coughed from the smoke rising off the molten rock and looked at her, "Did you get it?"

"No." She rolled her wrists and got two arrows ready. "This time for *sure*." She moved down the corridor to get a running start, then jumped across the cooling floor and fired while in the air. She planted her feet on the opposite wall, smoke rising from her leather shoes as she pushed off and jumped back to the group, firing as she did so. Dale watched her with a touch of hero-worship; he had never thought to attack like that. Perhaps he needed to start using more... how to describe it... aerial encompassing attacks? Include movement along all three dimensions instead of only remaining on the flat ground? Bounce off the walls to attack from odd angles?

Rose nodded to indicate that she had landed an attack on the creature and settled down to wait. Unless they wanted to backtrack and find a new way through the maze, they needed to let the stone cool enough to pass through. Assimilators only seemed to appear when they were near the center of the labyrinth, so it was a good bet that getting through here was their best option. They had been making a considerable amount of potential profit by going through the fourth floor again and again. Not only were Cores in abundance on this level, but they had pouches stuffed with tokens, creatures, and herbs.

Dale had stuck to his promise to only leave the dungeon for training and returning items to the academy, but each of the others cycled out for relaxation, baths, or their own personal reasons. It had been a week since they came in here, and the constant stresses and cultivation had been good for all of them physically, even if their mental state may have been in question. Hours of cultivating each day and night in an Essence-rich environment had propelled each person forward, even if it weren't enough for them to advance in rankings. Yet.

"I'm *almost* at C-rank six. *Then* she'll love me," Hans muttered to himself, moving his head slightly without looking so that the arrow coming his way landed in the wall instead of his head.

"Knock it off, Mr. *Dangerlicious*." Rose broke into a grin. "Even if I *wanted* to be with you, would my Grandmother approve of someone so... worldly?" The others chuckled at that, and Hans muttered about how much he hated that wayward Bard that had immortalized a story from his past.

They all relaxed for a few minutes, crossing the hallway after it cooled and harvesting the Assimilator. The ends of its tentacles had been determined to be a useful component for creating weapons that let you spray elemental assaults at enemies without messing with your aura. Tyler, the innovative weapon merchant and council member, had found an excellent way to attach these to a multitude of various weaponry. As the weapons were cheaper and even sometimes more effective than enchanted or Inscribed weapons of the same type, they were purchased en masse by F and D rank cultivators. Continuing to carefully explore, the party eventually made it back to the center of the maze.

The swirling steam and mist were a good indication that Snowball the Cat was awaiting them and that an ambush was likely. Dale glanced over at Hans. "Are you going to help on this one?"

"Nope. You're the one who wants to fight all the Cats and use them to get stronger. You four should have no problem working out how to take down the Boss. I'll try to step in before any of you die, but..." Hans shrugged and shook his head sadly. "Sometimes, things happen for a reason. Perhaps that reason is that you are weak."

"Very comforting." Adam rolled the golden orbs he called eyes, which did more to highlight their oddities than to show his displeasure.

"No warhammer." Hans pointedly stared at Tom until he reluctantly grumbled his assent. "Have fun, you crazy kids!"

Hans faded from view as the others stepped into the steam, giving Dale a flash of inspiration. He pulled on his aura, shifting it from earthen shielding and into a misty camouflage. To the others, Dale's feet faded, then the remainder of him, and finally, he disintegrated before their eyes. Before anyone could panic, he whispered to them quietly, "Don't worry; it's an aura trick. I might actually be able to get a sneak attack off on

Snowball because the dungeon seems to be busy doing something else today."

"Just make sure that you don't get between us and the Beast," Tom announced in a too-loud voice. "Else an errant attack could unintentionally fell you, and I feel that I would not be able to bear the shame of slaying yet another team member."

A loud growl rippled through the area, a sign that Snowball knew they were there... and that he was coming for them. Dale was getting excited and had to calm himself forcibly. Breathing hard or even a rapid heartbeat might give him away to the Cat. Dale softly padded away from the group, finding himself crouching near a steam vent. Snowball usually went around them when he wasn't relaxing or attacking, so Dale hunkered down and waited patiently. In a few moments, he heard a soft *shushing* sound that he had come to associate with Snowball's fur lightly brushing against the ground. Dale smiled, his teeth showing through the fog momentarily. White fur coats were the current fashion in Mountaindale, and intact pelts were going for a high price as winter progressed.

As the soft sound passed him by, Dale felt a disturbance in the mists of his aura. He launched forward, putting everything he could into a single attack. His fist slammed into Snowball's haunch, sending the Cat flailing and hissing with pain and surprise. Dale's smile faded as Snowball did something unexpected, using some form of ability that he had never seen before. The Cat inhaled and *roared* at the steam. It seemed that he took direct control of the vapor in the air because it shuddered at the tremendous volume and dropped to knee-height throughout the room... all of it but a human-outline of mist hanging in the air a few feet from the Cat.

Snowball sprang at the exposed cloud, but Dale hadn't stayed where he was. As soon as he realized that he was exposed, he had dropped to the floor and rolled toward the Cat. A roiling mist dispersed as Snowball tackled it, but Dale had managed not to get hit. His teammates had also reacted, and now, a full-scale fight had erupted. Snowball had already been weakened by Dale's attack, and his injury made it hard for him to deal with the multitude of attacks coming his way. He dodged away from a single arrow, but another took him in the flank and disabled his rear-left leg. Dale rejoined the battle then, springing out of his position on the floor and punching the Cat in the nose.

The move was... *surprisingly* effective. Given that Dale hit as hard as a bear with his current cultivation rank and that noses are notoriously fragile, Snowball's inability to respond to the blow was quickly capitalized upon. The fight ended a few exchanges later, as Tom's ingot hammers rapped out a staccato beat on the feline's skull. Dale was soon looking at yet another Core in his hand, excited about using it almost to the point of ignoring his team.

Hans slow clapped and sarcastically cheered for their group takedown of a Beast that was - by all accounts - much too strong for the group. Tom cleared his throat and countered the Assassin's condescending attitude. "My apologies, Hans, but I think that your sarcasm right now may be neglecting the fact that this Beast - by all rights - should be far too much for us to handle. Especially without powerful weapons like my warhammer. If you will pardon my saying so, you need to... tone it down? Is that the correct expression? With your current attitude toward our success, we can only make the assumption that you really and truly despise us. Perhaps this is the attitude that drives away the Lady Rose? That is, if you are *actually* interested in pursuing a relationship. None of us are currently certain of your sincerity."

"Or interest in *any* woman, for that matter," Rose agreed, flicking her sweat-soaked hair out of her face. "No one wants to hear negative comments all the time. It makes us despise being around you."

Hans had a genuinely grotesque look on his face by the end of this tirade, and his hands were frozen mid-clap. As the others got to work harvesting the now-red-furred Cat, Rose could hear him muttering, "Is that... *really* why I've been...?"

Chapter Twenty-Four

Dale walked out of the portal and into town, looking around with haunted, tired eyes. The week so far had consisted of sneak attacks from every angle, and his battle readiness was getting near its peak. He moved more fluidly, staying balanced and on the lookout for any danger, no matter the form it might take. He breathed out, fashioning his aura to shroud him in swirling white, and nearly vanished in the snowstorm as he walked. Right then, Dale decided that he might be in love with the myriad applications of aura.

He walked over to the area that had been designated to meet with the Elf and looked around with pure paranoia. The small field he had been ordered to in their last session was utterly filled with *snowmen.* Full-on, child fantasy, snowmen. Carrot noses, black rocks for smiles and eyes, and thin twig arms.

Dale flinched as his instructor's voice rang through the swirling snow. "Nice try with the aura, Dale. With that level of detail, you will only be able to fool humans up to the D-ranks *if* you are lucky. Most others won't bother to see who is trying to sneak around; they will just blast the area."

Dale felt a chill that had nothing to do with the bitter air. He hadn't even thought about what would happen if someone *did* see him. Anyone that would care would probably do exactly what the Elf had said and blast the oddity to kill a presumed thief. He grumbled a bit but dropped his camouflage aura completely.

"Excellent!" Dale was *anxious* about how cheerful the Elf seemed to be. "Today, we are going to be working on your *perception.* I *love* perception training; it gives me free rein to say 'you should have seen that coming'. Your test tonight, Dale, is a game I like to call 'monster or snowman'. If you get too close to a monster without attacking it, the creature will attack you. Hmm. Let me clarify. It'll actually attack you either way, but you'll get the first blow in. If you smash just a regular snowman... well, why ruin the surprise? You have until dawn. Then all the monsters that might be in there go free."

Dale stared at the field stuffed full of snowmen. *How* close did the Elf say he could get? ...He *didn't* say, did he? Dale moved forward a few more steps, then activated his Essence sight. The field lit up in swirling colors, but... it all looked like snow. *Just* snow. There were no distinguishing auras, nor were there any differences in the snowmen that he could see. He was just going to need to get closer and see what happened. Stepping next to one of the Snowmen, Dale stared at it, waiting for any sign of movement, any change in the immobile effigy.

When nothing jumped at him, Dale slowly got closer to a second Snowman. He kept an eye on the first, just in case there was a creature in there waiting to ambush him. Dale got to the third... fourth... soon he was surrounded on all sides by smiling snowmen. Were there no monsters? Was it all a trick to get him to attack something when he shouldn't? The Elf hadn't been overly fond of moral lessons so far - did that snowman just move? Dale stared at it, waiting for any sign at all that it had actually moved. There! It had moved... or the falling snow was messing with his eyes. Either was possible.

Dale decided that it was time to take a chance. He was pretty sure this one had moved, and he was going to run out of time if he did nothing. Nonchalantly acting as if he were approaching a different snowman, Dale whipped to the side and smashed his target with as much force as he could muster. The middle section of the snowman scattered into snow, and the top chunk fell to the ground. A blue light momentarily appeared over the site of his demolition, and he heard the Elf chuckle.

"*That* was a bad idea. I'm surprised and pleased that you waited until you were near the center. Bad for you, though; this is going to be entertaining." Dale still couldn't see the Elf, but he had a sick feeling in his stomach about this training. He staggered forward as a chunk of ice slammed into his back, then whirled around to see who had thrown it. Nothing appeared in his vision. No enemies, no monsters. Another chunk of snow-covered ice flew into his face like an obese homing pigeon.

Still, he couldn't see where it had come from. The only things visible were the snowmen. Who... had all turned to face him. Their smiles had also turned into frowns, which freaked him out more than he had a valid reason for. He heard a slight sound and dodged to the side. A chunk of ice sailed past him, slamming into another snowman and destroying its head. Another Elven chuckle, "Oh-ho! This is going to be fun."

Dale had to hold back a biting comment toward his 'teacher'. If he yelled at the Elf to teach him directly, the Elf *would*. Specifically, he would teach Dale 'respect' and beat him severely. It had already happened twice, and Dale was very interested in keeping that number as low as possible. Also, he had other things on his mind now. He was hearing the sound of something cutting through the air again, so he lashed out and shattered an ice ball with his right fist. As he felt the ice give way, another missile struck him, catching him right in the ear and making him yelp like a kicked dog.

As he recovered, he expanded his aura away from him in a diffuse cloud, one of the first things he had ever been taught to do. As two more ice balls flew at him, they entered his aura with the same feeling as someone pulling on his hair. Dale was able to get out of the way of the ice but winced as they once again impacted snowmen. He was fairly sure he knew what was going on: as more snowmen were broken and shouldn't have been, the remaining ones would conjure balls of ice equivalent to the amount destroyed.

Of the two snowmen that had taken a blow, one puffed into powder and released a blue glow while the other exploded with a sibilant *hiss*, expelling a dozen snakes that began slithering through the snow to him. Huh. It looked like there *were* monsters in some of them, after all. Dale was having a hard time keeping up with the current threats, as the snakes had spread out and were gliding toward him while he was forced to defend against three balls of ice every second. He slipped to the side as a snake lunged at him, punching out and smashing its head.

<What in the...? What did you just do? What was that? What's a snake?> Dale almost got bitten while wincing as he realized that he had just given the dungeon a new type of monster, one that was *particularly* scary to a majority of humans. <Why is there snow again? I thought I ate all the snow. What in the abyss is going on?>

"Busy... Cal!" Dale managed to get out as he slew the remainder of the snakes, taking the impact of an ice-ball without bothering to dodge.

<What is this, a human-made dungeon?> There was silence in Dale's head for a moment. <It's pretty sloppy; you can see where the monsters are hiding. If this was supposed to be an ambush, it was poorly done.>

"How do you find the ones with monsters in them? Dale quickly demanded, thinking that the dungeon seemed to be in a good mood tonight.

<Well, I mean, I can't *see* them, but it is easy to tell there is something there when I *can't* see it, you know?>

"I really *don't*." Dale finished off the last snake; luckily the cold had been affecting it pretty heavily, and it was moving rather slowly. Two more snowmen had been hit, so five ice balls were flying at him from various angles every second or so.

<It's pretty logical, Dale. Even *you* can feel with your aura to sense something's rank, right? Well, if you can't see *anything*, then someone or some*thing* is blocking you. Sweep your aura at something, if it rebounds - ya know, you can't scan it - then it is alive.> Cal's words resonated deeply with Dale, and he shifted his mindset on the spot. Sometimes what you *thought* you needed to look for was what led you in the wrong direction!

His aura was already extended, so he hurried through the field, testing each snowman. If it felt blank and not like snow, he blasted it. He was running out of time and not from dwindling night. Dale had already been shivering at the start of this exercise, but every fifth snowman that was broken without a monster inside added a ball of water that coated him in freezing cold liquid if it hit him. He wanted nothing more than to shift his aura to a fiery shield and bring it close to his skin, but that would make it impossible for him to determine if there were monsters nearby.

"You missed one!" the Elf called with delight. This threw Dale off, as the Elf had been silent for over a half hour. A set of snowmen fell over as a creature pulled itself out of the ground, bellowing a guttural *honk* at the lone fighter. Dale froze in place, shocked at the sight of a giant grey and white goose charging at him while flapping its wings. It didn't sound like a bird; it sounded like pure evil.

<He buried the Murder Honker *under* the snowmen. Clever.> Hearing the dungeon giving out compliments about trap-making made Dale nervous; it was going to be getting ideas from this. Dale ran at the goose, *needing* to stop it. The creature

was larger than he was, and it kept smashing aside snowmen. The air around Dale was now so thick with chunks of ice that he was sprinting and zig-zagging just to avoid being pelted to death. In fact... Dale dove at the goose as it tried to peck him. Beak him? No, peck was the right word. The cobra chicken honked in pain as it was clobbered by an ice storm, and Dale grabbed its legs and *clamped* down to make sure it couldn't escape or expose him.

He only felt a *little* bad as the ice beat it to death for him, especially with the noises it was making, but as soon as it went limp, the ice attacks abated. Pushing the goose off of him, Dale stood up and came face-to-face with his instructor. "Excellent progress tonight, Dale. You are truly one of those students that can't be taught in a classroom environment; you need to *feel* and *understand* why we ask you to do the things we do. You should go rest up, and as for those nasty bruises... maybe put some *ice* on them?"

The Elf turned away while chortling and vanished amongst the wreckage of a great snow war. Dale stared after him with hollow eyes. "...I'd like to *try* a classroom. How do you *know* this is the best method?"

<Hey, Dale?> The dungeon paused as Dale surveyed the field once again. <Are... are you gonna eat that?> When there was no response, the snowmen vanished, as did the snakes and goose. Dale shook his head, remembering how when he had been walking over here he had thought he was ready for *anything*. Who was prepared for snake-stuffed snowmen? Is *anyone* ever really ready for an angry goose?

Chapter Twenty-five

After eating all the new creatures and snow, I looked around Mountaindale and saw that the precipitation was not just in the training area. We had been in an almost tropical location recently, so I had forgotten to continuously absorb what was landing on me. I fixed that and looked around for Dani. She had been mysteriously absent for a few days, 'training' Grace. Every time I'd try to see what was going on, she would tell me that it was none of my business or that I didn't need to know.

Today was no different. I poked my mind into the room they were in and looked around in shock. The stone boundaries of the room - the walls, floor, and ceiling - were twisted, malformed, and *charred* in places. I looked over to see Dani bobbing in place, praising Grace. "Good job, sweetheart! Try once more; see if you can get that stone to shape into a spike this time."

<What is *happening* in here?> As soon as my voice was heard, Grace turned a happy pink and started flying around in circles.

Dani though... she turned red. "Get *out*! This is important training for *Dungeon Wisps*! Are *you* a Dungeon Wisp? Do you want us to send Grace off unprepared when she finds a good dungeon to bond to?" I recoiled from those words.

<That shouldn't *ever* be a problem! She doesn't need to find anyone else for a few hundred years. Right, sweety?> Grace zipped around, not quite understanding what was going on. I whispered the next part, <I'll *shatter* any dungeon who tries talking to you.>

"You will *not*, and you *will* get out!" She did... *something*, and my vision of the room disappeared.

<Hey! That's *my* Mana!> I shouted down the hallway.

A muffled reply drifted back to me, "*Our* Mana! What's yours is mine!"

<Razzem-frazzem.> I grumbled nonsensical words and looked around for something to break. My eyes landed on Artillery Bob. <Bob! How are those weapons looking?>

Artillery Bob looked up from the huge chunk of opal a few other Bobs were chiseling. He wiped his brow and nodded. "They are looking good, Great Spirit. My only concern is the Mana that you are planning to power them with. I'm not certain she can take the stress!"

<Don't personify a system, Bob.> I understood his concerns, but he needed to do this. <It's our only hope, Bob. I'll look it over before we use it and make sure there are no flaws. It has to be ***perfect***, and the Bobs are the only people I trust with this.>

Artillery Bob stood straighter, eyes shining as he saluted. "I will make it so, Great Spirit!"

<Many thanks.> I drifted away slowly. I was making a series of infernal cannons to try and hurt the S-ranker if he ever tried to absorb more of my dungeon, but there was no guarantee that they would work against the powerful being. I only had hope and, soon, cannons. For now though, our interests were beginning to align. I *wanted* to attack the necromancers that had taken Dani hostage, but the fact of the matter was that I was too weak to do so. This 'Barry' seemed to think I would be an essential factor in the war, but I didn't see how.

Oh. I think I *do* understand; it is *because* I can fly. They can use me as a mobile teleportation pad. They could be fighting on the eastern front, then five minutes later, have their entire force *anywhere* that they wanted. I was a huge, miraculous... *wagon.* They were going to use me as a troop transport, but at the same time, I had trouble believing that. I thoroughly doubted that they would be hanging around on me; I would either be their grand entrance... or their desperate escape plan. Uh-oh. I didn't like *that* thought at all. Would they run away and leave me as a treasure to be collected? Was I going to be the spoils of war?

The reason these thoughts were on my mind? That one was pretty simple: we were approaching the main Guild encampment. I couldn't see it directly, but I had Navigation Bob for that. I needed to adjust my far-sight Runes and make a projection for myself. From this point forward, we were going to be having an active role in the second 'great necromantic' war. According to Bob, even now there were several people flying toward us, leaving vapor trails in the sky as they broke the sound barrier. Please be Guild members, please be Guild members...

They touched down on me, remarking with good cheer on the density of Essence on my surface. Whew! I wanted to thank them and brag a bit, but my good cheer at their appearance vanished as Barry stepped out of a building and began moving toward them imperiously. As I glared at him, he looked around and grinned. "Oh, dear. I seem to have gained the dungeon's animosity. What*ever* shall I do?"

Let's see... two A-ranked Mages and an S-ranker. Hopefully, this one isn't a cesspit of a person like Barry is. He seemed to be the person who was going to do the talking, and as soon as the first oily words were out of his mouth, I cringed away. "Ah, Barry! *So* good to see you. Truly a *pleasure*, as always."

Huh. Was this guy bound to the **law** of butt kissing? He continued speaking, and I tried not to judge him by his opening lines. At least he seemed to be getting serious. "Our outpost is set up, and we are waiting on Shield Wardens and the Church to get their troops here. Until that point, I am temporarily in charge of our forces."

"Oh? *You* are in charge? 'Opportunistic Lord' Hendric?" Barry sneered at the opposing S-ranker, who paled at hearing his hated nickname. "*I* have the highest standing in the guild, *I* have the highest cultivation, and *I*"

"*You* want to be in charge? *You*?" Hendric sneered right back at Barry. "You think they would trust *you* more, '*Battalion Devouring Bartholomew*'? At least the troops know that I am trying to *help* them, and I won't *eat* the people pledged to me for a slight boost in my own power."

"You *dare* repeat that name to my face?" Barry clenched his fists, the ground around him shuddering and cracking as his emotions ran wild. "They were already *dead*; they just didn't know it! The corrupting mist had lain over them all night! They would have dissolved *painfully* and *horrifically* as the sun rose; I made it quick! There are hardly *any* who know the truth of this matter and spreading these falsehoods is grounds for me to *destroy* you!"

"You made it *quick*?" Hendric scoffed. "What of their *souls*?"

"They were *delicious.*" Barry's smile and shift in attitude were obviously not the reactions Hendric had been expecting, and the bloodlust washing over the area caused the A-ranked Mages to fall back. "You *will* cede control of this outpost to me, or I will *take* it."

Hendric struggled for a few moments, then rolled his eyes. "Fine! Take it, you abyssal psychopath! The regional Guildlord will be here tomorrow anyway, so enjoy your power over others while you can."

"I will. Let's start with *you.*" Barry pointed at an area off to the right of the camp. "I need a place for this mountain.

Check for anyone alive down there, since you obviously care *so* much about the fate of *fishies* and the like. Anything down there will be crushed, and it is unlikely that we will be mobilizing for any length of time. I don't want this thing spotted until it is too late for the corpse lovers to do anything about it."

Interesting. Landing may actually be of benefit to me, though I was loathe to do it without good reason. Without the need to stay afloat, I could rebuild my Essence reserves and finish tasks in *days* that had been projected to be completed in weeks. I informed Navigation Bob of our destination, and he altered our path slightly so that we would land gently on the specified area.

"See how well-trained I already have this dungeon?" I was taken aback as I heard Barry bragging. "I merely tell you where it will go, and it does the rest. Just wait until you see the improvements I made for our troops."

For that comment alone, I would make sure this man was a casualty in the war.

Chapter Twenty-six

I was as nervous as a new father as my mountain was set down on the plain. <*Carefully*! You can move slower than that!>

Navigation Bob was sweating heavily as he tried to follow my orders. I felt a *little* bad, but at the same time, it would take a tremendous amount of effort to reattach a part of Mountaindale that was not directly a part of the dungeon, such as the lake at the base. If that cracked or the water sloshed out, it was *gone* until I finally extended the dungeon proper to that point. "I am doing my *best*, Great Spirit. This is our first attempt at setting the dungeon down and not just getting *close*, so please bear with me."

<I am well aware, Bob. Just...>

"I have it well-handled, I think," Bob cautiously interrupted me. "Why don't you go check on *other* things and leave this to the people who can see where they are going?"

<That's cold, Bob. Fair, but cold.> I actually laughed, though; most of the Bobs were too 'respectful' to give me backtalk. <Fine, I'll get ready to divert the Essence into other projects. Any word on Minya? Has anyone seen her, heard from her?>

"Perhaps *another* Bob would be willing to help you, Great Spirit," Navigation Bob spoke through a clenched jaw as he used his whole body to shift a section of the Runescripting that was keeping us afloat.

I didn't reply, instead going to another Bob and asking. His response made me groan. "Why not try and contact her directly, Great Spirit?"

Because I forgot to do it, that's why. It hadn't really been a 'thing' I was used to doing because the last times I had attempted to do so, Minya had been in an area that was designed to interrupt our communication. I reached for our bond and sent my thoughts along it. <Minya! How are things? Did you get it yet?>

I waited a few moments, but there was no answer. Was she *still* in the dungeon? Was it blocking her attempts to communicate? I knew that *I* could do that and had in the past, but if it was something *all* dungeons could do, I needed to find a new method of communication. Actually, no, this should be the last dungeon we need to destroy for a long time. I glanced at the map of ley lines and found that the expanding lines had almost finished circling the entire globe. It had taken some convincing for me to believe that the world was a sphere, but the Bobs assured me that they could look out and see the world curving. I was still confused about how things stayed on the surface on the other side of the planet, but I saw strange things all the time.

I felt a shudder, then a thump, and then the entire mountain vibrated as it came to a stop. People and creatures stumbled as our momentum abruptly shifted, but I was pretty pleased with the final result. We had decided that hovering and gently lowering was a bad idea, as the mountain's momentum would need to go somewhere and might rebound on us even if we were moving *very* slowly. We had come down at a slight angle and let the ground get scraped up instead. As far as I could tell, it had been a success.

Navigation Bob did good work. I created a cookie for him and shifted all the power I had been using for flight back into myself. I was lifted out of my puddle - which splattered everywhere - as the Essence accumulated so rapidly that it overflowed onto the floor as liquid Essence. Luckily, I was *just* heavy enough to remain in my area; it would have been embarrassing to need to find a way back in. I hadn't moved my Core directly for a long time!

Converting the accumulating Essence into what I needed was easier than ever with such an overabundance. I returned the liquid power to its gaseous form and sent it through a pipeline that connected directly to the third floor. It was time to get my Goblins back! Luckily, there were very few people in the dungeon; most had gone to watch Mountaindale settle onto the ground. If a cultivator *had* been on the third floor right now, it would have been a dream come true in terms of easy cultivation. At least until I sent Snowball and the Hopsecutioners after them. Heh. If I ever start a band, that would be the name of it.

I twisted the Essence and, similar to the first time I had created this floor, the ground began to sprout stone. I remade the fortifications, the pathways, the plants, and even the Goblin hot spring baths. I then went to each spawning area and poured enough Essence into them to make a dozen Goblins at every fortification. *Still,* I wasn't even using enough Essence to keep up with the flow of power coming into my area.

I now had a moat of liquid Essence around the small hill that contained my Core, and the only reason it wasn't going further was the Runescripts. The liquid would get to the edge and stop, flowing higher as more flooded the area. If I didn't find a use for this Essence, I would soon have a pillar of liquid that reached the ceiling. Actually, that might be fun to see. I considered letting the Essence build up, but I decided that I may as well use it while I could.

After informing Mind Bob about all the bodies awaiting memories, he hurried to the floor with a happy smile. I guess being around only yourself all day *could* be a little annoying for other people. Being around *myself* was a delight for anyone who had the chance. Essence began to build higher, and I started to get nervous. Should I just work on absorbing it all? Convert it to influence and expand my control of the area? Feed it into the gigantic ritual that I was using to *create* the ley lines, thereby forming a feedback loop that would net me even *more* Essence?

That one. Yeah, I liked that last one. I opened a channel for the liquid and controlled its movement. I liberally poured power into the Cores powering the ritual, filling them to capacity. Then I empowered the Runescript directly and connected the channel of Essence to them. The liquid Essence could be used directly, and the Cores would add power again after I removed the alternate power source.

That should do it! My attention returned to my Core, and I frowned. That hardly *dented* the Essence accumulation. *Celestial feces* it took a ton of Essence to fly. I knew it was a *lot*, but... this was... wow. I made a pillar from ground level to almost be even with the hole I resided in under the Silverwood tree. Where else could I store this? I checked my reservoir through the small emergency portal that I kept, but even that was now full. Maybe I should make big tanks or barrels of Essence or something. Put it in flasks and see how many people drink it and explode? ...That could be fun.

<Hey Dale, want a training aide?> I winced as he looked up from his lotus position. His face was bruised so badly that I wouldn't have recognized him if I were an inferior being who relied on something as unreliable as eyesight. <Is that all from when you were being pelted by ice and goose?>

"Yeth," he lisped, nodding very gently.

<Wait, is that 'yes, I want the aide' or 'yes, the ice'?>

"Yeth ta aide, yeth th' gooth." He closed his eyes again; although, through the swelling, you could barely see that they were open in the first place.

<So, why haven't you been to a healer to get fixed up?> I kept my tone conversational as I created a large flask in front of him, directing pure vapor Essence into it and converting it back to liquid form. The vial, more like a jug, filled quickly. Dale's eyes were what I assumed was his approximation of 'wide-open' at the 'generosity' I was showing.

"Againth ta ruleth." Instead of drinking the now-full vial as I had expected, Dale covered the opening with his palm and began pulling it in through his meridians. Dang, he was smarter than I thought he was. I guess he did keep *some* of my characteristics. "Thith helpth. Thankth."

I wanted to say something, but he looked so abused right now that I figured I would be better served working with the overflowing Essence again. I placed a few small vials in chests on the first and second levels with just enough Essence in them to pop anyone below the C-ranks. I wanted to see who had more ambition than brains. This should be funny!

Next... hmm... I guess expanding influence? I went back to my Core, morbidly curious about how high the liquid had expanded. To my confusion, relief, and confusion again, the liquid had not gone past the base of the Silverwood tree. I could see the Essence pouring in and welling up, but it seemed to be vanishing after that. I had a stable amount of Essence and no more. Could it be that the... yup! The tree was taking it all in. I was impressed, awed, and a little jealous over its apparently endless capacity. There were no outward signs, and there was no overpowering aura coming from it; the tree was just... thirsty.

Not my problem, I guess. I connected to the veritable pool of Essence and began converting it into influence. I packed the influence into the ground and began expanding my body. If I hurried, I might be able to claim the entire Skyland as dungeon. If I *really* pushed, I might be able to take some of the surrounding countryside with me as well.

CHAPTER TWENTY-SEVEN

Dale sighed in relief as he sat in closed cultivation. This wasn't an extra-special process; it merely meant that he was in a locked room that held high Essence concentrations. The point of this setup was intended to be used to avoid interruptions while seeking enlightenment, but it was frequently used as a way to avoid people and decompress from stress. In Dale's case, he was using it for both reasons.

His team had requested a day off, which he agreed to as he was a *member*, not a dictator. Beyond that, he really didn't want anyone to see him right now. He was beat beyond recognition, had lost his Nobility, and had somehow gone from a champion of the people to a laughing stock overnight. Tom had even attacked him initially when he came back, which was why he was so happy to agree to a break. Tom had thought the bloated and malformed infected had returned to the dungeon, and only Adam's hasty intervention had saved him from a full-power warhammer smash.

Forcing himself not to roll his eyes at the memory - moving at all hurt - Dale looked around the small stone room he was in and gulped. Some water would be nice, but this was a 'breakthrough' room, designed as a sensory deprivation chamber for those that were close to ranking up and simply needed to clear their minds and let ideas come to them. Dale was using it as an escape as well as a hiding place. Who bothered those who were getting close to a breakthrough? He glanced at the mostly full jug of pure Essence in front of him. "Bethides the dungeon, I gueth."

His eyes closed once more, and he began directing the new Essence into his body while making new connections for his external aura. Without needing to constantly stop and restart after cultivating, he was building his aura at record-breaking speed. It was still tedious and time-intensive, but this liquid Essence jug held more Essence than he could gain from two dozen Snowball Cores. He closed his eyes and returned his mind to his aura. Loop. Twist. Loop...

At some point, Dale ran out of available Essence. He *knew* that he had, but he was in a trance of working. Building his aura had become rote, automatic and necessary for his mind. Darkness began to close in on him, and as his thoughts fell into tunnel-vision, a light appeared and began to peel away at the fringes of the encroaching void.

"Tut, *tut*, boy." The voice was familiar... Artorian? "Even if you are only my disciple in name, I can't have you dying from self-inflicted Essence withdrawal. Let's stop that working on the aura and get you to bed. How does that sound?"

"Thoudth good..." Dale muttered around his swollen lips.

"Those are some impressive bruises. Not healed, hmm? I bet your combat teacher is trying to teach you to 'fight through the pain' or some nonsense." Artorian swept Dale up and put him over his shoulder. "Bah. As if you wouldn't seek healing in some form or another during a battle."

A gentle warmth filled Dale as Artorian started to glow. "Sunlight helps everything, a least a little. Except for the undead. Melts them like butter." He chuckled once more, and that was all Dale remembered.

He awoke with a start, looking around in confusion. He was laying on a bed made of pillows, and when he tossed off his blanket, it turned out that he was *covered* in pillows as well. The 'blanket' he had tried to remove went sailing into the wall and exploded in a puff of feathers. Moving more carefully, Dale managed to crawl out of the pillow pit and get onto firm ground. "So much *floof!* I'm surprised he isn't a pillow Mage or something. Actually, that title seems a little... indecent."

He felt at the bruises on his face, but they had fully healed or were at least no longer painful and swollen. Dale wanted to find Artorian and thank him, but the man had apparently gone to do other things and was nowhere to be seen. Next... Dale felt entirely drained. His Essence was flickering, having barely restored itself from ambient Essence while he slept.

He sat down and began to pull in Essence, feeling relief wash through him as his starved body greedily ate the power. As his Essence started to increase rapidly, he felt his aura and was shocked. There were tens of thousands of miniscule connections that surrounded his body, over a hundred times what he had in place the day before. He continued to pull in Essence, pausing when a thought struck him. His cultivation was so *slow*, and there was someone he could blame for that.

"Cal," Dale firmly announced to the room. When there was no response, he glared and added a touch of Essence to his voice. "*Cal.*"

There was a tiny fluctuation in the ambient Essence, and Dale instantly looked toward it. <Whoa, that was creepy. Taking after your friend Adam now?>

"What are you talking about?" Dale's tired voice echoed in the room.

<How you looked at my point of view. It's not... a *normal* thing. Even S-rankers can usually only feel my presence, not the exact location.> The dungeon spoke with uncertainty, making Dale wonder what else was going on. The normal sarcasm and bad jokes were missing. <Anyway. What do you want?>

Dale took a deep breath. "Look, Cal. I need something from you."

<What a *shock*!>

"I'm serious, Cal. My growth is being impacted because of this." Dale's mouth set in a firm line, and he stared unblinkingly at the wall. "A while back, I had gotten a cultivation technique from the Dark Elves, and you ate it. I need it. All I have is the standard Guild technique, and it isn't really designed for someone like me. I've been overpowering it with all my affinities, but it isn't enough anymore."

Dale waited for a long minute, not speaking, moving, and barely even breathing. He wouldn't be the first to talk. If he did, he was *sure* the dungeon would turn this into a joke and run off. When the next words entered his mind, Dale's heart leapt into his throat.

<I... suppose I can do that.> There was a long, long pause. <This is *it* though, Dale. The armor, the special treatment, safe zones, and now a really, *really* good cultivation technique. Do you agree that we are equal in services if you get this? You did a good thing when you got Dani back for me... but this is *it*, right?>

Dale actually *hesitated*. Did he *really* want this to be the final favor he would ask for? Should he... no. He *needed* this. "I agree, Cal."

<Then here ya go!> The air in front of Dale thickened, and Essence began to swirl in front of him. There was a *throb* of power, and a solid item appeared in midair. Dale caught the gem in his hands before it could hit the ground.

He flinched as the voice inside his head suddenly shouted, <*A new hand touches the beacon*!>

"What the *abyss*, Cal! I nearly pissed myself!" Dale yelped, an instant headache forming from the mental strain.

<Heh. Just thought it'd be fun to see you flinch.>

Rolling his eyes and remembering the last time he had held a memory stone with this information, Dale pressed it against his forehead immediately. Information flowed into him, settling in place and becoming his own memories, his personal experience. He saw the Elf who had spent over a decade to form the initial stages of this technique and was startled to find that Cal had added in his own changes. Those changes increased the technique's ability to absorb essence by almost twenty percent, and Dale looked up with shining eyes.

"*Thank you*, Cal." Dale's voice was thick with emotion.

<Please, don't mention it. Ever.> There was a pause. <Really, withholding from you is kind of like damaging myself over time, isn't it? I have an excess... of good will right now, but it won't last for long. Go fix yourself.>

Dale waited to see if anything else would be added, but the fluctuation vanished and he knew he was alone once more. Remembering the details of the cultivation technique, he gulped nervously. Altering a cultivation technique was dangerous under normal conditions, and his had been put in place and sealed by Father Richard. Using this one would undo that seal, changing not only his fractal chi patterns but also the very *essence* of how he drew in the energy. A wry smile appeared on his face; that had almost been a pun.

Looking around the empty room, he decided that this was as good a place to practice as any other. He knew he could put the technique in place; he 'remembered' doing it properly and what was needed to make it happen. He also knew how painful this was going to be. He took a deep breath, reminding himself that at the end of this process, he would feel great. Dale turned his mind to his Center, his Core. With a thought... his chi spiral began unwinding. The fractal patterns reverted to unbound Essence, and the loose Essence threatened to swell out of control and explode outward if he didn't find a way to control himself. Dale gagged as his body screamed that it was dying since he could no longer draw in the energy of the heavens and the earth. He growled under his breath, "I'm *fine*!"

The body could survive for *years* without external Essence. It was just... unpleasant. Dale began weaving his Essence into threads, holding each string in place through force of will alone. For some reason, the experience transformed into a feeling like he was in a smithy heating metal. As each 'ingot' of Essence became 'hot' and malleable, he had to grasp it with his fingers and pull the near-liquid substance into a thin wire. It was a confusing sensation, as he had never spent time in a forge. Nonetheless, he continued to pull the cord and shape it into a complex configuration, a beautiful piece of elaborate jewelry that formed in his Core.

When he finished an unknown amount of time later, Dale smiled in satisfaction at his Masterwork. He was just handing the intricate jewelry to the King of... as the strange vision faded, Dale blinked, finding himself back in the Headmaster's quarters. It was night, but as he stood, a voice called out to him, "So, m'boy, it seems that you felt that you couldn't leave without saying goodbye, hmm?"

Dale turned and smiled at the hedonistic posture Artorian had taken. He was lying on a mound of pillows with a plate of fruit and a glass of wine, smoking from his hookah. A robe, possibly silk, was wrapped around him. Dale rolled his eyes at the excess, thinking that perhaps they had initially agreed to a salary which was far too high. "No, Headmaster, I was having a... breakthrough of sorts."

"Hmm. When I first came in, I honestly thought you had died sitting on my favorite pillows, and I would have hated to throw those out. No chi spiral usually means dead or crippled cultivator. Now though, *well*! You seem to be getting healthier by the second." It was true. Even the passive absorption of Essence with this technique outstripped Dale's previous by leaps and bounds. He could barely wait to see what the active cultivation looked like.

Dale wasn't sure how much to tell this man. Then again, he *had* saved his life and brought him into his home to recover. "The... dungeon and I have a special relationship. I did something for it recently, and it repaid me with a technique that I desperately needed."

"I... see." Artorian nodded, eyes half closed. "Well, I trust that you are well enough to head off? I do have some other things to take care of." Dale nodded and said his farewells, while Artorian thought long and hard about his next actions.

"I see no other *real* choice here. Excuse me, dungeon? I... would like to make a *deal*," Artorian spoke, and a small fluctuation in the ambient Essence assured him that the dungeon was listening.

Chapter Twenty-Eight

"Great Spirit, I have news!" Bob Prime was shouting into the third floor, his Mana-enhanced voice rattling Goblins and adventurers alike. A few started running to the exit, making me sigh as they avoided walking into traps or going for 'raspberries' from my sneaky monsters.

<Hello, Bobius Primius.> Bob didn't react to my teasing at all, so I just told him to report.

"Cartographer Bob has spotted Minya and two others flying toward us with all haste. There seems to be some form of... atmospheric disturbance behind them." Bob finished the last sentence hesitantly.

<Oh. They must have succeeded then.> I pondered what to do next. <Bob, you have heard that a dungeon can become a 'disaster zone' when it loses its Core, correct?>

"I have, but I do not understand exactly what that means," Bob confessed apologetically, even as he opened a secret panel and left the floor.

<Hmm. I'll use myself as an example.> I looked around and lit up a section of the wall. <Let's use this wall to explain. This section is made of a combination of cursed earth, dungeon grown stone, Runes, and is just *stuffed* with Essence. That's the *wall.* As we get lower in the dungeon, the items are formed with my *Mana* in some cases. As pure as my Essence is, I still *store* all of the corruption that I should have floating around in me. Now, my influence is also a factor here. Soon, this *entire* mountain, and then some, is going to be part of me. If my Core were to be taken out of here improperly, all of the Essence, corruption, and Runes that I keep in check would be... loosed.>

"So anything not in your Core... would start to leak into the surroundings?" Bob paled, and he swallowed as he looked around at the purple cursed earth.

<Over time. Then, as more gets loose, the remainder will get loose *faster*. Eventually, it will all go *boom* unless something takes control, absorbs the excess, or if it is exceptionally stable. I think the 'disturbance' behind them is the remains of the dungeon going 'boom'. I need to direct more power into the ley lines leading there. Let's see if I can't absorb the excess before things get weird.> I always liked a challenge.

These ley lines were fun toys, and extending the range from which I could absorb energies was very beneficial. I looked at the map and frowned as I found blank spots in areas around the world. One of the downsides of using basic Essence to power them was that a higher concentration of Essence or Mana could block the ley lines from expanding. Over time, I could *slowly* make them stretch into the area, but that wasn't good enough right now. I needed to make a statement here, to flex my power and take control.

Minya touched down on Mountaindale and ran toward the entrance to my dungeon. She started speaking on the first floor, her speed increasing as she flashed past bosses. "Cal, I'm holding a dungeon Core that is *very* unhappy to be held. It keeps trying to eat me, and if I put it in anything or let Essence touch it, it takes it all in, and I lose control."

Ah. That explained why she hadn't just taken the portal down to me. "Can you *please* take over this thing or give me access to something that'll get me closer to you!"

<Take a left, Minya.> She heard and obeyed, running toward a wall that slid out of her way. <Get ready, there is a bit of a drop.>

"A drop...?" She had gone past the wall and found that the ground simply ended. This was the most direct route down to me without a portal, a simple shaft that I used for air, Essence, and now Minya. "Ahhh!"

<Oh, knock it off, Minya. You can *fly*, can't you?> I saw the humor in her eyes as her descent slowed a tiny amount.

"Ah. I thought you were expecting a little drama." Minya patiently waited until the ground began to approach, then slowed and landed gently. She walked toward the Silverwood tree, cocking her head as she saw the liquid Essence sloshing around. "Is that...?"

<Yup. Liquid Essence. Can you put that Core on the pedestal there?> She did as I asked, and I stared at the Core. It had a tier-three Mana signature, which was... decently impressive. Earth and fire Essences... <Was this in a volcano?>

"Yes, also, it erupted just after we took the Core. The entire region is going to be having a hard few years." Minya looked so grim that I had to tune her out.

<Let's see here... hey. Core. Do you have a mind?> I projected my thoughts at the Core, and its colors began to swirl and shift. <I'm thinking 'yes'. Oh?>

<**Eruption**,> said a slightly feminine voice I had never heard before.

The previously almost inert Core launched a huge ball of liquid stone at me, more precisely, at the tree above me. <Oh, that just won't do. **Acme**.>

With a small puff of smoke, the attack was fully absorbed, converted into base Essence and Mana that I easily swallowed. The great thing about my Mana was if I was stronger than the attack coming directly at me, I could absorb it every time. Especially if I didn't need to deal with a being's aura weakening my own. <How to retaliate...? How about...>

I was speaking aloud intentionally to cow the Core into submission. My Mana expanded away from me, wrapping the Core in a suffocating cloud of dense power. When I say 'suffocating', I mean it. If the Core didn't give up soon, I was going to shatter it either by accident or design. That was when *another* new voice interrupted me.

"Please! Leave her alone!" A green Wisp came flying down the airshaft Minya had taken, and with a thought, I closed the wall. Whoops. That could have been bad. "She is just in pain, and terrified!"

I eased the pressure on the opposing Core, noting that a few imperfections flaked off of... her. <Can she speak?>

"Normally, yes, but I think she is in shock. She was just ripped out of her body; she isn't thinking *rationally*!" The Wisp seemed agitated. Heh. "My name is Xan; I'm her bonded Dungeon Wisp."

<You sound pretty proud of that, Xan.> I twitched, and my Mana retracted.

"I am. She is smart and had made over one hundred levels through an active volcano. That's... I mean, it's gone now, but she *did* it." Xan's voice dropped to a whisper.

<Is that what took you so long, Minya?> I looked over at the Mage, who was staring at the sloshing liquid Essence still.

"Huh?" She seemed to wake up. "Oh. Yeah. It was hard to get down, even harder to get back up through all the rising lava."

<Magma,> I heard a voice call out weakly. <It's only lava when it is out of the ground.>

<Ah, the guest of honor speaks!> I cheered with zero sarcasm. <I'm Cal, and I'd like to offer you a job.>

<What? I'm *dying*, Cal.>

<That's nice,> I responded brightly. <I need someone to take over a few of my floors so that I can do other things. I'm in the process of taking over and regulating the world's Essence right now. You have a name?>

<It... I'm Dregs,> the Magma Core responded. <Are you the one who kept tearing away at my Essence regeneration?>

<Yup, that was me. Kind of. Now I'm going to clean up your dungeon. One moment, please.> Bob had already been so kind as to isolate the ley line that led directly to the dead dungeon, and I had the map projecting on the wall right now. I touched the web of ley lines, pulling a breath of **Acme** from my Core. As the Mana passed through the air from my Core to the line, the air crackled and sparked, marks appearing in the air that took a long moment to heal. I touched the Mana to the line and sent it to empower and enhance the lines.

I watched on the map as the line I had just touched blazed. A pure white line was traced over the golden strings, and in moments, it had reached the blank spot of the chart. A sheet of white covered the empty spot, then slowly resolved into a series of individual lines. From there, white traced along a few connecting paths, but it all slowly returned to a bright gold, perhaps *slightly* more pale than the remaining lines. <And here... we... go!>

Mana and Essence were being sucked through the line, coming toward me. <Get ready, Dregs, we are going to see what you can do.> I directed the Mana into her Core as it reached us, and all the energy of an erupting volcano slammed into her. I heard her scream as she did her best to absorb all of her own Mana, but I was also watching her for when she couldn't take any more. Just before that point, I switched the flow to myself and swallowed *all* of the Mana at once.

<Yum.> I didn't allow anyone to see how much effort that had taken. <So, about that job.>

Chapter Twenty-nine

I installed Dregs as the controller of floors one through four. I still had everything in place; it was just her job to keep the traps and Mobs running smoothly so that I didn't need to bother with them. In return, she was able to draw in the pure Essence on these floors. Obviously, she didn't get it all *and* it was quite the demotion for her, but the other option for her was to become an intelligent weapon that I gave out as a special reward to someone. It would have been a whip that assisted the user, boosted control over fire and earth Essence, and... ah well. Maybe she would be terrible at her new job.

Then again, if she failed at such a simple thing, it would look bad for *me*. It would seem like *I* had failed. Maybe I should just... no, no. I needed to trust myself. The pursuit of **perfection** could *not* be a lonely road. I looked wistfully at the room Dani and Grace were in. I missed them. From the explosions, laughter, and bursts of energy, I could tell they were having fun. *Le sigh.*

The volcano that had been inhabited by Dregs had turned out to be a natural Essence accumulation point, a shaft from deeper in the earth where fire and earth Essences constantly spewed forth. My ley lines were now acting to regulate the energy, but it made me wonder if naturally formed dungeons served a purpose for the world. Did they fix what would otherwise be an imbalance in the Essence of the planet? At this point, so close to finishing the first layer of ley lines... did I care? Nope!

On another side note, I was advancing. I knew I was; although, for some reason, this advancement was oddly slow. Typically, there was a significant moment and boom! I advance!

This one, though... it felt like my soul was stretching. Not in the 'oh, I just woke up and feel good' way. More like 'put him in the rack and start pulling'! My cultivation settled into a plateau, and if I had lungs, I would have been gasping in pain.

<Dani, we need to talk.> She started to refute me, and I *knew* she was getting ready to kick me out again. I silenced her objections with a harsh repeat of my words. <Dani. We *need* to *talk*.>

Concern replaced her current haughty mood, and she floated out and toward my Core. "What's going on, Cal?"

I filled her in on what had been happening in the dungeon, the new Core and Wisp, and the pain of my recent advancement. She listened intently, not interrupting, which I was thankful for. When I was finished, she flew in circles around the glistening Silverwood tree for a bit, thinking. Grace splashed around in the liquid Essence, obviously enjoying the increased power and seeing what happened to things that the Essence landed on. She giggled as a flower mutated wildly out of control and burst into flames without consuming the plant. That's my girl!

Dani came to a stop, hovering above me. "So... the only thing I can think of is the next stage of Mana cultivation, which is applying your law within your soul. What this does is create a space, an actual physical location in your soul that is accessible. For most people, this is basically only enough room to store a single item, but... I'm not sure what you would be making. I could also be wrong, since this isn't normally started until the A-ranks."

I considered that. <Well... could it be that since I have such a high-tier **law**, I'd need to start that process early?>

"That's what I was thinking." She nodded along at my words, hesitating before speaking again, "Whatever you start making... you need to *finish* eventually. It needs to encompass your **law**, and if you make something too weak, you will severely limit your future growth. Weak Mages make something the size of a large box, strong ones make an entire palace, but the larger the creation, the more power will be needed to complete it."

<Does it all happen at once?>

"Hah! Not even close. Only the *concept* has to be made all at once." Dani chuckled as my dreams collapsed. "I think we are onto something here. Try *thinking* about what you will be making in your soul space, and when you are ready, try adding to the space that already exists. If *something* happens, you were ready for this. Otherwise, we will need to find some other way to help you."

Her instructions were helpful, but I was faced with the same issues I had when trying to cultivate perfection. What *embodied* perfection? What could I make that would be a sufficient stand-in for **Acme**? I pondered this question, but reflecting on perfection was as useful as staring into the void. There were no ready answers, and they wouldn't grant their secrets easily. I had real work to do now.

<Bob Prime, I have a job for you.> Bob perked up as I spoke into his mind.

"What can I help with today?"

<We are going to be working to change the Runescripting we have set up currently for the creation of the ley lines. I need to find an outlet for my power, and I've decided that I want to be moving the lines into stage two.> My words made him go still.

"Great Spirit, it might be *years* before stage one is complete. The blank spots on the map-"

<Are going to be overpowered by me,> I announced grimly. <I've found a bit of a bottleneck in my growth, Bob, and

I think the way to break through it is to devote myself to a few important tasks and learn more. When the preparations are complete, I will be connecting my Core directly to the diagram and powering it with my Mana. Anything trying to block us... I'm done trying to play nice. I am going to destroy them directly.>

"Is this... is this *wise*, Cal?" Oh? He called me by name?

<I can't say that it is, Bob, but I'm running out of time.> My mind looked upward, leaving Bob behind to follow my orders.

I watched as Barry ordered some Guild members around. "No, I'm glad the regional Guildlord was delayed. This camp is in shambles, and I only have a few days to fix a few *weeks*' worth of issues. We need our lower members to get going through the dungeon; it's a good training ground and gives out Inscribed weapons like a drug dealer gives out free samples."

I can't say that I cared for the comparison, but his point was valid. He continued speaking softly, though the people around him were stiff and silent, so his words were clear and audible, "The dead have been moving toward us; obviously, they plan to move to defeat our armies before continuing on to attack the High Elves in Citime-o Ka, the city of light. The Elves will be joining us, and our Dwarven and Northman allies will flank the army of the dead. This will be our only *real* chance to crush this foe. If we fall... if we fail... there will be no one left that can resist them."

"What was the purpose for bringing the dungeon here, Paragon?" an A-ranked High Mageous dared to ask. Paragon? Was that the title for an S-ranker then? Or just *his* title?

"We are going to use the dungeon to swoop around the dead and deposit our elite troops at the rear of the army, where the leadership will most likely be cowering and commanding their troops. If everything goes well, we will be able to cripple their chain of command in one. Fell. Swoop." Barry squeezed the table, which exploded into sawdust.

"When will we move out, Paragon?" another A-ranker spoke from the middle of the group.

"One week," Barry growled throatily. "In *one week*, this dungeon will take off, carrying the hope of the entire world with it."

Well, no pressure on me then, thank goodness. I snorted and moved away. I now had a deadline, and I needed to get to work on my pet projects. I moved over to where a few Bobs were working on an opal and asked them to step back while I inspected it. I went through the massive gem, whistling at the end. This thing had enough carats to feed a floor full of Bashers for a decade. There was a slight flaw, a crack near one end. I filled the microscopic crack, then congratulated the Bobs on their hard work. This is precisely what I had needed.

I washed my influence over the massive opal, dissolving it into my being. Using the new pattern, I exerted myself, and twelve identical opals appeared next to the nonplussed Bobs. <Now that we have our focus, it is time to start assembling the weapons.>

They nodded sleepily, which made me wonder if the crack I had found had been due to a sleep-related accident. <First, go get some rest. The energies we are going to be using are not something to play around with, and I don't want to have to clean your bodies up again.> Most of them nodded cheerfully and scattered away. A few went over to the corner of the room and fell asleep on mats that had seemingly been placed there for that exact reason.

I didn't envy their need for sleep. I looked over at the Runescript that Bob was layering on the original and went to offer my assistance. I was ready to taste the fruits of my labor, and the harvest was coming soon.

Chapter Thirty

Dale's thoughts were whirling as he strained his cultivation technique to the maximum he possibly could. He was having an issue similar to when he had first advanced to the D-ranks, where his chi threads were slightly fractured. All he needed to do was gather enough Essence to fill the gaps, but the issue was that he could only repair one section at a time. Once he got going, the usable portion would expand, rushing the remaining Essence toward healing. A snowball effect, if you will. His thoughts stuttered, and he shook off the memories of snowballs. If he never saw a snowman again...

He was sitting alone on the second floor, feeling that he would be best served doing this by himself. Dale tried actively cultivating again, and the air *shuddered* as Essence was pulled into him. He gagged as the pain of his chi threads reforming struck him, his technique faltering. Catching his breath, he grit his teeth and did it again and again. Each time he did so, he was able to devote more Essence to the threads and last a little longer. He was close; he knew it...

Pushing himself, needing Essence to reach his Core again, Dale pushed one last time. The air trembled, then *roared* as his chi spiral stabilized and began drawing in Essence. Dale was panting as the intricate workings of his new technique pulled power through every single affinity channel at the same time; his meridians began working overtime to bring Essence to his starving body. It took a few minutes before Essence actually began trickling into his Core, but once it did... the trickle became a flood.

The vibrations he was generating were causing the floor to shake, the air to *thrum*, and his body to rejoice. The last remnants of his injuries and bruises faded as his body took energy to heal and to enhance. In a few minutes, the power flowing into him returned to a trickle as the loose Essence in the air was depleted. It would replenish soon, but for now, this area was going to be useless to cultivate in. A few Bashers appeared nearby, drawn by the noise and shaking, but they seemed to get sick as they came closer. Dale watched them as they closed in, but a few hops later, they turned and ran away.

"What was *that* all about?" he muttered aloud, not expecting to get an answer.

"Well, Dale, they survive on Essence." Minya was seated off to the side, and he shrieked too shrilly when her voice reached his ears. "Wow. *That* was extra manly. Dungeon born flora and fauna in this world need a certain Essence density to survive. Just like when normal humans climb mountains and have a hard time breathing, Essence-enriched beings don't do well in depleted areas. In a dungeon, this is an effective tactic for keeping creatures away from you, which is in part what these new 'safe areas' in here do."

"Why are you here, Minya?" Dale questioned the Mage with a sigh. "Cal and I are on somewhat friendly terms now, and I have no need to be 'converted'."

Minya looked around, seemingly avoiding the question. "I'm just here... exploring how well the first few floors are being managed."

"What does that even mean?" Dale stood and brushed his pants off. He started edging toward the exit portal, his hand going toward his pocket where he kept a keygem. "Listen, it's good to see you, as always, but..."

"I *really* wouldn't do that if I were you." Minya smiled sadly at Dale. "I don't think you want to go up there right now."

"Might be better than hanging out with..." Dale took a deep breath and stopped himself. "I'm sorry, that isn't fair. If I am getting on friendly terms with the dungeon, I can't fault you for doing the same, if a bit more... *energetically* than me."

Minya nodded happily. "I'm glad you are finally coming around. The benefits of working with Cal... they're unbelievable. As I'm *sure* you've learned." Her smile was now mysterious and sly.

"Right. Well." Dale looked at the portal. "Why shouldn't I go up there right now?"

Minya's smile shifted to an annoyed frown. "The academy clerk that you've been giving your 'required items' to? You never got a receipt or a token of some sort to prove that you were making your quotas. If you go up there without fifty percent more than two weeks' worth of items, you will be dropped from the academy as soon as you appear."

Dale's jaw slackened, and he sighed deeply. "You know, I'm not a big fan of murder..."

"This is *your own* fault, Dale. You keep thinking that everyone else is going to be operating in good faith." Minya shoved him playfully, and he slammed into the wall. Dust rained down on him, and he slid to the floor groaning. "Oh, shoot, I'm so sorry. I forget that you are just in the D-ranks sometimes."

Dale muttered an inaudible reply, speaking louder after he was able to clear his head. "I turned in everything *yesterday*. I'm cleaned out. What *didn't* go to the academy went to Tyler's weapon shop. I cleaned out my bags to make room for the next trips."

"I'm sure they knew that, which is why a Guild member is waiting near each exit to ambush you and press you into service. I'm on my way out; would you like me to send anyone down here for you?" Minya smiled gently as Dale growled.

Thinking about the third floor and the Goblins it contained, Dale's eyes hardened. "No... I think I know what I want to do for now, and bringing others into this to save me from my own mistake wouldn't be fair. Thank you for the thought and the kindness you are showing me."

"I'm sure they wouldn't mind. You have a nice group of people on your team." Minya was no longer smiling and evidently thought Dale was being overly stubborn.

"I have a few kinks I need to work out of my fighting style, and right now, I really think this is what I need to do. Thank you for your concern though, Minya." Dale started walking toward the stairs, glancing back only once. Minya was already gone. Good.

He pulled his gauntlets over his hands and covered his face with his headgear, leaving only a tiny slit to see out of. Dale slipped into the breathing pattern he had been taught by the Moon Elves, maximizing the air he took in while minimizing movement. His walking pattern changed, and his aura began to shift to match the scenery. If Hans had seen this transformation, he would have recognized and complimented the deadly Assassin training Dale must have been going through.

Dale was excited for this opportunity, no matter what Minya had seemed to think. While he filled the role of a Fighter or Monk for his team, Dale's training had taken him down a different path. A path he didn't really want other people to see from him; one focused on lethal, instant, brutal attacks. An Assassin's path. He wanted to see how well he could do fighting against creatures at his own cultivation ranking. As long as he could avoid the powerful necromantic Goblin that appeared intermittently, he was confident that he could do well on this floor, *alone*. If nothing else, his armor, speed, and aura abilities would ensure that he could escape if he needed to, but he doubted it would come to that.

Padding along with silent footsteps, the only signs of his passage were the bending grass that he needed to step on while avoiding the paths. He spotted a raspberry bush, grinning as he got closer. Half the time, these things were mobs, and he wanted to see how close he could get before it noticed something amiss. Dale found where the creature had burrowed itself. The creature's head was barely peeking out, its eyes slowly scanning the scenery for prey. Dale stood directly in front of it, and it only blinked a few times to try and clear away its 'blurry vision'. Dale reached back... and *slammed* his fist into the creature's head.

One of the studs on his fist destroyed its eye socket, and the beast thrashed in pain. He punched again, and its skull fractured. The animal went still, though it still twitched every few seconds. Another blow and even that halted. Dale pulled a few spines off of it, planning to use the powerful sedative the thorns contained to control the amount of enemies he faced at any given time. Next, he harvested a few items that the Academy had on the list of goods accepted for contribution and started toward the hexagonal fortifications the Goblins could be found in.

There were guards on the fortress wall, but since they usually had a clear line of sight on any approaching adventurers, they were... *lax* in their patrols. This fort was in the center of the floor, not against the wall, so Dale couldn't recreate Hans' method of pressing against the wall to climb over. He pulled out a small throwing blade and used it to dig into the branches filled with sleeping poison, coating the small blade liberally. Calculating the force and angle needed to reach the Goblin on top of the wall, Dale took aim and threw the small blade.

Ting: The metal item bounced off the stone and fell back down, landing in the dirt a few feet away from him. Dale closed his eyes, hoping the Goblins wouldn't get alerted from this. He kept very still as the Goblin looked over the edge, attempting to identify the sound. Dale cursed silently; he thought that he was getting better at throwing the small daggers, but... that should have been an easy throw, and now his confidence was shaken. Glancing up, he saw the Goblin still leaning over the edge and narrowed his eyes. Plan 'B' then.

He reached out with his Essence and moved a line of power through the stone, shattering the wall right where the Goblin was leaning. The Mob fell with a yelp, landing awkwardly on the ground near Dale. That fall wouldn't typically be enough to kill a creature at this rank, but Dale was behind it as it started to stand. With a quick motion, he snapped its neck and crushed its windpipe just to feel satisfied. Then, before anything else came to investigate, he rushed around the wall to the opposite side and began to climb. A touch of power on his fingertips let him dig into the stone, and he peeked over the edge to check where he would cross over.

As he had expected, the majority of the Goblins had rushed over to the broken wall to see what was happening. Dale smiled even as he shifted his aura to match the stone more accurately and stealthily drew closer to the Goblins. It took a few minutes to circle the walls, but he heard some interesting conversations when he did.

"Shoddy walls maybe? The Lesser Spirit may not be as interested in making the walls solid for us."

"Don't lean on the walls, anymore, got it. Maybe it thinks that we are not allowed to *rest*? Should we ask the Great Spirit?"

"Don't be a fool."

Several variations of this conversation were being discussed as the gate opened and a few Goblins went to retrieve their fallen member. Dale retreated around the corner and pulled out the thorny branches once more, quickly stripping the thorns off with his gloved hands and moving around the bend to scatter them like caltrops near the clustered, *barefoot* Mobs. He waited a few minutes as the Goblins chattered, then seemed to remember that they had a duty to perform. They started walking away, a few of them snarling as they stepped on something sharp. Dale smiled. The poison took a few moments to have an effect if the thorns weren't still connected to the branch, but he could afford to be patient.

By the time they were back to their regular patrol sections, many of them were woozy and stumbling. Dale first targeted the few that were moving normally, taking out the first with two devastating kidney shots, making the Goblin stand rigid and unable to make a sound through the pain. Dale snapped his neck, shoving the fresh corpse into his spatial bag before moving to the next one.

The Goblin he came up on next was woozy, so Dale simply grabbed him by the back of his neck and slammed his head into the stone wall. This process was near silent, and another Goblin went into the bag. He continued around the wall in this manner, quickly finishing off the ranged Goblins. The melee Goblins might be harder to defeat with such attacks, but so long as he didn't need to dodge arrows at the same time, Dale was once again confident in his eventual success.

CHAPTER THIRTY-ONE

Dale climbed down a ladder set into the wall, getting close to the fighters that were clustered around small tables. They were working on various hobbies, sharpening weapons, or playing cards. Dale was shocked to see how similar the Goblins acted to members of the Guild when they weren't fighting. It was... Dale shook his head. No, he couldn't get sentimental about this; they were going *down*.

"Where are the archers?" Dale winced as one of the Goblins at the table looked up and scanned the wall.

"Maybe they fell off?" Another chuckled, stopping as the first held up a hand.

"No. Something is off; I think we are under attack." He stood, reaching for a massive sword that was always close to hand. His fingers grasped air, and he looked down at the imprint of his sword that had been *right there*. "Who took my sword?"

Dale grinned widely. The sword was safely stored in his bag. He had crawled around and collected any weapons not being held or not on a Goblin. He had to suppress his laughter as a small fight broke out. This was an excellent opportunity for him. While the others watched the match with amusement, Dale took out Goblins on the fringes of the area. He was burning through Essence, but a single strike to unarmored kidneys with his left hand would force a full quarter of the blood in their bodies to *shift*, and they would generally expire from the first strike.

If they did, they went into the bag. If they survived, a second blow to the base of the skull would finish the job, and they *still* went into the bag. Dale needed to replenish his Essence at this point. Without cultivating, draining their Essence with his other gauntlet, or opening the Goblins to take the Cores inside of them, he was starting to run low on available power. This wouldn't have been a problem if he hadn't recently drained himself and started a new cultivation technique, but right now...

"Stop! *Stop*!" The Goblins that had been fighting were now part of the only four that remained. "Where is everyone? What's happening?"

"They just went to check on the archers!" The one he had been fighting got in one more sucker punch, but the serious growl stopped him from throwing another.

"Fool, we are under *attack*! Group up!" The Goblins clustered, and Dale sighed softly. He didn't have confidence in his current ability to fight such a large group, and now that they were on the alert, he needed to leave. As the Goblins began searching, he moved in the opposite direction and opened the gate. There was only a simple and easy-to-remove bar holding it in place, making him smile. After quietly opening the gate, Dale walked away and found a small hill to sit on.

That could have gone better, but he was happy with the current progress. Taking a deep breath, he released his hold on his camouflage, setting a simple shield in place for now. With so many interconnected sections on his aura, the shield was able to be held with barely a thought and a hint of Essence, so it only made sense to keep them in place at all times. With a small happy sound, he opened himself up to his surroundings and *pulled*. The grass in the area bent toward him as the wind picked up, and the low rumbling of displaced air alerted anything nearby that something was happening.

Expecting that his cultivation would draw in Mobs, Dale kept his eyes open and tried to remain *aware* at all times. He smiled as he surpassed the amount of Essence he had been able to draw in on the previous floor. Since this floor was large and open, the ambient Essence quickly rushed to fix the imbalance created by his extraordinarily powerful draw. It took a half hour, but Dale - now panting and feeling bloated - finally needed to stop taking in more. His eyes were shining as he stood, flexing his empowered body. Applying more Essence than usual to his muscles, he took off running for the fort he had vacated.

As he sprinted, he smacked his lips. The Essence had held a more substantial hint of fire and earth than was usual, and he wondered if something had happened to a powerful lava cultivator here recently. The door he had used was still unlocked, and as Dale approached it, he shifted his aura and vanished from view. He slipped through the egress and looked around for the Goblins. They were calmly sitting with their backs to a wall, apparently expecting that their brethren would soon reappear and that the threat was past. They were very wrong. Only two of them held weapons still, so he decided to start with them.

He got close to the first, and its eyes jerked up as Dale stepped on some small scraps of metal. The group tried to get to their feet, but Dale abandoned stealth and punched the Goblin in the face, crushing its head against the wall. It slumped to the ground, and Dale ran at the others before they could get into a formation. He landed a few powerful blows against the Goblin with a weapon, but they were less effective since it could see the attacks coming and defend against them.

The Moon Elf hand-to-hand combat was *designed* to be used against single opponents but was easily able to be utilized against multiple foes. Dale would have taken a few scratches if he had not been wearing his armor, but even at his level of mastery, the martial art forms were more than sufficient to disable and destroy these Goblins. Dale straddled the last one, punching it in the face over and over while he screamed.

"How *dare* they take it all away from me? How could they just *do* that to me!" His bloodlust sated, Dale stared down at the unrecognizable lump of flesh on the ground, wincing as he realized the outlet his pent-up emotions had taken.

<That seemed cathartic, but can you *not* do that? They do retain some of their memories, and I'm pretty sure that if I don't take that memory away, this guy's future iterations are going to claim you as the focus of a blood feud.> Dale nodded, apologized for his loss of control, and stood up. He looked around, deciding to claim this area for the time being. Goblins wouldn't respawn if he was in here, and the density of the Essence was sufficient that he would feel safe working on his aura for an extended period of time.

He locked the doors of the fortress, double checked that he was alone again, and started cultivating. In terms of pure power, he had stepped into rank D-six. Dale shook his head, disgusted by the people who had been lying to him but also at his own insatiable need to meet their expectations. As his focus converged to a point, the connections in his external aura began to increase yet again. Dale wouldn't fall into a trance this time; he knew *that* for a fact. It slowed him down to keep a watchful eye, but relaxing here would likely be the last thing he ever did. He grinned wryly, thinking a dark thought: 'At least with this body'.

Dale worked through the night, cultivating when his Essence got low and increasing his aura when his power was full. With his new cultivation technique, he was never *out* of power for more than three-quarters of an hour. With all of his meridians open, he needed very little food or water to sustain himself. When he couldn't handle the tedium any longer, he would clear out a new fortification, always making sure not to take on too much. At one point, he realized that he was about to miss a training session with his Moon Elf instructor and had the dungeon send Minya with an explanation.

The Elf didn't seem to mind at first; in fact, he joined Dale in the dungeon and taught him there. As he was leaving, his ire became clear. He broke Dale's arm for making him go out of his way and then threw him over the wall of an intact Goblin fortress. Dale was pretty sure he left at that point because even though he took a nearly fatal beating from the Goblins, no help arrived. Dale's eyes blazed with silvery Essence. Good. He didn't *want* any help right now.

He could guarantee that the Goblins would. He also knew they wouldn't get any... at least not in time. He set the bones in his arm with a scream, then showed his teeth as the first arrow came his way. He arrogantly strolled forward, his smile growing wider by the second. Time to work.

Chapter Thirty-two

Filthy. That was the only word Dale could use to describe himself. The blood ran off of his clothes, the flecks of skin and bone would wash away, but he *stunk*. How long had he been down here? A day ago, he had felt the dungeon shudder as it lifted off the ground, but he didn't particularly care about those details. What he *did* care about was that his bag was nearly full of Goblins, Goblin weapons, and various items from this floor. No Cores, though. No, he wouldn't be giving any of those away. Those were *his*.

He felt a sense of exaltation, though. He had done it. He *knew* he had. His external aura was thick, dense, nearly *choking* him with power. It was complete, at least as much as he could make it at his current cultivation ranking. Now, when he made his shielding, it wasn't a pale shadow of a *real* shield. His was at least as powerful as other people he had been studying. When he made a sunlight aura like Artorian had taught him, it didn't *glow*. It *blazed* with light and life. When he made a regenerative aura, his wounds shrank at a visible rate; no longer was it a simple easing of pain.

Dale was at D-rank nine after his extended stay in the high-Essence environment with his new cultivation technique. He would have been in the C-ranks days ago if he hadn't bothered to devote his power to his aura. But... he had, and he would go to the *abyss* before he let any of his instructors tell him that he hadn't done as they asked.

The next step... next, Dale would work internally, trusting his armor to stop slashes and stabs. He knew from trial and error how easy it was to become concussed when struck, how easy it was to lose consciousness from a simple blow.

Enhancing his brain was at the top of his priorities, but for now... Dale looked at his bag, which was now dripping with blood that even it couldn't contain any longer. It was time to return to the surface.

Sneaking around the Boss of this floor, Dale stepped through the portal it protected. As the shimmering field of Essence vanished, an official approached Dale with a smug expression. "*Disciple Dale*, you are hereby informed that your tenure at-"

His words faltered as Dale's fingers came within an inch of his neck, stretched out in a claw shape and glistening with infernal-laced flames. Dale's eyes blazed with silvery light as the Essence imbuing them shone through. Dale's posture relaxed, his hands dropping to his sides. "Sorry about that. Extended training alone in the dungeon, really gets in your head. I'm sure *you* understand the risk of something getting *into* your head, or neck, I suppose. You have ten seconds to finish speaking before I leave. Nine."

"Uh. You..." the man coughed, regaining his posture, "you are to report for your failure to produce your required resources to the academy. If you do not appear to the headmaster and a quartermaster within thirty minutes of getting this message, you will be dropped from the academy and sent to the frontlines of the ongoing war."

Dale snorted. "I lose my protection from the war at the start of the C-ranks anyway, but yeah, sure, I'll play along. I assume they've already been alerted and will meet me somewhere?"

"You are to... um... yeah, they're going to meet you at the punishment hall." The man nervously scratched at the spot on his neck Dale had touched with his fist.

Dale turned and trotted away without a word. He was *done* being polite; he had done everything he could to be helpful, courteous, and charming in the past, and look where that had got him! Perhaps it was time to be ruthless. His foot hovered in the air, and he set it down slowly. Was this a realization that all cultivators eventually had? Was this why they all seemed to care so little for others, why they only respected power? He wanted to be different, but… his eyes hardened… but being different wasn't working out. Maybe he had merely stumbled upon the *truth*.

Walking into the punishment hall, he noted with a smirk that a large group had apparently been gathered to watch his 'disgrace'. Headmaster Artorian was the only one in the room that seemed anxious, but the others in the area seemed pleased when they noticed him. Some people were only happy when another person was suffering, was that what this was? He planned to wipe the smirks off their faces soon. *Very* soon.

"Dale, you are called here today to answer for your failure to produce results. Your contributions to the academy are *nil*, and unless you are able to produce a month's worth of such goods, you will lose your discipleship immediately," the quartermaster stated all this information dryly, neither happy nor sad about carrying out his duty.

"I'm sorry, Dale, there's-" Artorian was cut off as Dale reached for his bags.

"Sure, here you go." He upended the bag, fed it some Essence, and allowed weapons to pour out in a stream of clattering metal. As that faltered, he turned the bag, and preserved Goblin bodies began slapping wetly against the floor. A pool of blood rapidly expanded from the area the bodies were appearing, making the onlookers step away hastily. Dale turned the bag one more time, and various herbs and ores began falling onto higher ground. He wouldn't want to get the rare herbs bloody now, would he? When the last ingot bounced off the floor, Dale put the bag back on and glared at the quartermaster. "I assume this will *suffice*?"

"Plus an additional three weeks." The quartermaster nodded, ignoring Dale's attitude entirely. "Please ensure to get a receipt for all future deposits."

"This is absurd!" A student stepped forward, pointing at Dale. "He didn't make his contributions on time! Why does he get special treatment?"

The voice was familiar to Dale, but he couldn't place it. Artorian's sudden smile began to fade as the young man continued speaking. "He doesn't *deserve* a place here; he has cheated his way through *everything*! I challenge this *peasant* for his position as the Headmaster's disciple!"

Ah, that did it. Dale snapped his fingers. "Thomas Adams."

"I see you remember me, you scum. Thanks to you, my family was *humiliated* in front of the *Prince*!" Thomas roared theatrically, spittle flying as his eyes bulged.

Dale spoke over him, "If I remember *correctly*, it is this same attitude that got you in trouble *last* time. Are you sure you want to continue speaking this way to a Duke... *peasant*?"

"You are *no Duke*!" Thomas screeched shrilly, hand grasping for a weapon.

"I only lost my titles in the *Human* lands. Unlike *you*, I was assured of continued political allegiance by another people." Dale drolly and intentionally got the man worked up. "If you challenge me, it will not go well for you."

"My challenge *stands*!" Thomas spat while drawing his sword from its sheath. He was obviously confident in his ability to win, being at rank C-five.

Artorian coughed lightly. "A challenge has been issued... Dale, you do *not* need to accept it."

"Yes, *show* them that you are a coward!" Thomas taunted with a manic grin. "Run away; go back to herding sheep. If that is *all* you do with-"

"I accept the challenge," Dale stated calmly, vanishing from view.

"Huh?" Thomas blinked, staring at the spot Dale had stood. He took a step forward, not trusting his eyes. A shimmer in the air caught his attention, and Dale's *fist* caught him in the jaw, breaking it on the first strike. Thomas staggered backward, but Dale pressed his advantage and made a deposit at the bank of schnozz, breaking the sensitive olfactory organ with a sickening *crack*. The ex-Noble dropped to his knees, and Dale punched him twice more, once in the face and once on the chest, to send him awkwardly splaying onto the ground.

Dale looked around at the shocked faces, trying to make eye contact with anyone who dared. "I trust this matter is *settled*?"

"Did you kill him, Dale?" Artorian softly questioned the young man standing over the fallen, bloody ex-Noble.

"No," Dale responded grudgingly, getting a sigh of relief from the rest of the room. Why had they bothered to ask instead of just checking him with their Essence sight? "No matter my personal dislike of this man, that is, what others generously *say* is a man, every single one of us is another cultivator that can stand against the necromantic horde. He will be fine and just as unpleasant as ever after a cleric takes a look at him."

Satisfied with this outcome, Dale turned and walked out the door. He had a clerk to find. Why was he continually having trouble with people that were *supposed* to be doing their job correctly and with integrity, especially the ones that collected upon *other* people's hard work? Did the *insignificant* amount of power they had over others just naturally lend itself to enhancing their greed? Dale glanced into the collection point; happily, the person he was looking for was on duty. He waited a few minutes for the room to empty out, then stalked forward. To his surprise and fury, the clerk *smirked* at him.

"I'm *so* sorry; this area is only for *current* students. *Get out.*" The last bit was apparently an order and also one that the man thought would be enforced magically. When Dale simply kept walking toward him, he paled and tried to run.

Before he could take two steps, Dale was in front of the man and gripping his neck powerfully, choking the man as he lifted him off the ground. "I will make this easy for you. You owe me all of the supplies I gave you, the extra that was taken from me as a penalty, plus *another* week's worth for making me go out of my way like this. You have until this weekend to make it happen, and if I find that you did it by stealing from someone *else*, I will make sure you never have the option to do so again." Dale put his hand over the man's center, made a small cut with the sharpened Mithril knuckle, and pressed his palm against the fresh wound. With a *yank*, Dale forcibly pulled a strand of the man's Essence into his hand and absorbed it.

"D-*demon* cultivator!" the man hoarsely choked out. Dale backhanded him, bloodying his nose.

"Not even close, you *worm.*" Dale dropped him and walked away, not bothering to look back. "I'll see you in a few days. Better get *busy*... unless you want to go back to being a *fishy.*"

Chapter Thirty-three

"What did you do to yourself?" Craig stared at Dale, eyes narrow and searching.

Dale remained seated casually but cocked his head to the side at the question. "I'm not certain what you are talking about."

"Don't take me for a fool, Dale." Craig swallowed hard. "Are you... crushing Cores again? Do you not remember what happened last time? As far as anyone knows... it killed you. You haven't refuted these claims, so..."

"I'm not crushing Cores, Craig." Dale sat up and looked into the Monk's eyes to show his sincerity. "I have a new, *intensely* better cultivation technique."

"I'm not sure I can believe you, Dale. How do you explain your shift in attitude?" Craig's gaze sharpened further. "You nearly killed a young man today, I'm told. That isn't like you, Dale, but it does sound like someone who is doing things they shouldn't be doing. Heightened aggression, anger, sudden surges in power..."

Dale held up a hand. "I'm happy to prove it." He shifted in his seated position and closed his eyes. For a long moment, nothing changed. Before Craig could say anything else, the Essence in the room *trembled* and began moving toward Dale. *All* of it started moving. Craig's jaw dropped, and Dale opened his eyes in time to see the shift in his expression. The Essence stopped shifting as Dale laughed, almost falling over due to the Monk's shock.

"*So* much Essence absorption," Craig whispered reverently. "It's almost like... *ah-ha*! I see now."

Now it was Dale's turn to be concerned. "What? What did you just think of?"

"Hmm. No, he has also been in the dungeon consistently fighting... but if he hasn't been working his body hard enough... I bet he was nearly undamaged the entire time." Craig's mumbling was getting on Dale's nerves, but soon enough, the Monk looked up and explained himself. "Do you remember, a long time ago, we discussed how hard Nobles had to work themselves? How they would only cultivate a few hours a day, then work themselves *physically* for the remainder of the day?"

"I remember it vaguely." Dale swiped his hand through the air, motioning for the Monk to continue... and be quick about it.

"There are multiple reasons for this, ranging from stabilizing the Chi... to tempering the mind. Large and sudden increases in power are known to lead to a mental shift. *Arrogance* stands above the other risks, but wrath and a loss of concern for life also appear. If you do not keep yourself in balance, Dale, you may become something that you once despised." Craig waited to see if his words would reach the young man, but it seemed that Dale was already disregarding the words he was hearing. "I see. Well, let's get to training then."

Craig moved faster than Dale had ever seen, lightly touching Dale in the chest. The move was deceptive, as Dale went flying across the room before slamming into the wall. The Monk cracked his neck, walking toward the fallen man. "It seems that your Elven teacher knew you were already beginning to tread this path. If this is how it needs to be, *so* be it. I cannot, in good conscience-"

Dale jumped to his feet. He was surprised by the sudden attack, but for some reason, he was completely fine with it. He charged at the Monk, shifting into his combat forms and attacking as hard as he could. He knew he was out of his depth and only full power would give him a chance. Each of his thrown fists were deflected with almost contemptuous ease, and a wide kick was easily avoided. Craig slapped him in the chest again, sending Dale flying once more.

The young man got to his feet, spitting out blood and glaring at Craig. "To the *Abyss* with this! I'm leaving!"

"No. You aren't." Craig was now in front of the door, so Dale shifted into camouflage and tried to go around him. *Slap*! Once more, Dale was airborne. He screamed in frustration, grasping at the stone around him and trying to hurl it at the Monk. The rock lurched, but then stayed in place. Right. Craig was a more powerful and experienced earth cultivator than Dale was. A gold-tinged fire appeared in his hands and he pointed his palms at Craig, only to have his hands smacked and shifted away before he could launch an attack.

"A riddle for you, Dale." Craig took a step back and pulled some wraps off his hands. "If you have three, you have three. Two, and you have two. If you have only one, you have *none*. What is it?"

Dale ignored him, lunging for the wall, desperately trying to blast a hole through it. He failed, yet again.

"It's *options*, Dale. You leave me with only one choice, which is no choice at all. Essentially," Craig spoke calmly as he walked forward and proceeded to beat Dale methodically, "we need to give your body and mind something to focus on, other than your cultivation, that is. *Pain*. Pain is a good teacher, a decent motivator, and a *great* limiter. Ah, using your aura to heal yourself? Good, I can be a bit more... thorough."

By the time Craig left off with his brutal assault and let him lay on the ground whimpering, Dale was feeling thoroughly tenderized. He had deep muscle bruises over the entirety of his body, and Craig hadn't even spared the more *sensitive* areas. Something about needing to think with his *main* brain. Craig looked down at the quivering pile of purple meat named Dale and shook his head, "This should take some time and effort to fix, especially on your own, and as you do so... improve yourself. Start adding Essence to your body; don't just let it build up in your Center and allow your 'power' to go to your head."

"With your cultivation technique, you could be in the C-ranks *today*, if you wanted to ignore our advice. I wonder, though, how much *more* powerful would you be if you had the body of a C-ranker before ever even entering the new rank? How much more powerful could you *become* if you devoted your time in the C-ranks to only *empowering* your body and aura instead of needing to *build* it like everyone else in that rank?" Craig stood from his crouched position and walked toward the exit of the room, leaving Dale gasping in pain on the floor.

He paused for a moment at the door to deliver a parting line, "I admit, a part of me is simply curious... but another part, the part that has spent decades studying Essence... that part is telling me that this path would bring you to heights no person has ever been able to touch. I'll see you in two days for our normal session. Think on today's lesson so that we won't need to *repeat* it."

Once he was alone, Dale's rapid breathing slowly evened out. His eyes shot open. He tried to will fury at the situation, but he was far too hurt and exhausted to do more than grumble internally. Lying on the floor, he attempted to summon the energy to move, but while he was full of Essence... his body was simply too ravaged. His muscles were strained, his tendons expertly and gently damaged. He snorted impotently, almost impressed by the damage Craig had inflicted on his body. The

Monk had left him no choice *but* to empower his body if he ever again wanted to move normally.

There would be no help coming; Dale was sure Craig would make this a fact. He could heal himself over time, perhaps, but... Craig's warning and alluring words actually *did* give him pause. It was evident that this lesson would be repeated if Dale only healed himself, so he needed to find a better way. His eyes closed, and he took a deep, shuddering breath. Fine. He had already been taught how to use his Essence in such a way as to *permanently* enhance his tissue, but doing so required connecting his flesh to his Center, much like building his external aura had.

It meant that he would be sacrificing his cultivation base. He was on the cusp of the C-ranks, and doing this now... it would lower his ranking again. Dale wanted to be furious about this, but he saw the vast improvement his aura had given him already. Enhancing his body was sure to lend to even greater strength. Creating his external aura had also stunted his advancement because it was essentially devoting a chunk of his Essence to surround him at all times... but it was almost an 'invisible' cost. He had simply been devoting power as he got it and hadn't needed to lose his cultivation ranking to make it happen. Now... now it would be a very *visible* cost.

Dale grit his teeth and began the process. This was not something he could undo, which was the only reason he had been hesitating. Essence boiled out of his Core; Chi threads connected to each cell in his body. Those threads connected each of those cells to their surrounding cells, and slowly, the infusion of power began to enhance his body. Dale felt it like a blow when his cultivation dropped to D-eight, especially since only his heart had been fully improved by this point. Then he felt the benefit of his actions. His heart, which had been racing and straining to pump blood and repair his body, calmed and managed the same task for a fraction of the energy.

He smiled a real - if bloody - smile for the first time that day and allowed his outpouring Essence more leeway. More than anything else, he wanted to enhance and protect his brain, but he needed to do this in order. If he wanted to get at his brain, he needed to connect everything in a line from his center and upward. The connections reached the base of his skull, and he frowned. D-seven. He continued upward, and slowly, carefully, he enhanced everything until he finally reached grey matter. As the first connection took hold, his cultivation base *lurched,* and Dale passed out entirely.

Someone shook him. "Dale. Wake up. The process has completed, it seems." Craig was smiling at Dale, who looked up at him with bleary eyes.

"What... happened?" Dale managed, then his newly-enhanced brain kicked in, and his eyes dilated. "I see. The brain is an amazing organ, and it is so heavily interconnected that by inducing a single change to the system... the entire organ needed to be enhanced at once. It likely drew upon my Essence until it had finished, at which point consciousness once more became possible."

Dale blinked, felt at his cultivation, and paled. "Rank D-one...? I... I'm even lower than I started at..."

"You are likely the most potent and powerful D-ranked person on the planet." Craig shook his head in... admiration? "Dale, you have a full external aura and one-third of your interior enhanced, including the portion that is the most difficult and Essence-intensive. The only reason you are *not* ranked as C-two is the lack of available Essence in your Center. With your cultivation technique and access to the lower floors of the dungeon, you could finish your full aura and *still* enter the C-ranks in... I can't even estimate. Days? Weeks?"

"That's..." Dale shook his head, which felt clear and *aware*. "My thoughts are so much... *crisper*."

"Your brain has been enhanced past what is possible for non-cultivators. You are likely going to find that things that were difficult to understand before now are... undemanding." Craig smiled as he saw that the Dale he knew was back in control. "How do you feel, by the way?"

"I would have to say... embarrassed?" Dale admitted shamefacedly. "Did I *really* attack you? It feels like a dream or like the memories are from a memory stone."

Craig nodded sagely. "You were out of balance. Your spirit was full of power, and your body was strained to the breaking point attempting to keep up. This caused your mind to begin fracturing, and you looked to increase your fighting spirit above all else. While it is not *common* these days, it used to be. Back before we knew what these issues were caused by, people would begin to lose themselves to the draw of ever-increasing power, doing *anything* for even a small gain. It was an addiction. Now... well, like I said, it is at least *less* common."

"Thank you for making me understand." Dale stood up slowly, his body still in severe pain. "Why did you come back? I was certain you were going to just leave me here until I had finished my aura."

"Well, I *did* tell you that I would see you for our next scheduled training session, yes?" Craig smirked at Dale's expression.

"I've been lying on the floor there for *two days*?"

Chapter Thirty-Four

I'm flying again. This gives me a strange sense of freedom, even though I know that I am currently anything *but* free. Maybe I should roll the mountain like a barrel, just to see how many people fall off? ...but then I would lose all my lake water. Not worth it. Besides, the people I *really* want gone aren't going anywhere except to war, it seems.

Barry had come into my dungeon again and made the usual caustic threats. What was the main difference between now and the last time he had done so? Easy! I knew for sure that he was crazy enough to follow through with the threats he was spouting. I was honestly surprised that Xenocide had never abducted this guy and used him as a cultivation resource. There was probably a whole *mess* of madness wrapped up in Barry's nasty little mind. Once I had started moving, he wore a satisfied smirk and left the dungeon. He ordered me to a new position, simplistically telling me to 'head West until ordered otherwise'. This overpowered cultivator obviously thinks of me having intelligence similar to an animal: only able to understand the carrot and stick mentality.

My main issue is that it is *all* stick. There has been no benefit to me for working with this fiend beyond... staying alive. That still falls under the 'stick' category, though! It's a threat, a promise of slavery and a life of following the orders of the Guild. He thinks I'm a broken stallion, a creature of the wild that has learned to wear a harness. Soon enough, he'll learn that I'm a mimic. A creature that can hide its true self until striking at an opportune moment, slaying the unaware. I was looking forward to that *moment*.

"Copper for your thoughts?" Dani nudged my mind, breaking me out of the fantasy I was living in.

<Oh, not too much on my mind.> I hummed a short tune, turning the question back on her. <How are, um, things going with you?>

"You're *sure* nothing is going on? You were... cackling." Dani chuckled as I sputtered and tried to find an excuse for what I wished was a more abnormal activity. "You've been sounding very menacing the last few days. If you *remember*, right now we are supposed to be spending time together, watching the changing horizon as we fly along!"

<Right, right. Sorry about that. It is nice, isn't it?> I was silent for a few moments, watching on a projection as the vast plain slowly rolled under us like a verdant ocean. I had finally worked the kinks out. <It's just...>

"Here we go." Dani brightly laughed. "New superweapon? Awesome Mob? Hmm... a path to the A-ranks?"

<No, no, just planning our inevitable victory over the Guild. You know, nothing *extraordinary*. Just what I would be doing on a typical day.> My words caused her to fall out of the air and just lie on the ground for a moment. Wow. I was just being facetious; I hadn't thought I was being *that* aggravating.

"Oh, Cal." Dani flew up and started following lazy patterns around the Silverwood tree. "If anyone else were to say that, I would ignore them as I would *any* insane person. The Guild isn't just standard fighters and cultivators, you know. It includes all sorts of subsets like the Mages' Guild, an Assassin Guild, and even a branch of the Church. To most people, saying you are going to fight the Guild is the same as saying that you are going to fight civilization as a whole."

<Oh.> I hadn't thought they were *that* extreme. Did that change things? ...Maybe a little. I decided that I agreed with her

assessment. <Let me try again. No, no, just planning our inevitable victory over a certain member of the Guild.>

"Better. So what comes next, Cal? We are being used as a flying fortress, a mobile troop transport. How do we get out of this mess?"

<I hate to say it, Dani, but... if we need to, we will run away.> I stopped her before she could ask the obvious question. <I'm not talking about the *dungeon*, Dani. I mean you, Grace, and me. I have already shifted the ley line creation section to be out of the floating portion of the dungeon, so it will continue even if this place gets obliterated. I also have a small band of Essence I created that is holding me suspended over this portal; if something terrible happens and I am somehow no longer able to properly function, the Essence will dissipate, and I'll fall through this hole in space.>

"How would *we* get to you? What about everyone else, the Goblins, the memories of all these humans that...?" Dani's voice was soft as we discussed the worst possible outcomes.

<If I can no longer function, I am hoping that you two have already gone ahead. If we need to evacuate, you two are going first.> I paused, trying to keep the heated passion from my voice. I had been thinking about this a lot recently. <If we run, obviously, we will lose all the Cores and Stones we've been collecting, which will be a huge blow to me, but...>

I made sure Dani was looking at me. <The two of you are more important to me than *anything* else. If the entire world is going to burn, we will watch it happen from a distance, and we will be sad for a short while. Then, eventually, we will rebuild.>

Dani was silent for a full minute. "Wow, Cal, you would willingly give up *everything* else to keep us safe?"

<Yes, but at least we will have unlimited Essence!> I laughed as I ruined the serious moment. <That's all worst case.

We are talking *total* last option, necromancers closing in, everything else gone up in flames, Mountaindale overturning the earth as it falls from the sky...>

Dani cut me off before I could extrapolate further, “I get it. So we just fly through the portal under you?”

<Simple, right? That’s one heck of an easy escape plan.> I was inordinately proud of such a simple action. After all, sometimes simple was best, right? <Now if you had meant ‘what is next’ in the *really* short term... I think preparing for war is the only real option. I am making an army of Goblins to protect this floor and equipping them with all sorts of Inscribed silver weapons and armor so they are extra effective against undead and demons. I was thinking of calling them ‘The Silver Legion’. What do you think?>

“Sounds... good, I guess? I don’t think that silver is actually any more useful against them than other materials though. Why do you think that is?” Dani raised a good, fair, somewhat upsetting point.

<Are you *serious*? I was listening to a merchant on the surface telling all these students how much more effective silver was for killing infernal creatures because it is a ‘purified’ metal!> Did I really waste two whole days making silver equipment? <I got scammed. I got scammed so *bad*! No~o~o!>

Dani was laughing at me, and not with her usual chuckle. Mana was infusing her laughter accidentally, and the entire area was shaking and bouncing because of it. “Cal! Seriously? You got taken in by a *swindler*? This is just the best!”

<Why in the world would a merchant lie like that? It could get people killed!> I called indignantly.

“They are trying to make *sales*, Cal!” Dani groaned and rolled around in the air, trailing colored streams of light. “If the weapon is made correctly, it should kill the undead just as effectively as any other, but *just* maybe the knowledge that it is 'extra effective' might make them attack a little harder, go in for the killing blow, have a *little* more hope. That is what these merchants are really selling: hope. Or that's what they would tell you, anyway; they are really just selling anything they can to make an extra copper."

<It just seems wrong, somehow. People that come here *know* there is danger, but no one is expecting a trusted merchant to be a danger, even if it is just to their wallet.> I decided to move on; I couldn't really talk about 'ethical' things without some severe bias. <Well, my Silver Legion is still pretty awesome, and at a minimum, they look *really* cool. Extra shiny.>

"Plus anyone who sees them will think they are all wearing Mithril, since that is something you've used in the past," Dani chimed in. I froze, the gears in my head turning viciously.

<Make them expect one thing... and spring something different at them...> My tone returned to gleeful. <Oh, Dani, I think we have found an answer to a couple of our troubles. At the very least, I think I know how to take down Barry when the time is right.>

"Care to share your plans?" Dani hopefully questioned. I tended to be mysterious and circumvent explanations for fun, but...

<Sure.> I smiled when she went very still. <I'm going to use a decoy, like I did when necromancers came for me. Barry has been *walking* in, right? Not using the portals? Well, when he is coming to fight me directly, I'll have him walk into a false floor. He never bothered to go further than the third floor before, so...if I do this right, I won't need to sacrifice an *actual* level again. Oh, Dani. This is good. If this works... alright, here is the plan. Wait! Let me get Bob Prime first.>

Chapter Thirty-five

<At that point, if he walks to this position before attacking, we can use my spirit cannons to take him down!> I enthusiastically finished outlining my plans to my two most trusted compatriots.

"Hmm," Bob Prime made this sound deep in his throat, and Dani bobbed in agreement with his non-verbal disagreement.

<What is that all about? Why aren't you *thrilled* to hear that I've come up with such an excellent plan?> I was seriously stumped about this one.

"Well, it's..." Bob hesitated, then pressed forward, "Great Spirit, this plan relies on many, *many* assumptions and variables. What you just told me was: 'if he is here, in the right place, at the right time, and everything is ready, then *maybe* my prototype weapons will work against him *if* the rumors about his abilities are accurate'."

<Well, that's a *pessimistic* way of looking at things, Bob.> I looked pleadingly at my loving Wisp. <*You* think it's a valid idea... right, Dani?>

"It is a *totally* viable plan!" Dani trailed off with a nervous chuckle. "Maybe it isn't our 'go to' plan, though? Maybe we come up with something a little more, um, likely to work correctly?"

Dani looked over to see Bob rolling his eyes. She decided to amend her answer. "... Fine, It's a terrible plan, Cal."

<Oh, you guys are no fun. Next, you are going to want me to shove him through a portal to somewhere random and hope that he can't find us ever again.> I rolled my eyes at their lack of flair.

"Wait, can you do that?" Bob Prime latched onto my last statement with excitement. "That may be more likely than the hope that Barry will bother to fight your Goblin Warlord in a duel. I'm also not sure how we distract him for ten minutes with rabbits while you power up your weapons."

<With *Bashers*, Bob. Come on; you've been here *how* long?>

Dani cut me off before I could explain better, "I'm also not sure that he *will* fall into a pool of excreta, Cal. Most *regular* people will be able to recognize it, and S-rankers can likely do a lot more than that." She might as well be slapping me with these cold, mean facts. "That portal idea, though, that sounds interesting. What do you need for that?"

<Come *on*! That was literally the most boring thing I could think of to fight him! We aren't seriously considering->

"I vote for the portal plan;" Dani called out for a vote.

"Seconded!" Bob Prime replied with a smile. Evil! Pure evil! Humans were right about Goblins! I should have listened!

<*Guys*!> I whined, only to have Dani tell me to suck it up and figure out the details. Bah. What a boring way to fight someone. I'd do it their way, since... I mean, it did sound more realistic. I would work on 'plan S' behind their backs, though. If I had time. I don't think I would have time. I might put together *some* of it though. This is why I don't lay out my plans to other people. Why did I do it this time? Misplaced excitement?

"Great Spirit!" Navigation Bob was shouting into the air to get my attention, so I popped over to his area and saw what he was pointing at. "We are approaching the edges of a necromantic horde!"

<Thanks, Bob.> I was looking at the projection he was using, and if I had blood I would have blanched. What even *were* some of those things? A vast, grotesque, most likely smelly

army was marching in perfect step. The human-sized creatures were taking three paces for each one of the larger variants who were taking two steps for each one made by the massive abominations. There were three Tomb Lords that I could see, moving slower than others in their army so they didn't crush their own troops. They *had* to be Tomb Lords; nothing else I had ever heard of wore that much armor around a lump of decaying flesh. Those *things* were each A-ranked, and by themselves represented more military force than I could really comprehend.

To think we were coming up *behind* this force made me wonder what their front-line shock troops would bring to bear. I didn't usually feel bad for Humans, but this... this was... I shook off my awe, taking a moment longer to shake off my jealousy. I think that was the correct emotion to have, right? I wasn't a huge fan of the undead, but by the *abyss,* I wanted a cadre of A-ranked creatures to do my bidding! I enhanced the projection, zooming in closer to inspect some of the *things* walking around. It still surprised me how few living creatures were down there. It was almost as though a necromancer was a mobile dungeon because they were very similar to me. For instance: if the controlling necromancer fell, the creatures he controlled would either die instantly... or go wild and *then* die. Hmm. I didn't care for the fact that my abilities were parroted by such a noxious group.

I pulled myself away from the projection. At this distance, I had no way of knowing what the creatures were. I could see their form, but I wouldn't know *what* they were for sure until I heard them named by someone else. I'd have to wait until we got closer and the others could sense them or see them with their weak, fleshy eyes. It wasn't like I could invite anyone into the control room of the... but then, I didn't need *them* to come *here*, did I? I shifted the projection and controlled the light it emitted. It took a moment or three of finagling the details, but there was now a projection of what we were flying toward that appeared on the side of one of the academy buildings.

I zoomed in on one of the creatures that I wanted to learn the name of and waited for someone in the area to say something. What I *wasn't* expecting were the screams. Terror and horror filled the space, and the wall hosting the undead creature went *boom* as a Mage charged at the 'creature' and punched it. The structure detonated, injuring dozens of weaker humans as it collapsed.

"I got it, I think!" the Mage cheerfully called out.

"You moron, it's an illusion!" I think this guy was one of the remaining Spotters? Made sense that he was the first to recognize the projection for what it *basically* was.

A few minutes later, the wall was repaired, and over a hundred people were watching as the undead marched. Speculation ran rampant as people tried to figure out what was going on, and I was getting frustrated by the lack of correct guesses or information that I was hearing. I almost shouted for joy when someone noticed that the area we were flying over looked suspiciously similar to what had been projected recently. From there, the veil came down quickly. There was a collective 'celestial feces' moment, and someone must have run off to alert the Guild members because they appeared shortly after. When they confirmed what they could *clearly* see, people began moving around quickly.

Messengers ran to and through the portal, and merchants were suddenly swarmed with customers who had 'just remembered' that they needed an important or life-saving item. Barry tried to yell at me and give me orders to stop getting closer, but I continued with my facade of not being able to 'hear' him until he came down to at least the third level of the dungeon. After getting my new orders, I ever so slowly changed directions and continued following, albeit at a glacial rate along a zig-zag path. I still needed to gain Essence to fly freely because I was devoting most of the Essence now collected into other projects.

Barry was now back at the projection, speaking with the other members of the Guild that had been riding along. "As soon as we hear that the Guild is attacking, we will increase our pace. When we have word that our allies have flanked this *mass*, we will wait six hours and proceed at full speed into the undead. The heavy hitters amongst our groups - A ranked or above - will destroy the Tomb Lords and Abominations as well as any necromancers that we can find. Anyone B-ranked or lesser will fight against the standard undead and lesser necromancers at ground level. Are your orders clear? Does anyone have any question as to which group they will be in?"

Barry waited for anyone to ask a question, and sighed with relief when no one did so. "Thank goodness; I was *sure* someone would have forgotten their rank by now." People chuckled at his words. Wait a moment... was this guy *popular*? Was he liked and *respected* by the majority of his Guild? He continued to chat, and I looked at the people around him. It was *true*! They *liked* him! This cannibalistic monster clothed in the flesh of a man had people *fawning* over him! I was a little sick to my fifth floor over this! Great, now I can't *not* picture my fifth floor as a stomach. I blame Barry for *this*, too.

Let me see... escape plan in place, a growing group of Silver Legion Goblins setting up positions on the fourth floor, at maximum capacity for Mage-rank Bob production... all done. I can't really think of anything else to do right now. I suppose I could link myself to the Runescript set up for ley lines, but I figured that I would do that while the war was going on and I was in position not doing much else. Navigation Bob will make the call if we need to run for it, and I should be able to retaliate against anyone attacking me directly.

I was churning out anti-demon weapons, and all of my Mobs that could use these weapons were given them. Even my Bashers had tiny, little shoes with Inscribed silver claws on them. My troops were deadly *and* adorable!

Chapter Thirty-six

A voice boomed from the balcony of what used to be Dale's bedroom. The power-infused voice reached everyone on Mountaindale, even those within the dungeon. It took a second to register, but the voice resolved itself as Barry. "People of... *Mountaindale*. War approaches. The time you have spent here has likely been an excellent respite, a time safe from the constant struggle the rest of the civilized world has been embroiled in. Unfortunately, I must inform you all that your relaxation must now come to an end."

As the echoes faded, people began talking to each other. Barry interrupted once more; he had apparently been pausing for dramatic effect. Dale shook his head; he had waited too long to continue. In his opinion, everything now sounded stilted and poorly rehearsed. "War approaches. I hope that all of you survive. Though, I know many of you will not. This mountain is flying directly at the rear of the necromantic army, and in a few hours, the strongest members of the Guild will be arriving to assault the leadership of these monsters. We ask all cultivators to prepare themselves and all non-cultivators to remove themselves and either leave through the portal or seek shelter in the dungeon's... *workroom*? There's a *workroom* down there?"

Now it was obvious that the man was reading from a script. Not that there was anything *wrong* with that, but he didn't even bother to read through it beforehand. Just laziness. "*Ahem.* As I was saying, any cultivator attempting to avoid service to the Guild will be placed on the front lines of the battle *when* they are caught. *If* they survive, they will be slain after the battle has been won. Time is running out. Get moving."

Was 'get moving' his catchphrase or something? Dale shook his head to clear his thoughts; where had this constant mockery of other people's speech patterns come from? He hadn't done this in the past, had he? Dale felt at his aura, pleased with the progress he had made in the last few days. With the help of his team, he had been able to cultivate uninterrupted deep within the dungeon. His rank had increased back to D-three, but there was no comparison in terms of power from the first time he had been at this point. The *only* reason he was still in the D-ranks was because he had been devoting every spare drop of Essence to enhancing his body.

His cultivation technique had never been meant for humans or, really, *anything* that was able to move. Dale was using a B-ranked dungeon's *personal* cultivation technique, and the incredible results were obvious. All he had left to finish his aura entirely was his skin. From there, the way to increase in rank was to increase the flow of Essence to these areas. There were two more steps involved with reaching the Mage ranks from this point. Yes, the *Mage* ranks. Firstly, his body and external aura needed to be fully enhanced *and* empowered. Secondly, he needed to break through the barriers that limited his race. This was done by reaching the peak of the C-ranks and attempting to climb the Tower of Ascension.

Climbing the tower was... difficult to learn any *real* information about. Mages seemed to have different theories on why they were able to attain differing **laws**, but two facts were widely known. The more knowledge of a particular subject you had, the more likely you were to be able to grasp and bind to it. The second was you needed to have an affinity for it. The C-ranks were where people would *usually* open affinity channels, like Craig had done in the past in order to have three affinities. Of course, the one that had been trained to this point was going to be the most potent affinity, and the others could only be lesser or *just* about the same. There were... *mishaps* sometimes when opening affinity channels, but the process itself was known to be reasonably safe.

All of his channels were open, his aura was already almost built, and he should be able to gather the required Essence in *weeks* instead of years. Dale would be able to skip *all* the steps except for learning about the **laws**. If he attempted to jump into the Tower without the knowledge he needed, he would likely be stuck at the first tier... or he would die. It had happened in the past. Every single cultivator had heard the stories. People who skipped steps, who thought they could cheat, who cut corners... they died. Almost *always* in some spectacular fashion. That was the *real* reason that the world wasn't stuffed with Mages. Either the C-rankers were too lazy to push forward and learn all they could about their possible Mana paths, or they worked *very* hard and pushed for higher tier knowledge.

There was almost no in-between. There were very few people that would get to the peak of the C-ranks and be happy *only* reaching the first tier. The very few who were simply glad to be Mages... well, they tended to regret their decisions later on. Dale closed his eyes and smiled. He had a plan, a plan that would make others hate him if they knew about it; he was going to cheat. Dale burst into laughter, startling his team from their own cultivation or guard duty. They were already on edge from Barry's announcement to Mountaindale, and his random outbursts were not smiled upon. Dale simply kept his eyes closed to avoid the glares and thought through his plan.

Path advancement. That is what it all came down to. Dale would power through the C-ranks, and when he had the chance, he would throw himself into the Tower and climb as high as he could. He would be fine even if he took a first tier power because he knew from Rose that Madame Chandra had recently been able to upgrade her **law**. If she could do it just from the knowledge she had accrued plus a little nudge from the dungeon, Dale could as well.

He planned to take the several *hundred* extra years of life that reaching the Mage ranks granted and progress smoothly and continuously. As far as he knew... he was the first person *ever* to attempt something like this. There had been path advancements in the past, but they were always *mysterious.* They were not *planned* events and certainly not to the extent Dale was thinking of. Most dreamed that they may be able to advance once before the S-ranks... not him, though. He was going to climb until he was happy with his choices.

"I still can't believe what I'm seeing." Hans shook his head and sighed as he watched the Essence flow through Dale and connect each cell in his body to his Core. The weave was done with *pure* Essence, and the weave was so tight that Dale's body must have increased in durability and strength by a factor of ten. "You look like a *Royal* with that technique. If you ever find or make a spare of that... I have a hidden pit filled with platinum and gold coins I'd hand over."

Dale chuckled as he infused the skin on his palms, dust falling as his epidermis tightened and thickened. "Ouch! Wasn't supposed to do that. I'll see what I can do, Hans."

Chapter Thirty-seven

Dale's team walked out of the dungeon and looked around, utterly dumbfounded by the sheer chaos in the surrounding area. People were running toward the portal, Guild shock troops were coming out of it, the projection on the wall had increased in size and the undead were clearly visible, and merchants were basically under attack from cultivators trying to buy things. Over all of this was the *shouting*. Everyone was yelling about something, whether it was ordering another out of their way, screaming for some reason, or attempting to attract the merchant's attention. A few impromptu bar areas had been set up as well, and these were making money hand over fist.

"Over here, *pharmacist*!" a man shouted at Stefan. Dale only recognized him because of his unique name. "I was here first!"

Bedraggled and overworked, Stefan nodded painfully and slowly. "One potion of cure disease of sexual origin? Give me fifteen minutes..."

"Hey, hurry it up! If I don't have that potion ready by the time we are sent to fight, I'm going to *cut* you!" Stefan didn't react to this shout, moving at a continuous pace no matter the verbal assault thrown at him.

"I guess we're getting closer to the undead than I expected." Dale frowned as he looked at his team. They were all pretty worn down from the last few weeks of intense training and cultivation. "We should all split up and get some rest. Thank you all for helping me get to this point; I won't forget it. Sorry if I haven't been as invested in the team as I should have been recently."

Rose rolled her eyes. "Dale, you aren't the only person in the world. What do you think we do when we aren't working together, sit around drinking and longing for your company?"

"I mean, *I* do that." Hans batted his eyelashes at Dale.

"Oh, stop it. No! We train, hone our skills, and live our own lives. Also, when we party up like this, you aren't the only one who benefits. We've all been cultivating. We've all gotten stronger. You're fine; we work with you because it is mutually beneficial, and we all like each other." Rose glanced at Hans. "That is, we all like *most* of the group. Don't go all melodramatic on us again."

Dale froze, slowly losing his severe expression and laughing. "You mean to tell me that I *shouldn't* sacrifice myself to the necromancers in an attempt to appease them and halt this war? Well... there goes *that* plan." This got a few pity laughs, but the message was clear. They were all friends who would stick together without the need to promise rewards in the future.

"I will gladly take you up on the offer of rest, friend Dale." Tom clapped Dale on the back, frowning as his hand stung and Dale didn't budge an inch. "Huh. That is new. You seem to have become denser."

"That explains why we need to keep explaining things to him!" Rose called as she walked away.

The others chuckled and scattered to pursue their own interests, leaving Dale to plan his next move. He opened his bag and counted the gold and silver he had stored away. His bank account held more, but the large pile of gold he carried with him should do for now. He walked into one of the only places in the academy courtyard *not* stuffed with people and started shouting, adding to the noise. "Buying Cores in bulk! Sell your Cores for *gold* here!"

There were a few people giving him strange looks, but soon enough, students began drifting over to sell him their Cores. When word spread that he was paying good coin, the crowd around him increased quickly. Usually, Cores were graded and judged by the person buying them, but Dale gave a gold coin for any that held the density of an upper C-rank and half that for anything mid or low. No one offered him a B-rank Core, or he would have certainly bought that as well. When interest in his services waned, he went around to any merchant that was offering cultivation supplies and purchased any Cores they had. Finally, he went to the Guild store and purchased Cores until his coin ran out.

Looking through his bags, Dale could only smile as he saw the vast amount of gem-like objects gathered there. If the dungeon had been truthful, his meridians were more easily able to handle the large amount of Essence that shattering a Core would inject into his body. He needed to be careful, but if this worked, he would be able to get *so* much more Essence for his trouble. Cultivating while *holding* a Core worked far better, but it was too slow for his needs. He wasted less doing it *properly*, but it would take hours to drain a single Core. In a pinch, this would also let him empower abilities and supercharge his Essence attacks.

Dale needed to finish working with his skin. He was honestly surprised how long it took to work on this organ; you couldn't just infuse a patch of skin to completion, each layer of skin across the entire body needed to be slowly connected at the same time so that it wouldn't crack and separate from the other layers or the flesh around it. Dale was close to being done but still needed to devote time to making it happen. He rented one of the best empty rooms and took it for himself, barring the door and preparing himself mentally. He was nearly drained from the work he had done so far and so wasted no time in getting a Core out and forcefully crushing it.

Bamph! The Core exploded, and Dale grasped at all of the Essence that was now around him and on his body. He tried to pull it all in through his gauntlet but realized that he was being foolish. If there was Essence escaping, why not draw it in with his normal technique? Dale popped another Core and maintained his cultivation. This time, he was able to gain a large amount of Essence before the remaining power diffused into the area. Dale grinned, pleased he had been able to get one of the personal cultivation rooms at the academy. Being the headmaster's pupil *did* have some side benefits. There was a reason he had taken this particular room; it had weak but useful Essence gathering Runes throughout the area. Even though he was losing some of the energy from the Core, he would eventually get it back. There was no real escape for this Essence; he would have it all.

An hour passed, and Dale's bag full of Cores had been reduced by a quarter. He was absolutely sick of the feeling of Essence crashing into him like this; it felt like an instant drunken high followed by an immediate hangover. At the start, it had only felt good, but this was no longer fun. It was *work*, and that was all Dale needed to remind himself of in order to get the motivation to withdraw and crush yet another Core. His skin had finished infusing within the first ten minutes of this training, and his cultivation rank had skyrocketed. He broke one more Core and *shoved* the Essence against the barriers in his Center.

A common misconception was that if you had enough power, you would easily break the bottlenecks that held you in place. Unfortunately, the barriers to advancement were... elastic. 'Pushing' on them weakened them over time, but they were fine with expanding to a small degree. Cultivation usually stretched the barriers over and over until they finally gave out, but Dale was attempting to break the barriers as if they were rigid structures. If someone else was using sandpaper to scrape away, he was wildly swinging a hammer and hoping that it would hit a weak spot *just* right.

This method was painful, as the blockages were not in your physical body; but in your soul and your psyche. Dale crushed another Core and coughed, wiping away fresh blood that had begun dripping from his nose. He absorbed the Essence, and his barriers stopped expanding for a moment before deflating slightly. Dale felt this, and before his Center could use the Essence or remove it... he crushed another Core. The power rushed into him, and his barriers to the C-ranks began to crack. As he pulled in more and more of the Essence in the room, the barriers gave way with a groan like wood splitting. Dale felt the energy that had been used by his mind and body to maintain the barriers flowed back into him, condensing in his Core and wrapping his Chi spiral in a pearly substance.

Dale was gasping as he felt this process; he smiled through the pain as his Chi spiral became rigid and immutable. The benefits of the C-ranks were hard to ignore, but they were usually only a larger well of Essence and the start of aura control and creation. There was another thing that happened, but there was a massive argument about if it were a positive or not. The cultivation technique being used when someone broke into the C-ranks became an almost solid thing, almost like a pearl in a clam. This meant that if you wanted to change your technique after this point, you either needed to destroy your entire cultivation and start over in the F-ranks or make painstakingly slow changes to an almost solid Chi spiral.

Some people liked this fact since it meant they were genuinely committed to improving if they had to start over. Other people wanted the crystallization because it allowed

Essence to move much, *much* faster through the body. Dale tested this rumor by willing Essence to his hand, it- "Whoa! It's already..."

He shook off his wonder; his Essence was *incredibly* responsive. Even getting it to his hands before had taken a few moments of thought and direction. Now, it was simply *there*, ready to be used. He looked at his hands a moment longer before clenching them and standing. Dale took a deep breath, let it out, and took another. Then he screamed.

"*I did it!* I *did* it! I'm in the C-ranks! I'm *C-rank zero*!" Dale jumped up and down, his energy needing an outlet. He flipped in the air, punched the walls, and possibly even let a manly tear of joy slip out. After thirty seconds of this, he put his back to the wall and slid to the floor. His breath was coming hard, and he whispered once more.

"I did it."

Chapter Thirty-eight

"You disgust me." Hans glared at Dale as the young man walked toward them with a wide smile on his face. "It took me twenty-two years to get to the C-ranks. Twenty-two *years*, Dale!"

"Why does he disgust you?" Tom looked between them, his eyes slightly glazed from the Essence-wine he was sipping. "Those two statements seem entirely unrelated."

"Drink your wine, adults are speaking." Hans brushed Tom off, but the man didn't seem to mind, simply drinking more wine with a cheerful smile. "C-rank zero. Do you know that you are basically glowing to my sight? If I didn't know you were new to the C-ranks, I would assume you were at or near the end of the C-ranks and about to break into the B-ranks. You and ol' cloth-fist Craig have the same style of body aura."

"I feel *amazing*, Hans." Dale sat on the seat next to him at the Dwarf-run tavern, ordering the same Essence-wine that Tom was drinking. "My body feels like it was designed to have Essence moving through it. I literally feel ten times stronger than I was a single rank ago."

"Well, that is how progression is supposed to work. Remember? Each step in the rankings means that a similarly trained individual needs to have ten people a single step lower fight him at the same time in order to be reasonably assured of victory. Also, remember that this only holds true in the non-Mage ranks. From there on, the tiers from the Tower come into play, and everything gets super messy." Hans watched Dale throw back his drink with a wide smile. "At least I taught you *something*! Good lad, I was worried you would get all fastidious with what you eat like Craig did. He always says 'I'll eat what I want to in the Mage ranks'. Waste of good coin, though; it's hard for Mages to get good and drunk on anything affordable."

"I'm not going to get *drunk*, Hans! That was a celebratory glass and nothing more; we're going to war here soon." Dale twisted and caught Hans' fist as it was sailing at his arm.

"Oh? Interesting, you think you are up to the task of keeping up with ol' Hansel-bread, eh?" Hans' eyes were glittering with excitement as he imagined sparring against someone using Moon Elf fighting styles.

"Nah, but I think I could give Mr. Dangerlicious a run for his money." Dale laughed as the fight fell out of Hans, who was now pouting instead.

"I hate Bards," the Assassin muttered grumpily. He looked over Dale again with a critical eye, "So what is next for you? What **law** are you going to go for in the Tower? Some noble pursuit, I assume? You look like a Flesh Mage in the making to me."

"Ew, no. I want to be able to fight, not fix some lady's nose when she is sick of looking at it." Dale snorted at Hans' twitching face. "You were hoping to convince me and then get a discount on future work, huh?"

"Why do you *know* me so well?"

"If you aren't trying to get drunk, c-can I get that?" A tipsy dwarf reached for Dale's cup, taking it right out of his hand. "Thanks. Been a rough week to be a student. Name's Feljer Lynn, I was in a music class that got wiped out in the dungeon. You... Y-y-you should be nicer to bards. We... *they*... try so hard."

Hans looked at the drunk wreck of a Dwarf, looked at Dale, and worked to ignore the intruder. The young Dwarf drank down the contents of his ill-gotten mug and grimaced, light coming into his eyes. He was... sobering up?

The bartender behind the counter, a well-liked Dwarf named Steve, suddenly shouted into the room. "Alright, who in here is a cleric? Someone is regenerating people, and they are losing their buzz! Knock it off, or you are going to be buying everyone drinks to make up for it when we find you!"

"Agreed, I was having an enjoyable drinking session. Now, I am fully sober," Tom sadly told his companions.

"Hans, it might be time to go." Dale looked around at the patrons who were getting agitated. "I tend to hold a regeneration aura these days... I think it might be stronger than it used to be."

"It's *him*! It-" Hans' shout was cut off as Dale slapped a hand over his mouth and started pulling him to the exit. Tom joined them, not wanting to buy any more wine now that he was sober.

Dale let go of Hans and wiped his hand on his pants. "Did you *have* to lick my hand?"

"Yes," Hans replied seriously. "There are consequences for your actions."

"Why am I not surprised to see you three stumbling out of a bar right before we go into the most dangerous conflict of our lives?" Rose's voice was raised to be heard over the general hubbub in the area. Adam was strolling along beside her, his hair floating in the air like the man was underwater. His incredibly thick celestial corruption was still having an altering effect on his body, changing it in strange ways.

"Because you know me *so* well, my Rose!" Hans put both of his hands over his heart, pretending deep infatuation. "We are so comfortable together already, why don't we just make it official and-"

Rose whipped out an arrow and fired at him. Hans didn't move, and the arrow *thunked* into the armor covering his knee. He looked down at the arrow, back at her, and back at the arrow. "Are you invoking the Northman's courting ritual?"

"Ha!" Tom bellowed a single, deep laugh. "He's right; we call getting married 'taking an arrow to the knee'! You just got engag-" he sputtered to a stop as he looked at an arrowhead that was pointing at his eye.

"Will you three please stop flirting and get serious? Do we need anything else for when we fight against the undead?" Dale smirked as Rose obviously considered shooting Hans again, then Dale for his comment, but reluctantly put away her arrow.

"I am currently all set for the upcoming conflict. I have four days' worth of supplies and three times the amount of restorative potion that I would generally bring into an extended stay in the dungeon," Tom listed for the others.

"I have a similar amount. I also have anti-infection and infernal dismantling potions from the Church," Adam chimed in softly. He pulled the hood of his robe up, covering his hair since random people were stopping to stare.

"Everyone else?" Dale looked around and smiled. "Excellent. I also have extra Cores to empower some of my abilities if necessary. I made sure none of them were above C-ranked this time. Oh, and on that note, I advanced into the C-ranks this morning."

"What! Congratulations!" Rose gave him a quick hug while the others gave him appraising looks with Essence-empowered eyes. "Have you talked to your instructors yet? I'm sure they are going to want to see your progress!"

"Not yet, and if that image is correct, I think we are out of time. Good luck, everyone." Dale gestured at the enormous projection of the undead that they were approaching, drawing attention to the fact that some of the undead had turned around and were staring directly at them. "If they can see us, that means we are getting close enough that we are almost in combat range."

The projection flared, and black-tinged light surged from one of the Tomb Lords. A *dense* beam suddenly sprang from its eyes, growing larger at an alarming rate. *Something* flashed over their heads, the shockwave it produced knocking them off their feet. On the projection, a person appeared and absorbed the attack. They didn't take a hit; they *absorbed* the energy, and a moment later, the energy returned toward the undead below as an arc. The projection fuzzed from the amount of power discharged, and when the dust cleared after two minutes... Dale's mind had trouble understanding the amount of devastation wrought upon the forces gathered below. The landscape had shifted, and a new canyon had been created. Already, groundwater had begun pouring into the canyon, and a river had shifted its flow to pour into the chasm.

Of the forces that had been in the area, there was no sign. Dale was sick to his stomach over the thought of what would have happened to them if the Tomb Lord's eye-beam had impacted Mountaindale. At best, they would have needed to hold onto a chunk of superheated stone as it fell from the sky. At worst... well, he wouldn't have needed to worry about it. Rose made a choking sound before squeaking out, "We are going down to fight *that*?"

"No, no!" Hans cheerfully denied. "We are going down to fight on the ground *around* those things while the big ones fight *our* big ones. We fight the ones that, you know, got obliterated from the runoff of the first exchange. It'll be fun to try dodging friendly fire while re-killing the undead."

"Have you done something like this before?" Tom swallowed hard as the Tomb Lord picked up a chunk of stone the size of a village and hurled it with unerring accuracy at the floating Mountain. It seemed to be struck with something, falling out of the sky and slamming into the ground. A crater formed around the area, adding plumes of dust to the debris already in the air.

"Eh. It wasn't the undead, but the Guild was called to war once before. The entire conflict lasted an hour. When our heavy hitters walked onto the field, the other side surrendered in ten seconds. Half of their forces had already been wiped out by then; the Guild does *not* mess around. I had been fighting for twenty minutes at that point and had just got orders to go assassinate some of the leaders. If I had been faster, I would have been in the blast zone. I'm really sorry to have to tell you this, friends, but our survival right now depends on how lucky we are and how well we can dodge. Adam... do you know your job in all of this?"

"Heal and protect," Adam rattled off instantly.

"You *wish*," Hans stated without malice, only resignation. "You heal us if it is *absolutely* required, but your job is actually to keep an eye on the big fights and warn us if it looks like something is coming our way. You don't focus on *our* fight; you focus on *theirs*." He pointed at the projection, which showed one of the men Dale recognized as an A-ranker from the Guild. The man made an 'up' gesture, and a freaking *volcano* erupted under the Tomb Lord he was locked in conflict with. Balls of molten rock and pressurized gas ravaged the battlefield around the epicenter of the event, but the Tomb Lord only lost a bit of mass and stepped calmly out of the inferno.

"Also, Adam? You need to *really* pay attention," Hans grimly told him as the High Mageous simply ignored the volcano he had made and created more hazards. "Did you see how fast that happened? If you *think* something is coming, by the *abyss,* you *scream* it. We then make like sheep and get the *flock* out of there."

Chapter Thirty-nine

I was deep in meditation. My entire focus was at such a depth in my soul that I was having trouble extricating my thoughts from my being. I was finding what I needed, the concept I would model my soul around which would encompass all that my **law** had to offer. I had rejected everything that came to mind for what felt like weeks on end to my time-ignoring psyche. Now though... I think I had found it. The idea had come from exploring my cultivation technique, of all things. As I stared at the swirling galaxies that surrounded me, I realized that they may as well have been representations of what I already saw when I looked up at the night sky.

Where was I? I was in a place that *already* embodied **Acme**, a place that *already* had everything I needed. My inner soul space, therefore, would need to be a place where every other **law** could be represented in full. Only then could my inner self hope to reach **Acme**, the culmination of all other **laws**. Whew. That was wordy. In simple terms, my inner world had to be precisely that: a *world.* As I accepted this fact, a *vast* influx of Mana poured through my connection with **Acme**, and Essence emptied in from the area surrounding my physical Core. I took this as a good sign, as an acknowledgement of choosing correctly. As I watched, an entire planet was sketched out. My study of the maps in reality obviously impacted my thoughts, as my inner world reflected the outer one.

There were differences, though. Not all of the **laws** were equal, and different sections of the planet seemed to be wavering strangely. It was... it was *time* that was moving differently! I really hope that my irreverent attitude toward time wouldn't make this go poorly. I felt tiny *pops* in my consciousness as the Cores throughout my dungeon that I had been collecting corruption in burst and flooded into me. At first, I was shocked and nearly *sick* when the corruption hit me, *certain* that I was about to have a very bad time. My body had rejected every *hint* of this stuff in the past, after all, but, instead of tainting my cultivation, the corruption flooded into my ethereal world and began infusing the stones, water, light... *everything*. As more corruption entered me, my world became more robust - more *real*.

I didn't know what to do, and I didn't know what was happening. I had lost control. My collected corruption stopped pouring into me, what I had thought of as abundant Cores were *already* exhausted. A tiny *fraction* - about a half-acre - of the planet seemed solid now. I had just burned through *all* of the corruption I had stored in Cores since the inception of my current collection system. I gulped. This was going to be a long, *long* term project. On the plus side... I could tell that I had fixed the issue I had been having. I could feel that my cultivation path had finally opened up, and the suffocating feeling of 'nowhere to go' was now gone.

I 'blinked' and was once more aware of my surroundings. A feeling of vast emptiness yawning inside of myself caused me to groan with actual pain. I hadn't been this hungry since I was an F-ranked Core staring longingly at moss. The Essence that had been lapping around the base of the Silverwood tree was all used up, and a massive portion of my reservoir was once again empty. My goodness, that had taken a *lot* of power. <Oh, man... Dani, how are things going? What did I miss?>

"Hi, Cal!" Dani's voice perked me right up. She was so great. "Not too much going on in here, just playing with Grace."

I looked at the room they were in, taken aback by the twisted walls, demolished adventurers, and remnants of powerful

Mana usage. <What... um... what sort of games are you playing?>

"We're playing 'protect the Core', and a few adventurers got lost, so... we decided to 'invite' them to the game," Dani cheerfully informed me of the circumstances surrounding the massacre. "One of them got too close to Grace, so I needed to *convert* him."

<Convert him? Did he join Minya's cult?>

"No, I converted him to *corrupted ash.*" Dani giggled as Grace flew back to me and zipped around the Silverwood tree. She landed on one of the branches, and all the silver leaves around her took on a tinge of purple.

<Right. Don't let other people near Grace; message received.> I chuckled nervously. Unlike myself, Dani had full access to *directly* creating and using spells with my Mana. She had recently begun practicing and using it, which both amazed me and made me a *little* afraid of offending her. When I asked her about it, she had told me that in any relationship a healthy respect of your partner was needed. Also, that anyone who tried stealing from us or kidnapping one of us was going to have to figure out a way not to be turned into a torch during their attempt.

"Outside of here, I think that we have reached the necromancer's army. Bob said something about some creatures attacking the dungeon at range. Nothing hit us, though, so... I'm not sure what's going on. I should probably pay more attention, but I've been honing my skills here." Dani didn't seem too worried, which relieved me.

<Well, I certainly can't say anything about paying attention. I don't even know how long I was in meditation. Time is hard for me; I should really install an hourglass or something in here.> I looked at the projection of the battle we were facing,

going silent as I saw charred and smoking landscape. I was pretty sure that had been grasslands until recently. What *exactly* had I been missing out on seeing? <Hey, Dani, I... I think I need to work on this battle. Are you two okay without me here for a while?>

"No problem, Cal. We literally have forever together, a few hours apart here and there won't impact us at all." Dani flew over to Grace, snuggling in next to her on the branch. "It's nap time for her anyway."

<In that case... I'm going to monitor the situation. All the love!> I called as I moved my attention over to where Navigation Bob was allowing the other Bobs to watch the ensuing battle. So far, not too much had happened, at least not in the grand scale of the battle that was going to be playing out. There were tens of thousands of lesser undead, but in reality, they were not the overwhelming portion of the fighting force. The greater undead, the demons, and the necromancers were the *real* core of the troops. The lesser undead were good for tying up fighters and lesser cultivators as well as being used as occupational forces. That is, after an area was conquered, they acted as an army or policing force. Anyone who broke the law... well, they soon joined the police force.

The real threats were the higher undead and demonic controllers of the armies. The undead had no real will of their own; they were mainly hungry husks that were pushed in a general direction or controlled carefully to ensure they didn't turn on their masters. Thanks to the height of the dungeon coupled with our telescopic abilities, we could see the far fringes of the army as well as the closer ranks. We were on the only front that did not have a really *active* war being waged. This conflict spanned nearly thirty miles, and the entire perimeter was filled with flying Essence, Mana, debris, and especially blood.

Blood was everywhere. Some of it was rotting, but there was undoubtedly fresh red blood splashed liberally across the landscape. At this rate, there would be a *moat* of the sanguine fluid around the necromantic horde.

Here I was, powerless to do a single thing to help or absorb any of that power. I was too weak to help people survive this conflict, and I could only hope that the generous rewards and anti-demon weapons I had given out were going to be put to good use. I felt like... a group buffer, someone who could make the party stronger but was basically useless during actual combat. Oh, celestial, was I a *cleric*? Please no.... but all the signs pointed to yes. Anti-infernal weaponry, giving extra abilities and power to people, sitting back and not being useful... oh *no*! I shook off my melancholy, resolving to change this fact right *now*.

<Bob Prime, we have some work to do.> The Goblin I had called to perked up and walked out of the area to have a private conversation with me.

"What can I do for you, Cal?" Bob had dropped the 'Great Spirit' honorific, and I couldn't tell if I was happy about that or not. I had disliked it at the time, but... now I missed it a little. It reminded me of their arrival in my dungeon. I shuddered in revulsion at the memory. I decided that maybe it was better this way; natural Goblins were *nasty*.

<Bob, how close are we to finishing the changes to the Runescripting?> I fired a question without preamble. <The ley line stuff.>

He thought for a moment, leaning back and forth on his staff. "That's hard to say, Cal. We've used Mana in the past to power the Runes, but I haven't been able to find a good method of rejecting the corruption that would be pulled into you. In all other cases, when the Cores we are using input their Mana, they swiftly turn into corruption Cores. Their link to the Runes is nearly impossible to break, and even if they are removed from the Runes, there is a permanent sympathetic link and power flows through them and *into* them until they are destroyed either manually or by the energetic density. I am just... I'm not sure if this is a good idea. Ever. No matter *what* changes we make to the Runes."

How *very* interesting. <So what you are saying is that I would get a huge amount of Essence and corruption regularly from that point onward?>

"*Exactly*, Cal! I am relieved to hear that you see just how terrible of an idea this is." Bob Prime smiled and turned to go watch the screens again.

<This is exactly what I needed to hear. Let's *do* this!> My words halted Bob in his tracks, and when he finally stopped twitching, he looked up at me with a smile and asked a dangerous question.

"Have you talked to Dani about your plans for all of this?"

CHAPTER FORTY

"Everyone! Prepare yourselves!" a High Mageous was shouting at the cultivators that were already present on Mountaindale as well as the troops pouring through the portal to augment their combat power. The portal had been locked as 'one-way' until the end of the conflict. At this point, there was no escape; survival was the only option for leaving this place. "If you do not yet have access to flight or a flight-like ability, you will be deposited on the ground. Depending on the Mage setting you down, the ride might be rough. As soon as you land, get into a formation. You will only have a few moments to set up a defensive perimeter before getting swarmed by the creatures waiting below! If you die, please at least try to take a few with you."

"This guy should be a motivational speaker, hey, Dale?" Hans poked Dale in the side, trying to tickle a reaction out of the pale-faced youth.

"So what should we do after all of this?" Tom spoke with a wide smile. "I am thinking of visiting an exotic location, perhaps finding a secluded island and being revered as a god by the local women."

"Sounds like fun." Adam smiled and looked over at Rose, who was not paying attention to the conversation. "Any plans, Rose?"

"Hum? Oh, aim for the head, I guess," she responded somewhat distractedly.

"I... I meant after the fight?" Adam stammered as she turned her attention to him.

"Oh." She was silent for a bit. "Get some dinner I guess? One way or the other, I don't see this war lasting too long. There is a Mana haze here that screams 'the most powerful people in the world are present' to me. So... I'd say dinner time is an accurate guess-timate."

"A what, now?" Tom interjected. "I am unfamiliar with this word."

"Guess-timate." Rose cocked her head to the side. "A guess, an estimate. A guess-timate."

"Why do people have to keep changing the language with weird mash-ups?" Tom grumbled. "I have a hard enough time with it as it is normally; there are just too many consonants. Sounds like a bunch of snakes hissing at each other."

The Mage that had been speaking earlier began shouting again. "First groups! Lifting off in three... two... go!" Dale's party sucked in a deep breath as they were suddenly accelerated forward. To Dale, it felt like he was a ninety kilogram projectile being launched from a trebuchet to a point over three hundred meters away. In reality, their landing point was nearly a half kilometer away if the descent were included. The only reason the sudden velocity didn't damage anyone was that they were accelerated as a single piece, a unit, not grabbed and tossed. It was hard to describe the difference, but there was a notable one.

Dale watched as the ground approached at a rapid pace. The unspeakable abominations that were the undead - including actual Abominations - began turning toward the living flesh that was falling from the sky like a treat thrown to a hungry dog. Dale's section was not the first to touch down; that dubious honor went to a contingent of earth Mages who prepared their landing point and threw up some rudimentary defenses to slow the advancing nightmare fuel. From his current vantage, it looked like a group landed like a meteor and formed a crater when, in reality, they fell with prepared spells and walls sprang up around them. Either way, it was amazing to watch what he hoped to be able to soon accomplish under his own power. They landed not-exactly-gently within the sudden protections and hurried to the chest-level barricades to help hold back the flood of rotting flesh.

Moments later, Dale was fighting against zombies. He lashed out with his fist, and the skull of the first creature broke with a squishy *thud.* Dale was taken aback by the ease his first foe was dispatched, but another slightly alarming component was the infernal Essence that was absorbed by his gauntlet and absorbed into his Core. He was momentarily distracted, concerned that a necromancer would somehow gain a hold on him through his usage of his gauntlets, but he was forced to recover quickly. The dead were not waiting for him to resolve his internal crisis. Besides, after a moment, he could feel the corruption Core in his chest separate out the taint and suck it into itself. He should have nothing to fear from fighting as usual.

Right, left, right, left. Dale's punches were nearly as regular as a drum beat playing a marching cadence as he beat down the undead rushing at him. There were already bodies and skeletons piling up around the basic fortifications. Their opponents were starting to use the rotting corpses as a platform to jump at them or to gain the high ground and swing at them from above. Fire and celestial cultivators were working overtime in an attempt to destroy or consecrate the bodies so that the approaching Abominations couldn't pull them into themselves and become stronger.

Dale could only continue to punch, kick, and dodge. Sometimes he wished he had a longer range weapon, but his body was more durable at this point than many of the items he could buy, and his gauntlets were Inscribed and effective. Dale took a deep breath as he eyed the mounds of flesh that were shambling to their location. They didn't bother to avoid the other undead as they traveled, simply crushing them with each step and slurping up their broken forms to add to their own mass. The first of them reached the line of consecrated bodies, absorbing them and continuing forward. Having expected a different outcome, Dale debated reaching for a Core to throw an enhanced attack at the creature. It was *too close* and was standing eight feet taller than him at this point. It hesitated for the first time, quivering as the consecrated bodies deposited their payload of celestial Essence directly into the greater undead.

Blisters began forming on it, turning into weeping sores in seconds as the Abomination worked to expel the consecrated flesh and bone. It did, finally, needing to sacrifice a more substantial chunk of its body in order to package and regurgitate the damaging 'food' it had swallowed. A large sack of meat and bones fell out of the humanoid, looking for all the world like it was defecating on the battlefield. The smell of the creature didn't help either, as the rotting meat already smelled worse than - *boom.* A pillar of holy light seemed to fall from the heavens, and the squatting Abomination disintegrated, the ashes flowing upward and vanishing.

"Looks like the Mages finally woke up." Hans panted as he lashed out with his daggers yet again. Dale didn't know what he was attacking at first, then saw a few zombies drop a half dozen feet from them. He must be using his wind affinity to increase the range of his attacks. Probably because... Dale looked at Hans. Yup. Perfectly clean still.

"Your reluctance to get filthy in combat is *song worthy*, Hans!" Dale called over, breaking the tension and putting smiles back on the faces of his friends.

"Don't you *dare*! Oh, and *I'm* sorry that I don't want rotten meat and blood on me. I'm no Mage; I can still get sick from this nasty stuff." Hans slashed the air, cutting deep into a pair of sprinting ghouls. "Ew, I hate the running ones. They splash when you cut them down."

Everyone else in earshot was surreptitiously trying to clean particles off their hands or faces as Hans' words registered. Most people here hadn't lived through the last necromantic war, but the tales of disease and pestilence from that time were nearly as legendary as the war itself. Everyone winced as screams tore through the air behind them; an Abomination had broken through the defenses and was able to smash a hole through the defenders, swelling in size as fresh meat and blood empowered and emboldened it. A Mage sent it flying away from the area to impact a swarm of skeletons that were using the breach as a gateway.

"Someone close that hole! Where is the Mage that was supposed to be watching this area? Stop sitting on your thumbs and get *fighting*! Now is not the time to be *conserving Mana*!" Dale looked at the unknown person shouting orders, trying to figure out the chain of command here.

"We need to move," Adam calmly stated to the group. "Not just us five, *all* of us. I am seeing a ripple in the area, the kind that washes through time when a cataclysmic event occurs. I'd say we have less than two minutes to get away from this area."

Hans' eyes widened, then narrowed. "Guild members! I am invoking martial clause twenty-five bravo! We need to shift our position a hundred-"

"Two hundred, at the minimum," Adam interrupted quietly.

"Two hundred and fifty meters south, *now*!" Hans easily incorporated the new information and disseminated it.

There were wide eyes all around as people were forced to move. A Mage stepped forward and parted the bodies, making a corridor of death that the formation charged through. The Mage then caught up and sprinted alongside Hans with furious eyes as they moved, speaking quietly, "If you *flippantly* made us leave a fortified position in the middle of a war, I will ensure that you pay for every life we lose. I don't know *how* you have the authority to declare a state of emergency in the middle of a battlefield-"

"That's fine, but in that case, you'd *better* make sure my team gets the accolades for saving every single person in the company that *survives* when we are done here," Hans returned darkly, his serious tone making the Mage raise a brow and go silent. They both had good reason for their concerns, as the undead collapsed upon them from all sides now. Shambling zombies, sprinting ghouls, clacking skeletons, and moaning Abominations did their *very* best to grow the numbers of the dead. In too many cases, they succeeded. Anyone below the C-ranks had a difficult time against anything but the zombies or skeletons, and fighting the Abominations was reserved almost exclusively for Mages.

When they reached their new position, the fighters all needed to work together to push the dead far enough for the earth affinity cultivators to raise solid barricades again. The seconds ticked by, and tempers started to rise against Hans as nothing happened to their old position. The entire fighting force of the Guild that had deployed in the area were well-spaced out so that a single blow couldn't eradicate them, but now, they were cut off from any *chance* of reinforcements. Before their anger could boil over, a Tomb Lord fell out of the sky and impacted their old position so hard that the flesh within its armor turned to paste.

Barry stood solidly in the air above it, exhaling a green mist that washed over everything in the area. A word from the midst of the cloud in front of him shattered the very air, and thunder was heard as all the mass in that section was converted into a hand-sized sphere of energy. The thunder was generated from air rushing to refill the empty space as the green cloud returned to Barry's body. The sphere of power started moving toward him as well, but as he caught it, the S-ranker snorted and tossed the silver orb deep into the ranks of the dead. There was a detonation nearly a half mile away as the energies contained in the globe were released, and the shockwave knocked over roughly half of the undead. Then Barry vanished, returning to do battle in the air at speeds that lower ranks simply couldn't even *see*.

The Mage next to Hans glanced over, taking a deep breath. Hans spoke first, "I got it, and we are all set here. Same team, right? Also, we'll take the bonus in gold, please. So you know, this is the man that was doing the scrying for us." He jerked his head at Adam and continued to fight.

Adam nodded at the Mage. "Don't worry too much; I'll keep an eye out."

"Please do. I am granting you the same authority *he* used to get us here; if you see something, make sure we *all* hear it." With that, the Mage hopped into the air and went to take his position. The war was nowhere close to being over, and there was no time to waste.

CHAPTER FORTY-ONE

An hour later, Dale was *brimming* with energy. He cheerfully smashed yet *another* skull in the endless tide, absorbing the small amount of Essence that was keeping the corpse moving. The people around him, fighting just as hard as he was, were forced to switch out as they ran low on stamina and Essence. Dale was certain that he should be sore or weary, but his powerful aura, as well as his new ranking, kept him from falling out of the line like the others. Hans eventually came over and gripped his arm, pulling him into the center.

"I know you *feel* fine, but you need to take a break or the mental stress might break you. Battle trances can be really hard to break out of, and if the rumors are true, you have a bad history with overdoing it in trances." Hans forced him to sit and drink some water, and the ice-cold thrill as the liquid hit his stomach made him remember that he was starving. Then he nearly fell asleep in seconds as the adrenaline wore off. Having enhanced his *entire* body meant that the chemicals keeping him going also had a more powerful effect. Dale's hands shook, and then he *actually* fell asleep in the middle of a battle.

He was shaken awake fifteen minutes later to the unpleasant sight of Tom urinating a few feet from his head. He was upright in a second as the others laughed. Rose shrugged at him while chuckling. "Well, we couldn't use the outer edge as the latrine. A zombie would have bit that off of him."

The others winced at the visual, and she rolled her eyes. "Seriously? We are in the middle of a war where... you know what, forget it. Dale, we could use you on the line with us again; we need to cycle back in."

"That's fine. I'm feeling refreshed even if my masculinity is feeling a *little* threatened right now." Dale's eyes flicked to Tom as he sighed in loud relief.

"Ahh, that's the good stuff. I try to stay hydrated, and this is the price. Fear not, Dale. Most men would be having insecurities right now." Tom grinned as Rose's cheeks went pink and Hans rolled his eyes.

"Just wait until the C-ranks, Tom," Hans told him. "You can get up to an inch extra each rank. Just ask Dale."

Dale nodded with a straight face. "If anything, Tom, I was feeling a little bad for you."

Tom's hands twitched, as though he were hoping to take their necks and *squeeze*. "The two of you are not funny. If these were true facts, there would not be a man alive who didn't do his utmost to enter the C-ranks."

"Well, you got me there." Dale smiled as they tapped a few people, signaling that they should switch. The punching began anew, and Dale was soon absorbing infernal Essence once again. His Core did separate it, but he was starting to feel a little ill after collecting the mess of filthy energy. Remembering what Artorian had taught him, Dale shifted the output of his auric Essence and carefully shifted to an aura of starlight. There was still a regenerative property to this version, though it was far less pronounced than what he had been using. The real difference became apparent as he landed a punch and the skeleton's skull not only broke as usual but *melted* for a few seconds after landing on the ground.

"Well, *that's* new. I like it," Hans commented as the bone bubbled and popped. Dale would have responded, but the downside to his aura had just become apparent. The dead were staring at him, and his aura was painting a beacon of hate for them to target. Dale had been dealing with waves of zombies and skeletons, but now there were *ghouls* sprinting at him as well. The long-clawed undead were faster, smarter, and overall more deadly than their lesser counterparts, even though they were lesser undead themselves. If a comparison had to be made, ghouls fought in a manner similar to rogue-types. They could deal a tremendous amount of damage in a short amount of time with their teeth and claws, using their enhanced strength to tear off chunks of meat.

Dale wasn't overly concerned about these fiends - as his armor would prevent their main weapons from cutting into him - but the mass of dead now focused on him was still unnerving. *Thud, thud, thud.* Dale's fists beat out a metronome, and bodies began to pile up in front of him. Unbidden, his armor unrolled itself, ensuring that only the *smallest* sliver was left open for his vision. An arrow took a jumping ghoul in the eye socket as it dove at Dale, too late to arrest the undead's momentum as it tackled the man from the side and brought him to the ground. It began sizzling and melted onto him as his aura interacted with it, but by then, more ghouls and zombies were coming through the slight opening in the lines.

The people that had been resting were forced to join in the battle and beat back the encroaching horde. As the last were cleaned up and tossed out of the ring of warriors, Dale had to grip the arm of someone who assumed he was dead and was trying to throw him as well. This had the unfortunate side effect of having the man scream like he was being murdered, and Dale very nearly *was* slain as his friends came to 'rescue' the man. Dale waved his arms and shouted that he was alive, but the man still fell back mumbling, "You were dead!"

"I was never *dead*; I was just covered in bodies!"

He shook his head violently while whimpering, "Dead things should *stay* dead!"

"I *wasn't dead*!" Dale yelled as the man stumbled away.

Hans pulled Dale back into his position before it could be overrun again, pausing as the blood splatter that had managed to land on him boiled and vanished into vapor from Dale's aura. "Oh, I like that a *lot*. I think it'd be worth opening some affinity channels if I can get an instant bloodstain remover. Listen, Dale, some people handle the stresses of combat easier than others. Look at Adam, he's barely freaking out. Tom is laughing and coating himself with as much gore as he can; he's going to need a healer after this. Rose is more of a 'fire and forget' sort of person, so she seems fine. That guy was in shock, pretty obviously. You get that sometimes."

"Tom! Get closer to me here, would you?" Dale called to the overly large Barbarian. "You are going to get a nasty infection if you keep doing what you are doing!"

Tom kept laughing and swinging his hammers, crushing undead as he stepped a few feet closer to Dale. Black blood began to boil off the redhead, revealing bright red bulging arms. Tom's arms were *hot* from constant use, and if he were not in a battle frenzy, he would have been in serious pain from his strained and damaged muscles. Dale's aura began to sink into the man's skin, and the tight muscles relaxed and began to heal at a faster-than-natural rate. It wasn't what he truly needed - a cleric - but it kept the man from suffering possibly permanent damage to his limbs. It also allowed Tom to last longer before he would need another rest.

Tom's commitment to the battle, even at the expense of what must be *severe* pain, helped Dale stay grounded and focused even though the dead began surging against their lines harder. Heavily armored Death Knights started joining in against the Guild, their hard-to-damage forms keeping the attention of the cultivators while standard units used them as a distraction to pile onto the living and bring them down. The Death Knights weren't hindered by the stone barricades, simply smashing through them when they charged with ground-shaking steps. Defensive Mages reinforced the walls quickly, and the next few Death Knights bounced off or flipped over the chest-high walls, becoming easy prey if the humans were able to take advantage of their position.

The death toll began to build as more and more Guild members fell and joined the opposing forces. A cleric-Mage in the center of their group flew into the air, hands clasped before him in supplication. He shouted to the sky and released an immense wave of golden Mana that rolled over their formation and into the undead surrounding them. The Mage's eyes rolled back into his head, and he fell out of the sky, luckily caught by his team waiting below. The undead who were caught in the light dropped like puppets with their strings cut, instantly consecrated and banished from the world.

"What is going on? Why have they gotten so much more aggressive?" Rose shouted, her ears ringing from the blast of power.

"I don't know!" Dale shouted back, his ears equally impacted by the thunderous noise. There had been a strange dichotomy of pain and pleasure as the healing energy washed over them, but the noise had followed the light and so was the most recent thing to affect them. As the sounds of the battlefield started to resurface, they quickly learned why everything was starting to go downhill. Walking across the small gap were three smiling demons. Before the dead closed around their path, Dale also saw a few men in purple and black robes. Not only demons then; the necromancers themselves had arrived to wipe them out.

Chapter Forty-Two

"Why *hello* there, filthy mortals." The demon's voice was difficult to listen to. The intonation was pleasant enough, but worms of infernal Essence seemed to crawl across the skin and ears of everyone present. "Our Master has authorized us to give you a chance to flee. Take it, and be gone from this area. Quit the field, leave the war, run away like a scared little *Forest Elf*! Pretty please, run in terror. Flee before us, and show to the world that the so-called 'Adventurers' Guild' will always leave them to their fate in order to save themselves!"

It was evident that the creature was intentionally taunting them. It had no interest in letting them leave, but it had to follow its orders even if it only *technically* did so. While everyone else stood frozen, including the Mages, Rose took the initiative and answered for the Guild. She whipped out an arrow from a side quiver, sending it speeding at the demon as a flashing streak of silver. The demon casually held up a hand and let it *thunk* into its palm.

"Oh, look, she used *silver*. How *cute*." The demon's casual tone vanished as the banishing Rune on the tip of the arrow took effect. "What? You *filthy-*" He vanished with a flare of infernal and fire Essence. The Guild members cheered wildly as the other demons stared toward them with fury - and *maybe* just a tinge of fear - outlined on their faces. Then, in sync, they squinted and ordered the dead to attack instead. Creatures that had been slow and unfocused in their attacks before were now being directly controlled; they had become fast and coordinated. The necromancers empowered them with bolts of infernal Essence, and the demons directed dozens of attacks at once.

Before this point, only their overwhelming numbers were a serious concern. Now, even the lowest powered minion was a strong and deadly threat by itself. If a bolt of dark power connected to a skeleton, they would be wreathed in dark flames and subtly change. Their boney fingers would sharpen, and a hint of the deepest darkness would appear in their joints and along their bones. Dale punched one in the face, and instead of the skull shattering, it only *cracked.* Putting a bit more effort into it, he lashed out again, and the entire skull was blown into fragments that knocked over a few beings that had been behind his target. A more substantial portion of infernal Essence was sucked into him, and he took a sharp breath as it reached his Core.

"I'd say somewhere *between* the strength of those two strikes, Dale," Hans quipped easily while never failing to dispatch zombies and ghouls that were coming at him. For some reason, his ranged attacks tended to glance off the skulls of the skeletons now. That was fine because Tom was happily smashing skulls left and right with his ingot hammers and powerful arms but was having trouble with the more meaty heads of the zombies. Rose ran out of regular arrows and had to leave her position to stand in line to get a fresh crate of them transferred to her bag from a Guild supplier.

Dale rolled his eyes, not that Hans could see it. "I figured that out, thanks, *Hans.*"

"Always happy to teach the newest generation how to do things properly!" Hans flipped the dagger in his hand, using the hardened pommel to smash a skull that was clattering at him. "I don't mind the skellies getting close, I suppose. They aren't very leaky."

As they were bantering, a Mage lifted out of their group in preparation of using a large-scale spell. As her hands began forming symbols, a demon sprinted across the combat area and *leaped*, snatching her out of the air like a dog catching a ball. She screamed once, a sharp cry that made everyone wince as she vanished among the dead. Someone else shouted an order, "No more flying!"

"What? *Why*?" Dale muttered sarcastically as he began increasing the pace of his attacks. After he had given himself a bit of breathing room, he pulled two small items out of his bag. They were the ends of the tendrils of Assimilators, specifically the Runes for fire and celestial projection. Holding a Core in each palm, Dale began directing Essence through his corruption Cores and gauntlets into the organic Runes. With a grunt, he crossed the Runes and a wash of celestial-enhanced fire sprayed from him in a cone. This naturally drew attention, and as the flame began to sputter out, Dale saw a black-eyed demon sprinting at him with a malicious grin. As it closed in, sure of its kill, Dale smiled in return. The demon saw his expression shift and tried to react, but for *once,* Dale was faster.

The Cores in his palms shattered, and Dale grasped the entirety of the expanding Essence and directed it through the Runes. This time the fire was almost a *solid* as it projected outward, obliterating the dead it touched and coating the demon in holy fire. It screamed an unearthly *buzzing* scream as the flame stuck to it and seemed to draw ever more flame to itself. Almost as a mercy but more in terms of practicality, Hans whipped a spike at the being. This was a spike pulled from Manny the Manticore and was an effective banishing device. With a *pop* and a blast of Essence, the entity vanished, taking the flames and spike with it.

The organic Runes in Dale's hands crumbled to ash, scattering in the wind before they ever touched the ground. He took a moment to slap Hans' outstretched hand, grinning as he did so. "Two down, one to go?"

"They can summon more, so what we really need to do is take down the necros," Adam interjected quietly, scanning the horizon for hints of danger. There were massive exchanges of power in the distance as the powerful members of the armies clashed, but since they were alive and still here, it appeared that there wasn't a decisive victor yet. This made Dale wonder exactly *how* powerful The Master was. He knew there were powerful people in his army, but if the might of the *entire world* was being fought to a standstill right now...

"Son of a... an S-ranker is making a move in the area!" one of their remaining cleric-Mages shouted. "The dead are moving!"

"No kidding, moron!" someone jeered to a round of chuckles. "We've been fighting them all afternoon!"

"Not the ones still *standing*, fool! The ones we've been destroying!" the Cleric bellowed with a high-pitched tone. Indeed, the dead that they had dismantled were being pulled away by an invisible force, shattered bones and rotting flesh that had been ignored to this point were yanked deep into the enemy forces. A towering being began to take shape, the decaying materials flowing up and connecting together. Bones collected over each other. Skin, muscle, and sinew lashed the gargantuan bones into single chunks, and a towering form took shape.

"Someone is making a Legion Dreadnought Bone Lord!" Dale heard this shout and almost laughed despite the seriousness of the tone.

"Seriously, pick a name. Am I right, Hans?" He looked over with humor in his eyes, but Hans was staring at the towering creature that was forming and gasping deep breaths. "Hans? *Hans*!"

Hans started moving again, jerkily slashing and stabbing. He didn't answer Dale, instead looking over at Adam. "Anything? What do you think?"

"Too nebulous of a threat," Adam responded darkly. "*Everywhere* is threatened right now. I can't get a read on where it will go, and nowhere within leagues will actually be *safe*."

"Talk to me, please! How worried should we be? Please explain what that is!" Dale barked at the two, who simply changed the scope of their conversation to include him.

Hans explained the nomenclature as quickly as he could, "Bone Lord, fairly obvious. Bigass undead Golem made mostly of bone. Dreadnought, heavily armored and *really* hard to stop, does a lot of damage. Not as hard to stop as a Juggernaut-classed one, but it is reinforced with Spiritual energy so that point is basically moot. Legion type: this means that there is a demon bound to each limb that can control it independently and one *more powerful* demon controlling and coordinating the entire body as a whole. If that thing comes at us without us having S-ranked support, we die. I'd just go ahead and be *very* nervous, Dale."

"What can we do about it?" Dale was hoping for anything but the answer he got in reply.

"Hope it doesn't come after us and try to run away if it does?" Hans' speech was slowing, so Dale nodded and got back to his own fight.

"In that case, all we can do is continue, right? Let's trust that our people will recognize the threat and take care of it before it becomes an issue for us." Dale's words flowed evenly and powerfully, raising the spirits of the others around him. Their morale, that is. Not some kind of phantasm. He wasn't a necromancer.

"It's forming a weapon," Adam stated almost blandly as his eyes stared unblinkingly at the monstrosity.

"Let me guess, a scythe, right?" Tom laughed as eyes turned toward him. "These sorts of things always have a scythe in the stories!"

Adam shook his head, looking like he was going to be sick. "No, it looks like it will be using something similar to a cat o' nine tails with ends similar to a morningstar. This is bad. This is *really* bad."

"What's the matter, Adam? How does this get *worse*?" Rose shouted over the growing sounds of terror in their group of Guild members.

Clearing his throat, Adam had to swallow before speaking in a squeaky voice, "Four legs, three arms, three weapons. Those weapons also have an entity bound to them. There are *eleven* powerful demons in that thing. This thing has to be *at least* SS-rank. It has to be a personal summon of The Master."

CHAPTER FORTY-THREE

<Kind of a nice updraft coming from the battlefield down there. Plenty of Essence and Mana drifting up too, barely even have to keep Mountaindale flying around.> Navigation Bob didn't respond with more than a grunt, keeping his eyes and limbs in constant motion as he made subtle changes to our flight trajectory. <Yes sir-*ry*! Beautiful day for a war.>

"Cal, now is not the time for you to be messing around and distracting Bob!" Dani chided me sharply. I didn't hold it against her; she was really nervous about the changes that I was making against everyone else's recommendation. "You should be *triple* checking every last Rune, making sure that you have done plenty of research on the possible side effects, and-"

<It's all been done, Dani,> I gently interrupted the ranting Wisp. <At this point, there is nothing to do but to make it happen. You *know* me; I wouldn't do this if I had even an *inkling* that I would be making the wrong choice, Dani. I really think that, at this point, there is no other option for my advancement, Dani. If we want to grow, if we want to live without fear, we need to fight against our instincts of self-preservation and *change* what would otherwise be our destiny. Dani, I don't want us to be *mediocre*, Dani. You don't want that for us either.>

"If you say my name in a soothing tone *one* more time, I'm going to throw something at you." She growled deeply, making me and the Bobs in the area laugh.

<Fair enough, my bad!> I chortled while checking the Runes *one* more time just to appease her. Looky there! No changes, still perfect. <Everything looks good on my end. Is everyone ready? Nav Bob, you have control of the flight? Bob

Prime you have the dungeon respawners all good to go? Loot generators?>

“We are all set... Great Spirit.” Bob Prime spoke morosely, which may have set me off a little.

<Hey, I’m going to be right here! I’ll be fine. This is going to be beneficial to all of us! Stop acting like I’m going to break; that isn’t even a valid concern.> There were half-hearted smiles and a smattering of false cheer around the room. Ugh. Bunch of whiners. <Alright, here we go! I’ll do the honors myself if that is fine with everyone.>

The stone around me swiftly vanished into my influence, removing the hill and exposing my Core and thousands of roots from the Silverwood tree. I watched with just a *twinge* of regret as my puddle of Essence splashed to the now-flat ground, leaving me totally dry for one of the very few times in my life. I was still held up by a small pillar of stone, looking for all the world like a stereotypical Mage’s staff. Pfft. They *wish* they had something as awesome as me on their weapons; though I’d make sure to be the most cursed item *ever*. The pillar shrank away, leaving me only with a thin band of metal supporting me in the air. It wasn’t actually a metal ring; it was two different metals set to spring apart and drop me through the tiny portal below me in case of emergency. Sometimes simple means are still the best means.

The Runescripted stone flowed across my floor, which would have been an impressive feat if there were anyone carrying it. No need for that here; in here it was just another chunk of area under my control. I lowered the stone that was already around me, the Runescript that collected Essence, and set the new section in its place. The original still functioned correctly and would even disperse the power to me just as easily, so there was no issue with using this new setup. I shifted everything around so that I was comfortable and took one last look at my surroundings.

My army of silver-clad Goblins stood in formation, Dani was flying around nervously while Grace followed, roots were everywhere... this is why I needed to become better, stronger, more powerful, so that I could protect all of *them.* Sure, a not-so-small part of me wanted to grab power just to *have* power, but what I was seeing right now was my drive, my motivating factor. I re-formed the hill around me, which I'm sure was a relief to the Silverwood tree. This was the first time the Goblins had ever seen my actual Core, and they were acting entirely too reverent. <Someone tell them to keep an eye out like they are supposed to be doing, please?>

The Goblins in the ranks snapped to attention, glaring around like someone had tricked them into sneaking a peek. I chuckled and let the metal holding me sink downward. Now, I was still suspended in the air but was also in the center of the Runescripting. I was about to become the power source as *well* as the receiver of all the power and corruption that would move through here. With a deep sound of inhalation - since I didn't actually breathe - I connected my Mana directly with the activation sequence of the incredibly dense Runescripting.

Power began to flow out of me, moving along the lines of precious metals, corruption-transference minerals, logic gates, gemstones... if you could see it, the activation was a beautiful sight to behold. I tried not to get bored, but I had expected something like what had happened in the past. Boom! Power flows like crazy, instant results! I was getting spoiled. As the last portion of the new Runescript was activated using my **Acme** Mana, my literal worldview began to expand and not in an existential way. As my Mana began to filter through the myriad of powerfully scripted Runes that formed the ley lines, I could *see* the area that the ley lines moved through in a way similar to the influence of my dungeon.

I could also get a hazy view of the areas the ley lines weren't directly impacting. All of this information was just too much for my mind to process, so I needed to follow a single point at a time to really *understand* what I was seeing. I could describe everything about it, the earth, minerals, underwater rivers, and the ocean... but what I was able to understand and comprehend in a moment was simply too much to voice. It was also... hard to *hold* all of that information at once, and so I funneled it into my soul space. The concepts, the design of things, the very fabric of the world's surface... all of that was grabbed by the model inside of my soul which subtly altered *everything*.

The flaws, the deep mysteries hidden from view, the fantastic sights, it was all replicated. At least, it was reproduced in the same way an artist might replicate their sight with a pencil. Everything was mutable and could be changed for now. I had a feeling that this may not hold true if I 'solidified' these sketches with corruption. My thoughts were jerked out of myself as I felt a sudden strain. The final few ley lines already in place were now fully empowered with a thin layer of my Mana. I was drained beyond belief, but the connection to the world was worth it. There were a few... let's call them *holes,* in the lines that we hadn't noticed on the map, but once I had restored my Mana, I should be able to simply *shatter* whatever was blocking me in those spaces.

Now came the easy part, depending on how I looked at it. With a single thought, I turned the lines from 'outgoing power' to 'drawing in power'. What do you think happens when a universal receiver and a perfect conductor for all forms of power opens itself to overabundant ambient energy? That instant gratification I had been missing before decided to grace me with its presence. I was forcibly returned to my standard dungeon view as the unbound Essence and Mana in the world started to pour into the ley lines and through them into me.

<Hey, Dani?>

“Cal! You are alright! Did everything go okay? Are you hurt?” Dani zoomed around frantically.

<Dani!>

“What, Cal!” she practically shouted at me.

<You remember a long time ago when I talked about making a giant Rune to draw in all the Essence of my dungeon?>

“...Yes?”

<I did one better. What would you say about getting to the A-ranks before the end of the week?> I smiled at her excellent reaction.

“If it were anyone else, Cal, I would tell them it was a nice dream and to go back to bed.” Dani glowed brightly and happily. “Coming from you, I say... *let’s do this*!”

CHAPTER FORTY-FOUR

<Great! I mean, I can't guarantee that we are going to get that rank, but, you know, I'm glad you approve.> I chuckled as she quivered with barely suppressed rage.

"*Cal*! I'm gonna... *argh*!" she shouted into the air, making a few of the Goblins in the area shake with laughter that they worked *very* hard to hide.

<'Argh'? What are you, a pirate?>

"Why do you need to take *every* serious situation and turn it into a giant joke?" Dani groaned as she settled back onto the Silverwood tree. "Would you like to explain yourself to me? To *us*, I guess?"

Fair enough. It looked like there were plenty of people trying to listen in. I expanded my speech to include them. <Sure. Listen up, friends. I just connected to the surface of the *entire world.* Any minute now, Essence and Mana from around the globe are going to start arriving. I am *out* of Mana right now, but after I regain some, the ley lines we have created will begin to engrain themselves deeper into the world. This will form a feedback loop that will bring in a nearly endless amount of power. So far, we have been fine with the Essence in the area, a bare trickle through the ley lines. I believe this will now be a *flood* of power.>

I could keep speaking endlessly - as I didn't breathe - but I thought it would be best to let them imagine a few grand scenarios on their own. <It can only increase from there. I am hoping to absorb *everything*, but that isn't realistic. It is highly likely that there will be spillover, which means evolutions for the creatures in here, more open space, and more powerful forms for everyone!>

The Goblins cheered softly, needing to remain on task, but the Attendants went *wild*. Clapping their hands, dancing in place, hugging... they *really* wanted to leave their humanity behind. I could help with that. After all, to err is *human*. If I didn't need to have that beaten out of them, all the better. I hadn't even thought to offer to mutate them; most species tended to have an inherent superiority complex, and the thought of leaving it behind should be abhorrent. Maybe I really *did* get lucky with the people that Minya had gifted me? At least the ambition for power was something I could respect. Perhaps the majority of them simply had no way to get started?

<All of this will take time, but what do we have if not time?> There were a few polite chuckles at this, as all of them were now functionally immortal unless something happened to me. <Right, well, anyone not on duty, make sure to get plenty of rest. We are at war, so... yeah.>

I cut off my words to everyone but Dani, feeling almost shy. I didn't often speak to large crowds. <Was that okay? I didn't go overboard, right?>

"You did fine, Cal. Wow. Who would have guessed that you were a shy public speaker?" Dani teased me lightly. "By the way, holy *roots*! No wonder the Elves have never figured out a way to safely move one of those things; they must be tied to the earth so tightly that it's near impossible to budge, even with earth magic!"

<Oh? Yeah, I guess. We've seen Dwarves chop off the top of a mountain peak before though, so I'm not so sure it only has to do with the ground. I bet that it needs a highly-concentrated place of power to live. I've been watching it ever since it was a seed, ya know. I always see growth spurts after we increase in power or add a new floor. Also, I'm *pretty* sure it is intelligent.> I had projected the last few sentences, and it was

gratifying to see the shining silver leaves above me react slightly. Not enough that a being that relied on eyes could see it happen, but still. I had befuddled a tree. I feel that this was a real accomplishment.

<I *saw* that!> I jokingly taunted the tree. It was doing a better job acting now, and it didn't react to my teasing.

"You saw what, Cal?" Dani seemed worried that I was going insane. She must have been listening to the old rumors.

<Eh. Don't worry about it.> I 'winked' at the tree, or at least I sent the conceptual idea of winking at it. There was another tiny reaction as a single leaf tilted slightly to the left. Real communication between us might prove to be difficult. <Hey, do you hear that?>

"What?" Dani didn't get a chance for a follow-up question as a torrential flood of Essence sprayed into the reservoir below me. The flow of power was so extreme and so *filthy*, that I almost cut off the portal reflexively. I stopped myself and took a deep, calming moment to myself. Four million liters of liquid Essence filled the reservoir to capacity in under a *minute*. I may have made a mistake; I may have overestimated my abilities while underestimating the amount of power that would be coming.

I had only ever used standard Essence or Mana to power the Runes in the ley lines, and filling it with a perfect superconductor in the form of the ultimate type of Mana was giving me... *different* than standard results. Oops. <Dani, you should back away - *Glub glub.*>

Liquid Essence merging with mixed Mana types was squirting in a high-pressure stream through my portal, and in a few seconds, the mass of power had almost reached the ceiling. There was now a column of liquefied energy encasing my tree in a perfect pillar of swirling, crackling candescence. Fortunately, I was held in place, or I would have been floating around the room screaming by now. I had made the drowning noises as a joke, but Dani seemed to be freaking out about it. <I'm fine, sorry, was just having fun! It! Is! Time! To! *Eat*!>

No lungs? No need for air? All that means is that there is no need to slow down when eating! I opened myself entirely to the energies around me, bypassing the need to cultivate properly and simply *swallowing* the power. The hole in my soul expanded by a tiny degree, and the pillar that had surrounded me and my shiny tree became a whirlpool. Oops, looks like a few Goblins died. Lightning had formed as friction caused the air to charge, and it seemed that the silver armor my legion were wearing had been a great path for the lightning to play. Well, we had to learn somehow. The screaming humans were getting on my nerves though.

<Hey! Tree! Help yourself to this power; take what you can get while you can. If you don't eat it, I will!> I watched as the Silverwood tree pretended it couldn't think for another long moment, then it gave in and the leaves shone with a soft silver-and-purple glow. Its trunk became more porous, and I paid careful attention to what forms of Essence and Mana it ate. I couldn't be too sure that this is what it would *always* want, but if I took care to feed it treats it enjoyed, maybe it would open up to me more.

After making my offer, I ignored everything else and focused on draining the power into myself. It was an uphill battle, as more power continuously flowed into the area, but I was making progress. When the glorious food - that is, the mysterious power of the world - was back to a manageable amount and flowing into me and not the room, I took a look at where it was actually going. Diving into my soul space, I took a look at the forming world. I was still absorbing a hundred thousand liters of Essence and Mana every few seconds and adding it in directly, so I found the results to be disappointing. Only a single cubic foot of the world was solidifying per five seconds.

What if I tried to direct the power to turn into air instead of earth for a while? I did so and found that I was fortunate to be incorporeal. A cubic foot of air formed from the convergence of Essence and corruption that was so dense it created *solid* air; solid like a *rock*. What happened next shocked me. Not *actually*, I didn't form lightning, but it was somewhat startling. There was a massive, *explosive*, decompression of air. The ground that it had formed over was blasted apart, and for a half-dozen feet, the earth was churned and tossed around. Well. Oops. Glad I did this now instead of later. Changing the point of air creation, I started in on making an atmosphere for my burgeoning planet. The various corruptions went to their respective areas to sketch out molecules and such - of course - but the Essence to create and solidify them was being fully devoted to making an atmosphere.

I watched as a solid cube of air decompressed and filtered out to fill about a hundred and thirty feet of space. The density wasn't anywhere near high enough to be breathable, but a few weeks at this rate... who knows? I left my soul space and returned to reality, happily telling Dani all of the details. She was impressed and nodded along as I explained everything, or at least, she acted that way.

"Good work, Cal!" Her bright words made me as bubbly as my puddle had been. Oh. Now I'm sad again. "This is really interesting! You have somehow reached 'foundational' cultivation without getting to the A-ranks, though I have to say I don't doubt that will be reached soon."

<Wait, I thought foundational was a type of energy?>

"No, you are thinking 'fundamental' energy. In a sense, though, yes, your foundation is a conceptual source used in the A and S-ranks. You use the concepts and things stored there as images that you can then impose on your Mana, allowing you to reach greater heights. It is rare to find anyone in the A-ranks that is willing to discuss this information, so a lot of this will be trial and error for us. What you are doing now is called 'building a foundation' and has different connotations for different cultivators. It is as varied as the types of Mana themselves."

My goodness, Dani is smart. I should just take a few years and get all the knowledge she has in her head moved into mine.

CHAPTER FORTY-FIVE

I almost feel like I'm cheating. This type of power delivery system is slowly but surely increasing my power, and I'm not having to do much for it. Actually... you know what? No! I *deserve* this. Did anyone else set up a world-spanning power collection array? This is the result of hard work, and I should just reap the benefits of all the effort I had to put in to get to this point without concerning myself with minor details.

I had been playing with my inner world, trying to see if there was anything I should or *could* be doing better. The forming world mirrored the real one, at least superficially, but did I want it to be an *exact* replica? Maybe... maybe not. For instance, the fact that almost all of the landmass was concentrated into a single massive area, followed by the rest of the world being underwater was kind of dull. Once you were past land, it was just blue as far as you can see. Sure, there are volcanic islands, but... I wanted my world to be more interesting.

I spent a few days fiddling with the mechanics of my soul world but didn't really come up with an answer to my restlessness. Dani got my attention with a ping of Essence, and I returned to reality once again. She was impatiently waiting on something, and when I had no idea what to say she made a frustrated noise and jumped into it, "Ugh, I gave you three hours to play with yourself, but you can't just sneak into a dark corner forever. Now, what should we do to help in the war down there?"

<What do you mean?>

"The *war*, Cal. Come on; I know that you didn't forget about-"

<No, not that! I was working on my foundation for *days*, Dani. Three hours? Are you sure?> I was getting excited; I must have a temporal distortion in my world! Did time run faster than in reality?

"Pretty *sure*, Cal." Dani paused a moment and seemed to squint at me. "Are you telling me that you thought you left Grace and me *alone* during a *war* for *three days*? You were *fine* with that?"

<No idea what you are talking about, my sweet firefly. So, the war, huh? What do you think we should do?> My too-casual tone didn't convince her, and I'd have been sweating if it were physically possible.

"Well..." Dani let the word draw out ominously, and I felt physical relief when she allowed the subject to be changed, "we need to figure out a way to do *something*, but you should really look at the battle before we make a final decision."

I watched as a monstrosity formed, finishing its growth at a hundred feet tall and half as wide. The power radiating from the creature was palpable even through the projection I was using, and I gasped as it began to move. Son. Of. A. Biscuit. Then it started doing that infuriating 'I'm way more powerful than you and thus too fast to be seen' thing. It had left the ground, shattering a quarter kilometer of earth with the force needed to counteract gravity. It appeared on the other side of the battlefield, a half dozen brilliantly shining High Elves forming a barrier in front of its descending weapon.

That must be the Elven leadership, the S-rankers that form their top level of government. I winced as the shockwave of the blow reached Mountaindale, causing the entire mountain to tilt dangerously. <I need to either get higher or lower if we are going to survive this!>

"Go down! Their blocking is deflecting the force upward; look at the clouds!" Dani directed my attention to the clouds that had been gathering due to the massive releases of Mana and Essence in the area. A half second after I switched my point of view, the cloud imploded like a pillow punched through a hole in a wall. The gathered power scattered, clearing the sky and allowing the bright light of the sun to wash over the area once again. Yikes. Down it was. We dropped for a moment, just enough to get below the current shockwaves being produced. Really, there was no need for all the screaming coming from the humans on my surface; they landed with hardly *any* broken bones!

The battle between the S-ranked Elves and SS-ranked demon thing would have been over in short order if the Elves were doing anything except defending. To have a minute *chance* at victory, they would need at least ten S-rankers fighting against this thing in perfect synchronization. I wanted it to continuously focus on the Elves and others rushing toward it and ignore me completely. Sadly, Dani didn't seem to agree with my assessment. "How can we help destroy that thing?"

<Dani, I could drop this entire mountain on that, and it would probably brush me off like an annoying fly, turning us to dust as an afterthought! You want me to get involved in *that*?> I turned her attention to the airborne bone demon as infernal fire wreathed its head. The Spiritual energy version of **Malice** Mana - shaped as a flaming skull - flew at the Elves. A few more S-rankers had joined the Elven defenders, and a reinforced barrier took the blow. There was a detonation that hurt my soul to look at, and the shielding power reshaped and deflected the blow. The malicious energy flew away into the sky like a reversed meteor strike, and I was sure it would eventually destroy something up there.

"Well..." Say nothing, say no, say anything but- "yes, I think we should do something."

<Quite frankly, Dani, and I mean this with all the love possible... no.> She scoffed at me, and I kept talking to head off her complaint. <I don't have anything that could damage it, even if I *was* able to figure out where it would be by the time an attack got to it. Drawing its attention can only mean death for us!>

She was quiet, which was always nerve-mangling, and her eventual words didn't fill me with the confidence that she understood my limitations. Apparently, I needed to be less awesome. "If you *do* think of something, just promise that you will join the fight."

<This is unlike you, and I will *not* make that promise.> My decisive and icy answer seemed to startle her. <You are essentially asking me to throw my life away as a distraction to help people I have no affiliation or loyalty to. No. *Our* safety and people come first. If this world is overrun with the dead, then we will go to the sea. If the sea is conquered, we will fly into the sky. If the air is taken, we will strike out and leave this planet behind! But no matter what else happens, I won't put you in danger again.> With that thought in mind, I took a glance at the portal on my surface that connected me to other cities.

The *unguarded* portal that is not currently in use or protected. Nom nom nom. I slid a section of stone away, and the portal dropped into my depths. The stone slid back over its previous location, making it look like the portal was ripped away by something clawed. That should throw them off the trail when they were looking for the culprit if I was not fast enough. When the portal finally stopped moving downward, I studied it with my Mana and dissolved the artifact after removing its active connections. No need to tear a spatial rift through myself. I snorted at the horribly inefficient and shoddy workmanship, disgusted that *this* was the culmination of centuries of gathered human knowledge.

I replicated the portal with a thought, making the exterior appear the same but replacing the internals with Essence instead of Mana. I restored the connections it previously had, and as the portal came to life, it no longer had the infernal whooshing-buzzing sound that had been its trademark in the past. Actually... that might give away my changes. I made a screaming rock, adjusting the Rune on it over and over until it matched the buzzing sound nearly perfectly. I put that in the base of the new portal and pushed it upward, placing the portal back in its old location.

From now on, the portal Mages would *think* they had control and would still be able to change the location it connected to, but I could cut the power off whenever I wanted. *I* would also be able to change the location it linked to. When I made my escape, I wanted it to be a *clean* escape. I didn't need adventurers anymore, but I'd continue building up my dungeon for the simple fact that I still needed to protect myself. Not a lot would change, at least not soon, but at least I was getting *ready* for it!

CHAPTER FORTY-SIX

"Ah, if it isn't my *star* pupil! Get it? *Star* pupil?" Dale flinched at the voice that sounded near his ear. He glanced back to see Artorian studying him. "Yes, good, good. How *impressive* that you were able to create a derivative of my sunlight aura from a simple conversation on the Essence ratios! Your comprehension must be off the charts! C-ranked as well, now? Astounding."

"Headmaster, what brings a nice guy like you to a *dead*-end place like this?" Dale wryly questioned as a lance of light extended from his palm and began melting a Ghoul's head. Artorian nodded approvingly at Dale's formed Essence.

"Hmm, a decent application of light. Good for conserving energy if you can retrieve it, but not great application for this large of a crowd. Allow a demonstration." Artorian nudged a *very* tired Dale out of the way, extending his hand. His palm faced the ground, and his fingers were pressed together to form a wedge. "Now, while energy conservation is good for a long fight like this, what we need right *now* is fewer enemies around us. So, as the average height of the undead is based on the average height of our fallen people, we position our attack thusly and allow the light to move in a line, actually a wave if you pay attention closely."

His extended arm glowed strangely with much less light than Dale expected. He had only thought about increasing the brightness or concentrating the light, so watching Artorian do... *something* was a little confusing. Artorian stepped back and nodded. "That should do it, did you catch all that?"

Dale looked at the unchanged view, frowning skeptically. "I'm sorry to say that I don't see any difference."

"Hmm? Oh, give it a second. They are all propped up due to the high enemy density. Now, this isn't something that works well for extended fights," Dale's jaw dropped as a long, *long* line of undead simply slumped to the ground with partially melted skulls as the others around them moved onward, "but it can grant a reprieve, as you can see, even if the Essence cost is astoundingly high."

"H-how?" Dale sputtered even as he punched another zombie that tried to fill the gap.

"It's a simple usage of light." Artorian cocked his head to the side. "Ah, I see. You are only using the visible spectrum. Well, I guess experience will always win out. I used a combination of focused, high-spectrum light along with the inherent properties of celestial Essence; in other words, I consecrated the portion of the skull that necromancers connect to in order to direct movement. Light naturally travels through certain materials easily, but, as I said, high Essence cost. Also, this works to damage regular people as well, so you can't just fire it off willy-nilly."

"I... I don't understand. Spectrum? What do you mean light goes *through* things? That's just *false*!" Dale was so agitated that he missed an incoming attack and had a boney fist slam into his face. Luckily for him, it was a skeleton that did the attacking, and its hand broke as it contacted Dale's cheek.

"We will have plenty to talk about, it seems." Artorian smiled gently as he joined in the fight more directly. "There is always more to learn, Dale. Again, this is simply a matter of experience. You will be able to do something similar in the near future, I am certain. In the meantime, I notice that you are having some trouble taking down Ghouls before they land an attack on you. Extend your senses and attempt to learn."

Artorian's palm began to glow fiercely, though it also contained the same glowing not-light as the long-range attack he had used previously. "This is the basic form my attacks take, a simple palm strike. Now, I'll walk through all of the instructions you will need to follow my ability. It should synergize well with your current hand-to-hand fighting abilities."

"The user's celestial Essence is condensed, massively, into the legs, spine, arm, and hand. This will prevent you from hurting yourself. Usually. The speed at which you move when completed perfectly *should* cause a 'boom' to occur shortly after the first few steps have been taken. When I arrive at the destination and target, my foot is planted in front of them, forcing all of the velocity and momentum to push forwards and spiral up along my body and into my arm. I then deliver all of that force and energy into the target with a palm strike in a single go. This makes me appear to have arrived at an abrupt standstill while the target proceeds to cease existing as it takes on all of the force and energy I generated." Artorian then followed his words up with action.

Boom. The ground indented where Artorian had been standing, and he appeared a few feet away.

Boom. Shattered shards of bone went flying in all directions.

Boom. Artorian began panting as three Ghouls corkscrewed through the air before dropping to the ground, the remains of their heads following soon after. "As you can–*pant*–see, the perfected form is a bit hard on your body and would normally be used only on enemies much stronger than these. The–*gasp*–Ghouls will be good training targets until you are able to have perfect understanding of this technique."

He then performed a less-potent version, still destroying anything he touched with a simple slap but no longer using the maximum force possible. “Get back in there, Dale; we’re wasting daylight. For me, that’s a *terrible* thing to waste.”

Dale was having trouble reconciling the hookah-smoking, grape-eating, hedonistic headmaster with this undead-obliterating starlight warrior. He got back into the fight, punching vigorously - if somewhat mechanically - as the potent aura coming off Artorian refreshed the muscles and reduced the fatigue of everyone near him. Dale grumbled good-naturedly; he had really thought he had the starlight aura perfected, yet Artorian was able to produce better results without blinding the people around him. Trying out a palm strike, Dale winced as the blow did hardly any damage. There was so much he had yet to learn! This fact made him smile and attack with renewed vigor. He had things to do, and this war was getting in the way!

Hans jumped in the way as a demon reached out of the pressing dead and grasped at Rose. The demon laughed as Hans seized him, switching targets and slowly dragging the Assassin forward. Not knowing what to do, Rose froze in place. Hans shouted loud enough to be heard over the other sounds of combat, “You’re gonna have to make it up to me *later*, Rose, if you know what I mean!”

On instinct, she whipped out an arrow and shot it at Hans’ head. Gasping as she realized what she had done, Rose took a half step forward as Hans effortlessly predicted the incoming arrow and shifted his head to the side. The projectile slid through Hans’ ear and the demon’s cheek. Cackling laughter cut off as black fire washed up and started traveling over the wooden shaft between them. The demon’s eyes were hungry as he was pulled through the rift of banishment, doing his best to take the rogue with him. Hans twisted, tearing a chunk of flesh out of his ear as the arrow and demon vanished entirely.

"I knew you'd scratch me with one of those eventually." Hans grinned at Rose, and a watery smile formed on her lips.

Screams rang out behind the team, and Dale glanced back just in time to see an entire section of their defensive ring collapse. Adam whipped his head around and glared at the demons that were gleefully pummeling fallen warriors, blood spurting as their punches went *through* chests and struck the earth below. Striding toward them, Adam swung his topaz-tipped staff and struck the lead demon in the chest. Contrary to expectations, the previously gleeful demon was *blasted* away with a smoking crater in his chest. Anyone watching felt sick to their stomach; the collision of the opposing Essences had created a small dodecahedron of chaos.

"*Seeds*!" Madame Chandra's voice rang out, and a nearly undetectable ripple of Mana followed along with the Incantation. The churned earth of the battlefield suddenly sprouted greenery, drinking spilled blood and feasting upon rotten flesh to grow into bizarre corruption-mutated plants. "There is a wave of Abominations approaching led by a Tomb Lord! This should slow their growth as they near your group, but *don't touch* the plants! They will eat living flesh as happily as undead tissue!"

Dale watched the spot where she had been floating, as she had vanished abruptly as soon as her speech had finished. This entire battle was confusing to him. There was a literal tier system in place here, where B-rank and below stayed on or near the ground, A-rankers fought in the air above them, and the S-rankers and above were keeping their combat even higher in the sky. He was uncertain why they were even fighting, as soon as one side's S-rankers won, they would crush everyone else. Were they *literally* there as a distraction for the top-ranked fighters?

"*Someone* get rid of that blasted demon!" The hole in their lines had closed, but the final demon from the last wave was now among their forces causing havoc. It was darting back and forth, stabbing, burning, and cackling. Dale turned to help, but Tom was there first.

With a smile on his face, Tom swung the massive hammer in an uppercut at full strength, right as the infernal being turned toward him. Now, lesser demons were considered to be equivalent to B-ranked Mages, but even they were subject to the whims of physics if they were unprepared. When the warhammer cut into the being's chest, the force enhancement Runes activated and attempted to send the creature into orbit.

"Four!" Tom shouted gleefully as he watched the creature shoot upward, only to be caught in the crossfire of A-rankers battling above them. There was a flash of black fire, and the demon was banished. Painfully. "That's the fourth demon I've landed a hit on today!"

"Ah, I was wondering what that meant." Hans slapped the Barbarian on the back and smiled. "Good job, my star pupil!"

Tom - still holding a smile on his face - fell to the ground. Hans could have caught him, but he was so shocked that he didn't even attempt to do so. Hans swooped down and checked the large man's vitals, sighing in relief when he found that he was only unconscious. "Lack of Essence collapse! I *told* him that using that warhammer in extended combat was a bad idea." Hans called to a cleric, who nodded and helped him drag the redhead into the protected center area. Dale's group sighed with relief and got back into position.

"I'm so sorry about this. It's really the only way the rest of us make it," Adam said to no one in particular, gaining looks of concern when he spoke his next words. "Dale, remember...

when you have only one option remaining, you have no options at all."

Just as they refocused on the battle, a flicker appeared in the air in front of Adam and coalesced into a demon with a still-smoking crater in his chest.

"That *hurt*," he hissed into Adam's ear just before backhanding the cleric with all his might. A sickening *crack* rang in Dale's ears as Adam's twisted body was propelled into the lines behind them.

Chapter Forty-Seven

The demon vanished with a furious roar as a knife with a Rune of banishment embedded itself into his side. Hans' face was full of cold fury, obviously wishing he could cause more pain to the vanishing being. Rose ran to check on Adam's condition, but when she pulled back his hood, it was obvious that his neck was broken in multiple areas and his face had been caved in.

"Celestial *feces*," Dale whispered as Rose attempted to straighten their cleric's neck.

"C-c'mon, Adam," Rose whispered softly as she re-aligned his vertebrae. "You're *stuffed* with celestial corruption, a little damage like this shouldn't be an issue for you to fix!"

"Rose," Hans stated quietly. "You need to-"

"*Adam!*" Rose shouted down at the prone man. "Adam, come *on*! You... you can't..."

Once more, Hans' voice reached her ears, "Rose."

She whirled on him furiously. "Don't! Whatever you are *thinking* of saying, just *don't*!"

Hans took another step forward, wrapping her in a tight hug that she struggled to break free from. "Rose, he's g-"

"*No*! Shut your *abyssal* mouth!" Rose stared at Adam, her eyes widening as his skin began to glow with a bright golden light. "Look! Look, he's fixing himself!"

Dale, Hans, and Rose stared at their friend's unmoving body as it began to glow brighter and brighter. Rose's joyous expression faded as his skin started to flake away as a golden energy that flew like sparks, vanishing into the air above them. "*No*!"

Stepping closer to Adam's disintegrating body, Dale put one hand on the cleric's vanishing head and whispered a goodbye. Dale blinked, and in the moment his eyes closed... Adam's body vanished with a blaze of golden light that shot upward. An almighty thundering *boom* echoed across the entire battlefield as the Legion Dreadnought Bone Lord - wrapped in an unholy aurora of hellfire - appeared in the air above them and *bounced* off the layer of hardened celestial Essence released by Adam's body. Instead of landing on the two hundred or so cultivators remaining around Dale, it tumbled through the air and fell amongst the dead. A flood of black flame washed over the area of impact, cleansing the dead for nearly fifty feet and leaving behind a disk of molten glass as the Dreadnaught sprang back into the air to engage the S-ranked beings chasing after it.

Dale watched all of this happen with abject fear holding him in place. The thought that there was a battle happening above them on a scale he couldn't imagine made him sick to his stomach. He looked over the empty robe and clothes left behind by Adam, genuinely feeling the loss of a close friend. He stored the Mithril laced robe, leathers, and finally, the topaz-tipped staff in his bag. They would honor his sacrifice... eventually.

Suddenly feeling a strange *lurch* in the air, all of the cultivators in the area went a little green. The overabundant spent Essence and Mana in the area were no longer wafting upward and around wildly; now the energy was moving slowly but surely to the ground. At first, this seemed to be an incomprehensible technique that someone was using as an attack, but as time went on and nothing seemed to happen, the oddity was ignored.

Twenty minutes later, Rose collapsed, fully spent. Dale didn't blame her; he was getting close as well. Though he was constantly refreshing his Essence, the mental and emotional toll was starting to impact his performance. He had needed to be healed twice so far when a Ghoul or small swarm of undead had been able to bring him down and break a few bones. Just as Dale was considering giving in and trying to switch out, he saw a flash of purple and black. There was a necromancer hiding in a group of the dead! The man was at least twenty paces away, but at that moment, Dale had something approaching a mental break.

Ignoring the shouts of concern, he jumped over the chest-high barricade and sprinted forward. Sprinted was a bit of a misnomer, as the only path forward was by using the heads of the undead below him as stepping stones. A throwing dagger caught him in the back of the knee, causing him to stumble. He knew that dagger; it was Hans'. Dale was furious for a bare second, but then a demon that had jumped for him passed through the space he would have been in if not for the thrown knife.

Turning the stumble into a roll, Dale jumped forward and was suddenly face-to-face with a befuddled necromancer. Utilizing his training to its maximum, Dale delivered a full force punch to the man's slightly open jaw. The Mage stumbled back, not hurt in the slightest but still thrown off and confused by Dale's actions. As he straightened, something *clinked* against his teeth... from the *inside*. His eyes widened a fraction as the pre-crushed beast Core Dale had shoved into his mouth gave way and detonated with all the stored Mana Manny the Manticore had once contained.

Headless, the smoking body of the necromancer toppled to the ground. A hideous *wailing* filled the area as small portals opened and sucked several demons back to their plane of existence. A large portion of the dead surrounding Dale, as well as those around his fellow defenders, simply stopped moving and lifelessly slumped. A ragged cheer came from his group as the Mages stepped out to collect or destroy the fallen bodies before they could be taken by a different necromancer. Dale raced back to his group, a much easier task now that there was open space surrounding them.

More undead were coming, and Dale was sure other necromancers would target them for vengeance... but it was worth it. Seeing the number of undead that had fallen, Dale *knew* that this necromancer had been the one responsible for the assault on them and the death of his friend and teammate. Even if it *had* been murder by proxy, this man was the one controlling the *things* that had done the deed. Feeling triumphant, Dale arrived back to his position, expecting cheers or even nods of appreciation. Instead, only silence greeted him, and nearly everyone was staring at him. No... they were looking *past* him. Dale glanced over his shoulder and paled, then hurried to get behind friendly lines again.

Enormous meat slimes, the swift-travel form of Abominations, were rolling toward them. Once they had gotten close enough to attack, they would take on a form with limbs and smash through the living with extreme prejudice. A Tomb Lord was tromping along toward them as well, quite a way behind the rolling globs of meat. Doing their very best to prepare, the C-rankers formed up while the Mages prepared their most destructive spells.

"Alright, that is quite enough now," the twisted voice was heard by everyone at the same moment, belying the idea that it was simply *spoken*. "While I am enjoying the show, I was asked to end the war, and I'm–*heehee*–going to oblige this wish."

"That voice..." Dale muttered with wide eyes. "That's..."

"I said that was *enough*!" the voice screamed, **Madness** obvious in the tone. The SS-ranked Dreadnought was suddenly visible and torn out of the air. It *smashed* into the ground and bounced back into the air, then did so again and again. Each bounce was half the height as the one previous but also seemed to strike the earth with double the force. By the time the bounces were less than a half inch off the ground, the effect was so strong that the demons were banished from *pure physical force*, something thought impossible to this point.

Only a strangely steaming liquid paste remained of the unholy being when Xenocide appeared in the sky. "Hello, everyone, and thank you for attending my ascension into the Heavenly ranks. How should I put this...? I couldn't have done this without you? Thank you for the centuries of insanity that you propagated? Universal constants are a physical quantity that are generally believed to be both universal in nature and have constant value in time, so there is nothing that you could have done to avoid this outcome?"

He seemed to ponder for a moment, but his form flickered near constantly even while appearing not to move. People all over the field that had tried to use the lull to attack exploded into bloody mist. "Well, no matter. I did need you to do what you did, and now I need you all *not* to exist. Also, I finally have the power to do it! I am about to solve all of the issues our planet has faced for millennia!"

Xenocide's voice rebounded crazily over the entire area, his speech echoing at odd angles. There were times that Dale heard his words before his mouth moved or where bizarre chanting or whispering was laced through the **Madness** cultivator's words. "Hunger, poverty, subjugation of others, inequalities... and finally, *finally*... war! I'm ending it all! You can't thank me later! Ha! Ha-ha! *Haaa-ha-ha*!"

The land the war had been fought on began to churn, and all the blood, juices, bodies, and detritus generated throughout the entire battle began to *shift*. All of it raised off the ground and formed itself into a massive Runescript, a formation... a ritual. A dark, twisted, **Madness**-designed ritual. The S-rankers that had been fighting each other instantly came to an agreement and turned their attention to Xenocide... and a new war began. A war they couldn't win; a war to subdue **Madness**.

Chapter Forty-Eight

<See? It all worked out, Dani!> I cheerfully watched the unfolding drama. <I didn't need to risk my neck, and that extra-armed demon thing was still taken out. Not that I have a neck to risk, but the analogy is valid.>

"Cal, this is an even *worse* outcome! Look at that formation; what do you think that massive Runescript is going to do?" Dani practically shouted at me.

<Hmm. Let me see... I mean, it can't be too bad right? He said he was going to fix all those problems, and I've heard a *lot* of people complaining about them.> I looked over the behemoth, *unbelievably* intricate, spinning Runes. I was actually a little jealous about the apparent ease in which he created them. *I* wanted to be able to do that.

"I'm pretty sure he meant 'fix' those issues in the same way you offered to 'fix' people with interesting bodies," Dani ominously informed me.

<Oh, so you mean he is going to slay anyone who has those issues?> I paused and pondered a long moment. <That makes sense. Too bad, I guess the races of the world had a good run, though.>

"*Cal!*" Dani bawled at me, making me 'wince'.

<What did I do *this* time?> The placement of the Runes suddenly clicked in my mind. <Oh, hey, that's bad. Dani, that gigantic setup is designed to pull two objects together. I have no idea how he is going to power it, though. I'm pretty sure that sucker is designed to latch onto the smaller moon around the planet and pull it close enough to collide with the world. Even a triple S like he claims to be shouldn't be able to generate that kind of power.>

"What if he had the help of *all* the other S-rankers from *all* the races?" Dani's quiet voice interrupted my thoughts.

<I suppose, but I highly doubt that the other S-rankers and such would willingly end their world like that. It is more likely that->

"Cal, not *willingly*, but... look." Dani directed my vision to the projection that every other being on this floor was watching. We were watching a few seconds behind reality, as we needed to slow down the projection to a level of speed we could follow.

Xenocide stood tall as Essence, Mana, and Spiritual energies assaulted his position. Instead of tearing holes in the world or ripping him asunder, Xenocide was able to direct every bit of power into the blood-soaked activation sequence of his floating formation of Runescript. Abandoning long-ranged attacks, the most powerful beings of the respective races worked together to contain all power and attack Xenocide physically.

The deranged cultivator somehow avoided all attacks by moving into strange, confusing or provocative poses. I laughed out loud when he put his index finger to his lips and bent forward, sticking out his butt and lifting a single foot in a sexy pose, somehow just *not* being included in the attacks of *eight* different S-rankers. Dani's glare made my laughter peter off, and I was happy she couldn't see my mirth when I kept from being loud. A human would be rolling on the ground if they were having this much fun!

A glint of something sinister appeared in Xenocide's eyes, and his hand flashed out and caught a startled cultivator. He tossed the S-ranked man as easily as a C-ranker tosses a ball, and the thrown man splattered against the Rune. In an instant, all of his collected energies were drawn into the Runes, and that was when I saw that there was a dungeon Core being used to draw in the power. I zoomed in on the odd-shaped Core and heard a gasp from Dani.

"That's...!" She sounded absolutely sick. "That's *Kantor*! That means... mom..."

<Dani, I'm so sorry.> If Kantor, the Dungeon Core, was being used as a ritual component, that meant he was already gone... as was his bonded Wisp. Another thought tickled my mind even as I tried to comfort Dani: if the Core of an S-ranked dungeon was being used for this Runescript, it would be far more potent than I had originally credited. If this Runescript were fully powered... there would be no stopping it.

<We need to do something,> I demanded decisively. <All troops, prepare to attack. We are going after that ritual. We need to break it, and we need to do it now. Anything that can fight physically, get to a portal. Abandon banishing weapons, and grab any force enhancing or piercing weapons and get moving.>

Creatures began moving, sprinting to follow the orders of the dungeon. Me that is. My orders. I felt sick. They were all *going* to die because I was ordering them to. I was ninety-nine percent sure of it. <Navigation Bob, take us up. We are going to break that Runescript even if we need to sacrifice the entirety of Mountaindale and the dungeon to do so. Pour on the speed; power is not an issue.>

I diverted a large portion of the Mana and Essence I was getting into the flight controls. We began gaining altitude even as my creatures swarmed to my surface. The Mobs were going to begin jumping as soon as we were over the massive Runic circle, but Manny suddenly thundered his war cry and *squeezed* out of the entrance to the dungeon. He was much the worse for his travels, scales caked in mud and blood. He snarled at the assembled Mobs, "Fools! Return to the dungeon! I shall step in, and whether I fail or succeed... your deaths would have been in vain!"

I would have teared up if it were at all possible. Seeing a single file line of Goblins, Bashers, Cats, and Golems ready to jump over the edge so that they could *possibly* do something to help me was heartbreaking. Suddenly, having them all back... there was no way to thank the selfless Manticore. We climbed higher, and soon, it was almost time to throw our lives away. I shuddered at the intrusive thought, but I really believed that this was what was about to happen. My Mobs traveled deep into the dungeon and entered the workshops. I directed all of them to lay on the gravity Runes and increased the power of them until there was no way for the various creatures to fly away or be rattled from an impact. At least, I hoped this was the case.

Manny and I were even with the clouds that had begun to creep back into the area and were soon able to see the smaller of the two moons as it glowed unnaturally brightly in the late afternoon sun. If I were a romantic and didn't know what was going on, I would try to woo my lady tonight, claiming that the moon had never seemed bigger or brighter. Now, the sight just made me wince; the connections between the Runes and the Moon must be forming vigorously for the light reflecting off the moon to be wavering like this. *Celestial feces*, I needed to speed this up. The humans on the surface of Mountaindale were falling to the ground one after another, unable to get enough air to breathe. If there had been many cultivators left there, this wouldn't have been such an issue, or they could have saved the mortals. Whoops.

Manny launched his attack, jumping and diving off the cliff. I knew what he was going to do, and I was already horrified. He was going to slam himself into the Runes and use the destruction of his Core to enhance a single attack. We were both hoping that his ability to corrode nearly anything would weaken the spot I would be targeting. As he got closer, I couldn't bear to watch.

I looked down at the spinning Runes of Xenocide's formation, then up at the oscillating light surrounding the moon... and released my version of a sigh. Drat. Self-preservation was king; what was I *doing*? Before I could talk myself out of it, I let go of the power holding up me upright and began to fall. <*For Kantor*!>

The projection of my target so far below, the Runescript *shimmered* as the base of Mountaindale began to heat up. Soon, the stone was cherry-red and glowing, the friction with the air causing lightning to form and crackle along my surface. I adjusted my course a tiny bit, seeing the space my Manny was going to attack. It was one of the few stationary points on the massive, flowing Script, and as Manny detonated into corrosive poison and pure force... the Runes were painted red with his blood. I *really* hoped that had done what we needed. Now I had a target to aim for, and as much as I hated to admit it, Manny's actions had helped me go through with my own selfless action.

A small part of me noted that Xenocide was cheerfully shoving his hand into an unknown cultivator dressed like a necromancer in elaborate dark robes. I saw the instant he noticed the falling mountain and frowned, but he failed to move in time to block me as the obviously high S-ranking man grabbed and distracted him for the quarter of a second I needed in order to be too close to stop. The entire mountain and dungeon slammed at terminal velocity into the section of Runes that had been painted in the blood of my Manticore, sending molten stone to the ground and crushing or burning hundreds of beings on the battlefield below.

As my projection cleared of the dust and loose energy, I noticed something unexpected. The mountain was still above the Runescript. *We had bounced off of it.* I hadn't been able to destroy the Runes, though I saw a tiny stream of power escaping the Runescript from a crack that had formed. A *crack.* All of that for a *crack.* Xenocide appeared next to the energy stream, inspecting it with insane fury on his face. When his expression transitioned to relief, I got very, very nervous.

"Tsk, tsk. Bad dungeon! *Punishment!*" Xenocide smiled directly at *me* somehow, raised a hand, and smacked the mountain that was hovering in the air above him. A massive chunk of stone on the side of the mountain was blasted into dust, at least a few hundred tons worth. The rest of the strike sent me spinning through the sky. By 'me' I, of course, meant the *entire abyssal mountain.* If I had a stomach, it would have been emptied on the floors, walls, and ceilings. As it was, the humans that remained on my surface and outdoors were tossed off and sent falling to the ground far below. The ones indoors... I would try to clean them up before anyone saw them.

There was nothing I could do for several minutes. Even after the initial force of the strike wore off, I was now off balance and still out of control. It took a full half hour until I was able to compensate for the instability and spinning, and by then... well... the war was over. My dungeon was empty of everything but my Attendants and the Mobs that had been held to the walls and floor, and they were all heavily damaged. I had lost a tenth of my overall size, and my lake was gone. The Wisps were fine, but Grace was so dizzy that she kept falling into the floor and accidentally causing corkscrew spikes to form when she came back out.

"Well," Dani paused to heave, causing a trickle of glitter to fall to the ground, "I'm glad you didn't draw attention to yourself during combat. You were—*hurk*—right... all along. We should have just run."

<Dani.> I gazed at her form as she stared at me. <I know.>

CHAPTER FORTY-NINE

"War is over, go home?" Hans was still supporting an exhausted Half-Elf as he queried the Mages hovering above them.

"This is bad. Dale, where are you?" Princess Brianna appeared among the combatants, causing a few people to curse loudly and one man to fire a stream of rocks at her. She dodged and ignored the small attacks, calling for Dale once again.

"Over here," Dale called apathetically as he helped Tom get to his feet and stand on wobbly legs. "Please don't tell me that it is worse than it looks."

"At least it isn't raining!" someone called brightly, obviously trying to lighten the mood. A lake's worth of water suddenly sloshed to the ground a few hundred feet away, causing decomposing bodies to be washed toward them. Exhausted water Mages directed the flow around the group but glared daggers at the too-cheerful man.

"Dale, we should speak in... no... everyone needs to hear this." Brianna took a deep breath and enhanced her words with wind, carrying them across the field, "Every S-ranker in the guild, the High-Elves, Dwarves, Northmen, Humanity... my *Mother*... they were *all* killed here. They were *all* used to power that monstrous Runescript floating in the air. Without an S-ranker, the Guild law states that-"

"Not *every* S-ranker, Assassin." Dale stifled a groan as Barry's voice echoed through the area. A sick smile was on his face even as a huge portion of the survivors began to cheer wildly. "I am *quite* sure that I am the highest ranked Guild member remaining, so I will take over from here."

"First of all, we will need to find a way to destroy this infernal floating Rune and reverse the course of that moon." Barry started, only to be cut off.

Xenocide's voice drifted over, unenhanced and nonchalant. He had paused in the middle of doing sit-ups and was sitting on his Rune smiling at them. "Good luck with that! Also, the Church has a few S-rankers left! You should bring them here; I'd love to play catch with my boy a few times before the world ends!"

Barry paled, his hands trembling as he looked at the insane person who was staring back at him. He cleared his throat, resuming his speech, "As I was *saying*, we all have much to do. I look around this field and see undead roaming around, which tells me that we have not wiped all of the necromantic filth from this world; we will remedy that."

"*Will* you, now?" A *crack* resounded through the area as Barry was backhanded and sent spinning to the ground. A man in tattered, once-intricate robes stood in the air where Barry had been only moments ago. Blood was leaking from his mouth and flecked the air whenever he spoke. "I am fairly *certain* that your only hope, the only hope for *all* of us, is to join together and launch a counter initiative. Once again, *Barry the Devourer*, your mouth is getting you into trouble."

Chandra joined the group, looking up at the man who could easily swat an S-ranked man out of the air. There was only one explanation for his overwhelming power. "Why would you do this, Ra-"

"I go by *The Master* now, *Madame*." The Master's voice had lost a bit of its frigidness, and a touch of sadness had entered his tone. "We were all wrong. We were manipulated, we lost sight of everything we had hoped for, and all of the world events in the last five hundred years that brought us to this point were calculated and plotted."

"What? Who would...?"

Chandra's voice faltered as Xenocide waved at them lazily. "That was me! Thank you for the recognition! Do you have *any* idea how hard it was to convince the entire world to hate each other? Alright, fair enough, not *that* hard, but still, it is nice to be noticed for your dedicated efforts. Nap time!"

"There is no way a triple S-ranker needs sleep," Dale muttered as Xenocide fell backward and snuggled up to a no-longer-animated zombie bear. Snores drifted to them in moments.

"We should strike *now*!" Barry was pulling himself out of the crater his impact had created and was intentionally not looking at The Master.

"Shut up, *Barry*," the Master ordered coldly. "We are all exhausted, our forces are devastated, and if we couldn't defeat him with the most powerful combined forces of the entire known world, what could we do now that he slew them? Listen, all of you. We were all led astray; it is clear to me now. Things in my past that confused me, the reasons people acted the way they did to my powers and the power of my followers... all of the blame rests at the feet of Xenocide."

"Aww. I'm blushing."

The Master grimaced and ignored Xenocide's words. "We need to quit the field, and those of us that remain need to find peace amongst ourselves, no matter our *personal* feelings. I want this to happen, but I will warn you only once: attacking my people means that you forfeit your life."

There was silence on the field, but slowly, the surviving people began grouping together. It took three hours for everyone to cross the massive battlefield, but soon, Elves stood by

Dwarves, Northmen stood near Amazons, and Guild members uneasily eyed black-robed necromancers. The tension in the air proved that the only thing keeping these people from attacking instantly was the shared fear of what loomed above them. The Runes in the air shifted again, the once pure red was now tinged with green and creating a sickly light. The Master strode forward in the air, looking at the assembled people with tired eyes.

"Alright. Please, believe me when I tell you that this war is the absolute last thing I ever wanted. It should have never progressed to this point, and if pride, *tradition*, and fear hadn't gotten in the way... we would be living in a much better world right now." The Master took a deep breath, and in that moment, one of the Amazons tried to derail the conversation.

"Was destroying our society *twice* not enough for you, *male*? Wouldn't this *issue* never have happened if *you* had followed the law!" Instead of a question, her words were an admonition.

"I had no interest in being a slave, nor did I care for your rules or what happened to males that learned how to cultivate. Murdering a *child*? That is what you wanted to do? *Don't speak*; I know the answer. I was *there*, wasn't I?" The Master's words were a command with a touch of power in them, and the Amazon found that her mouth would no longer open.

The Master continued, now uninterrupted, "Everyone, I am uncertain what your individual cultures and practices are, but I doubt any of them include dying without a purpose. I am uncertain how much time we have before this Rune pulls down the moon, but I am certain we can do nothing about it right now. We need to gather the new leadership of nations and unite as a world to combat this threat."

"We don't even know for *sure* what this Runescript is doing! I say we call for Spotters to inspect it!" a new voice shouted out. "As far as I know, it is making illusions and you are working to set yourself up as the leader of the world!"

Power rolled off of The Master, causing everyone but Barry to be forced to their knees on the sodden ground. Even Barry was bending heavily, panting as he pushed himself to ignore the power. The Master's voice *thundered* in the air, causing noses and Essence-enhanced ears to bleed, "Do you think I would need to *ask* to rule you? Your leaders are *dead*, slain by that madman! You want to resort to *bureaucracy* as the world is literally *ending*? I should castrate you here and now so that your genes don't spread!"

"I have thirteen children," the man whimpered in a desperate plea to be released.

"Of *course* you do." The Master sighed and reined in his power. The pressure eased, and he looked around. "Find yourselves new leaders, gather the remnants of your societies, and gather on the flying dungeon. It... where did it go? I'll go get the dungeon, you all have a day. Do *not* make me come dig you out of whatever place you think will be safe. I will guarantee this: it won't be."

He vanished in the direction he had last seen the dungeon, and soon, people were muttering and looking at each other with distrust. With no one overly powerful enough present to protect them, the necromancers started a hasty retreat. A few people discussed going after them, but after the world-shaking events of the day, no one had the energy to act upon their grumbling.

Tom looked around, searching the sky. "The dungeon really left us here?"

"Did you see what that slap did to it?" Rose shook her head sadly. "I would have fled if it were possible. Right now, though... I think we are stuck here until this ends one way or another."

CHAPTER FIFTY

<Gotta run, gotta run now! Move spritely!> I sang lightly as I flew as fast and as far as I could. I was staying low to the ground, which... frankly, I wasn't sure if that would help. I was a *mountain.* I didn't exactly do inconspicuous well. Although... I looked at the Elven Embassy that had been built above me and started absorbing it. <Nom, nom.>

"You seem a little loopy, Cal," Dani stated unnecessarily. "Did that slap rattle you harder than I thought it did?"

<No, no. I'm just excited to be making a break for it. How long has it been since we got to hang out with only people that we wanted to hang out with? Maybe we should seal the entrances for a while and dive really deep into the ocean. I bet it'd be hard to find us down there!>

"Ha, as if! We'd never survive the deeps!" Dani chuckled like I had made a joke, and when she realized that I was serious, her tone completely changed. "Cal, you *do* know that the most powerful beasts in the world live in the deep oceans or deep underground where the Essence concentrations are highest...?"

<I guess that figures.> I sighed as I felt feet touch down on my surface. <Well, it was a beautiful dream while it lasted. Someone's here. I suppose we should greet them.>

My attention turned to my entrance as The Master walked in. You could have heard a pin drop as the tension mounted in the air between us. I created a pin and dropped it on the second floor to test this theory. Yup. His head twitched as the tiny noise reached him. He cleared his throat, which was probably just as useful for him at the S-ranks as it was for me not having organs.

"So. Dungeon." The Master's powerful voice shook dust from the ceiling. I really needed to clean the place up. Xenocide's slap had done a number on me. "I came here... to apologize. To you and your Wisp both."

<What?> My voice was inaudible to him.

"*What*?" Dani's screech could be heard five floors away. "Oh, *abyss* no, you don't get to walk in here and-"

My pleading voice cut off the incoming tirade, <Dani, he can really do whatever he wants to do. Let's not irritate the man that can kill us more than *once*?>

"I hear that your Wisp remembers me." The Master sighed deeply, running a hand through his hair. "Listen, the both of you. I have been experimenting with Dungeon Cores for a *century*, and I have never encountered one that could be considered actually intelligent. Every single one of them was nothing more than a bundle of instinctual hunger. I had no reason to believe that Wisps were any different. I had heard legends of Wisps and Cores and assumed that binding them together was what *made* the intelligence of a Core happen. I didn't realize it was... more."

He paused, either deep in thought or pretending very well. "Little Wisp, when I had captured you, I was *shocked* that you were able to speak aloud. By then though, I stayed the course despite my better judgement. I have now learned *why*. Xenocide's power is far-reaching and insidious. I met him when I was but a child, and he gave me something that allowed me to attain great power. I now am able to break past his control but only because I finally recognized it for what it was. A seed of **Madness**."

Dani didn't answer, though she could hear him clearly. The Master started walking deeper into my dungeon. "I know you have no reason to listen to me, and you certainly have no reason to *trust* me, but I do need your help. There are a lot of people that are stranded in a field between fallen Kingdoms that have no way to send aid. I need you to come back and be the bridge that connects us together. We are likely all going to perish to Xenocide's plans, but without you, this becomes a *certainty*."

<What would you like me to do, Dani?> I knew what I *wanted* to do. I also knew what I *should* do, but Dani was pretty great about making me do the *right* thing.

"If I may offer an opinion?" One of the Human Attendants piped up, breaking the current mood. This was one of the ones who was planning on taking the slow but easy route to his growth. "Can we convert them..."

<That sounds pretty good. We get something out of it; they get to survive->

"...into corrupted ash?" the man finished his thought, my words only now penetrating his thick skull. I made a note immediately that this man was never to be given a position of power over another person. Or animal. Probably not crops, either. When there was no response; he slunk to the back of the group and pouted.

<Dani, do you want to step in here?> I watched as she trembled, multiple colors and emotions playing across her body.

She bobbed in the air, her version of a nod. "Fine, Mr. Master. We will *consider* helping you."

"I do thank you." He stepped out of nothing, appearing in the room with all of us. The collective butt clench could have created a diamond if there had been a Mage nearby that could harness the sudden pressure. "There are so many lives that we can save, and that is all I've ever been after."

<You've been trying to *save* lives?> I waited for an answer for too long before I realized that he couldn't hear me. <Will *someone* please translate for me?>

"Cal! The *Master* is coming to drag you back to the battlefield!" Minya burst through a portal that connected to the surface, the sudden shouting causing the already tense Goblins to react in certain ways. A few squeaked, a few got into battle positions, and one fainted. Huh.

<Got that, Minya.> I watched the look of horrified realization cross her face as she saw the man himself in front of her. <Actually, you have perfect timing. I needed a translator. Can you speak for me?>

Her incomprehensible squeak of terror answered *that* question easily. I was going to ask Dani to step in, but Minya rallied and straightened her spine. "I will speak for you, Great Spirit!"

<Oh, not this again!> I groaned as nervous chuckles rolled through the room. I looked over to see The Master looking around in shock. Were those *tears* in his eyes?

His hand moved fast enough that I was certain no one else noticed, and the droplets were gone. He swallowed deeply, nodding a few times. "I have missed laughter. Actual laughter, not the... maniacal cackling version. No one laughs around me anymore, and even with my abilities... hearing it always catches me by surprise. I have only greater respect for you, dungeon. If your people are comfortable laughing near you, you are doing something very right."

<Ask him if I need to turn around,> I directed Minya. She repeated my words, and the Man nodded. With a *twinge* of dismay, I turned Mountaindale in a wide arc and began flying back the way we had come, albeit slower. No need to be wasteful or get there just for Xenocide to decide it was killin' time. <Will you ask him if he has a plan? I'd *really* like for there to be a plan in place before we do anything. Having a plan is a good plan.>

"Calm down, Cal," Dani whispered soothingly.

"Cal? So that *is* your name, dungeon?" The Master got nods from all around the room. "Interesting! I only met one other dungeon that had a name, and Kantor was a worthy foe."

The absolute silence that followed his words caused the incredibly powerful man to shift with discomfort. "Once again, I would like to reiterate that I-"

"Was it *you*?" Dani whispered darkly. Her colors were icy blue, and she was pulsing like a poorly created Rune. "Were *you* the one that killed them?"

The Master looked down at the ground. "I can neither confirm... nor *deny* that statement. I pledged to never speak of it, and so I cannot *deny it* without breaking my word."

For some reason, Dani calmed down when she heard his words. She pulled in a deep gust of air and spoke normally again, "I see. Thank you. Is there anything you *can* speak about? The bound Wisp?"

<Why are you so calm? He might have...> I tried parsing the conversation, but Humans were confusing. If I didn't have Dani helping me out, I would almost certainly get in trouble pretty often.

"I cannot say." He sadly shook his head. "Please, once more, forgive me for what I tried to do to you, for what I tried to do to *both* of you. I need to get back, and I will see you soon. We... can we talk?"

He stared at the air, and in an inexplicable way *through* the air. Without awaiting an answer, The Master stepped forward and *into* something, vanishing without a trace. I watched the spot where he had been trying to detect *any* differences in the Essence or Mana of the area. Nothing. How bizarre. I looked at all the uncomfortable faces in the room and directed my thoughts to only Dani and Minya.

<Did anyone else notice that he was bleeding? Why would he be bleeding?>

CHAPTER FIFTY-ONE

Rose was having trouble with the loss of Adam. They all were, but she didn't seem to understand his heroic sacrifice. "I don't *care* what he said at the end, Dale! If he had just told us, we could have found another way!"

"Rose, you *know* how Adam-" Dale was forced to drift to the side, letting another arrow skim past his head. Dale decided that Rose had been getting considerably more violent.

"Don't you tell *me* how Adam... Hans, what are you doing? Do not get *any* closer to me!" Hans was staring at Rose, his face a blank slate. He trod forward with heavy steps and used his daggers to deflect the arrows she sent at him. With a scream, she swung at him with her bow, only for him to gently use her momentum against her and leave her wide open. He stepped forward once more, sweeping her up in a tight hug.

Dale could see Rose struggle violently, but Hans turned his head slightly and whispered something in her ear that was too soft to be heard from this distance. The fight seemed to go out of her, and she collapsed onto him shaking with shirt-muted sobs.

Tom stood near Dale, nodding at the horizon. "The dungeon's on its way. See that dot? Pretty sure that is it, but take a look for yourself."

Dale nodded as well, turning away from his friends and peering at Xenocide. The man always seemed to lock eyes with him whenever Dale looked over, and it was creeping him out. The man waved from his perch in midair, causing Dale to shudder and look away for the umpteenth time. He looked up, seeing that night was falling and the moon was extraordinarily bright. It was still crossing the sky, so at least it wasn't moving so fast that nature lost *all* of its patterns.

In fact, as the darkness around them deepened, the moon finished crossing the horizon and vanished from sight. The Runes that had been casting a nauseating light went dark in an instant and ceased their erratic spinning. Dale's eyes lit up in opposition to the shadows, and a hushed whisper left his mouth, "A *reprieve*."

"*Brianna*!" Dale shouted into the night, causing several battle-damaged people to scream in terror. The Dark Elf appeared beside him in moments, nodding at him.

"I noted the change as well. I'll seek out the others and... this *Master*," she spat the name, "and call for a meeting. We may have more time than we thought we had."

"Thank you, Brianna." Dale reached out for her as she turned to go. "Is... is it *Queen* Brianna now?"

Brianna smiled at him sadly. "None of your abyssal business."

She vanished, leaving Dale looking at her previous location incredulously. "Aren't I a Duke? I feel like this is something I should know. Is she my Queen now?"

He shook his head, fighting off the fatigue of the day. Hans and Rose were now sitting and talking, and Tom had two fresh-faced female clerics healing his 'wounds'. Dale really hoped there weren't more serious cases because they seemed fixated on repairing Tom's torn and strained muscles. For some reason, they swore they needed to massage him to 'heal', but Dale just rolled his eyes and looked away. What was it about the mountain of a man that drew ladies to him like flies?

A commotion near the edge of camp drew his attention, and he drifted over to hear what was going on. Two men were shouting at each other, a necromancer and a Mage. The Mage was being the loudest. "What do *you* mean I can't take this armor? I killed the *thing* wearing it, and it has excellent Runes of protection on it!"

"You can't loot *our* undead!" the necromancer bellowed in return. "How many times have you threatened us now when we got close to the people *we* killed?"

"They were our *friends*!" the Mage snarled, eyes getting a bit too wild for comfort. "You touch them, and we'll tear you apart!"

"These were *our* creatures! You think they equipped *themselves*? I paid through the *nose* to get that armor crafted. Boris was my main defender!" Black air was whipping around the necromancer's hands, and it looked like they would come to blows over this issue if no one stopped them. Dale waited, but no one else stepped in. Everyone seemed ready to *join* in, but no one looked like they would stop the fighting from beginning. He strode forward to put an end to it but was knocked backward and off his feet as the Mage slapped the air like it was water and a shockwave erupted from him.

"Feces." Dale twisted in the air and landed on his feet, looking over at a scene from earlier in the day. Undead were rushing to the conflict, and Mana was zipping through the air, charging it with power. People were bashing each other at full strength, but thus far, no one had been *too* injured.

"Are you *all* as insane as the man sitting up there and giggling at you?" Barry appeared over the battle and screamed at the people below him. "Enough of this, you are all *mine*."

Green light coalesced in front of his mouth, and his eyes went blank. He breathed out, and a thick green mist coated everyone below him. Fear filled Dale; Barry hadn't particularly cared about accuracy, and the wall of fog was rapidly approaching him. The Master appeared next to Barry and shoved a single finger into the crackling energy. Lines of black and silver raced over Barry's technique, and the fog split and rushed back to him. Barry shuddered and fell to the ground gasping.

"I was gone for *thirty minutes*," The Master snarled, his fury palpable and crashing over the assembled people. "You are telling me that you couldn't even go for a full hour without trying to kill each other? I'm disappointed in my people. As for the rest of you, thank you for reinforcing our stereotypes against you the very first chance that you got."

The necromancers recoiled like they had been whipped, but the Mages would have ignored The Master if it were possible. "Greed, avarice, fear of the unknown or something *different*. That is how you are seen by my people. I will change how *all* of you interact with each other, by *force* if needed. If you cannot change, you will not last long in this new world order."

There was silence that lasted only until the two sides had retreated a few dozen feet from each other. Then they all began talking, grumbling, perhaps plotting. The Master shook his head and turned to leave. Dale took the opportunity to call out to him, "Excuse me! The Master!"

The Master appeared in front of him on the ground, seemingly just an average man in damaged robes. "Who are you and why should I care about what you have to say?"

"Yeah. This is just as intimidating as I expected it would be, thanks for that." Dale swallowed and tried again. "So, The Master, I was-"

"Just call me 'Master' when you are talking to me." The man rolled his eyes and motioned for Dale to continue.

"Right. Listen, I am the owner of the flying dungeon, at least legally with the Guild. That's not the point of this, though!" Dale promised when The Master started to snarl. "I'm not asking for special treatment; I'm just trying to establish my credibility with you! Listen, I had a council of people that helped me choose the best path for increasing our abilities and that of the dungeon. The entire point of it was to see things that other people didn't and try for the best outcome. I'm... I'm rambling, sorry. Listen, I want us to work together."

"I'm not overly interested." The Master started to turn but paused at Dale's next words.

"My council consisted of the Dark Elf Princess Brianna, King Henry, Queen Marie, High Mageous Amber of the portal guild, and *Madame Chandra*," Dale's voice firmed. He didn't include Tyler; there was no benefit to telling The Master things that wouldn't matter to him. "Chandra has been trying to advocate for you, for peace, and for discussion ever since you reappeared in the world. Not only that but we, together, represent a large portion of the races' leadership. Please, come with me and talk to them. We may be helpful, certainly more so than you seem to think we will be."

The Master was considering; Dale could see it and so didn't interrupt. The Master shifted on his feet and shrugged. "Why not? At worst, I might even be able to have a conversation with... an old friend."

Dale and The Master walked together through the middle of the fortifications, drawing whispers and causing strange conversations to start. As they walked past a tight-knit group, a familiar face stepped forward. Thomas Adams, the man who had lost his Nobility, had a look of absolute *glee* on his face. "I should have *known*. Of *course* you were helping the necromancers; it all makes sense now!"

"Shut your mouth, or I'll break your nose again and mess up your face bad enough that it'll take a flesh Mage a month to fix it." Dale's aura shifted, and bright flames dripped from his fingers.

Thomas smirked and bowed sarcastically, stepping back into his group. "Yes, *overlord*."

Dale and The Master walked on, but now Dale was fuming. "I hate rumors. I do. Why are people morons, though? The planet won't survive the moon smashing into it! Why can't we fix the issues we are having before playing these *games*?"

A small smile played over The Master's lips. "It is interesting to hear my words spoken by someone entirely different from my own people."

They walked in silence for a few more feet, but then The Master asked a question that nearly made Dale fall over, "So you and the dungeon share a soul. How did that happen?"

Chapter Fifty-Two

Dale's head was spinning. "How in the *world* do you know that? I swear if you say 'you just told me', I'm going to be *so* mad."

"Dale. Dale, right? I'm not great with names. You'd think with a perfect memory..." He trailed off, noticing Dale's stare. "Souls are *kind of* my thing, aren't they? I can see at a glance that not only are your souls linked, they are actually the *same*."

"You aren't a necromancer, though; how do you see souls?" Dale countered, getting a rush of pleasure from the shock on The Master's face.

"*How* do you know that?"

"You just told-"

The Master cut him off impatiently, "None of that; I didn't do it to you. This is actually important."

Dale stammered out a reply, "Um. Madame Chandra has told us that several times."

"So she *knew*. I had hoped, but this entire time, she *knew* it wasn't me who..." The Master stopped talking, but if Dale wasn't terrified of the man he would have shaken the rest of the sentence out of him. "To think... all this time I was afraid she would despise me. Perhaps we could even..."

"Dale? What are you doing with *him*? If we needed him, *I* would have found him." Princess Brianna was looking up from a table that had apparently been grown in that spot, and she did not look happy. At least it hadn't been The Master's fault that her mother had been slain to power the Runes floating in the sky. That would have made this conversation extra awkward.

"We are here to discuss what we need to do to combat Xenocide," Dale firmly stated, meeting her eyes. "The Master is by far the most powerful person that will be joining us in this venture, so he needs to be informed of the plan as *well* as be a part of it."

"The Master," Chandra greeted the man cordially, if a bit coldly. Dale swore that there was a hint of pain in The Master's eyes for a moment, but any personal feelings were swiftly hidden behind his standard stoic facade.

"Madame. It is good to hear that you achieved your childhood desire." The Master spoke politely, but his words caused her face to twist in a strange series of emotions: sadness, anger, pain... longing?

"And you, yours. I am happy for you but not for the world. Your dreams were built upon the death of thousands." Chandra stared at him, and he shrugged.

"What can I say? I am a product of my environment." His flippant answer almost brought tears to her eyes, and she turned her head to look away. Dale really, *really* wished he knew what was going on. He also knew that asking right now would only gain him silence, possibly anger if they were both hurting like he thought they were.

Dale decided that the best course of action was to move on quickly and try to pry the story out of them if they all survived. "I'm very sorry to interrupt, but there may be a moon crashing into us in the near future... I'd like to stop that from happening."

"Fine." The Master tore his eyes off of Chandra and focused on Dale.

"Fine." Madame Chandra did the same.

Ahem. Dale cleared his throat as arguably the most powerful people in the world turned their full attention on him.

His full council, The Master, and Barry were now around the table, staring at him with various levels of amusement or animosity. "Before anything else, we need to discuss what we know. One: Xenocide has set in motion a plan to crash the moon into the planet."

"Hello!" a voice drifted down to them. Brianna closed her eyes in annoyance and inhaled sharply, but Dale ignored Xenocide and continued.

"Two: we would like to stop this from happening. Three: this Runescript is powered by the death of over a dozen S-ranked people. Can either of you shed some light on what that means for us?" Dale looked at Barry and The Master, who shrugged.

"Entering the S-ranks means becoming *more*," Barry stated abruptly, catching Dale off guard. He hadn't exactly been forthcoming in the past. More... murder hobo? "It is the final act of understanding the **law** that you have bound yourself to. It is becoming an *incarnation* of that **law**. This is different for each person, so attempting to tell you how best to disperse their combined power? Laughable."

"I hate to agree with the walking stomach, but he is correct," The Master grudgingly stated. "For those Runes to have absorbed all of the variations... it must be powerful beyond compare. The dungeon literally dropped a mountain on it from near-orbit, and it made a hairline crack. I had thought I was about to die, or I would have stopped the dungeon myself. Releasing that much concentrated power into the area would have devastated the entire continent."

"Wait, I saw that! You stopped Xenocide from moving to block Mountaindale? Does that mean you were fine with *all* of us dying?" Brianna's voice was filled with horror at how close their demise had brushed by them.

"I thought I was going. I planned to take him with me." The Master spoke without a trace of regret. "At least there would have been survivors. Somewhere. Most likely."

No one had an answer to that, so Dale, once again, had to get the conversation moving. "What were we at? Third? So, third-"

"Fourth," Tyler interjected, squirming as soon as eyes landed on him. "Um, we were at number four."

"A mortal?" Barry looked at Tyler with twitching eyebrows. "How are you here and alive?"

"I, um, sir, I came down to hand out supplies and specialty weapons. I have a weapons shop that-"

Tyler was cut off as Dale continued, "So *fourth* in our list, we know that the Runes above us seem to power down when the moon is hidden by the curvature of the earth." Dale resolutely ignored the looks he was getting from the others. "What we need to do is find a way to stop those Runes from working, stop the moon from crashing into us, and find a way to survive Xenocide through all of this."

"That sounds difficult!" Xenocide chimed in from hundreds of feet above them. "How*ever* will we make it happen?"

"That is actually a good question, but we need him not to hear us." Dale sighed as Xenocide chuckled.

"I can do that." The Master looked around, gauging the distance around them, and grunted. Something odd happened to the air, and all sound from outside of their group was cut off. All the light vanished as well, though Dale's sunlight aura fixed that easily. "We are not *technically* in a different plane of existence, but we are cut off from outside influences here. We have about thirty minutes of air, less if anyone panics."

He looked pointedly at Tyler, who did his best to regulate his air intake. Dale looked around at all of the people, getting ready for the inevitable arguments. "So what does everyone think we should do?"

"We can't beat Xenocide, and we can't outright destroy the Runes." Madame Chandra tapped her chin as she thought out loud. "I guess that leaves-"

"Blowing up the moon!" Barry finished her sentence with his own thoughts.

"Idiot," Chandra spat out. "How did you ever reach the rank you have attained? I was going to say compromising with Xenocide to stop this from happening. Not everything needs to be about killing. Perhaps there is something he wants."

"How likely is it that he is actually going to go through with this? He is going to die too if the planet is destroyed!" Brianna growled with a tired voice. "He would have to be-"

"Insane?" The Master finished for her with an arched eyebrow. "I think that has been established. If this is how he plans to reach into the Heavenly rankings, nothing we will ever do will be enough to stop him. No, what we need is a way to get rid of those Runes. They are working to bind the moon, but I don't think that the earth is being pulled as well or there would be other things happening to us. Could we get the Runes off this planet? Have the moon dragged elsewhere? For celestial's sake, just bury them! If the curvature of the earth is enough, put them in a pit and cover them up!"

Silence greeted this suggestion, and it was the only option that sounded viable. Destruction was impossible without mutually assuring their own demise, and negotiation was also out. Redirection... that might be possible. Dale looked over at High Mageous Amber. "This is your area of expertise. Is it possible?"

"Putting them in a pit? No. There is a difference between a layer of dirt and the entire planet being between them. The other option? Getting rid of them? It depends on the amount of time we have to make this happen. If we are talking days... it is unlikely. If we have weeks and a way to generate the Runes and resources needed, then maybe. If it were as simple as waving a hand... humph. Xenocide must have spent *decades* putting all of this together. The Runes were fueled with S-rank power to function, yes, but his setup cost over a hundred thousand bodies and their blood, not to mention the Essence and Mana they had accrued. Ritual magic is poorly understood, but it is powerful." Amber shook her head and fell silent.

"The dungeon is our answer to all of this." Dale's eyes were wide, and pieces were starting to fit together. "It can create perfect Runes, it can generate materials, and it uses rituals for various things. I've seen it. Rituals are just well-connected and timed Runescript after all, aren't they?"

"If you want to use the most generalized thoughts on the subject, how you would explain it to a child, then yes, that is what rituals are." The Master smirked at Dale's eye roll. "No one has dared to scoff at me in a decade or more. It's... I forget if I dislike it. I think you have a point. We need to bring this to the dungeon. If it will work with us... we may be able to make this work. We might all survive."

"I'll ensure that ritual magic is taboo after this," Barry quietly muttered. "The only use it has is to destroy, and the cost is too high. It is an unsustainable magic, tricks for people who don't have personal power. A joke."

"A *joke* that could kill us *all*, Barry." Chandra's voice was a whiplash. "The *Master*, can you return us to our previous location on the dungeon so that we can get this project moving?"

The Master nodded solemnly. Sound and light washed over them a moment later. A necromancer ran over, braving the hostile looks from the people he passed. "Master! Something is happening to the undead! We can't prove who is doing this to our summons, but somehow, someone here is severing our link to them."

The Master looked over the assembled people coldly. "Right now, this doesn't matter. Bring everyone here. *Everyone.* We are going to the dungeon."

CHAPTER FIFTY-THREE

I was maintaining a five kilometer minimum distance from Xenocide. I knew it wouldn't help if I upset him or he decided to destroy me, but I was taking an 'out of sight, out of mind' approach. I was trying to, at least, but every time we looked at the projection, he would look at me, and our gazes would lock. He would always wave, too. No idea how he knew when or knew where I was watching from. Even my vision was passive light collection; I wasn't sending anything back out!

<This guy is the ultimate creepy creep.> It was time to distract myself. <Dani, how are we doing on Essence and Mana collection? Should I be focusing my abilities elsewhere or just continuing to dump it into my foundation?>

"One moment, Cal." Dani's distracted voice told me that she was trying to stop Grace from doing something. Her next words confirmed that. "Grace somehow lit this thing on fire, and I can't put it out. Not only that, but it keeps... I'd almost say dodging?"

<What?> I took a look, and sure enough, there was a ball of fire on the ground one floor up. Dani sprayed water at it, and it rolled wildly to the side. <What was she doing up there?>

"She was playing with the Golems, and one of them broke." Dani growled as the fireball hopped away. "She started playing with the broken chunks, and..."

<Hold on, Dani. Stop trying to kill that.> I was watching the fireball hop around and got more and more excited. <This is it! *This* is what I've been trying to figure out!>

"What are you talking about, Cal?" Dani was trying to kill the fireball by staring at it, I could just tell. She didn't like Grace playing with 'dangerous' materials. I decided not to tell her about the lightning room I had built to train Grace's dodging abilities.

<I have been trying to decide where to go after Golems weren't cutting it anymore. Look at that fireball, Dani! It is a Core surrounded by pure Scarletite! The mineral that has the highest fire corruption potential!> I waited for a response, but I'd have been there all day if I'd have waited for a comment. None was forthcoming. <Ugh, Dani! I've been making them into humanoid creatures, but *why*? Because that's what I was used to! This one is tiny and weak, but if I do it like this...>

I pulled a Core filled with water corruption and Mana over and wrapped it in Gallium, then modeled the pattern of Mana release from the tiny fireball. <Boom. Water elemental.>

There was no reaction. I mentally prodded the double-fist sized item and waited a second longer. <Hmmm.>

"I have an idea." Dani directed the water she had been using, spraying the mineral-wrapped Core. Instead of spraying everywhere, the water hit and collected on the surface. Soon, there was a massive blob of water twisting and turning. It looked around, at least I assume, before spotting the tiny fireball and chasing it. I wanted to see what would happen, so I let the blob catch the fireball. The fire persisted but was quickly growing dim. The water in that spot began boiling, but then the fire Core cracked, and Mana spilled into the water. Steam started pouring off the blob, but it neither dissipated nor was reabsorbed. A quick check told me that the elemental had eaten the Core and used the material it was wrapped in to upgrade itself.

<I may be in love with this creature,> I told Dani, who mimicked an eye and rolled around.

"I don't know; it reminds me of a basic slime." Dani critically inspected the blob of steamy water.

<No way, major differences.> I looked at the blob lovingly. <I'm going to name you Bath. I bet you are just the perfect temperature, aren't you?>

There was no response, which was exactly as expected. Perfect. If it had somehow talked, I might have screamed and tried to figure out what was going on. Water wasn't supposed to speak. Of course, who was I to get upset about typically inanimate objects talking. <Okie-dokie, time for the next test!>

I built up a Core with various Mana types and tried to match the minerals to it. I used all sorts of material, but... nothing I did worked to make a higher form of elemental. I couldn't even replicate Bath! I even destroyed him and absorbed him, but... there was nothing that should have allowed him to be animated like he was. There must be some property of corruption that allowed it to function as it did, but it was energy. Energy was supposed to only be a tool, not a deciding factor in animation. There was only one thing to do.

<I'm gonna make a new floor!> I shouted to the beings in my dungeon. There were whoops and cheers, but most of it was a cheerleading attempt. They all knew they would likely not be visiting this new floor. I had previously been working on carving out a space and infusing it with my influence, but I had given up on actually putting anything down there for a long while. This war and my forcible inclusion in it had eaten my attention for *far* too long. It was time to be a dungeon again, and I had missed my experimentation.

So, a massive empty room that needed creatures. Creatures that needed to eat others of their kind to increase in power and complexity. This should be fun. I thought about making the room become filled with rings to battle through, but I decided to try something else that would be interesting and potentially deadly. The walls moved at my direction and closed in around the room until there was a huge conical shape created from the stone. The rim, the highest portion of the room, would be the start. The tip of the cone would be at the bottom. Was it a waste of space? Maybe, but it was only a few hundred feet deep.

My real concern was people flying. I needed a way around that, and I decided that I had figured it out. <Dani! Want to come see something neat?>

"What are you up to, Cal? You've been quiet for a while now." Dani flew to where I directed her, Grace tagging along and bounding through the stone to create oddly flowing patterns in the rock. It was cute, so I left her art wherever she made it.

<So I had an idea for a new floor...> I trailed off, letting her mind play a few tricks on her. When she was sufficiently twitchy, I continued, <And I'd like your feedback before I continue.>

"Oh, thank goodness." She breathed a sigh of relief while I chuckled. "What are you thinking?"

<I have this as the base model,> I let her look over the cone, <and was wondering how I should grant access to it? I want the exit, portal, and tree all down there, but hidden in a side room. I am going to chain gravity Runes together so that the strength of them increases the further down you go. What do you think?>

"That sounds neat. I'm guessing the Runes are to mess with flying people?" I confirmed her guess, and she thought for a moment while Grace played around. "We could... Grace!"

The tiny wisp had made a corkscrew spike grow from the ground and giggled when she heard her name called. Dani paused and looked at the spiral. "Well, there we go. How about a ramp that spirals around the entire thing? Take it from a cone to a screw. Two ramps. Start them at opposite ends and meet at the bottom. How does that sound?"

<Sounds like a plan!> I shifted the stone and began to carefully draw out the gravity Runescript. It took a few hours to get done, and when I finished, I had Bobs start going over it to double check my work. While they did that, I started making elementals. It was as fun to me as feces are to a monkey. I could direct the ones I made in terms of movement and attacking, so it was exciting and frustrating that I couldn't direct their growth.

Another interesting fact to me was that the elementals could only be earth, wind, water, or fire based. How do you give celestial or infernal to an elemental? I created the elemental cores for them anyway, assuming correctly that the basic types would eat them to expand themselves. Neat. I made *swarms* of elementals and forced them to wait to do anything. There were various sizes of each of them so that the... beasts? Creatures? Entities? There we go. So that the entities could change in large or subtle ways as they fought. I'm sure that the celestial and infernal Cores would be useful for growth as well.

After the final Bob had given the Runes their seal of approval, it was nearly morning. I was getting *much* faster at this sort of thing! When the Bobs had left, and the Silverwood tree and I were safely hidden at the bottom of the cone, I released the reins on the elementals. It. Was. Awesome. I had kept all the types separated, and most of them ignored their own kind unless they were twenty percent smaller than themselves. Then they would latch on and absorb the smaller entity. The edges of the groups began to blur as elemental combat erupted. A water elemental went over the edge, not on a ramp, and began falling.

When it reached the bottom of the slope, it was so compressed that it was basically a superfluid. The Core of it stopped rolling and shattered, spraying water and Mana everywhere. I was so glad that I had thought to reinforce this area to an extreme. It was basically a panic room that even A rank-seven Mages would have trouble destroying in a single hit. They could do it, but they would need to put extra effort into it. I highly doubted they would bother.

The battle kept raging, and some of the elementals began moving down the ramps. Upon doing so, their bodies would become somewhat more compressed. This gave them an advantage over the non-compressed versions, and they quickly defeated and ate their closest rivals. If they progressed too quickly, they would break under the pressure and be scooped up by the others or their power would return to me. By the time one of them reached the base of the cone, they would be incredibly powerful.

If I could have purred in pleasure, I totally would have done so. I tried to make a similar sound, but only got an odd look from Dani. I ignored it; I was happy. So what if I'm a little strange? You have to be a little odd to be number one.

CHAPTER FIFTY-FOUR

Daylight started to touch my surface which always made me a little ticklish. Or something similar, I suppose. How could I be tickled? It seemed fun...? An issue for another time. I saw the light flare from Xenocide's Runescript as the moon breached the horizon once more. What *incredible* power those Runes contained. I simply had nothing that I could compare it to. A miniature version of the sun? It didn't give off heat or light, so no, but something about that comparison tickled my mind.

Speaking of power, my ley lines had never stopped expanding, even if they had only moved downward fractions of an inch. That was over the entirety of the planet, so it was still pretty impressive. Whatever power not used by me directly or for my purposes was directed back into expanding the lines. Loose Essence continued to flood into me, but I was also starting to notice the lack of Mana storms in the area. From all the power thrown around yesterday, I would have absolutely expected the world to attempt to purge it from the atmosphere in the form of a Mana storm. That it hadn't... I was pleased.

This was the first direct confirmation I had gained that my ley lines were ironing out the overly concentrated areas of power in the world. Now, I wasn't absorbing all of it, but as one area of high power concentration was removed, it would stop leaking power into the surroundings. When areas with *low* concentrations were drained, energy would flood in from a more highly concentrated area. I had several Bobs working to take samples of the power density, and they were making a second map to set over the first.

They called it a 'power overlay'. Pretty basic, but easy to understand. Now, the hope was that we could increase draw on ley lines in the areas with the highest concentrations. Doing so could only be beneficial, at least to us. It was likely that powerful monsters would not appreciate their lairs weakening, but that was someone else's problem or, at least, an issue for the future. Oh! I should extend my influence to the base of my mountain so that I can crush things and absorb their pattern! That would be my next goal after fine-tuning my elemental cone.

I was getting the warm and fuzzies from watching the rapid evolution of my new elementals. I felt like a real dungeon again and not just a ride or cash-cow for the powerful. How long had it been since I made a new monster? Made a new Rune? I had all the Runes the Spotters *publicly* knew about, but what had I done to seek out or create new ones? I was in a creative tizzy, and I felt like I was myself again after weeks of stress and uncertainty. Do you know what happens when you overstress a Core? *Boom*! I'm glad I avoided that.

The strongest of the elementals had reached the halfway point of the cone and had undergone significant changes. No longer were they blobs of basic elements. As the pressure had increased, they had been forced to branch out from their weak forms. Limbs were made, appendages, whip-like tentacles, but still no heads or other sensory organs. Why would they need them? The one I was rooting for had started out as a giant fireball and focused mainly on attacking and eating earth and infernal types. It must have killed a spider or something because, otherwise, I had no idea how it decided to make similar limbs.

It was now an infernal magma elemental and had twelve legs. It looked like a darkly glowing ball of molten stone, and it was interesting to watch. When it walked, it raised the front and back two legs - so four legs total - and used them as piercing weapons. It never had to turn: it only needed to use different legs. This gave it *amazing* mobility, even though I had originally thought it would be a weakness to need to change which legs you were using. What would *I* know about leg usage though? I called it Aranea infernum or Aranea for short. What can I say? I'm a very literal Core.

This elemental was directly across from one that I had been subtly guiding to be its opposite. This one was Bath version two: Imbrem Aureum. Strange name, but very fitting. It had started as a *massive* water elemental and had been eating air and celestial types like Dale ate jerky. Too fast for their own good is what I mean. Soon, water was no longer dominating, and it had turned into a Core with celestial-infused raindrops swirling around it at high speed. I was really interested to see what would happen if these two ever met and fought. Would the outcome be a chaotic lightning superfluid elemental? Want. I want it *bad.*

Unfortunately, their progress had stagnated. They couldn't continue downward for fear of the pressure crushing them, and they couldn't move upward without being overwhelmed by swarms of their brethren. They had to hold their ground and destroy challengers that came after them. I had started dropping caches of Cores along the path that matched their current progress, just so that they could continue to progress. I thought of it as a leader bonus. Everything else had to destroy to empower themselves, but the leader needed incentive to stay ahead of the rest. I loved it. Survival of the strangest! Imbrem closed in on a challenger, and the spinning droplets shredded its opponent in moments. Those drops... whew. They had the force of B-rank four Mana behind them.

Speaking of ranks, I could feel my path opening before me. I was sitting at B-rank *nine* right now, trying to find the key to unlocking the A-ranks. I was certain it would be an esoteric truth, an understanding of myself and my **law** that would drive me forward into great power. If it was something obvious, I would almost feel cheated. I wouldn't mind, but I wanted to rise in the ranks in an awe-inspiring way, not quietly and surreptitiously. I wanted to hear the humans say: 'Celestial feces, we should run.' or something similar.

I just *had* to think of humans again, didn't I? Almost as soon as I had, I felt footsteps on my surface. It was like a summoning spell. What the...? How many were arriving? I took a look; it appeared that the entire army of mixed races had flown here. Ew, necromancers. So *many* of them, too. I had gotten over my hatred of them, but having them around made me nervous. The Church tended to be less than careful when exterminating the 'heretics', and I had heard stories of entire cities falling. Of course, most of the Church's most powerful had been slain...

"Go oversee the arrival of the new leaders of each race." The Master's voice made dozens of people start toward the portal, obviously thinking he was talking to them directly. It just had *that* kind of quality. I saw his lips twitch in either a grimace or laughter as the people tried to figure out who was supposed to be in charge. His next mutter was too soft to be heard, "Like herding *cats*."

I could appreciate that sentiment. I was still trying to get some of my Cats to give up the special weapons and armor I had equipped them in, and I could supposedly *force* them to do it. Somehow, I kept finding *one* more Cat playing with the shiny superweapons. Dale landed with a group and walked toward The Master with Tom in tow. I also noticed that Hans and Rose were walking toward the tavern together. What had *happened* down there? She must have taken a blow to the head.

Dale was looking around, seemingly surprised by the lack of motion on my surface. "I guess everyone left through the portal to wait out the war?"

Wrong. The smart or lucky ones did. I wasn't going to be the one to break it to him, though. As they got closer to The Master, Tom stepped forward, glaring at the powerful man. "Can I hit you?"

"What?" The Master seemed taken aback by this question.

Tom started pulling his warhammer out of his bag. "One of my friends died down there to prevent your summoned creature killing *all* of us. I would like a free hit."

"Ah. A Northman. I understand and will allow this in thanks for the time your people saved me from the Valkyries." The Master nodded, pulling open his tattered robe and baring his chest. "This will end things between us?"

"As is custom," Tom ruefully agreed. "*Hans*! *Rose*! Come over here before you do other things."

The two that had been walking toward what they didn't realize was an empty building stopped, looking over and slowly approached. Their walk became even slower when they saw who was standing shirtless in front of them. Tom looked at the Master, swallowing. "I understand that this will not actually hurt you, but please do not hold yourself in place."

"I will take the blow," The Master stated noncommittally. Tom nodded, knowing that he was getting a chance he would never have otherwise. A crowd was starting to gather, but Tom wasn't going to wait. Taking a few deep breaths, he enhanced his body to the absolute maximum he was able, got a running start that would make him into a blur in front of an average person, and swung his hammer with all the force he could possibly put behind it. *Clang*. The Master was hit in the chest, and though the warhammer bent and warped from the force, there was no visible damage to The Master.

He did allow the force to turn into momentum and was launched off the ground and upward several hundred meters. He slammed through a granite building, reducing the wall to rubble and a cloud of dust. As the people watched the dust mushroom into the air, The Master spoke from beside Tom. "Let this matter between us be settled. My mistakes will haunt me forever, but you have proven that my scars must remain mental."

Tom nodded deeply. "I have proven that the strength of my arm cannot match the depth of my loss and so lose my claim against you. May we move forward in peace and prosper as we go our separate ways." They each made a fist and tapped their forearms against the other person's, creating an 'X' in the air. They stepped back, and Tom turned and strode toward Hans without another word.

The Master watched him go for a moment before turning to talk to Dale. "I spent quite some time learning from the Northmen. They are a brutal people, but their honor and traditions are the purest I have ever witnessed. If I had been able to have my way, I would have never left them. I would have adopted all of their ways and lived as they do. So... *so* many things I wish had gone differently."

"Why did you need to leave them?" Dale asked the question before he could stop himself.

The Master looked over, hesitating before answering, "Their prince was assassinated, and his new bride was destroyed because of it. A faction of the Northmen used the chance to purge outsiders from amongst them, becoming even more insular than they already were. I... I was an outsider. Exile or death, those were my options. I had just started making a life there, and it crushed me to leave it behind. I left, and from there found a group of other exiles. That path led to the first great necromantic war, our desperate bid to gain a home."

"You are not at all what I expected." Dale reached out his hand and carefully set it on The Master's shoulder. He was glad the man had already put his robe back on. "You sound like... just a normal guy looking to find his way. I'd love to know what happened."

The Master snorted so hard that the air around him *thrummed*. "Would you believe me if I told you I was once one of the lowest in the Queendom and my greatest aspiration was to be a journeyman butcher? I was given an apprenticeship as a Butcher Boy, and... well, it is not only my story to tell. As you know Madame Chandra, it would not be fair for me to discuss her family without her permission."

Dale wanted to shake the story out of him, but he really liked having his arms attached to his body. "I know how that goes. I was a failing shepherd when I stumbled across a dungeon on my mountain."

"Ah yes, is that where *this* happened?" The Master waved his hand at Dale's body. "I had thought that this dungeon was the product of my attempt to create a dungeon over a decade ago, but the soul involved is too different for it to be one of mine. What do you know of that?"

Dale was quiet while he decided how much to say. "Depending on how you look at it, this dungeon was created either well over a decade ago or just a month or so. When we attacked the Tigress Queendom to regain the dungeon's Wisp, the necromancers tried to escape through a portal. Most made it, but as the final few were escaping, the portal was impacted by chaos. I... somehow... the portal connected through *time*, and I was sacrificed to create this dungeon. The current-day dungeon had been holding open the portal and took my memories back into itself. We share a soul because I was killed to create the dungeon, and Cal remade my body to rid itself of its newfound human morals."

"That... that is the most incredible thing I have ever heard in over five hundred years of life," The Master said after he had fully processed everything Dale was saying. "Is this common knowledge?"

"It wasn't, but I have no doubt that it is about to be." Dale looked around and noted how many eyes shifted away swiftly. "Ugh."

CHAPTER FIFTY-FIVE

"Dungeon!" The Master spoke aloud, trying to get my attention without shouting. "Cal, we have need of your assistance."

<Dale, would you please tell the scary man that I am busy doing dungeon things? If he's going to threaten me like Barry did... I'm not sure what I'll do, but I might just slam this whole place into the ground and see what happens.> I had already agreed to play 'horsey' for all these people again; if they tried to make me do stuff I didn't want to, I might seriously start smashing things.

"Whoa, easy, Cal." Dale at least sounded concerned about this; he must be able to tell that I was serious. "We are here to ask a favor. We aren't here to attack you or anything like that, *right*, Master?"

"Of course not." The Master seemed upset by the tone of the conversation. "I'm guessing the Guild was telling him they were going to cause damage? Maybe they gave a show of force? Morons. That is just asking for trouble. If someone doesn't want to work for you, there will always be ways they can hurt you. Dun- that is, Cal, we would like your help in stopping Xenocide. We need to find a way to dismantle those Runes or possibly send them away."

I waited a moment so that Dale would panic a little. That never got old. <So... what do *I* get out of this?>

"Well, the planet might be destroyed, so you get a place to live," Dale shot right back.

<Pretty sure I'll be fine either way, Dale. I'll go to the other side of the planet and hang out in the ocean. After the planet breaks up, I'll work on eating all of it. The amount of

power generated would likely make me more powerful in moments than I can imagine.> I didn't really think that, but it was a good back up plan. Dale didn't need to know that tidbit.

Dale pulled a face, and The Master correctly guessed the reason for it. "Cal, just a hint of what this might entail. We are going to be attempting to send those Runes off our planet, to draw the moon away from our world. We would be pooling all of our most rare resources and esoteric knowledge to make this happen. I have forbidden Runes, dark knowledge that humanity was forbidden from ever learning for hundreds of years. Would you like to be a part of this venture, or should we do it ourselves... somewhere else?"

Water was pouring off of the ceiling near them, a visceral reaction that I stopped as soon as I noticed it. I don't think I had ever drooled before. <Please let the very nice gentleman know that I would be happy to assist. Also, let him know that if I were in the A-ranks, I would be able to be far more helpful.>

"What do you mean by that?" Dale looked around, trying to find a hint of my advancement. "How high have you reached in the last few days? ...Are you the reason there was no Mana storm? Did you go and absorb all of it?"

<In a way,> I responded evasively. <I got to B-rank nine, but that isn't super important. Please go ahead and tell this guy what's going on. He's looking impatient.>

That snapped Dale back to reality. He repeated my words to The Master, who nodded. "Excellent. I'm happy to learn of your progression; it will be more helpful than you know. Hmm."

He rubbed at his chin, then looked around. "B-rank nine... I remember it well. This rank is a difficult one to break through, and even when you do, it may not be apparent right away. The others all seem to have clearly delineated objectives, such as gaining a spiral, reaching a certain amount of power, forming an aura and empowering it, or gaining Mana. The A-ranks is all internal, within your mind and soul, and begins with the laying of your foundation. Only when you have gained a certain amount of *solidity*, when your foundation is *settled*, do you reach the A-ranks. In fact, perhaps it is simpler than I think, and I can tell you the key to the A-ranks right now. Being able to manifest your **law** and combine a portion of your foundation into it."

"In fact, perhaps that is *it*. When you can store an item in your world, you will need to have settled your foundation. That seems to be the minimum requirement for anyone I have ever met in the A-ranks. Of course, you won't be storing a *living* thing. You would need to create a soul-key for that, which requires that you sacrifice a portion of your soul. While people do it... they are typically beast tamers or some such. It is *very* dangerous and wasteful in the extreme if done without a purpose. Also, most people's foundation simply cannot handle the inclusion of external life. Their souls would fight each other. Now, the benefits for those who can properly utilize..." The Master looked at the stunned people around him and smiled. "I always wanted to teach."

"You know, we have been looking for an instructor in the infernal wing of our academy," Dale stated hopefully, getting only a short laugh in reply. It had been worth a shot.

A young man cautiously approached the group. He bowed several times as all eyes in the cavernous room turned to rest upon him. "I am *so* sorry to bother you, but I was tasked with coming here and informing you that the Dwarves have arrived. The... um... their leader. King, I think? I-"

"We understand," Madame Chandra jumped in to rescue the youngster from his babbling. "Thank you; you can leave."

The boy bowed once more and ran away, obviously terrified of the ominous 'Master'. Brianna stepped through the shadows and stopped next to Dale. "I suppose we should get moving then. Dwarven metallurgy and their talent with shaping the earth will be paramount to this project. Cal might be able to replicate it or even do a better job with the initial creation, but there is no one more versed in *altering* metal."

"There was an actual reason to call the races together, then?" Dale looked askance at the Dark Elf. "I really thought that it would just end up being a power play."

"It will," the Elf responded pessimistically. "There is no other choice than for *him* to demonstrate his power. There will be someone, some insignificant *speck* that won't listen to reason, who won't see this as the end of the world but as a chance to add some gold to the pile. So The Master will obliterate them to show the rest how easy it was for him to do so. There will be no uprisings after that. No. If Xenocide doesn't want to do it, The Master will rule the world by the end of the day."

Silence followed her grim proclamation, even The Master unsure of how to respond. Madame Chandra let out a harsh bark of laughter and glanced at him. "Just like you always talked about when we were kids, huh? This whole event has sped *all* your plans up, didn't it?"

"I wanted to do it through diplomacy, through words and deeds that sway the hearts of the people. You know better than anyone that I would have never chosen this path!" The Master angrily turned her words against her.

Dale joined into the conversation when it was obvious that no one else would, "Can we just go meet with them and start working on a plan? There is the possibility that they will understand the gravity of this situation, isn't there? That we will be able to point at Xenocide and get them to understand that fighting is futile?"

"All we can do is try," Tyler chimed in, having caught up to the group just as Brianna had turned glum. He wilted under the gazes sent his way and busied himself with a roll of vellum that he had brought with him.

"Dale." Chandra reached out and brushed some dust off his arm, "I don't think that you should attend the upcoming meeting. I know that it is a weakness of the powerful to see lower ranks as lesser, but the fact remains that you will hurt our chances of resolving this peacefully by your mere presence."

Narrowing his eyes at her, Dale folded his arms to cover the fact that his hands were balling into fists. "You aren't joking, are you? Madame, *I* have been the one who-"

Brianna impatiently stopped his speech, "No one is doubting your contribution or intellect, Dale. Those of us who *know* you understand, but for now, just shut your mouth and find something else to do for a while. Take this order from your new Queen, please and thank you."

Dale looked at her somberly. "I'm... I'm sorry for your loss, Brianna. Long live the Queen?" Still, he took a breath to argue his point. Brianna flicked him in the forehead, sending him spiraling into unconsciousness against Tyler, who needed to scramble to keep him from falling on his face.

"Brat," she murmured affectionately. "You need to learn to follow before you can lead, my Duke. Let's get moving."

The powerful members of the council vanished in a whirlwind of displaced air, leaving Tyler holding Dale's limp body. Tyler started dragging him toward the entrance, moving faster and beginning to sweat when he saw a few curious Bashers approaching them.

CHAPTER FIFTY-SIX

<A good, old-fashioned power grind,> I told Dani with satisfaction as I looked back over the progress of my foundation. I was extra happy with my choices to this point; the fact that I had been creating air instead of earth allowed me to shift around what I wanted to see in my inner world. Why did I need to create a copy of the world I lived in? Because it was easy? That wasn't my usual process!

I projected an image of what I saw to Dani and started detailing my thoughts, <I was thinking of *splitting* the world like *this*. I'll create seven very different sections and arrange them to be free-floating under my control. That way, I can make *wild* variations of climate, resources, and training zones. A dungeon literally *within* a dungeon!>

I paused and waited to see what Dani's reaction would be. She pondered long enough that I was concerned about her final decision. "I like it, but you are missing a lot of details. What about the oceans that you will likely need to bring along with you? What if you make *six* landmasses, then another area that is ocean? You can freeze portions of it, boil others, and then you can always use it as a source of easy water if you need to instead of creating it fresh every time."

<Great idea, Dani!> I combined a floating landmass with one of the others, then had to split it up when it was so much larger than the rest of them. Once it was nice and even, I created an image of a planet's worth of ocean and lake water. I covered the plane in a layer of ice and made massive rivers of water that reached out to each of the other planes of my inner world. Now it looked like there were six continents orbiting a colossal sphere, connected by rushing waters. For fun, I also found a way to

connect huge sheets of ice between the planes. I could freeze or melt them on a whim and laughed as I realized that I had accidentally decided to model my world *almost* exactly after the mythology of a city I had passed a long time ago. I wonder why I had never seen anything from those people again?

As a salute to their influence on my construction, I decided to name my new sketches of areas. The connective water would be a 'bifrost bridge', as it had two states: frost or steam. If I could replicate this in the real world or even do it in my inner world, I would have a lot of fun. Right now, I was only playing with my mental projection, but it felt *right* somehow. By my naming scheme, would that make my ice and water world 'Hel'? Sure, why not. I could then– *Oof.* I felt like I had been punched directly and quickly needed to turn my eyes inward. What I saw was... not shocking but still very interesting.

My foundation was splitting, following the patterns I had designated in my mental projection. It wasn't perfectly smooth, and I needed to intervene multiple times, or there would have been some catastrophic collisions, but my mental vision was soon realized within my soul. It was amazing how much my mind impacted everything I did, especially to my own being. If I had a head, I would have been shaking it in wonder. As the corruption-sketched landmasses settled into their positions, I felt like I had finally decided upon the shape my foundation would take. Something within me *clicked*, and the Essence in and around me vanished.

There was a small clap of displaced air as my Core took *every* bit of *available* power from the area around me, but other than that, I felt no different. Hmm. What was it that Master guy had mentioned? Was I in the A-ranks now? I focused on a small rock near me and tried to *will* it into my Core instead of absorbing it. I kept staring at it, pulling, pulling... and with a small *pop*, it vanished. There was no increase in the amount of Essence coming into me, so I hadn't accidentally dissolved it with influence. Did I pull it into my inner space?

I looked around but quickly realized that I was looking for a small rock in an area with the landmass of a planet. Then again, it was my *soul*, so I felt like there should really be a way for me to scan the contents quickly and see what didn't belong. I poked around for a moment or thirty and reeled back as I figured out the different ways to look. Everything in my soul had a certain 'feel' to it, and when I was looking at the world like this, I could feel what wasn't entirely 'me'. Even though I had created the rock in the real world, it was still by using what was available out there. There was no perfect way to describe how it felt, only that the difference was instantly apparent to my mind. The rock had found its way into the massive orb of water and was hidden by the sketches of what would be millions of gallons of water and ice. No wonder I hadn't seen it.

Now, though, I had confirmation that I was in the A-ranks! At least by the metric given to me by the second-least trusted man on the planet. Still. <Hey, Dani, am I in the A-ranks now?>

"Cal, if you need to ask, you probably... oh. Yeah. It appears that we are. I didn't even notice; that was the smoothest transition to a new rank. Wow, yeah. A-rank." Dani seemed unsure how to handle the transition.

<...We did it!> I cheered with a *ton* of exaggeration. That was the most anti-climactic...

"Cal! Look at the Silverwood tree!" Dani broke my grumpy mood with a simple statement, and I turned to look at the Silverwood tree, which was *blooming*!

<Look at those flowers! Look at that *pollen*!> I was stunned by the majestic beauty of the flowering tree. <We are

going to be fighting off Elves *so* soon! If they aren't here in an hour, I'll be shocked beyond belief.>

"I can't believe how good that smells!" Dani sighed happily at the heavenly scent that I couldn't experience. "Wow, we should definitely steal this scent for our own uses."

<Already copied the chemicals in the air,> I told her with glee. Just because I couldn't experience the smell myself didn't mean I couldn't use it to lure in prey. I looked around and saw that my newly increased power was already benefiting the elementals.

My two current favorites were absorbing the passively increased Mana in the air at a prodigious rate, and right then, I realized something amazing about my power. Not only was I able to absorb any type of Mana from others, it seemed that my own power could feed them as well. I was a universal receiver as well as *donor.* The power of my Mana was not only meant to boost myself, it could be used to power Mana-based creatures directly! It seemed that I had been underutilizing my powers to a vast degree and that I had kept the same ability that I had with Pure Essence. I had been splitting the power into its constituent parts and only feeding them Mana that fit their current archetypes, but for the elementals - at least - that was unnecessary. Interesting!

Naturally, I started running tests right away. I tried treating my Mana in the same way I handled my Essence-based influence, just to see what would happen. Instead of an invisible gas-like power, my Mana-based influence created sparkles in the air that caught any light and reflected it like glitter. The first time one of these 'sparkles' touched an elemental, their power would substantially increase. Careful testing showed that increased sparkles were beneficial but not nearly as much as I would have expected it to be. For instance, no matter the amount of sparkles

I devoted to my new infernal lava spider, Aranea, it never reached my own ranking. As usual, the same rules for growth seemed to apply. No creatures at my own strength level without somehow making it happen either by luck or disaster, and even if I were able to... controlling it would be near impossible.

Back to my original realization, Aranea and Imbrem Aureum were swelling in size, then taking a few steps deeper down the ramps and being compressed by the gravity Runes again. They were both *blazing* with power now, having reached the mid B-ranks. When your entire being was compressed Mana surrounding a Core, rapid growth was more than possible; it may as well have been a requirement. Somehow, I had also unknowingly found the key to their progress by increasing the gravity to such intense levels. If the gravity in here had been merely standard, they would have simply become larger and larger blobs, almost certainly reaching a critical mass and losing control.

There was another aspect to these elementals that had me laughing with maniacal glee; they *were* almost purely Mana. Not only did this make them nearly immune to standard damage, it also meant that they had *impeccable* control of their Mana and were *vastly* more powerful than a standard Mage of the same rank. If a B-one Mage fought a B-one elemental, the fight was almost certain to turn in favor of the elemental.

My two highly favored beings were slowly and steadily moving toward the base of the room, so I made a pile of high-powered Cores on the ground to entice them further. Then I sat back to watch as they pushed and strained to become stronger, seeming to understand that the first being to make it there would become the first Boss of this floor. I loved being a dungeon.

Chapter Fifty-Seven

Queen Brianna looked away from the 'negotiations' that were currently happening, wiping blood off her face as it tickled its way down her cheek. That Dwarf had been *far* too stereotypical, unable to change or bend in the face of overwhelming power and evidence. She *knew* this would happen, yet it was still disappointing. Something... something had changed, though, and it took her two more deep breaths to figure it out.

"It smells like... *Silverwood pollen*!" her hushed voice rang through the sudden silence, the words leaving her lips before she could consider *not* saying them. She cursed the faux paus as people tried to slip away from the negotiations as soon as they understood the gravity of the situation. With a touch of power, she called Moon Elves out of various locations and had them reveal themselves. "No one leaves. Secondly, the Dark Elves own all products of the tree according to a deal with the landowner that the *Guild* promised to uphold, so before you get any *ideas*, understand that we will slay anyone we find stealing pollen."

"Your Majesty, permission to collect pollen?" The Moon Elf Elite that instructed Dale on fighting stepped into the room and bowed, a team of four others matching the movement.

Brianna nodded and spoke, "Permission granted-"

"Gomei." The Moon Elf interrupted her. "It is something Dale started calling me that I thoroughly enjoy, and I would like to be known by this name in this location if you would allow it."

"Understood. Is there any significance to the name?" Brianna noted The Master's eye twitching as he held himself back from commenting on the derailed discussion.

"Ah. Yes." Gomei almost smiled, and even the slight twitch showed more mirth than Brianna had ever seen from him. "Dale calls me 'Grumpy Old Moon Elf instructor' under his breath and turned it into an acronym. He thinks I don't hear him, but I plan to use it as a training aid for our next lesson."

The tension in the room broke when Gomei and his team vanished at the end of his explanation. Chuckles rang through the room, and The Master used the shift in attitude to press forward and extract promises of aid from all the races. The Dwarves were the hardest to convince after the recent display of power, but they knew there was no real choice. The fact that The Master offered certain powers and rare resources that were needed by each of them may have also played a part in their attitudinal shift. He was not above bribery.

After he had gained binding agreements from each of them, The Master turned the conversation over to High Mageous Amber of the Portal Guild. She stood in front of the room and began detailing her needs and the requirements of each of the people present. "...so not only do we need you to put forward the effort at a breakneck pace, we need it to be perfect. I'm sure I don't need to remind you all that the fate of the world, the actual *world* is at stake here. There will be no surviving this *calamity*, this *madness.* Xenocide threatens every single person, being, and object on the planet. Only through our *newly born* alliance do we have a chance to hold off the *desolation* of our homes!"

After her slightly odd-phrased but impassioned speech, the groups slowly scattered. They left the floating dungeon through the portal, eager to get their people working. They didn't have an abundance of time, that much was obvious. As the representatives of the different races moved around the skyland, the black-clad Moon Elves were moving toward the Silverwood tree. The unseen squad ran through the final layers of the dungeon, quietly remarking upon the Mage's Recluse and making plans to visit and claim a place to live.

When they got to the last known location of the Silverwood tree, they found the guards on duty standing around with faces filled with either panic or longing. Gomei stepped out of the shifting shadows and took them by surprise. "Where is the tree?"

"Oh, abyss," the guard leading the group muttered as quietly as he could. "High Lord-"

"Gomei. Just Gomei from now on."

"Right. Um. Lord... I mean, Gomei, the dungeon created a new level and has descended. We attempted to follow, but... we are not sufficiently strong enough to survive the next floor. We believe the dungeon reached the A-ranks, and the power of the monsters on the next floor attests to this fact. We sent a message to the Princess but have not gained a response. Frankly, I thought that you were here to investigate." The guard seemed to become more at ease as he spoke, relieved to have such a powerhouse coming to take over. His tension returned when Gomei spoke.

"Foolish child." Gomei's voice was tight with anger. "Has anyone else gone down there?"

"No, Lord-"

"Do you not smell the... ah... you are all so young and have never had the chance to produce offspring. I see." Gomei's word made the guards flush with embarrassment and resentment. "That scent in the air, the sweet tang of the unknown and unpredictable? The Silverwood tree is blossoming, and pollen is available for collection. Learn this scent well, for it means the continuation of our race. Stand aside, and ensure that only Dark Elves progress. Any others that you cannot stop... ensure you learn who they are so we can end them."

The Moon Elves moved forward as a single unit, sweeping past the Dark Elves who were now *focused* on ensuring that no one would pass. Gomei started leading his people along a strange staircase leading downward. The stairs had hard turns that hid what was both above and below, making him feel itchy, like a trap was awaiting him. Gomei glanced at everything portrayed along the walls, knowing that the dungeon liked to offer hints toward what was coming.

"*Turn back! Only death awaits!*"

"*Yoo-hoo! Big summer blowout!*"

Gomei ignored the screaming stones that tried to startle them or induce fear; they had been a constant companion in the tunnels leading to and past the Manticore. What actually bothered him was the utter *lack* of information on the walls. There were oddly-glistening spiders etched into the walls, strange abstract shapes that held hints of knowledge. Spotters would be trapped here for weeks if they ever managed to reach this level, only looking for the 'hidden meaning'. Gomei shook his head in disgust. Seeking knowledge for no purpose, only to *suppress* that knowledge anyway? Pointless.

They reached the end of the stairs and paused as they took a collective inhalation. The air here was suffused with the scent of the Silverwood tree, but more than that, it was filled with *power*. There was a battle royale playing out between beings that made a near-zero amount of sense to Gomei. They were blobs of... Mana? They were *generating* power though, not losing it like typical constructs do. Not only that, but their basic attacks were as strong as full-powered incantations from human Mages.

That one seemed to be pure lightning! It crawled across the ground at speeds the others couldn't match, targeting a water-based being that had no defense against it. As the water boiled, the lightning beast seemed to *feed* upon it, taking on a new form and slipping over the rim of a gigantic hole in the ground.

"This is unusual," Gomei spoke aloud for the benefit of his followers. "Be on your guard; we need to attack a lesser version of these things and learn the weaknesses."

A few brutal blows later, they had determined that the only way to destroy the creatures was to either smash or remove the Core they carried around. This was no easy feat, as the Core was surrounded by a shell of minerals and Mana. Attacking the body of the creature may separate some of its power, but it did no permanent damage. If they had been much weaker, the Moon Elves would have been in serious trouble. When they had removed a Core, the other beings in the area had swarmed after them. The simple expedient of tossing the Core away had caused the Mana-things to fight each other instead of them, and so they had taken to using a removed Core as a way to clear a path to the rim of the hole.

Looking over the edge nearly killed one of the others as he was pulled forward by a strong force, but Gomei reacted swiftly enough to yank the oddly heavy Elf back to safety. "What was that? What did you see?"

The Elf, though internally shaken, responded smoothly, "There appears to be a powerful gravitational force in the pit. There are two ramps leading downward which are filled with these things in various forms. A light at the bottom of the pit seems to indicate that the tree and dungeon Core are hidden in an adjacent room. Also. Good catch."

Gomei nodded at the thanks, not bothering to waste time making eye contact. "Let's go."

They stepped onto the ramp and could instantly feel the increased weight. Gomei stopped them and looked closely at the Inscriptions that seemed to flow around the entirety of the conic hole. "I see. These Runes are all linked. The weight will be extreme at the base; if at any point any of you are too encumbered to fight correctly, we will set you as rear guard. Make sure to speak up. Do not damage the Runes."

He pointed out the linkages throughout as he spoke, then looked them all in the eye to denote his seriousness. "You see how this place is shaped? Destroy the Runes, and we couldn't run fast enough to escape the blast. I doubt we would escape unscathed, though I have no doubts the dungeon and tree will be fine. With Runes breaking... who knows what could happen? We might even survive it but be sent elsewhere."

They began walking downward and tossed an elemental off the ramp to see what would happen. The creature screamed like a boiling teapot as it was crushed in midair, shattering its Core before ever even reaching the bottom. The water released from its death hit the ground like a chunk of granite tossed from a building, slightly deforming the ground. Gomei spoke softly once more, "Don't fall off. That might even be enough to severely damage us if done too fast. Until we can test it, assume it is deadly."

They continued downward, finding it harder and harder to progress. Not only were they hampered by the gravity - which was somehow becoming strong enough to actually impede them - but the elementals were starting to become powerful threats. As they went deeper, the Mana was at such a density that their weapons were becoming useless without powerfully enhancing them. Gomei was still able to smash through with his techniques, and unless the others did something similar, the Mana - and therefore the Cores - were strong enough to resist instant destruction.

A little over halfway down, one of the Elves stopped and nodded, indicating that this was as far as he felt safe going. Gomei tried not to be disappointed, but he understood. His students were fresh into the A-ranks, and Gomei himself was only at A-five. These... *things* were strange and attacked in nerve-fraying ways. Not a single one of them followed the same attack pattern, which was frustrating to the logical Assassin. Another Elf needed to stop a short while later, and a third was forced to stop by Gomei when the Elf began sweating. That was a reaction he hadn't seen on an A-ranker in a long time and showed the massive strain he was under.

The final Elf and Gomei were looking at a much more solid-looking construct, a sickly, boiling-stone spider. They were only a short distance from the bottom, and Gomei made a mistake in his impatience. Instead of smashing the creature, he tossed it over the edge. He had evidently expected it to be destroyed, and it almost happened. Instead, the spider landed on the ground. Specifically, it landed on a cache of Cores and began draining and incorporating them right away. Added to that was the fact that I started dropping the floor, and soon there was five feet of open space between the last gravity Runes and the new floor height.

The spider, no longer forced to maintain a perfect shape, began ballooning upward and was now precisely five feet tall and nine feet wide. Gomei saw the transition happening and rushed forward, diving past the spider and into the room with the Silverwood tree. "I'll get the pollen, the rest of you get out of here!"

The molten spider watched the Elves flee, even as its power continued to skyrocket. Over the course of ten minutes, as

Gomei gently scraped pollen from the tree, the spider being reached B-rank nine. It watched consideringly as its nemesis, the golden water elemental, slowly and continuously worked to gather power. It would eventually challenge the spider, but the new boss would be ready. It folded its legs and shrank down, appearing to become nothing more than a darkly glowing boulder. Every time a new Core appeared on the ground, a fiery leg would grab it and pull it in. At this rate, it would reach the A-ranks in days.

Gomei looked at the palm-sized purple bag he held in his hand. It was filled to the brim with pollen and would be enough to birth a thousand new Elves. He bowed to the tree and the Core that resided under it, giving his respects. His race had been on the brink of destruction; this would save it. "I thank you both. I shall return to collect the next batch in a decade. Dungeon, I want you to know that this room is going to become the training grounds of the Moon Elves. I have never found an area for resistance training that was this beneficial to my people."

Obviously, there was no response, but Gomei felt as though the dungeon approved. A swirling portal snapped into place, and Gomei could see the fourth floor through it. He stepped through, allowing the gateway to wink out behind him. It seemed that this was a floor that the dungeon wouldn't allow others to skip. Gomei nodded approvingly; that floor could have even been dangerous for *him*, so he agreed that others should need to prove their mettle with each attempt.

Chapter Fifty-Eight

<Hey, Dani?> My lovely Wisp had seemed to run out of easy things to teach Grace and had taken to hanging out with me more often. <I forgot to add a portal to the other floors in my dungeon, but I had a one-way setup nearby that I dragged over last minute. Um. That Elf guy seemed to like it; should I make a keygem so they can get a portal to this level?>

"Nah, I kinda like the idea that people can't just pop down here." Dani grabbed a stray bit of Mana, burping lightly as she absorbed it. "Mm! I like those. I know they don't actually do anything for me, but they are super tasty. Right, the portal. Keep it as a one-way, in my opinion. Maybe put a really high-payout token station in here though? Also, there was no loot from the elementals."

<The Cores were supposed to be loot, it isn't my fault they used them like lures!> I may have been getting too defensive. <But I suppose a few tokens would be a good idea. Maybe Hans will visit or something.>

"Plus, that Elf basically just promised that we would have high B-rankers and low-to-mid A-rankers in here." Dani was getting excited at the prospect. "Just think how much more power we are going to be able to get from them! We are going to be the training ground of the *Moon Elves*!"

<You think they will let other people onto the floor?> My words acted like a bucket of cold water. Actually... I found Dale and saw he was sleeping. I poured a pails worth of ice water on him, and he woke up sputtering. Heh.

"You think they will stop other people from coming onto the floor? Oh, I hope not!" Dani was now zipping around being agitated, so I took a few moments to create a bubble around

Grace that repelled Mana. I had been doing it manually, but if I needed to turn my attention away, I didn't want her accidentally popping. Now, she chased after the sparkles, and they would curve around her no matter how creative she got. Why did it feel so wrong when I laughed at her failed attempts?

<I think we are fine, Dani. We don't really need to eat people anymore, right? I mean, it's tasty and all, but *need* to? Nah.> I felt a ripple pass through ambient Mana in the area and looked around. The Master was standing at the top edge of the cone, looking down at the view below. He stepped over the edge, landing lightly on the floor.

Aranea unfolded its legs with a high-pitched hiss as the humidity in the air was boiled. A heat haze settled over the area, obscuring the spider with a mirage of shifting light. It reached its full height... and impacted the back wall with enough force to crack the stone and make pieces of the protective coating around its Core flake off. Dani, being the brave ball of light that I knew and loved, zipped out to hover a few feet from the man as he approached the side room where my Core was contained.

"Hey! Listen up! You're a jerk, and I really dislike that we have to work with you," Dani's voice made the man freeze up, his eyes narrowing a bit. "That said, I think that going forward, I can put the past behind us. I know that you had something messing with your mind, making it hard to see right and wrong. You're still going to need to earn my trust, no matter how strong you are. Also, thank you for not breaking Aranea. Cal really likes it."

"You are a whirlwind of conflicting emotions, Wisp," The Master let a grin appear on his face, "but I like how upfront you are. I am here bearing gifts."

He upended a storage device onto the table. "This contains the majority of my personal Runes, both ones I know and ones I have collected but cannot understand. Over here... these are the secret materials each race has found. Their conductivity for the basic affinities are-"

"We know all of those. Also? Rubies? Really? We know that Scarletite is at least five times as effective." Dani's words made The Master's jaw drop, the first *really* human thing I had seen from him.

"These are some of the most jealously guarded secrets of the races, and you shout them at me because I got them *wrong*? I know craftsmen that would *kill* to learn these secrets, and you shout them in anger. Just. I am amazed. Are the Runes at least useful?" The Master winced when he saw that the books and stacks of paper he had brought were gone.

<Let him know that they were very tasty. Also, there were many I had never seen before. I'll test any of the unlabeled ones and let him know what they do.> I paused as Dani relayed the information. <Also, can you please ask him what I should be doing to help the cause? Would he be willing to slay Barry for me when this is over? The usual questions. Also, figure out how long he has to live.>

"I can... wait. *What*?"

Dani's voice made The Master's face crumble. He knew from her tone that she *knew*. "Drat. I had hoped it wasn't so obvious. Well, abyss. I hope I can hide the fact long enough to save everyone."

"You mean he is *right*?" Dani seemed to be having a hard day. She flew over and landed on the Silverwood tree to calm down.

"Indeed, he is," The Master confirmed solemnly. "If we are going to do this, we need to do it right and *fast*. Faster than even I had hoped. Here is how you can help..."

DALE

"Ahh!" Dale shouted in fury as icy water poured over him. "Fight me, Cal!"

As expected, there was no answer. Dale grumbled for a moment, then went silent in rage as he remembered his last few moments of consciousness. He went outside of the medical tent he was in, grumbling about water and wondering why he wasn't at the church's medical area. The teeming masses of people moving around caused his mouth to close with an audible *click*. He had never seen so many variations of sentient beings walking around together without fighting. To be fully truthful, there were often tense moments, especially when the Northmen and Amazons walked past each other.

Dale ran around Mountaindale, searching all of the usual places that his group members were fond of. After fruitless calling and searching by not only himself but messengers as well, Dale decided that they must be in the dungeon but was wondering why they would go without him. Deciding that he would simply need to find out later, Dale decided to go into the dungeon and take out his frustrations on the Goblins. Maybe he would stay down there for a few days... why not?

He left a message to his friends and team at the academy; as soon as a messenger saw them, it would be delivered. Until they came to collect him or for four days, he would be fighting Goblins. Dale was just leaving the academy to jump into fighting when he heard a voice calling out to him. "Dale, m'boy!"

"Headmaster, good to see you. I'm sorry to be blunt, but I was just going into... are you a *Mage*?" Dale had just turned to look at the older man and was now gaping at the aura he saw in front of him. "What in the world kind of...?"

Artorian laughed heartily, taking a deep breath and wiping a tear away. "Lad, you aren't going to believe it. I got to the *top* of the tower. I wanted to thank you for bringing me to this amazing place."

"But... what...?" Dale sputtered, trying to get a sense of the raw might coming from the man.

"Do you really want to know?" Artorian frowned at the youngster.

"*Yes*!"

"It's ***Love***." Artorian began laughing anew as Dale's expression turned thunderous. "Oh yes, sunshine and **Love**. That's Headmaster Artorian."

"You are messing with me."

"I swear that I am not." Artorian's words rang with Mana; there was no way for him to have made that promise and survived if he were lying. "Anyway, let me know if you need anything. I'm off to play with my new powers."

Dale stood there trying to deal with the new information as Artorian became translucent and flew away faster than Dale had ever seen another Mage move, vanishing with a fading *Whee!* "Sunshine and love. Just... at least he didn't find some **law** for pillows. Now I *really* need to hit something."

He went into the dungeon, bypassing the early levels and popping out into the Goblin area. Bloodlust radiated from him, and a smile played across his face as he charged at the nearest fortress. He still needed to be careful, as sometimes, a wandering Bob would appear, which meant Incantations and Runic traps. Those weren't something that Dale was ready to fight against. At least, not head-on. Yet. He ran straight at the fortress wall, leaping off the ground and tumbling over the sentry on duty. The Goblin didn't even get a chance to see him or raise an alarm since Dale crushed his head from above in passing.

Now, a good chunk of the Goblins in the area were D-ranked, with the wandering Shaman, Bob, appearing every once in a while. This meant that there were wild variations in the average power levels of the Goblins, anywhere from upper D-ranked to upper C-ranked. Dale had just entered a fortress with *only* D-ranked Goblins. They never even saw him, though they understood that they were under attack. The human simply killed them with brutal and efficient assaults from invisibility, moving on as soon as they stopped twitching.

When the last Goblin fell, Dale was dissatisfied. He moved onto the next fortress, finding that it too was only home to D-rankers and a single Goblin in the C-ranks. "Cal, what's with the Goblins on this floor?"

<Dale? What? Oh. Yeah, I've been using the others for a... special project. Plus, I was getting a lot of complaints. Minya had me shift things around so that there would be a more balanced setup on that floor.> Dale made a 'continue' gesture. <Fine. Look, I'm swamped right now trying to manufacture the stuff needed to keep us all from getting squashed. In general, get closer to the next floor, get higher powered Goblins. Have fun, and if you die, I am going to wait a week before bringing you back.>

"Won't be a problem." Dale looked deeper into the dungeon and cracked his knuckles. It was time for a proper fight.

Chapter Fifty-Nine

Dale left the dungeon four days later, bruised, bleeding, and in a bad mood. He eventually found his companions, stopping and staring at them darkly. "Rose... are you wearing a *dress*? What in the abyss is going on? Why didn't any of you come find me?"

"Dale! You are just in time!" Hans walked over wearing nice clothes and a wide smile, patting Dale on the back hard enough that he could actually feel it. "We didn't get you because there was no point! We are taking it easy before the end of the world, and if we survive, there will be plenty of time for training afterword! What have you been up to?"

"Still, you couldn't pop down and tell me that? I was so worried that you would arrive as I was leaving that I couldn't force myself to come up for air!" Dale growled at the Assassin, who only smiled in reply. "I spent the last day working to perfectly hold my aura no matter what, and I made a ton of progress. We need to get back to training!"

"Sorry, Dale, not today." Hans handed over a small box. "Hey, can you put this on?"

"What? Why?" Dale's questions went unanswered as Madame Chandra appeared among them.

"Oh good, Dale made it in time." Chandra looked over at the others with a frown. "Are we sure that this is the best course of action? We have a lot of work to do, and I can't have you four vanishing for days on end like you have been."

"It's what we want, Grandma." Rose smiled sweetly at Chandra before turning to face Dale.

"Alright, *someone* tell me what is going on!" Dale barked in frustration at their expectant expressions.

Hans laughed, causing the others to join in. "Well Dale, we're getting married, and you are my best man. Let's go. Put that flower on, will you?"

"*What*?" Dale hollered as the doors to the church opened. He hadn't even realized where he was standing. "Are you *kidding* me? She hates you!"

"Nah, we got that all worked out. Flower, Dale." Hans motioned at Dale to move, and when he didn't, Chandra *tsked* and made a motion. The flower popped onto his chest and firmly grasped his shirt. "But... but!"

"No butts, let's go!" Hans grabbed him and ran to the front of the church, and Dale watched as the surreal ceremony flew by. When the newlywed couple started walking out, Dale followed in a daze.

"Am I dreaming?"

<Yes.> The mind-voice made Dale look around in shock, expecting the scene to fade away. <Ha! Had you for a second there. Nope, they got married. Surprised me, too.>

"I have just... absolutely no idea how to handle this. There was no warning, no lead-up!" Dale confessed to Tom as they watched Hans and Rose step through the portal for lands unknown. They would be back in a day or two, when the assembled races of the world would launch their initiative against Xenocide.

Tom bobbed his head in understanding. "I agree, this is quite the shocking turnaround. I admit, though I *did* see it coming. Her physical attacks against him were an obvious sign of interest, and after she actually shot him, they were technically engaged by Northman standards."

Dale looked sideways at the tall redhead. "Your country is weird."

"I know." Tom smiled halfheartedly. "I do miss it, though."

"Have you tried...?"

"Not right now, Dale. I will if we survive this." Tom looked away, leaving Dale feeling like an absolute jerk. "My family... it is not so easy as explaining that I have found a way to fix my issue as a berserker. I will be tested and tested and not allowed to heal."

"When you say tested...?" Dale was cut off by a hand wave.

"Berserker rage has a chance to appear when you taste blood... or when you are close to death. Both... both forms will be tested." His voice was heavy and dark, so when he stopped talking, Dale simply nodded.

"Any word on the portal? Or whatever it is they are trying to do?" Dale asked as they walked toward the tavern. They both needed a drink after the day's sudden shifts.

"All I know is that it is going poorly. Though the materials are present, and the experts are working on it..." Tom looked up at the moon, which was looming large in the sky and put his fist up. It barely covered the moon from his perspective. "They think it will not be fast enough. Xenocide laughed at us this morning and *left.* He *left*, after saying that he knew exactly what we were doing. Then he told everyone that he had been staying on the Runes so that he could devote more power to them, and he was telling the truth. They are so much more potent that I overheard The Master saying that if the moon impacting doesn't destroy the planet, the Runes breaking from the impact *would.* Not might, *would.*"

Dale shook his head and thought longingly about the small comfort that Hans and Rose had found. It made him realize that he may never have that or find it for himself. He slowed, then came to an abrupt stop. Tom continued a bit longer before noticing that Dale wasn't with him. "Dale? What are you doing?"

"Possibly something very, *very* stupid." Dale turned and started looking for The Master.

Tom watched him walk away, shrugged, and followed after. "Why not? Should at least be interesting."

They walked into the academy just as a large structure lifted out of the floor of a warehouse Dale had never seen before. It was dug into the ground and was in the dungeon's domain because of it. <Whew! Someone tell the Master guy that I need more work if he is going to try to get the other teams caught up.>

"You really want me to tell him that?" Dale spoke out loud, getting a few people to look at him.

<What? Abyss no! This man is a demon, I tell you!> Dale winced as the voice in his head reached new heights of volume. <He is making *me* tired, Dale! I didn't even know that was possible! I was being facetious, and *of* course that's when you show up!>

"Got it, sheesh." Dale walked up to the craftsmen that were working at a frantic pace to try and build a mobile portal that they could send Xenocide's Runes through. "Excuse me, The Master? I need a moment."

"No." The response was swift and brutal. "Far. Too. Busy."

<What are you up to, Dale?>

"Something stupid." Dale's words to the air made The Master glance over.

"Oh, it's you. Good, Minya needed to leave, and the only other person who can talk to the blasted dungeon is Artorian. *I* can't convince him that he needs to focus on this, all he wants to do is play with his Mana! I've never seen a more unreliable... get over here and help me work with the dungeon." The Master's words cleared up a lot of confusion from Dale's mind, especially how Artorian was able to progress to such a high tier of Magehood.

"Sorry. Listen, are you going to make it?" Dale looked directly into The Master's eyes, waiting for the man to spout a platitude or lie outright.

"At our current pace..." The Master hesitated but forced himself to continue, "we will complete the project too late to turn the moon, let alone send it away. We still need to try."

"I have an idea," Dale spoke heavily, swallowing deeply as he thought about his next words carefully, "but I need your help to stay alive. Can you give me a moment?"

The Master saw the look in Dale's eyes and forced himself to look at the people around him. What he saw were drawn faces, terror, and absolute exhaustion on people that typically never even needed to sleep. They had not rested, had not stopped continually using their power, for days. "I can spare a moment. The rest of you... go get some sleep. Be back in thirty minutes."

There were protests, but even the staunchest of them stopped working when they saw the Master leaving the room. They may be enthusiastic about survival, but the pace they had been setting was brutal even by The Master's standards, and he usually had tireless undead doing the work. They went to get food or quietly sat and took a short nap among those that had recently been racial enemies. A common goal and the threat of eradication was a good motivator for drastic shifts in mentality.

"Alright, Dale. You have my attention. What can you do for this that we cannot?" The Master listened patiently as Dale spoke, his eyes bulging slightly. When Dale had finished, The

Master rubbed his eyes and released a long, slow breath. "You're sure? Can you do it?"

"I see no other option." Dale's mind suddenly flashed back to Adam's last words to him, and he felt like he had been punched in the gut. Was this what he had meant? His mind said yes... but his heart told him that this was not going to be his hardest tribulation.

"Then we try it your way, Dale."

Chapter Sixty

<Tell me again why we aren't figuring out some way for me to do this, Dale,> I told Dale as I ordered his powerful cursed weapons and armor to fall off of him.

"I mean, technically you *are* doing it," Dale quipped as he donned simple wool clothes.

<Don't be snarky with *me*.> I may have been taking my frustration out on him, but I was so mad that he had come up with a viable solution.

"Look, *can* you do it without shattering the Runes and killing us all?" The hope in Dale's voice made it even harder for me to admit that I couldn't. Not for sure, and not in such a localized area.

<...No,> I finally admitted, seeing his face fall a little even though the answer was expected. <Not without leaving my dungeon behind, and that would... well, that would be bad for everyone.>

"Then here we are."

<Dale, we might be able to get the portal to work in time.>

"You know what Xenocide said. He would know better than any of us at this point what his Runes were capable of. If he thinks that all our plans end in our failure... even though he is obviously insane, I have no reason to think that he is *wrong*. Our only chance is to do something *as* insane and hope that it works out."

<I really don't like that... I want to call it logic, but I feel that is being too generous to the words coming out of your mouth.>

"Too late now, Cal. I'm committed."

<It's *not* too late, and you should *be* committed.> Dale ignored the words and walked out to stand with the people waiting for him. One last sentence entered Dale's mind, <Good luck, Dale.>

"Thanks, Cal," Dale muttered under his breath as he stood before the others.

The Master looked him in the eye. "Are you *sure* about this? Once you start, failure means that a lot of people will die, including yourself."

"Been there, done that," Dale breathed the words softly, looking up at the now *very* concerned Master. "I'm ready. Let's do this while we still might have time to succeed."

"Then here we go." The Master, Barry, and the group of Mages ranging from A to B ranks were airborne in an instant, flying toward the Runes Xenocide had left floating in the air. They were shining, the connection they created pulling the smaller of the two moons toward their planet at what must have been extraordinarily high speeds. As Dale settled into a seated lotus position on the swirling Runescript, he breathed deeply and evenly.

The Mages were a whirlwind around him, moving at breakneck speeds as they set up and activated various Runes of their own. None of them trusted what they were doing, as, in their words 'the blasted dungeon made this in a day, and it has never been tested'. Barry and the Master waited until everything was in the proper position, then used their own energy to bring the Runes to full power.

When the new Runescript was humming with the same mysterious frequency as the Runes made by Xenocide, The Master nodded at Dale. "Feel free to begin when ready. At this range... I think it will be hard for you to fail. Just..."

"Get ready, Master," Dale spoke in a dreamy tone, having been pushing to enter a state of trance-like calm. "I am about to start."

The Master nodded, then stood back a few feet. If this didn't work as hoped, being further away wouldn't help at all. He watched as Dale's aura shifted all at once, going from radiating light and peace... to becoming a slight sheen of water that began to collect on his skin. Not only that, but Dale suddenly became an aberration to the Master and to everyone watching. Instead of appearing as a human, as anything living or even *inanimate*, Dale became a black hole to their senses.

There was no Essence, no Mana, *nothing* where Dale was... unless they looked with just their eyes. Then all they saw was what appeared to be a sweaty, sodden young man who was breathing heavily. The 'sweat' collecting on Dale began to run off of him and drip onto the Runes below. The Runescript gave off a sinister *hiss*, like a powerful acid touching bone. Wherever the water touched, the Runes would darken for a long moment.

"It's not doing anything!" Barry snarled at the waiting people. "It's not *enough*!"

"Patience, Barry. The show hasn't even started." The Master's words were *just* enough to make Barry stop, but his frustration was evident to all. "Disenchanting water is barely known, and I have never met someone who could actually *produce* it. All it does is turn the amazing into the mundane, and who would want to do that?"

Dale raised his hand slowly, forming his fingers into a shape the Moon Elves called 'wyvern's talon' and let the water collect on his fingernails. Just as it was about to drip, he *slammed* his fingers into the space between his folded legs, simultaneously disenchanting and breaking a section of the Rune beneath him. As the S-ranked energy began to return to the space below him, the part he had smashed began to leak vast amounts of power. Whenever the incomprehensible energy touched Dale, it simply... ceased to be.

Still, power was blazing around him, and Dale sank into the Rune as it crumbed from the outrushing energy. He focused harder, generating more of the water to not only protect himself but regulate the power seeping past him. The Runes The Master and the others had activated began to grab the energy, channeling it into a space a few feet above Dale's head. The ball of power that formed was not within a human's normal visual spectrum, even when their eyes were enhanced by Mana. Instead, the area shifted to a gray monotone that expanded rapidly. The Master narrowed his eyes and shifted more of his power into activating the Runes. The gray ball stopped developing but didn't condense any further.

Dale was now surrounded by S-ranked power, perhaps all the way to SSS, but it never fully touched his skin. If it had, it would have disintegrated his body entirely and nigh-instantaneously. Dale was trapped deep within his own mind, doing everything he could to hold this aura perfectly. He couldn't mess it up for an instant, or everything would fail catastrophically.

The reasons he couldn't ask the dungeon to do this was simple. The dungeon would have needed to find a way to send the disenchanting water *through* the energy stream as well as making it pool perfectly on the Runes. A single breeze, a single shift in *anything*, and no one would be left alive to know what had happened. Now, the dungeon *could* have managed to simply douse a section in the water if they only needed to stop the Runes from functioning, but... the moon was too close, and the Runes had been protected by Xenocide until this point. That issue was what the new Runescript around Dale was created to fix.

The ball of grey light collecting above Dale reached critical mass. Dale became entirely obscured by the strange light, and a torrential amount of power was now pouring out of the area around him. The power could not go side to side; it could not go down. So, following the **laws** of the world, it took the path of least resistance and went *up*. And up. And up. Now that the Runes had been set in place and the energy was in motion, the remainder simply followed the created path. In three minutes, they got to see what was happening in the sky far above them.

The energy reached the moon, seemingly doing nothing for one... *long*... second. Then the moon simply collapsed inward like a melon that had been hit by a club. There was no sound. There was no air, no way for the vibrations of its violent desolation to reach them. All they could do was watch as the moon that had been circling their planet for time unknown was blown up, shattered into millions and millions, of pieces.

The Master only noticed that they were falling because someone bumped into him. Looking around, he saw that the others were starting to make the same realization. No one had yet grabbed Dale, and the multiple tons of bones and various materials that made up the Runes they had been standing on were only a few dozen feet from the ground. The Master moved, grabbing Dale and gently pulling his unconscious body into the air.

"I suppose you weren't able to get any air in there, were you?" The Master laughed harshly. He had heard rumors about Dale, but he hadn't given them any thought. This young man kept accomplishing impossible feats of bravery and somehow surviving them. At that moment, The Master noticed Dale was nude. "Ugh. Just because you were untouched doesn't mean your clothes weren't, hmm? Good thing I noticed; that would have cast a pall on your triumphant return."

Dale's aura flickered to life, just a neutral network of pure Essence. And... something else. The Master looked down at the boy in wonder. No... could it be? He turned and made for the dungeon, appearing at the deepest levels and dropping Dale amongst the branches of the Silverwood tree.

<Of all the times for someone not to be able to hear what I am saying, this has me the most annoyed.> I heaved a sigh, then screamed, <Dani! I need you!>

"I know it, glad you realized... oh. What happened?" Dani flew into the area and inspected Dale.

"He succeeded." The Master's voice was still tinged with worry, making me wonder what was happening. "Wisp, he's-"

"I can see that he's unconscious. Oh man, Xenocide is going to be *angry*," Dani snapped at the man. "Cal, can you take care of him?"

<Dani.> My voice, tinged with wonder and concern, stopped her cold. <I can't do anything but drench this area in Essence. He's not unconscious. I don't know how, I don't know why, but he's *ascending*. Dale's mind is in the Tower of Ascension.>

Epilogue

Dale stood on a vast, silver plane. He knew part of what was happening, but he didn't know why. "This... I'm not seeing a tower. What's happening?"

"**Dale**," a voice came from above him, and Dale was blasted away. He landed over a mile from his starting point, flat on his back and somehow unhurt. Thanks to being on his back, he ended up staring up at a huge ball of *something*. "**I am sorry, Dale. I do not mean to hurt you by existing, but that is simply an aspect of what I am. What *you* are as well.**"

Each word sent Dale flying, buffeted by sheer power. If he had been here as a physical presence, he would have been slain and splattered across the ground from the first syllable.

"Please tell me what you can, in as *few* words as possible." Dale coughed once he could 'breathe' again.

"**Your soul is already bonded to a Law. It is bonded to Me. You are here to see what awaits you upon your return, what awaits you all.**"

"And who... *what* are you?"

"**I am Acme.**" A flood of knowledge he was not prepared to handle entered Dale's mind. Just before he began to lose his sanity, **Acme** shielded him with a sigh. "**See.**"

Dale watched as the world he lived on was destroyed. There was no doubt that nothing would survive, or at least, very little. The reason wasn't even the debris from the falling shards of the moon, though that would wipe out almost everything and change the surface of the planet drastically. There was a simple truth that was utterly undeniable.

"Cal has killed us all," Dale whispered as he saw the planet wither. The creatures and people that somehow survived the shards of moonstone, survived the freezing of the planet from long decades of winter caused by the ash and dirt in the air... they all died of Essence starvation as all loose Essence was torn out of the air and forced through Cal's ley lines.

"Not. Just. Yet."

New images appeared, humanity living on. The other races, the races that needed Essence and Mana to *survive*... none of them walked the earth again. Humankind thrived, though they were reduced to a dark age. Years - centuries - passed. All the while, humans improved themselves. Needing to progress, they took a different route and began learning all new concepts of technology. Essence, Mana, and everything about it was labeled taboo or faded into mythology, becoming a joke to the world. War became increasingly prevalent as chaos-infused smoke was released by transportation devices, to heat homes, or to generate a subpar lightning Essence. The impact of the raw chaos was noticed but chalked up to other various scientific reasoning, the real matter of the base elements not even being *considered.* Tears filled Dale's eyes as he stared at the planet of the future, at the far-reaching impact of the dungeon's grand plans.

But then, as if to tease Dale's ability to cope, a light appeared. Cal somehow changed, became *more*, and Essence and Mana began returning to the world. With the return of the life-giving energy came the return of the races and destruction turned to exaltation. Dale watched as a golden age of knowledge, thought, and peace ruled over the world. The vision faded, and Dale stared up at the Node, stared up at **Acme**.

Tears filling his eyes, Dale asked the question he was dreading. "How? How can I do it, how can I save them?"

"Work has already begun, even if it was not known. Cal is the only one who can save all of them, but there is only one way for this to work, only one way they survive: *you* have to

make the hard choice. I warn you, what you saw... was the *best* possible outcome.”

Dale blinked and found himself in his body, staring at silver leaves swaying in a breeze that he couldn’t feel. His body *roared* with power, and his back arched in pain and pleasure as he was remade by Mana. When he settled on the ground, he looked around to see one awed face and two Wisps.

“What...” The Master licked his lips, which were suddenly dry. “What tier? What type of Mana?”

Dale’s voice echoed with power that he didn’t know how to contain yet. “I gained... I have gained **Acme**. I’m so sorry, there is no time to discuss this right now. We have to make a plan. Cal... we need to save the world.”

<*Celestial feces*, Dale. We *just* did that! How about you go play hero, and I work on being a better dungeon? I think that I could just vanish into the horizon and->

“From you, Cal.” The newly minted Mage shook his head, cutting off the tirade. “We need to save the world from your dungeon’s desolation.”

AFTERWORD

Thank you for reading! I hope you enjoyed Dungeon Desolation! Since reviews are the lifeblood of indie publishing, I'd love it if you could leave a positive review on Amazon! Please use this link to go to the Divine Dungeon: Dungeon Desolation Amazon product page to leave your review: geni.us/DungeonDesolation.

As always, thank you for your support! You are the reason I'm able to bring these stories to life.

THE DIVINE DUNGEON UNIVERSE

THE DIVINE DUNGEON

Dungeon Born (Book 1)

Dungeon Madness (Book 2)

Dungeon Calamity (Book 3)

Dungeon Desolation (Book 4)

Dungeon Eternium (Book 5)

THE COMPLETIONIST CHRONICLES

Ritualist (Book 1)

Regicide (Book 2)

Rexus (Book 2.5)

Raze (Book 3)

About Dakota Krout

I live in a 'pretty much Canada' Minnesota city with my wife and daughter. I started writing The Divine Dungeon series because I enjoy reading and wanted to create a world all my own. To my surprise and great pleasure, I found like-minded people who enjoy the contents of my mind. Publishing my stories has been an incredible blessing thus far and I hope to keep you entertained for years to come!

Connect with Dakota:
Patreon.com/DakotaKrout
Facebook.com/TheDivineDungeon
Twitter.com/DakotaKrout

About Mountaindale Press

Dakota and Danielle Krout, a husband and wife team, strive to create as well as publish excellent fantasy and science fiction novels. Self-publishing *The Divine Dungeon: Dungeon Born* in 2016 transformed their careers from Dakota's military and programming background and Danielle's Ph.D. in pharmacology to President and CEO, respectively, of a small press. Their goal is to share their success with other authors and provide captivating fiction to readers with the purpose of solidifying Mountaindale Press as the place 'Where Fantasy Transforms Reality'.

Connect with Mountaindale Press:
MountaindalePress.com
Facebook.com/MountaindalePress
Twitter.com/_Mountaindale
Instagram.com/MountaindalePress
Krout@MountaindalePress.com

Mountaindale Press Titles

GameLit and LitRPG

The Completionist Chronicles Series
By: Dakota Krout

A Touch of Power Series
By: Jay Boyce

Red Mage: Advent
By: Xander Boyce

Ether Collapse: Equalize
By: Ryan DeBruyn

Axe Druid Series
By: Christopher Johns

Skeleton in Space: Histaff
By: Andries Louws

Pixel Dust: Party Hard
By: David Petrie

APPENDIX

Adam – A mid-D-ranked cleric who joined Dale's group. He was corrupted by a massive influx of celestial Essence which may have given him powerful abilities.

Adventurers' Guild – A group from every non-hostile race that actively seeks treasure and cultivates to become stronger. They act as a mercenary group for Kingdoms that come under attack from monsters and other non-kingdom forces.

Affinity – A person's affinity denotes what element they need to cultivate Essence from. If they have multiple affinities, they need to cultivate all of those elements at the same time.

Affinity Channel – The pathway along the meridians that Essence flows through. Having multiple major affinities will open more pathways, allowing more Essence to flow into a person's center at one time.

Amber – The Mage in charge of the portal-making group near the dungeon. She is in the upper A rankings, which allows her to tap vast amounts of Mana.

Artorian – The new Headmaster of the Academy. He made a deal with the dungeon to swiftly advance to the Mage ranks.

Assassin – A stealthy killer who tries to make kills without being detected by his victim.

Assimilator – A cross between a jellyfish and a Wisp, the Assimilator can float around and collect vast amounts of Essence. It releases this Essence as powerful elemental bursts. A pseudo-Mage, if you will.

Aura – The flows of Essence generated by living creatures which surround them and hold their pattern.

Barry the Devourer – A powerful S-ranked High Elf with the ability to turn all matter within a certain range into pure Essence and absorb it.

Basher – An evolved rabbit that attacks by head-butting enemies. Each has a small horn on its head that it can use to "bash" enemies.

Beast Core – A small gem that contains the Essence of Beasts.

> Flawed: An extremely weak crystallization of Essence that barely allows a Beast to cultivate, comparable to low F-rank.
>
> Weak: A weak crystallization of Essence that allows a Beast to cultivate, comparable to an upper F-rank.
>
> Standard: A crystallization of Essence that allows a Beast to cultivate well, comparable to the D-rankings.
>
> Strong: A crystallization of Essence that allows a Beast to cultivate very well, comparable to the lower C-rankings.

Beastly: A crystallization of Essence that allows a Beast to cultivate exceedingly well, comparable to the upper C-rankings.

Immaculate: An amalgamation of crystallized of Essence and Mana that allows a Beast to cultivate exceedingly well. Any Beast in the B-rankings or A-rankings will have this Core.

Luminous: A Core of pure spiritual Essence that is indestructible by normal means. A Beast with this core will be in at least the S-rankings, up to SSS-rank.

Radiant: A Core of Heavenly or Godly energies. A Beast with this Core is able to adjust reality on a whim.

Brianna – A Dark Elf Queen that intends to build a city around the dungeon. She is a member of the council and knows that the dungeon is alive and sentient.

Cal – The heart of the Dungeon, Cal was a human murdered by Necromancers. After being forced into a soul gem, his identity was stripped as time passed. Now accompanied by Dani, he works to become stronger without attracting too much attention to himself. Too late.

Cats, dungeon – There are several types:

Snowball: A Boss Mob, Snowball uses steam Essence to fuel his devastating attacks.

Cloud Cat: A Mob that glides along the air, attacking from positions of stealth.

Coiled Cat: A heavy Cat that uses metal Essence. It has a reinforced skeleton and can launch itself forward at high speeds.

Flesh Cat: This Cat uses flesh Essence to tear apart tissue from a short distance. The abilities of this Cat only work on flesh and veins and will not affect bone or harder materials.

Wither Cat: A Cat full of infernal Essence, the Wither Cat can induce a restriction of Essence flow with its attacks. Cutting off the flow of Essence or Mana will quickly leave the victim in a helpless state. The process is *quite* painful.

Celestial – The Essence of Heaven, the embodiment of life and *considered* the ultimate good.

Center – The very center of a person's soul. This is the area Essence accumulates (in creatures that do not have a Core) before it binds to the Life Force.

Chandra – Owner of an extremely well-appointed restaurant, this A-ranked Mage is the grandmother of Rose. She has an unknown history with The Master.

Chi spiral – A person's Chi spiral is a vast amount of intricately knotted Essence. The more complex and complete the pattern woven into it, the more Essence it can hold and the finer the Essence would be refined.

Cleric – A Cultivator of Celestial Essence, a cleric tends to be support for a group, rarely fighting directly. Their main purpose in the lower rankings is to heal and comfort others.

Corruption – Corruption is the remnant of the matter that pure Essence was formed into. It taints Essence but allows beings to absorb it through open affinity channels. This taint has been argued about for centuries; is it the source of life or a nasty side effect?

Craig – A powerful C-Ranked monk, Craig has dedicated his life to finding the secrets of Essence and passing on knowledge.

Currency values:

> Copper: one hundred copper coins are worth a silver coin
> Silver: one hundred silver coins are worth a Gold coin
> Gold: one hundred Gold coins are worth a Platinum coin
> Platinum: the highest coin currency in the Human Kingdoms

Cultivate – Cultivating is the process of refining Essence by removing corruption then cycling the purified Essence into the center of the soul.

Cultivator – A cultivator is one who cultivates. See above. Seriously, it is the entry right before this one. I'm being all alphabetical here. Mostly.

Dale – Owner of the mountain the dungeon was found on, Dale is now a cultivator who attempts to not die on a regular basis. As a dungeon born person, he has a connection to the dungeon that he can never be rid of.

Dani – A *pink* dungeon wisp – Is that important? – Dani is the soul bound companion of Cal and acts as his moral compass and helper.

Distortion Cat – An upper C-Ranked Beast that can bend light and create artificial darkness. In its home territory, it is attacked and bound by tentacle like parasites that form a symbiotic relationship with it.

Dregs – A Dungeon Core that has limited intelligence. It was installed into Cal's dungeon to control floors 1-4 so Cal could focus on other things.

Dungeon Born – Being dungeon born means that the dungeon did not create the creature but gave it life. This gives the creature the ability to function autonomously without fear that the dungeon will be able to take direct control of its mind.

Dwarves – Stocky humanoids that like to work with stone, metal, and alcohol. Good miners.

Egil Nolsen – Known to the world as 'Xenocide', this man is of unknown ranking and fully insane.

Elves – A race of willowy humanoids with pointy ears. There are five main types:

High Elves: The largest nation of Elvenkind, they spend most of their time as merchants, artists, or thinkers. Rich beyond any need to actually work, their King is an S-Ranked expert, and their cities shine with light and wealth. They like to think of themselves as 'above' other Elves, thus 'High' Elves.

Wood Elves: Wood Elves live more simply than High-Elves, but have greater connection to the earth and the elements. They are ruled by a counsel of S-ranked elders and rarely leave their woods. Though seen less often, they have great power. They grow and collect food and animal products for themselves and other Elven nations.

Wild: Wild Elves are the outcasts of their societies, basically feral, they scorn society, civilization, and the rules of others. They have the worst reputation of any of the races of Elves, practicing dark arts and infernal summoning. They have no homeland, living only where they can get away with their dark deeds.

Dark: The Drow are known as Dark Elves. No one knows where they live, only where they can go to get in contact with them. Dark Elves also have a dark reputation as Assassins and mercenaries for the other races. The worst of their lot are 'Moon-Elves', the best-known Assassins of any race. These are the Elves that Dale made a deal with for land and protection.

Sea: The Sea Elves live on boats their entire lives. They facilitate trade between all the races of Elves and man, trying not to take sides in conflicts. They work for themselves and are considered rather mysterious.

Essence – Essence is the fundamental energy of the universe, the pure power of heavens and earth that is used by the basic elements to become all forms of matter.

Father Richard – An A-ranked Cleric that has made his living hunting demons and heretics. Tends to play fast and loose with rules and money.

Fighter – A generic archetype of a being that uses melee weapons to fight.

Frank – Was the Guild Leader of the Adventurers' Guild. He had his Mana bound to the concept of kinetic energy and could **stop** the use of it, slowing or stopping others in place.

Grace – A *purple* dungeon wisp – Is that important? – Grace is the offspring of Dani and Cal.

Hans – A cheeky Assassin that has been with Dale since he began cultivating. He was a thief in his youth but changed lifestyles after his street guild was wiped out. He is deadly with a knife and is Dale's best friend. Now Rose's husband.

Incantation – Essentially a spell, an incantation is created from words and gestures. It releases all of the power of an enchantment in a single burst.

Infected – A person or creature that has been infected with a rage-inducing mushroom growth. These people have no control of their bodies and attack any non-infected on sight.

Infernal – The Essence of death and demonic beings, *considered* to be always evil.

Inscription – A *permanent* pattern made of Essence that creates an effect on the universe. Try not to get the pattern wrong as it could have... unintended consequences. This is another name for an incomplete or unknown Rune.

Mages' Guild – A secretive sub-sect of the Adventurers' Guild only Mage level cultivators are allowed to join.

Mana – A higher stage of Essence only able to be cultivated by those who have broken into at least the B-rankings and found the true name of something in the universe.

Meridians – Meridians are energy channels that transport life energy (Chi/Essence) throughout the body.

Mob – A shortened version of "dungeon monster".

Necromancer – An Infernal Essence cultivator who can raise and control the dead and demons.

Noble rankings:

> King/Queen – Ruler of their country. (Addressed as 'Your Majesty')

Crown Prince/Princess – Next in line to the throne, has the same political power as a Grand Duke. (Addressed as 'Your Royal Highness')

Prince/Princess – Child of the King/Queen, has the same political power as a Duke. (Addressed as 'Your Highness')

Grand Duke – Ruler of a grand duchy and is senior to a Duke. (Addressed as "your Grace")

Duke – Is senior to a Marquis or Marquess. (Addressed as "Your Grace")

Marquis/Marquess – Is senior to an Earl and has at least three Earls in their domain. (Addressed as 'Honorable')

Earl – Is senior to a Baron. Each Earl has three barons under their power. (Addressed as 'My Lord/Lady')

Baron – Senior to knights, they control a minimum of ten knights and therefore their land. (Addressed as 'My Lord/Lady')

Knights – Sub rulers of plots of land and peasants. (Addressed as 'Sir')

Pattern – A pattern is the intricate design that makes everything in the universe. An inanimate object has a far less complex pattern that a living being.

Raile – A massive, granite covered Boss Basher that attacks by ramming and attempting to squish its opponents.

Ranger – Typically an adventurer archetype that is able to attack from long range, usually with a bow.

Ranking System – The ranking system is a way to classify how powerful a creature has become through fighting and cultivation.

> G – At the lowest ranking is mostly non-organic matter such as rocks and ash. Mid-G contains small plants such as moss and mushrooms while the upper ranks form most of the other flora in the world.
>
> F – The F -ranks are where beings are becoming actually sentient, able to gather their own food and make short-term plans. The mid-F ranks are where most humans reach before adulthood without cultivating. This is known as the fishy or "failure" rank.
>
> E – The E-rank is known as the "echo" rank and is used to prepare a body for intense cultivation.
>
> D – This is the rank where a cultivator starts to become actually dangerous. A D-ranked individual can usually fight off ten F-ranked beings without issue. They are characterized by a "fractal" in their Chi spiral.
>
> C – The highest-ranked Essence cultivators, those in the C rank usually have opened all of their meridians. A C-ranked cultivator can usually fight off ten D-ranked and

one hundred F-ranked beings without being overwhelmed.

B – This is the first rank of Mana cultivators, known as Mages. They convert Essence into Mana through a nuanced refining process and release it through a true name of the universe.

A – Usually several hundred years are needed to attain this rank, known as High-Mage or High-Magous. They are the most powerful rank of Mages.

S – Very mysterious Spiritual Essence cultivators. Not much is known about the requirements for this rank or those above it.

SS – Not much is known about the requirements for this rank or those above it.

SSS – Not much is known about the requirements for this rank or those above it.

Heavenly – Not much is known about the requirements for this rank or those above it.

Godly – Not much is known about the requirements for this rank or those above it.

Rose – A Half-Elf ranger that joined Dale's team. She has opposing affinities for Celestial and Infernal Essence, making her a chaos cultivator.

Rune – A *permanent* pattern made of Essence that creates an effect on the universe. Try not to get the pattern wrong as it could have... unintended consequences. This is another name for a completed Inscription.

Silverwood Tree – A mysterious tree that has silver wood and leaves. Some say that it helps cultivators move into the B-rankings.

Soul Stone – A *highly* refined Beast Core that is capable of containing a human soul.

Tank – An adventurer archetype that is built to defend his team from the worst of the attacks that come their way. Heavily armored and usually carrying a large shield, these powerful people are needed if a group plans on surviving more than one attack.

Tom – A huge red-haired barbarian prince from the northern wastes, he wields a powerful warhammer and has joined Dale's team. He is only half as handy to have around right now.

Xan – A *green* dungeon wisp – Is that important? – Xan is the wisp bonded to Dregs.

Printed by Amazon Italia Logistica S.r.l.
Torrazza Piemonte (TO), Italy